P9-ARC-731

The House of God

The House of God

a novel by Samuel Shem, M.D.

Richard Marek Publishers, New York

Copyright © 1978 by Samuel Shem

All rights reserved. No part of this book may be reproduced in any form or by any means without the prior written permission of the Publisher, excepting brief quotes used in connection with reviews written specifically for inclusion in a magazine or newspaper. For information write to Richard Marek Publishers, Inc., 200 Madison Avenue, New York, N.Y. 10016.

Library of Congress Cataloging in Publication Data

Shem, Samuel.
  House of God.

  I. Title.
PZ4.S54573Ho   [PS3569.H39374]   813'.5'4   78-18368
ISBN 0-399-90023-3

Printed in the United States of America

The author wishes to express appreciation for permission to quote from the following:

"The Man with the Blue Guitar" by Wallace Stevens from *The Collected Poems of Wallace Stevens* © 1971 by Alfred A. Knopf, Inc.

Lines from "Let the Mermaids Flirt with Me" are by Mississippi John Hurt, copyright © by Wynwood Music.

To J and Ben

*We shall forget by day, except
The moments when we choose to play
The imagined pine, the imagined jay.*

—Wallace Stevens
   The Man with the Blue Guitar

Contents

I.   France   9
II. The House of God   19
III. The Wing of Zock   285
Laws of the House of God   376
Glossary   377

I. FRANCE

Life's like a penis:
When it's soft you can't beat it;
When it's hard you get screwed.

—The Fat Man, Medical Resident in the House of God

1

Except for her sunglasses, Berry is naked. Even now, on vacation in France with my internship year barely warm in its grave, I can't see her bodily imperfections. I love her breasts, the way they change when she lies flat, on her stomach, on her back, and then when she stands, and walks. And dances. Oh, how I love her breasts when she dances. Cooper's ligaments suspend the breasts. Cooper's Droopers, if they stretch. And her pubis, *symphasis pubis,* the bone under the skin being the real force shaping her Mound of Venus. She has sparse black hair. In the sun, she sweats, the glisten making her tan more erotic. In spite of my medical eyes, in spite of having just spent a year among diseased bodies, it is all I can do to sit calmly and record. The day feels smooth, warm, pebbled with the nostalgia of a sigh. It is so still that a match flame stands upright, invisible in the clear hot air. The green of the grass, the lime-white walls of our rented farmhouse, the orange stucco roof edging the August blue sky—it is all too perfect for this world. There is no need to think. There is time for all things. There is no result, there is only process. Berry is trying to teach me to love as once I did love, before the deadening by the year.

I struggle to rest and cannot. Like a missile my mind homes to my hospital, the House of God, and I think of how I and the other interns handled sex. Without love, amidst the gomers and the old ones dying and the dying young, we had savaged

11

the women of the House. From the most tender nursing-school novitiate through the hard-eyed head nurses of the Emergency Room, and even, in pidgin Spanish, to the bangled and whistling Hispanic ones in Housekeeping and Maintenance—we had savaged them for our needs. I think back to the Runt, who had moved from two-dimensional magazine sex into a spine-tingling sexual adventure with a voracious nurse named Angel—Angel, who never ever did, the whole long year, to anyone's knowledge, string together a complete sentence made of real words. And I know now that the sex in the House of God had been sad and sick and cynical and sick, for like all our doings in the House, it had been done without love, for all of us had become deaf to the murmurs of love.

"Come back, Roy. Don't drift off there, now."

Berry. Finishing our lunch, we are almost to the hearts of our artichokes. They grow to enormous size in this part of France. I had trimmed and boiled the artichokes, and Berry had made the vinaigrette. The food here is exquisite. Often we eat in the sun-dappled garden of our restaurant, under the lattice of branches. The starched white linen, delicate crystal, and fresh red rose in the silver vase are almost too perfect for this life. In the corner, our waiter attends, napkin over his arm. His hand trembles. He suffers from a senile tremor, the tremor of a gomer, of all the gomers of the year. As I come to the last leaves of the artichoke, their purple surpassing their edible green, and throw them toward the garbage heap for the farmer's chickens and glass-eyed gomer of a dog, I think about a gomer eating an artichoke. Impossible, unless it were pureed and squirted down the feeding tube. I remove the thistly hairs, green abundant, covering the mound of choke, and come to the heart, and I think back to eating in the House of God, and to the one best at eating, best at medicine, my resident, the Fat Man. The Fat Man shoveling onions and Hebrew National hot dogs and raspberry ice cream into his mouth all at once at the ten-o'clock supper. The Fat Man, with his LAWS OF THE HOUSE and his approach to medicine that at first I thought was sick but that gradually I learned to be the way it was. I see us—hot, sweaty, Iwo Jima-heroic—hovered over a gomer:

"They're hurting us," the Fat Man would say.

"They've got me on my knees," I'd reply.

12

"I'd commit suicide, but I don't want to make the bastards happy."

And we'd put our arms around each other and cry. My fat genius, always with me when I needed him, but where is he as I need him now? In Hollywood, in Gastroenterology, in bowel runs—as he always put it—"through the colons of the stars." I know now that it was his zany laughter and his caring, and that of the two policemen of the Emergency Room—the two policemen, my Saviors, who seemed to know everything and who almost seemed to know it in advance—that had gotten me through the year. And despite the Fat Man and the policemen, what had happened in the House of God had been fierce, and I had been hurt, bad. For before the House of God, I had loved old people. Now they were no longer old people, they were gomers, and I did not, I could not love them, anymore. I struggle to rest, and cannot, and I struggle to love, and I cannot love, for I'm all leached out, like a man's shirt washed too many times.

"Since you drift off there so much, maybe you'd rather be back there after all," says Berry sarcastically.

"Love, it's been a bad year."

I sip my wine. I've been drunk much of the time we've been here. I've been drunk in the cafés on market day as the clamor ebbs in the market and flows in the bars. I've been drunk while swimming in our river, at noon the temperature of water, air, and body all the same, so that I can't tell where body ends and water begins and it's a melding of the universe, with the river curling round our bodies, cool and warm rushes intermingling in lost patterns, filling all times and all depths. I swim against the current, looking upstream where the winding riverpath rests in a cradle of willow, rushes, poplar, shadow, and that great master of shadow, the sun. Drunk, I lie in the sun on the towel, watching with blossoming arousal the erotic ballet of the Englishwomen changing into and out of swimsuits, glimpsing an edge of breast, a wisp of pubic hair, as so often I had glimpsed edges and wisps of nurses, as they changed into and out of their costumes before my eyes, in the House. Sometimes, drunk, I ruminate on the state of my liver, and think of all the cirrhotics I have watched turn yellow and die. They either bleed out, raving, coughing up and drowning

13

in blood from ruptured esophageal veins, or, in coma, they slip away, slip blissfully away down the yellow-brick ammonia-scented road to oblivion. Sweating, I tingle, and Berry becomes more beautiful than ever. This wine makes me feel like I'm bathed in amnion, breathless, fed by the motherblood-flow in the umbilical vein, fetal, slippery and tumbling over and over in the warmth of the beating womb, warm amnion, warmnion. Alchohol helped in the House of God, and I think of my best friend, Chuck, the black intern from Memphis, who never was without a pint of Jack Daniels in his black bag for those extra-bitter times when he was hurt extra bad by the gomers or the slurping House academics, like the Chief Resident or the Chief of Medicine himself, who were always looking at Chuck as illiterate and underprivileged when in fact he was literate and privileged and a better doc than anyone else in the whole place. And in my drunkenness I think that what happened to Chuck in the House was too sad, for he had been happy and funny and now he was sad and glum, broken by them and going around with the same half-angry, half-crushed look in his eyes that I'd noticed Nixon had had yesterday on our French TV, as he stood on the steps of the helicopter on the White House lawn after his resignation, giving a pathetically inappropriate V-for-defeat sign before the doors closed over him, the Filipinos rolled in the red carpet, and Jerry Ford, looking more flabbergasted then awed, put his arm around his wife and walked slowly back to the presidency. The gomers, these gomers . . .

"Damnit, everything makes you think of those gomers," says Berry.

"I hadn't realized that I'd been thinking out loud."

"You never realize it, but these days, you always do. Nixon, gomers, forget about the gomers. There aren't any gomers here."

I know she's wrong. One lazy and succulent day, I am walking by myself from the graveyard at the top of the village, down the catnapping winding road overlooking the château, the church, the prehistoric caves, the square, and far below, the river valley, the child's-toy poplars and Roman bridge indicating the road, and the creator of all this, the spawn of the glacier, our river. I have never taken this path before, this path

14

along this ridge. I am beginning to relax, to know what I knew before: the peace, the rainbow of perfections of doing nothing. The country is so lush that the birds can't eat all the ripe blackberries. I stop and pick some. Juicy grit in my mouth. My sandals slap the asphalt. I watch the flowers compete in color and shape, enticing the rape by the bees. For the first time in more than a year I am at peace, and nothing in the whole world is effort, and all, for me, is natural, whole, and sound.

I turn a corner and see a large building, like an asylum or a hospital, with the word "Hospice" over the door. My skin prickles, the little hairs on the back of my neck rise, my teeth set on edge. And there, sure enough, I see them. They have been set out in the sun, in a little orchard. The white of their hair, scattered among the green of the orchard, makes them look like dandelions in a field, gossamers awaiting their final breeze. Gomers. I stare at them. I recognize the signs. I make diagnoses. As I walk past them, their eyes seem to follow me, as if somewhere in their dementia they are trying to wave, or say *bonjour,* or show some other vestige of humanness. But they neither wave nor say *bonjour,* nor show any other vestige. Healthy, tan, sweaty, drunk, full of blackberries, laughing inside and fearing the cruelty of that laughter, I feel grand. I always feel grand when I see a gomer. I love these gomers now.

"Well, there may be gomers in France, but you don't have to take care of them."

She goes back to her artichoke, and the vinaigrette accumulates on her chin. She doesn't wipe it off. She's not the type. She enjoys the oily feel of the oil, the vinegar sting. She enjoys her nakedness, her carelessness, her oiliness, her ease. I feel that she's getting excited. Now she looks at me again. Am I saying this out loud? No. As we watch each other, the vinaigrette drips from her chin to her breast. We watch. The vinaigrette explores, oozing slowly down the skinline, heading south toward the nipple. We speculate together, without words, whether it will make it, or if it will veer off, toward cleft or pit. I flip back into medicine, thinking of carcinoma of the axillary nodes. Mastectomy. Statistics crowd in. Berry smiles at me, unaware of my regression toward death. The vinaigrette stays on line, oozes onto the nipple, and hangs. We smile.

15

"Stop obsessing about the gomers and come lick it off."

"They can still hurt me."

"No they can't. Come on."

As I put my lips to her nipple, feeling it rise, tasting the sting of the sauce, my fantasy is of a cardiac arrest. The room is crowded, and I am one of the last to arrive. On the bed is a young patient, intubated, being breathed by the respiratory tech. The resident is trying to put in a big intravenous line, and the medical student is running round and round the bed. Everyone in the room knows that the patient is going to die. Kneeling on the bed, giving closed-chest cardiac massage, is one of the intensive-care nurses, a redhead with great thighs and big tits, from Hawaii. Tits from Hawaii. It had been her patient, and she had been first to arrive at the arrest. I stand in the doorway and watch: her white skirt has ridden up her legs so that as she bends over the patient, she flaunts her ass. She wears flowered bikini panties. I can almost see the petals through the seams of the white stretch pantyhose. I think of Hawaii. Up and down, up and down her ass is moving up and down in the middle of all the blood and vomit and urine and crap and people. Waves of surf on volcanic beaches up and down up and down. Fantastic plush limousine of an ass. I go up to her and put my hand on it. She turns and sees who it is and smiles and says Oh hi Roy and keeps on pumping. I massage her ass as she moves up and down, around and around my hand goes. I whisper something raunchy in her ears. I take both hands and pull down her pantyhose, and then pull her panties down to her knees. She beats on the body. I take my hands, and slip one into her crotch and run the other down the inside of her thighs up and down and up and down in time to the chest compressions of the resuscitation. She takes her free hand and undoes the buttons of my white pants and grabs my erect penis. The tension is incredible. There are shouts for "adrenaline!" and "the defibrillator!"

Finally they're ready to put the paddles of the defibrillator on the patient's chest, to shock the dying heart. Someone shouts: "Everybody off the bed!" and the Hawaiian slides down onto my penis.

"Shock him!"

SSZZZZZZ!

They shock the patient. The body convulses up off the bed as the muscles contract from the 300 volts, but the cardiac monitor is flat line. The heart is dead. An intern, the Runt, enters the room. The patient is his patient. He seems upset. He looks like he's about to burst into tears. Then he sees the Hawaiian and me going at it, and his eyes show his surprise. I turn to him and say:

"Cheer up, Runt, it's impossible to be depressed with an erection."

The fantasy ends with the young patient dead and all of us consoling ourselves in sex on the blood-slippery floor, singing as we rocket toward orgasm:

"I wanna go back to my little grass shack in Kooalakahoo Ha-WAAAAA—EEEEEEE! . . .

II.   THE HOUSE OF GOD

We came here to serve God,
And also to get rich.

—Bernal Diaz del Castillo, *History of the Conquest of Mexico*

2

The House of God had been founded in 1913 by the American People of Israel when their medically qualified Sons and Daughters could not get good internships in good hospitals because of discrimination. A great tribute to the dedication of the founders, it soon attracted red hot doctors, and was blessed with an affiliation with the BMS—the Best Medical School—in the world. Built up to this status, internally it had broken down into many hierarchies, at the bottom of which now lay the very people for whom it had been constructed, the House Staff. Consistently, at the bottom of the House Staff lay an intern.

While the straight shot down from the top of the medical hierarchy got the intern, the intern was at the bottom of the other hierarchies only indirectly. In many tricky ways he had the opportunity to be abused at any time by Private Doctors, House Administration, Nursing, Patients, Social Service, Telephone and Beeper Operators, and Housekeeping. The latter made the beds and regulated the heat, cold, toilets, linen, and general repairs. The interns were completely at their mercy.

The House medical hierarchy was a pyramid—a lot at the bottom and one at the top. Given the mentality required to climb it, it was more like an ice-cream cone—you had to lick your way up. From constant application of tongue to next uppermost ass, those few toward the top were all tongue. A mapping of each sensory cortex would show a homunculus with a

21

mammoth tongue overlapping an enormous portion of brain. The nice thing about the ice-cream cone was that from the bottom, you got a clear view of the slurping going on. There they were, the Slurpers, greedy optimistic kids in an ice-cream parlor in July, tonguing and tonguing and tonguing away. It was quite a sight.

The House of God was known for its progressiveness, especially in relation to the way it treated its House Staff. It was one of the first hospitals to offer free marital counseling, and when that failed, to encourage divorce. On average, during their stay, about eighty percent of the married medically qualified Sons and Daughters would make use of this suggestion, separate from their spouses, and take up with some bombshell from Private Doctors, House Administration, Nursing, Patients, Social Service, Telephone and Beeper Operators, and Housekeeping. In a further progressive gesture, the House believed in introducing its incoming interns to the horrors of the year in a gentle fashion, inviting us to an all-day talk session broken by a lunch catered by the B-M Deli, taking place on Monday June the thirtieth, the day before we were to start. At this meeting we were to be exposed to representative members of each hierarchy.

On the Sunday afternoon before the B-M Deli Monday before the horrific Tuesday July the first, I was in bed. June was ending with a final sunny flash, but my shades were drawn. Nixon was off on yet another summit junket to masturbate Kosygin, "Mo" Dean was breathless in her agony over what dress to wear to the Watergate hearings, and I was in pain. My pain was not even the modern pain of alienation or ennui, the kind that many Americans currently felt while watching the TV documentary on "The California Family: the Louds," with their expensive ranch house, three cars, kidney-shaped pool, and no books. My pain was fear. Despite always having been a red-hot, I was scared out of my mind. I was terrified of being an intern in the House of God.

I was not alone in bed. I was with Berry. Our relationship, having survived the trauma of my years at the Best Medical School, was blossoming, rich in color, woven with liveliness, laughter, risk, and love. Also in bed with me were two books:

22

the first, a gift from my father the dentist, an "internship" book, something called *How I Saved the World Without Dirtying My Whites*, all about this intern rushing in at the last minute, taking over, crisply barking orders which saved lives in the nick of time; the second book I'd bought for myself, something called *How to Do It for the New Intern*, a manual that told you everything you needed to know. While I ransacked this manual, Berry, a Clinical Psychologist, was curled up with Freud. After a few minutes of silence, I groaned, let the manual drop, and pulled the sheet over my head.

"Help, hellllp," I said.

"Roy, you really are in terrible shape."

"How bad is it?"

"Bad. Last week I hospitalized a patient who was found curled up under the covers just like that, and he was less anxious than you."

"Can you hospitalize me?"

"Do you have insurance?"

"Not till I start the internship."

"Then you'd have to go to the State Facility."

"What should I do? I've tried everything, and I'm still scared to death."

"Try denial."

"Denial?"

"Yes. A primitive defense. Deny that it exists."

So I tried to deny that it exists. Although I didn't get very far with this denial, Berry helped me through the night, and the next morning, B-M Deli Monday, she helped me to shave, dress, and she drove me downtown to the House of God. Something stopped me from getting out of the car, and so Berry opened my door, coaxed me out, and pressed a note into my hand that said "Meet you here at five P.M. Good luck. Love, Berry." She kissed me on the cheek and left.

I stood in the steamy heat outside a huge urine-colored building which a sign said was THE HOUSE OF GOD. A ball and chain were demolishing one wing, to make way, a sign said, for THE WING OF ZOCK. Feeling like the ball and chain were swinging back and forth inside my skull, I entered the House and searched out the "function room." I sat down as the

Chief Resident, named Fishberg and nicknamed the Fish, was giving a welcoming speech. Short, chubby, scrubbed to a shine, the Fish had just completed his training in Gastroenterology, the specialty of the House. The position of Chief Resident was smack in the middle of the ice-cream cone, and the Fish knew that if he did a good job that year he'd be rewarded by the higher-up Slurpers with a permanent job and become a permanent Slurper. He was the liaison between the interns and everyone else, and he "hoped that you will come to me with any problems you might have." As he said this, his eyes slithered over to the higher-up Slurpers arrayed at the head table. Shifty, slimy, he oozed. Too cheerful. Not in touch with our dread. My concentration waned, and I looked around the room at the other new terns: a smooth black guy slouched down in his chair with his hand wearily shading his eyes; more striking was a giant of a guy with a bushy red beard, wearing a black leather jacket and wraparound sunglasses, twirling a black motorcycle hat on his finger. Far-out.

" . . . and so, day or night, I'm available. And now it gives me great pleasure to present the Chief of Medicine, Dr. Leggo."

From the corner where he'd been standing, a thin, dry-looking little man with a horrific purple birthmark on the side of his face walked stiffly to the center of the speaker's table. He wore a butcher-length white coat and a long old-fashioned stethoscope wended its way across his chest and abdomen and disappeared mysteriously into his pants. A question flickered across my mind: WHERE DID THAT STETHOSCOPE GO? He was a renologist: kidneys, ureters, bladders, urethras, and stagnant urine's best friend, the Foley catheter.

"The House is special," said the Chief. "Part of its being special is its affiliation with the BMS. I want to tell you a story about the BMS, that showed me how special the BMS and the House are. It's a story about a BMS doctor and a BMS nurse named Peg. It showed me what it is like to be affiliated with the . . ."

My mind wandered. The Leggo was a less chubby version of the Fish, as if, given the fact that the Leggo had published rather than perished to become Chief, all the human juice had been sucked out of him, and he had been left drained, dehy-

24

drated, even uremic. So this was the top of the cone, when finally, and with all men, as Chief, one was perpetually more slurped against than slurping.

" . . . and so Peg came up to me with a surprised look on her face and said 'Doctor Leggo, how could you wonder whether that order had been done? When a BMS doctor tells a BMS nurse to do something, you can be sure it will be done, and it will be done right.' "

He paused, as if expecting applause. He was met with silence. I yawned, and realized that my mind had gone straight to fucking.

" . . . and you'll be glad to hear that Peg will be coming—"

"HHRAAAK! HHRAAAK!"

An explosion of coughing from the tern in the black leather jacket, doubling him over, gasping, at his seat, interrupted the Leggo.

"—coming from the City Hospital to join us here at the House later in the year."

The Leggo went on to make a statement about the Sanctity of Life. Like the Pope's statements, the emphasis was on doing everything always for everyone forever to keep the patient alive. At the time, we couldn't have known how destructive this *nuncio* would be. Finishing, the Leggo returned to his corner, where he remained standing. Neither the Fish nor the Leggo seemed to have a firm grasp on what went into being a human being.

The other speakers were more human. A House Administration type in a blue blazer with gold buttons gave us some advice on how "the patients' charts are legal documents" and told us that the House had gotten sued recently because some tern, as a joke, had written in the chart that the Nursing Home had left the patient on the bed pan so long that stasis ulcers developed, which led to death on transfer to the House; an emaciated young cardiologist named Pinkus remarked on the importance of hobbies in preventing cardiac disease, his two hobbies being "running for fitness and fishing for calm," and then went on to say that every patient we would see during the year would seem to have a rumbling systolic heart murmur which in fact would turn out to be the jackhammers from the Wing of Zock and we might as well throw our stethoscopes

25

away now; the House Psychiatrist, a sad-looking man with a goatee, turned his pleading eyes on us and told us that he was available to help. Then he shocked us all by saying:

"Internship is not like law school, where they say look to your right and look to your left and one of you will not be here at the end of the year, but it is a strain, and everyone has a hard time. If you let it go too far, well . . . Each year the graduating class of at least one medical school—maybe two or three schools—must step into the ranks just to replace colleagues who commit suicide—"

"HAA—RUMPH! HAAA—REMMM!"

The Fish was clearing his throat. He did not like this talk about suicide and was clearing his throat of it.

"—and even year after year right here in the House of God we do see suicides—"

"Thank you, Dr. Frank," said the Fish, taking over, greasing the wheels of the meeting again so that it could roll on to the last medical speaker, a representative of the House Private Doctors, the Attendings, Dr. Pearlstein.

Even at the BMS, I'd heard of the Pearl. Once the Chief Resident, he had soon abandoned academics in pursuit of cash, had snatched the beginnings of his own practice from his older partner when the latter was away on a Florida vacation, and with a quick entry into computer technology that fully automated his office, the Pearl had become the richest of the rich House Privates. A gastroenterologist with his personal X-Ray machine in his office, he serviced the wealthiest bowels in town. He was the retained physician of the Family of Zock, whose Wing of Zock jackhammers would make us throw our stethoscopes away. Well-groomed, glittering with gems, in a handsome suit, he was a master with people, and in a few seconds he had us in the palm of his hand:

"Every intern makes mistakes. The important thing is neither to make the same mistakes twice nor to make a whole bunch of mistakes all at once. During my internship, right here at the House, a fellow intern, eager for academic success, had had a patient die, and the family had refused permission for the postmortem. In the dead of night, this intern wheeled the body down to the morgue and did the autopsy himself. He was caught and punished severely, being sent to the Deep

South, where he practices in obscurity to this day. So remember: don't let your enthusiasm for medicine get in the way of your feeling for people. It can be a great year. It started me on the way to what I am and what I have today. I look forward to working with each and every one of you. Best of luck, boys, best of luck."

Given my aversion to dead bodies, he needn't have bothered to warn me. Others felt differently. Sitting beside me, Hooper, a hyperactive tern whom I'd known as a classmate at the BMS, seemed to get off on the idea of doing the autopsy himself. His eyes gleamed, he rocked back and forth in his chair, almost quivering. Well, I mused, whatever turns you on.

The token humanitarian statement having been made, we turned to computers, the Fish passing out our day-by-day schedules for the year. A large-breasted adolescent stood up to guide us through the maze of paperwork. She spoke of "the major problem you will face in your internship: parking." After going over several complex diagrams of the parking in the House, she passed out parking stickers and said, "Remember: we do tow, and we love it. With the Wing of Zock going up, you'd better put your stickers on the inside of your windshield, because the past few months the construction workers have ripped off all the stickers they could find. And if you're thinking of riding your bikes, forget it. Every night the teen gangs rip through this place with bolt cutters. No bike is safe. Now we fill in our computer forms, so we can get paid. You all brought your number-two pencils, right?"

Damn. I'd forgot. My whole life has been trying to remember to bring those two number-two pencils. I couldn't remember when I'd ever remembered. And yet someone else always did. I filled in the circles of the forms.

The meeting ended with the Fish suggesting "you might want to go to your respective wards to get acquainted with your patients before tomorrow." Although this sent a shiver through me, since I wanted to continue to deny that it exists, I filed out of the room with the others. Lagging behind, I found myself on the fourth floor walking from one end of the corridor to the other. Ten yards down the corridor were two armchair recliners, in which sat two patients. One, a woman with bright yellow skin signifying severe liver disease, sat with her

27

mouth open to the fluorescent lights, her legs spread apart, her ankles puffed and her cheeks gaunt. There was a bow in her hair. Next to her was a decrepit old man with a frantic thatch of white hair spilling over his veined skull, who was yelling over and over:

HEY DOC WAIT HEY DOC WAIT HEY DOC . . .

An intravenous bottle was running yellow stuff into his arm, and a Foley catheter was running yellow stuff out of his vermilion-tipped schlong, which lay across his lap like a pet snake. The caravan of new terns had to wend its way single file past these two lost ones, and by the time I got to them there was a traffic jam and I had to stop and wait. The black guy and the black motorcycle guy waited with me. The man, whose name tag said "Harry the Horse," kept yelling: HEY DOC WAIT HEY DOC WAIT HEY DOC . . .

I turned to the woman, whose name tag said "Jane Doe." She was singing, a chromatic phonetic scale of increasing intensity:

OOOO—AYYY—EEEE—IYYYY—UUUUU . . . .

In response to our attention Jane Doe made motions as if to touch us, and I thought "No don't touch me!" and she didn't but what she did do was squeeze out a long liquid fart. Smells had always gotten to me, and that smell did then, and I felt like vomiting. Nope, they weren't going to get me to see my patients yet. I turned around. The black guy, whose name was Chuck, looked at me.

"What do you think of this?" I asked.

"Man, it's pitiful."

Looming over us was the giant with the black motorcycle gear. He put on his black jacket again and said to us: "Guys, in my medical school in California, I never saw anyone as old as this. I'm going home to my wife."

He turned, walked back down the corridor, and disappeared into the down elevator. On the back of his black motorcycle jacket was spelled out in shiny brass studs:

***
EAT MY DUST
EDDIE
***

28

Jane Doe farted again.

"Do you have a wife?" I asked Chuck.

"Nope."

"Me neither. But I can't take this yet. No way."

"Well, man, let's go have a drink."

Chuck and I had poured a good deal of bourbon and beer into our bodies, and had gotten to the point of laughing at the farting Jane Doe and the insistent Harry the Horse asking us to HEY DOC WAIT. Having started by sharing our disgust, we proceeded through sharing our fear, and were in the process of sharing our pasts. Chuck had grown up dirt-poor in Memphis. I inquired as to how from this humble beginning he'd gotten to the pinnacle of academic medicine, the BMS-affiliated House of God.

"Well, man, you see, it was like this. One day when I was a senior in high school in Memphis, I got this postcard from Oberlin College, and it said: WANT TO GO TO COLLEGE AT OBERLIN? IF SO, FILL OUT AND RETURN THIS CARD. That was it, man, that was all. No College Board tests, no application, no nothin'. And so I did it. Next thing I know, I get this letter saying I'd been accepted, full scholarship, four years. And here the white guys in my class were all trying like crazy to get in. Now, I'd never been out of Tennessee in my life, I didn't know anything about this Oberlin, 'cept I asked somebody and he told me they had a music school there."

"Did you play a musical instrument?"

"You gotta be kiddin'. My old man read cowboy novels as a night janitor, and my old lady cleaned floors. Only thing I played was roundball. The day I was supposed to leave, my old man says, 'Son, you'd be better off joinin' the army.' So I take the bus to Cleveland and then I was supposed to change for Oberlin, and I didn't know if I was in the right place but then I see all these dudes with musical instruments and I say yup this must be the right bus. So I went to Oberlin. Majored in premed 'cause you didn't have to do nothing, read two books—the *Illiad*, which I didn't dig, and then this great book about these red killer ants. See, there was this dude trapped, tied down, and this army of red killer ants came marchin' and marchin'. Great."

"What made you decide to go to medical school?"

29

"Same thing, man, same ezact thing. In my senior year, I got this postcard from the University of Chicago: WANT TO GO TO MEDICAL SCHOOL AT CHICAGO? IF SO, FILL OUT AND RETURN THIS CARD. That was all. No Medical Board tests, no application, no nothing. Full scholarship, four years. So there it is, and here I am."

"And what about the House of God?"

"Same thing, man, same ezact thing. Senior year, postcard: WANT TO BE AN INTERN AT THE HOUSE OF GOD? IF SO, FILL OUT AND RETURN THIS CARD. There it is. Sumthin' else, huh?"

"Well, you sure put one over on them."

"I thought I did, but you know, seeing these pitiful patients and all, I think those guys sending me the postcards knew all along I was tryin' to fool them by gettin' all this, so they fooled me by givin' it all to me. My old man was right: that first postcard was my downfall. I shoulda joined the army."

"Well, you got to read a good story about the killer ants."

"Yeah, I can't deny that. What about you?"

"Me? I look great on paper. For three years after college I was on a Rhodes Scholarship to England."

"Damn! You must be some ath-a-lete. What's your sport?"

"Golf."

"You gotta be kiddin'. With those little white balls?"

"Right. Oxford got fed up with the dumb Rhodes jocks, so they went in more for brains my year. One guy's sport was bridge."

"Well, man, how old are you, anyway?"

"I'll be thirty on the fourth of July."

"Damn, you're older than all of us. You're as old as dirt."

"I should have known better than to come to the House. My whole life has been those goddamn number-two pencils. You'd think I'd learn."

"Well, man, what I really want to be is a singer. I got a great voice. Listen to this."

In *falsetto*, shaping the tones and words with his hands, Chuck sang: "There's a . . . moone out too-night, wo-o-o-ooow, and I know . . . if you held me tight, wo-o-o-owww . . . "

It was a lovely song and he had a lovely voice and it was lovely, all of it, and I told him so. We both were real happy. In the face of what faced us, it was almost like falling in love. After a few more drinks we decided we were happy enough to leave. I reached into my pocket to pay, and came out with Berry's note.

"Oh, shit," I said, "I'm late. Let's go."

We paid and walked out. The heat had disappeared under an umbrella of summer rain. Soaking wet, with the thunder blasting and the lightning rattling, Chuck and I sang through the car window to Berry. He kissed her good-bye, and as we left him, walking toward his car, I yelled out: "Hey I forgot to ask you—where are you starting tomorrow?"

"Who knows, man, who knows?"

"Wait—I'll look," and I fished out my computer schedule and saw that Chuck and I would be together for our first ward rotation. "Hey, we're gonna work together."

"That's cool, man, that's cool. So long."

I liked him. He was black and he had endured. With him I would endure. July the first seemed less frightening than before.

Berry was concerned about my lacing my denial with bourbon. I was silly and she was serious, and she said that this first forgetting to meet her was an example of the problems we might have during the year. I tried to tell her something about the B-M Deli, and could not. When I, laughing, told her about Harry the Horse and the farting Jane Doe, she didn't laugh.

"How can you laugh at that? They sound pathetic."

"They are. I guess denial didn't work."

"It did. That's what your laughter's about."

In my mailbox was a letter from my father. An optimist, he was a master of the conjunction, his letters patterned in the grammer of: (phrase) conjunction (phrase):

> . . . I know there is so much to learn about medicine and it is all new. It is fascinating all the time and there is nothing more amazing than the human body. The hard physical part of the job will soon become usual and you must watch your health. I had an eighty on Wednesday afternoon and am putting better . . .

Berry put me to bed early and went back to her place, and I was soon wrapped in the velvet robe of sleep, heading toward the kaleidoscope of dream. Pleased, happy, no longer scared, with a smile I murmured "Hiya, dream," and I was soon in Oxford, England, at lunch in the Senior Common Room of Balliol College, a Septcentenary Fellow at each elbow, eating dull food off bone china, discussing how the screwy Germans, after fifty years' work on their vast Dictionary compiling all the Latin words ever used, had gotten only up to the letter K, and then I was a kid running out into the summer dusk after supper, baseball mitt in my hand, leaping up and up in the warm twilight, and then, in a whirlwind of dread, I sighted a traveling circus falling from a cliff into the sea, the sharks savaging the succulent marsupials as the drowned clown's painted face dissolved in the cold inhuman pickling brine . . . .

3

It must have been the Fat Man who first showed me what a gomer was. The Fat Man was my first resident, easing my transition from BMS student to intern in the House of God. He was wonderful, and a wonder. Brooklyn-born, New York City-trained, expansive, impervious, brilliant, efficient, from his sleek black hair and sharp black eyes and bulging chins through his enormous middle that forced his belt buckle to roll over on its belly like a shiny fish, to his wide black shoes, the Fat Man was fantastic. Only New York City could have bounced back from his birth to nourish him. In return, the Fat Man was skeptical of whatever wild country existed to the west of that great frontier, Riverside Drive. The only exception to this urbane provincialism was, of course, Hollywood, the Hollywood of the Stars.

At six-thirty in the morning of July the first, I was swallowed by the House of God and found myself walking down an endless bile-colored corridor on the sixth floor. This was ward 6-South, where I was to begin. A nurse with magnificently hairy forearms pointed me to the House Officer's On-Call Room, where rounds were in progress. I opened the door and went in. I felt pure terror. As Freud had said via Berry, my terror was "a straight shot from the id."

Around the table were five people: the Fat Man; an intern named Wayne Potts, a Southerner whom I'd known at BMS, a nice guy but depressed, repressed, and kind of compressed,

33

dressed in crisp white, pockets bulging with instruments; the three others seemed eager, and this told me they were BMS students doing their medicine clerkship. Each intern was to be saddled with a BMS, each day of the year.

"It's about time," said the Fat Man, biting a bagel, "where's the other turkey?"

Assuming he meant Chuck, I said, "I don't know."

"Turkeys," said Fats, "he'll make me late for breakfast."

A beeper went off, and Potts and I froze. It was the Fat Man's: FAT MAN CALL THE OPERATOR FOR AN OUTSIDE CALL, THE OPERATOR FOR AN OUTSIDE CALL, FAT MAN, RIGHT AWAY.

"Hi, Murray, what's new?" said Fats into the phone. "Hey, great. What? A name? Sure sure yeah no problem hang on." Turning to us, Fats asked, "OK, you turkeys, what's a catchy doctor's name?"

Thinking of Berry, I said, "Freud."

"Freud? Nah. Gimmee another. Stat."

"Jung."

"Jung? Jung. Murray? I got it. Call it Dr. Jung's. Great. Remember, Murray, we're gonna be rich. Millions. Bye-bye." Turning back to us with a pleased smile, Fats said, "A fortoona. Ha. OK, we'll start rounds without the other tern."

"Great," said one of the BMSs, leaping to his feet. "I'll get the chart rack. Which end of the ward do we start on?"

"Sit down!" said Fats. "What are you talking about, chart rack?"

"Aren't we going on work rounds?" asked the BMS.

"We are, right here."

"But . . . but we're not going to see the patients?"

"In internal medicine, there is virtually no need to see patients. Almost all patients are better off unseen. See these fingers?"

We looked carefully at the Fat Man's stubby fingers.

"These fingers do not touch bodies unless they have to. You want to see bodies, go see bodies. I've seen enough bodies, and especially bodies of gomers to last me the rest of my life."

"What's a gomer?" I asked.

34

"What's a gomer?" said the Fat Man. With a little smile he spelled out "G-O . . ."

He stopped, his mouth still set in the "O," and stared at the doorway. There stood Chuck, wearing a collar-to-toes-length brown leather coat with tan fur ruffles at the edges, sunglasses, and a brown leather hat with a broad rim and a red feather. He walked clumsily on platform heels, and looked as if he'd been up dancing the night away.

"Hey, man, what's happenin'?" said Chuck, and slid into the nearest chair, slouching down, covering his eyes with a weary hand. As a token gesture, he unbuttoned his coat and threw his stethoscope on the table. It was broken. He looked at it and said, "Well, I guess I broke my scope, eh? Rough day."

"You look like some kind of mugger," said a BMS.

"That's right, man, 'cause you see, in Chicago where I come from, there are only two kinds of dudes—the muggers and the mugged. Now, if you don't dress like a mugger, man, you automatically gets youseff mugged. You dig?"

"Never mind dig," said the Fat Man, "pay attention. I was not supposed to be your resident today. A woman named Jo was, but her father jumped off a bridge and killed himself yesterday. The House switched our assignments, and I'll be your resident for the first three weeks. After what I did as an intern last year, they didn't want to expose the fresh terns to me today, but they had no choice. Why didn't they want you to meet me, your first day as a doctor? Because I tell things as they are—no bullshitology—and the Fish and the Leggo don't want you to get discouraged too soon. They're right—if you start to get as depressed now as you'll be in February, in February you'll jump off a bridge like Jo's pop. The Leggo and the Fish want you to cuddle with your illusions, so you don't give in to your panic. 'Cause I know how scared you three new terns are today."

I loved him. He was the first person to tell us he knew about our terror.

"What's there to be depressed about?" asked Potts.

"The gomers," said the Fat Man.

"What's a gomer?"

35

From outside the room there came a high-pitched, insistent cry: GO AVAY GO AVAY GO AVAY . . .

"Who's on call today? You three interns rotate days on call, and you only admit patients on your on-call day. Who's admitting today?"

"I am," said Potts.

"Good, 'cause that awful sound comes from a gomer. If I'm not mistaken, it's from one Ina Goober, whom I admitted six times last year. A gomer, or rather, the feminine, gomere. Gomer is an acronym: Get Out of My Emergency Room—it's what you want to say when one's sent in from the nursing home at three A.M."

"I think that's kind of crass," said Potts. "Some of us don't feel that way about old people."

"You think I don't have a grandmother?" asked Fats indignantly. "I do, and she's the cutest, dearest, most wonderful old lady. Her matzoh balls float—you have to pin them down to eat them up. Under their force the soup levitates. We eat on ladders, scraping the food off the ceiling. I love . . ." The Fat Man had to stop, and dabbed the tears from his eyes, and then went on in a soft voice, "I love her very much."

I thought of my grandfather. I loved him too.

"But gomers are not just dear old people," said Fats. "Gomers are human beings who have lost what goes into being human beings. They want to die, and we will not let them. We're cruel to the gomers, by saving them, and they're cruel to us, by fighting tooth and nail against our trying to save them. They hurt us, we hurt them."

"I don't get it," said Potts.

"After Ina you'll get it. But listen—even though I said I don't see patients, when you need me, I'm here with you. If you're smart, you'll use me. Like those dolled-up jets that cargo the gomers to Miami: 'I'm Fats, fly me'. Now, let's get on to the cardflip."

The efficiency of the Fat Man's world rested on the concept of the three-by-five index card. He loved three-by-five cards. Announcing that "there is no human being whose medical characteristics cannot be listed on a three-by-five index card," he laid out two thick decks on the table. The one on the right was his. The duplicate deck on the left he split in three, and handed a stack to each of the new terns. On each card was a patient, our patients, my patients. The Fat Man explained how on his work rounds he would flip a card, pause, and expect that tern to comment on the progress being made. Not that he expected progress to have been made, but he had to have some data, so that at the next cardflip, a condensed version later in the morning with the Fish and the Leggo, he could relate "some bullshit or other" to them. The first cards flipped every day would be the new admissions from the tern who'd been on call the night before. The Fat Man made it clear that he was not interested in fancy elaborations of academic theories of disease. Not that he was antiacademic. To the contrary, he was the only resident to have his own reference file on every disease there was, on three-by-five cards. He loved references on three-by-five cards. He loved everything that was on a three-by-five card. But the Fat Man had strict priorities, and at the top was food. Until that awesome tank of a mind had been fueled via that eager nozzle of a mouth, Fats had a low tolerance for medicine, academic or otherwise, and for anything else.

Rounds over, Fats headed to breakfast, and we headed out to the ward to get to know the patients on our cards. Potts, looking green, said, "Roy, I'm as nervous as a whore in church." My BMS, Levy, wanted to go see my patients with me, but I shooed him away to the library, where BMSs love to be. Chuck and Potts and I stood at the nursing station, and the hairy-armed nurse told Potts that the woman on the stretcher was his first admission of the day, named Ina Goober. Ina was a great mass of flesh sitting upright on a stretcher, wearing, like a uniform, a gown that had blazoned across its front, "The New Masada Nursing Home." Glowering, Ina clutched her purse. She was yelling a high-pitched: GO AVAY GO AVAY GO AVAY . . .

Potts did what the textbooks said to do: introduced himself, saying, "Hello, Mrs. Goober, I'm Dr. Potts. I'll be taking care of you."

Upping her volume, Ina screamed: GO AVAY GO AVAY GO AVAY . . .

Potts next tried to engage her using the other textbook meth-

37

od, grasping her right hand. Quick as lightning Ina struck him a southpaw blow with her purse, knocking him back against the counter. The sinister violence of it shocked us. Potts, rubbing his head, asked Maxine, the nurse, whether Ina had a private doctor who could provide information.

"Yes," said Maxine, "Dr. Kreinberg. Little Otto Kreinberg. That's him over there, writing Ina's orders in her chart."

"The private doctors are not supposed to write orders," said Potts, "that's a rule. Only interns and residents write orders."

"Little Otto is different. He doesn't want you writing orders on his patients."

"I'll talk to him about that right now."

"You can't. Little Otto won't talk to interns. He hates you."

"He hates me?"

"He hates everyone. See, he invented something having to do with the heart thirty years ago, and he expected to get the Nobel Prize, but he hasn't, so he's bitter. He hates everyone, especially interns."

"Well, man," said Chuck, "sure is a great case. See you later."

I was so scared at the thought of seeing patients that I had an attack of diarrhea, and sat in the toilet with my *How to Do It* manual spread on my knees. My beeper went off: DR. BASCH CALL WARD 6-SOUTH RIGHT AWAY DR. BASCH . . .

This scored a direct hit on my anal sphincter. Now I had no choice. I could no longer run. I went out onto the ward and tried to go see my patients. In my doctor costume, I took my black bag and entered their rooms. With my black bag I came out of their rooms. All was chaos. They were patients and all I knew was in libraries, in print. I tried to read their charts. The words blurred, and my mind bounced from *How to Do* cardiac arrests to Berry to this strange Fat Man to Ina's vicious attack on poor Potts and to Little Otto, whose name rang no bell in Stockholm. Running through my mind, over and over like Muzak, was a mnemonic for the branches of the external carotid artery: As She Lay Extended Olaf's Potato Slipped In. And even there, the only one I could remember was Olaf's, which stood for Occipital. And what the hell use was that?

I started to panic. And then finally the cries coming from the

38

various rooms saved me. All of a sudden I thought "zoo," that
this was a zoo and that these patients were the animals. A little
old man with a tuft of white hair, standing on one leg with a
crutch and making sharp worried chirps, was an egret; and a
huge Polish woman of the peasant variety with sledgehammer
hands and two lower molars protruding from her cavernous
mouth became a hippo. Many different species of monkey appeared, and sows were represented in force. In my zoo, however, neither were there any majestic lions, nor any cuddly
koalas, or bunnies, or swans.

Two stand out. First, a heifer named Sophie, who'd been admitted by her Private Doctor with a chief complaint of "I'm depressed, I've got headaches all the time." For some reason her
Private, Dr. Putzel, had ordered the complete Gastrointestinal
workup, consisting of barium enema, upper GI series, small-
bowel follow-through, sigmoidoscopy, and liver scan. I didn't
know what this had to do with depression and headache. I entered her room and found the old lady with a balding little
man who was sitting on her bed patting her hand affectionately. How sweet, I thought, her son has come to visit. It was not
her son, it was Dr. Bob Putzel, whom Fats described as "the
hand-holder from the suburbs." I introduced myself, and
when I asked Putzel about the reason for the GI workup for
depression, he looked sheepish, straightened his bowtie, murmured "flatulence," and, kissing Sophie, hurried out. Confused, I called in the Fat Man.

"What is it with this GI workup?" I asked. "She says she's
depressed and has a headache."

"It's the specialty of the House," said Fats, "the bowel run.
TTB—Therapeutic Trial of Barium."

"There's nothing therapeutic about barium. It's inert."

"Of course it is. But the bowel run is the great equalizer."

"She's depressed. There's nothing wrong with her bowels."

"Of course there's not. There's nothing wrong with her, either. It's just that she got tired of going to Putzel's office, and
he got tired of calling at her house, so they both pile into his
white Continental and come to our House. She's fine, she's a
LOL in NAD—a Little Old Lady in No Apparent Distress. You
don't think Putzel knows that too? And every time he holds

Sophie's hand, it's forty of your Blue Cross dollars. Millions. You know that new building, the Wing of Zock? Know what it's for? The bowel run of the rich. Carpets, individual changing rooms in radiology with color TV and quadraphonic sound. There's a lotta money in shit. I'm searching for a GI fellowship, myself."

"But with Sophie it's fraud."

"Of course it is. Not only that, it means work for you, and Putzel is the one making the money. It sucks."

"It's crazy," I said.

"It's doing medicine the House of God way."

"So what can I do about it?"

"Start by not talking to her. If you talk to these patients, you'll never get rid of them. Then sic your BMS on her. She'll hate that."

"Is she a gomer?"

"Does she act human?"

"Of course she does. She's a nice old lady."

"Right. A LOL in NAD. Not a gomere. But you're sure to have a gomer on your service. Here, let's see. Rokitansky. Come on."

Rokitansky was an old bassett. He'd been a college professor and had suffered a severe stroke. He lay on his bed, strapped down, IVs going in, catheter coming out. Motionless, paralyzed, eyes closed, breathing comfortably, perhaps dreaming of a bone, or a boy, or of a boy throwing a bone.

"Mr. Rokitansky, how are you doing?" I asked.

Without opening his eyes, after fifteen seconds, in a husky slurred growl from deep down in his smushed brain he said: PURRTY GUD.

Pleased, I asked, "Mr. Rokitansky, what date is it today?"
PURRTY GUD.

To all my questions, his answer was always the same. I felt sad. A professor, now a vegetable. Again I thought of my grandfather, and got a lump in my throat. Turning to Fats, I said, "This is too sad. He's going to die."

"No he's not," said Fats. "He wants to, but he won't."

"He can't go on like this."

"Sure he can. Listen, Basch, there are a number of LAWS OF

THE HOUSE OF GOD. LAW NUMBER ONE: GOMERS DON'T DIE."

"That's ridiculous. Of course they die."

"I've never seen it, in a whole year here," said Fats.

"They have to."

"They don't. They go on and on. Young people—like you and me—die, but not the gomers, Never seen it. Not once."

"Why not?"

"I don't know. Nobody knows. It's amazing. Maybe they get past it. It's pitiful. The worst."

Potts came in, looking puzzled and concerned. He wanted the Fat Man's help with Ina Goober. They left, and I turned back to Rokitansky. In the dim half-light I thought I saw tears trickling down the old man's cheeks. Shame swept over me. My stomach churned. Had he heard what we'd said?

"Mr. Rokitansky, are you crying?" I asked, and I waited, as the long seconds ticked away, my guilt moaning inside me.

PURRTY GUD.

"But did you hear what we said about gomers?"

PURRTY GUD.

I left, and stopped by to listen to Fats on Ina Goober.

"But there's no indication for the bowel run," Potts was saying.

"No medical indication," said Fats.

"What else is there?"

"For the House Privates, a big one. Tell him, Basch, tell him."

"Money," I said, "there's a lotta money in shit."

"And no matter what you do, Potts," said the Fat Man, "Ina will be here for weeks. See you on Visit Rounds in fifteen."

"This is the most depressing thing I've ever done," said Potts, lifting up a pendulous breast as Ina continued to shriek and attempt to whack him with her tied-down left hand.

Under the breast was greeny scumlike material, and as the foul aroma hit us, I thought that this first day must be even worse for Potts. He was a displaced person, from Charleston, South Carolina, to the North. He came from a rich Old Family who owned a dream house on Legare Street amidst the magnolias and yellow jasmine, a summerhouse on Pawley's Island, where the only competition was between waves and winds, and an upriver plantation, where he and his brothers would sit out on the porch of a cool summer night and peruse Molière. Potts had made the fatal mistake of coming north to Princeton, and then compounded his mistake by coming to the BMS. There, over the stiffs in the Path course, he'd met a classy female BMS from Boston, and since up till that time Potts's sexual experience had consisted only of "an occasional recreational encounter with a schoolteacher from North Charleston who was fond of my blue-steel throbber," he'd been assaulted by the female BMS in both intellectual and sexual terms, and, like a false spring in February when all the bees hatch and are killed by the next frost, there had blossomed in these two BMSs something each called "love." The wedding had been held just prior to both internships, his in medicine at the House, hers in surgery at the MBH—Man's Best Hospital—the prestigious BMS-affiliated WASP hospital across town. Their on-call schedules would rarely coincide, and their joy of sex would curdle to their job of sex, for what erectile tissue could stand two internships? Poor Potts. Goldfish in the wrong bowl. Even at BMS he'd seemed depressed, and each choice since then had served only to deepen his depression.

"Oh, and by the way," said the Fat Man, poking his head in again, "I've written an order for this."

In his hand was a Los Angeles Rams football helmet.

"What's that for?" asked Potts.

"It's for Ina," Fats said, strapping it on her head. "LAW NUMBER TWO: GOMERS GO TO GROUND."

"What does that mean?" I asked.

"Fall out of bed. I know Ina from last year. She's a totally demented loxed-out gomere, and no matter how securely restrained, she'll go to ground every time. She cracked her skull twice last year, and was here for months. Till we thought of the helmet. Oh, and by the way—even though she's dehydrated, whatever you do, do not hydrate her. Her dehydration's got nothing to do with her dementia, even though the textbooks say it does. If you hydrate her, she stays demented, but she gets incredibly abusive."

42

Potts's head turned to watch the Fat Man go, and somehow, her left hand free, Ina slugged him again. Reflexively Potts raised his hand to hit her, and then stopped himself. The Fat Man nearly keeled over with laughter.

"Ho ho, did you see that? I love 'em, I love these gomers I do . . ." And he laughed his way out the door.

The manipulation of her head intensified Ina's screams: GO AVAY GO AVAY GO AVAY . . .

And so, leaving her tied down six ways from Sunday, the ram horns curling around her ears, we proceeded to Visit Rounds.

Being an academic House affiliated with the BMS, the House of God had a Visit for each ward team: a member of the Privates or the Slurpers, who held teaching rounds every day. Our Visit was George Donowitz, a Private who'd been pretty good in the prepenicillin era. The patient presented was a generally healthy young man who'd been admitted for routine tests of his renal function. My BMS, Levy; presented the case, and when Donowitz grilled him about diagnoses, the BMS, straight from the library of obscure diagnoses, said "amyloidosis."

"Typical," muttered the Fat Man as we gathered around the patient's bed, "typical BMS. A BMS hears hoofbeats outside his window, the first thing he thinks of is a zebra. This guy's uremic from his recurrent childhood infections that damaged his kidneys. Besides, there's no treatment for amyloid, anyway."

"Amyloid?" asked Donowitz. "Good thought. Let me show you a bedside test for amyloid. As you know, people with the disease bruise easily, very easily indeed."

Donowitz reached down and twisted the skin on the patient's forearm. Nothing happened. Puzzled, he said something about "sometimes you have to do it a bit harder" and took hold of the skin, wadded it up, and gave it a tremendous twist. The patient gave a yelp, leaped up off the mattress, and began to cry with pain. Donowitz looked down and found that he'd ripped a big chunk of flesh from the guy's arm. Blood was squirting from the wound. Donowitz turned pale and didn't know what to do. Embarrassed, he took the piece of flesh and

43

tried to put it back, patting it down as if he could make it stay in place. Finally, mumbling, "I . . . I'm so sorry," he ran out of the room. With a cool expertise the Fat Man put a gauze compression bandage on the wound. We left.

"So what did you learn?" asked Fats. "You learned that uremic skin is brittle, and that the House Privates stink. What else? What do we have to look out for in this poor bastard now?"

The BMSs ventured several zebras, and Fats told them to shut up. Potts and I went blank.

"Infection," said Chuck. "In uremia you gotta watch for infection."

"Exactly," said Fats. "Bacteria City. We'll culture for everything. If it hadn't been for Donowitz, that guy would be going home tomorrow. Now, if he lives, it'll be weeks. And if he knew about this, it would be Malpractice City."

At this thought the BMSs perked up again. The BMS now comprised a majority of minority groups, and "Social Medicine" was a hot ticket. The BMSs wanted to tell the patient so he could sue.

"It won't work," said Fats, " 'cause the worse the Private, the better the bedside manner, and the higher the patient's regard. If a doctor buys the TV illusion of 'the doctor,' so does the patient. How can the patient know which are the 'Double O' Privates? No way."

" 'Double O'?" I asked.

"Licensed to kill," said Fats. "Time for lunch. We'll see from the cultures where Donowitz last stuck his finger before trying to murder that poor uremic *schlump*."

The Fat Man was right. Colorful and esoteric bacteria grew out of the wound, including one species that was native only to the rectum of the domestic duck. Fats got excited about this, wanting to publish "The Case of Duck's Ass Donowitz." The patient flirted with death but pulled through. He was discharged a month later, thinking it usual, even a necessary part of his successful course of treatment in the House, for the skin to have been ripped off his arm by his dear and glorious physician.

When the Fat Man went to lunch and we did not, the terror

returned. Maxine asked me to write an order for aspirin for Sophie's headache, and as I started to sign my name, I realized I was responsible for any complications, and I stopped. Had I asked Sophie if she was allergic to aspirin? Nope. I did. She was not. I started to sign the order, and stopped. Aspirin causes ulcers. Did I want to have this poor LOL in NAD bleed out and die from an ulcer? I would wait for the Fat Man and ask him if it was all right. He returned.

"I've got a question for you, Fats."

"I've got an answer. I've always got an answer."

"Is it all right to give Sophie two aspirin for her headache?"

Looking at me as if I were from another planet, Fats said, "Did you hear what you just asked me?"

"Yes."

"Roy, listen. Mothers give aspirin to babies. You give aspirin to yourself. What is this, anyway?"

"I guess I'm just afraid to sign my name to the order."

"She's indestructible. Relax. I'm sitting right here, OK?"

He put his feet up on the counter and opened *The Wall Street Journal.* I wrote the order for the aspirin, and feeling dumb, went to see a gorilla named Zeiss. Forty-two, mean, with bad heart disease, Zeiss needed a new IV put in. I introduced myself, and tried. My hand shook, and in the hot room I got sweaty, and the drops of sweat plopped onto the sterile field. I missed the vein, and Zeiss yelped. The second time, I went in more slowly, and Zeiss squirmed, moaned, and cried out:

"Help, nurse! Chest pain! Get me my nitroglycerin!"

Terrific, Basch—your first cardiac patient and you are about to give him a heart attack.

"I'm having a heart attack!"

Wonderful. Call a doctor. Wait—you are a doctor.

"Are you real doctor or what? My nitros! Fast!"

I put a tablet under his tongue. He told me to get lost. Crushed, I wished I could.

Filled with great moments in medicine, the day wore on. Potts and I clustered around the Fat Man like ducklings around a mother duck. Fats sat there, feet up, reading, ostensibly into the world of stocks and bonds and commodities, and yet, like a king who knows his kingdom as well as he knows his own body, who feels the rages of a distant flood in the pulsating of his own kidneys, and the bounty of a harvest in his own full gut, he seemed to have a sense for any problem on the ward, instructing us, forewarning us, helping Potts and me. And once, only once, he moved—fast, unashamedly a hero.

A scheduled admission, named Leo, had arrived for Potts. Gaunt, white-haired, friendly, a little breathless, Leo stood at the nursing station, suitcase at his feet. Potts and I introduced ourselves and chatted with him. Potts was relieved that here at last was a patient who could talk to him, who was not deathly sick, and who would not slug him. What Potts and I didn't know was that Leo was about to attempt to die. In the midst of a chuckle at one of Potts's jokes, Leo turned blue and fell down on the floor. Potts and I stood there mute, still, frozen, unable to move. My one thought was "How embarrassing for poor Leo." Fats glanced over, leaped to his feet, yelled out "Thump him!" which we were too panicked to do and which I thought would be rather melodramatic, ran over to us, thumped Leo, breathed Leo, closed-chest-cardiac-massaged Leo, IV'd Leo, and organized with a cool virtuosity Leo's cardiac arrest and Leo's return from the world of the dead. A large crowd had arrived to assist in the arrest, and Potts and I had been pushed out of the action. I felt embarrassed and inept. Leo had been laughing at our jokes, his attempt to die was surreal, and I had denied that it existed. Fats was marvelous, his handling of the arrest a work of art.

When Leo had returned to life, Fats walked us back to the nursing station, put his feet back up, opened the paper again, and said, "All right all right so you panicked and you feel like shit. I know. It's awful and it's not the last time neither. Just don't forget what you saw. LAW NUMBER THREE: AT A CARDIAC ARREST, THE FIRST PROCEDURE IS TO TAKE YOUR OWN PULSE."

"I guess I wasn't worried about him because he was an elective admission and not an emergency," said Potts.

"Elective doesn't mean shit around here," said Fats. "Leo would have died. He's young enough to die, you know."

"Young?" I asked. "He looks seventy-five."

"Fifty-two. Congestive heart failure's worse than most cancers. It's ones his age that die. There's no way he'll become a gomer, not with a disease like that. And that's the challenge of medicine: gomers gomers gomers where you can't do anything for them, and then, suddenly—WHAM!—in comes Leo, a lovely guy who can die, and you gotta move fast to save him. It's like what Joe Garagiola said last night about Luis Tiant: 'He gives you all his herky-jerky stuff and then, when he comes in with his heater, it looks a whole yard faster.'"

"His heater?" asked Potts.

"Oh, Jesus," said Fats. "His fast ball—HIS FAST BALL!—where did they get you guys, anyway?"

By that time I was wondering the same thing, and so was Potts. Both of us felt incompetent. For some reason, Chuck was different. He didn't need help. He knew what to do. Later that afternoon I asked him about how he seemed so competent already.

"Easy, man. See, I never read nuthin'. I just did it all."

"You never read anything?"

"Just about them red ants. But I know how to put in a big line, tap a chest—you name it, I done it. Ain't you?"

"Nope. None of that," I said, thinking about my piddling around with Sophie's aspirin.

"Well, man, what all did you do at the BMS?"

"Books. I know all there is to know about medicine in books."

"Well, it looks like that was your failing, man, that right there. Like my not joinin' the army. Maybe I still . . ."

Standing in the streaming July light was a nurse, the afternoon and evening nurse. She stood with her hands on her hips, reading the med cards, legs apart, rocking first one foot on its lateral edge, and then the other. The sharp sunlight made her costume almost transparent, and her legs flowed in smooth lines from her thin ankles and calves all the way up to where all seams meet. She wore no slip, and through her starched white dress I could see the bright patterns on her panties. She knew they would show through. Through her dress showed her bra strap, with its pleading unhookable hook. Her back was to us. Who could know about the front? I

47

half-wished she would never turn around, never spoil the imagined breasts, the imagined face.

"Hey, man, that's somethin' else."

"I love nurses," I said.

"Well, man, what is it about nurses?"

"It must be all that white."

She turned around. I gasped. I blushed. From her ruffled front unbuttoned down past her clavicular notch showing her cleavage, to her full tightly held breasts, from the red of her nail polish and lipstick to the blue of her lids and the black of her lashes and even the twinkly gold of the little cross from her Catholic nursing school, she was a rainbow in a waterfall. After a day in the hot smelly House, after a day of being whacked by the Privates and the Slurpers and the gomers, she was a succulent chilled wedge of an orange squirting in my mouth. She came over to us.

"I'm Molly."

"Gurl, the name's Chuck."

Thinking to myself is it true what they say about interns and nurses, I said, "I'm Roy."

"This your first day, guys?"

"Yeah. I was just thinkin' of joinin' the army instead."

"I'm new too," Molly said. "Started just last month. Scary, eh?"

"No foolin'," said Chuck.

"Hang in there, guys, we'll make it. See ya round the campus, eh?"

Chuck looked at me and I looked at him, and he said, "Sure does make you glad to be spendin' time in here makin' it with the gomers, don't it?"

We watched Molly disappear down the corridor. She stopped to say hello to Potts, who was talking to a young Czech patient, a man yellow from liver disease. The Yellow Man flirted with Molly, and then ogled her as she, giggling, wiggled down the corridor. Potts came over to us and picked up the lab results from the morning.

"Lazlow's liver functions are getting worse," he said.

"He looks mighty yellow," said Chuck. "Lemmee see. Too high. If I was you, Potts, I'd give him some roids."

"Roids?"

"Steroids, man, steroids. Whose patient is he, anyhow?"

"He's mine. He's too poor to afford a Private doctor."

"Well, I'd give him the roids. Never know if he don't have fulminant necrotic hepatitis. If'n he does, unless you hit him with the roids now, he's gonna die."

"Yeah," said Potts, "but the tests aren't that high, and steroids have a lot of side effects. I'd just as soon wait a day."

"Suit yourself. Looks awful yellow, though, don't he?"

Thinking about what the Fat Man said about the young dying, I got up to do some work. When I returned to the nursing station I saw two LOLs in NAD peering through their thick cataract-defying glasses at the blackboard on which were written the names of the new interns on the ward. They mentioned my name, and I asked them if they were looking for me. Tiny, a foot below me, huddled together, they peered up at me. "Oh, yes," said one.

"Oh, aren't you the tall young doctor."

"Handsome and tall," said the other. "Yes, we want to hear the news about our brother Itzak."

"Itzak Rokitansky. The professor. Brilliant, he was."

"How is he, Dr. Basch?"

I felt trapped, not knowing what to say. Fighting the impulse to say PURRTY GUD, I said, "Well . . . I've only been here a day. It's too early to tell. We'll wait and see."

"It's his brain," said one. "His marvelous brain. We're glad you'll be taking care of him, and we'll look for you tomorrow. We visit every day."

"We spend much of our time now visiting the ones who are ill. Good-bye Dr. Basch. Thank you so much."

I left them, and noticed them pointing at me to each other, pleased that I would be their brother's doctor. I was moved. I was a doctor. For the first time that day, I felt excited, proud. They believed in me, in my art. I would take care of their brother, and them. Take care of the whole world, why not? I marched down the hallway with pride. I fingered the chrome of my stethoscope with a certain expertise. Like I knew what I was doing. Far-out.

It didn't last. I got more and more tired, more and more

caught up in the multitudinous bowel runs and lab tests. The jackhammers of the Wing of Zock had been wiggling my ossicles for twelve hours. I hadn't had time for breakfast, lunch, or dinner and there was still more work to do. I hadn't even had time for the toilet, for each time I'd gone in, the grim beeper had routed me out. I felt discouraged, worn. Before he left for the day, the Fat Man came by and asked if there was anything else I wanted to talk about.

"I don't get it," I said. "This isn't medicine, this isn't what I signed up for. Not writing orders for cleanouts for the bowel run."

"Bowel runs are important," said Fats.

"But aren't there any normal medical patients?"

"These are normal medical patients."

"They can't be. Hardly any of them are young."

"Sophie's young; she's sixty-eight."

"Between the old people and the bowel runs, it's crazy. It's not at all what I expected when I walked in here this morning."

"I know. It's not what I expected either. We all expect the American Medical Dream—the whites, the cures, the works. Modern medicine's different: it's Potts being socked by Ina. Ina, who should have been allowed to die eight years ago, when she asked, in writing, in her New Masada chart. Medicine is 'bedrest until complications,' Blue Cross payments for holding hands, and all the rest you've seen today, with the odd Leo thrown in to die."

Thinking of the Rokitansky girls, I said, "You're too cynical."

"Did Potts get socked by Ina, or did he not?"

"He did, but all of medicine isn't like that."

"Right. In the teeth of our expertise, the ones our age die."

"Cynic."

"Ah, yes," said Fats, eyes twinkling, "no one wants you to know all this yet. That's why they wanted you to start with Jo, and not me. I wish I could lie. Doesn't matter, 'cause I can't discourage you yet. Like sex, you gotta find it out for yourself. So why don't you go home?"

"I've got some more work to do."

The House of God

"Well, you won't believe this either, but most of the work you do doesn't matter. For the care of these gomers, it doesn't matter a damn. But do you know to whom you're saying good-bye?"

I did not.

"To the potential father of the Great American Medical Invention. Dr. Jung's. More money than in the bowel run of the stars."

"What the hell is this invention, anyway?"

"You'll see," said Fats, "you will see."

He left. I felt scared without him, and troubled by what he'd said. Got to find it out for myself? In fifth grade, when I'd asked an Italian kid why he liked having sex, he'd said, " 'Cause it feels good." I couldn't understand someone doing something because it felt good. What sense was there in that?

Just before I left I wanted to say good-bye to Molly. I found her carrying a bedpan toward the disposal. I walked with her, the shit sloshing in the pan, and said, "It's not a very romantic way to meet someone."

"The romantic way has gotten me into all kinds of trouble in the past," she said. "This is much more realistic."

I said good night and drove home. The sun was a foreign diseased thing, glowering down a hot red contagion on the city. I was so tired that I had a hard time driving, the white lines weaving back and forth across the road like the visual aura to an epileptic's seizure. The people I saw seemed strange, as if they should have some disease that I should be able to diagnose. No one had a right to be healthy, for my world was only disease. Even the braless women, sweat collecting in the hollows of their breasts, nipples poking out with the full expectation of a lush and sultry summer night, their eroticism magnified by the scents of the July blossoms and of their aroused bodies, were less the stuff of sex and more the specimens of anatomy. Diseases of the breast. I hummed, of all things, a bossanova: "Blame it on the carcinoma, hey hey hey . . ."

In my mailbox was a note: "I think of you all night, I think of you in white. It's hard to be an intern, but I know you will return. Love, Berry." Undressing, I thought of Berry. I thought of

51

Molly, I thought of Potts and his blue-steel throbber, but my own blue steel was throbless that night, for they had started in on me and I was through with feeling anything more for that day, including sex, including love. I lay down on top of the cool sheets, which felt soft as the sole of a baby's foot, soft as the inside of a baby's mouth, and I thought of this puzzling Fat Man and that even if summer is green, death is an odd number, an odd odd number.

4

As I walked onto ward 6-South the next morning, my fear tempered by expectation, I saw a bizarre sight: Potts sat at the nursing station, looking like he'd been shot out of a cannon, his whites filthy, his straight blond hair tangled, blood under his fingernails and vomit on his shoes, his eyes pink, a sick rabbit's eyes. Next to him, strapped to a chair and still wearing the Rams football helmet, was Ina. Potts was writing in her chart. Ina freed herself, screamed: GO AVAY GO AVAY GO AVAY . . . and took a swing at him with her left fist. Enraged, Potts—gentle Molière-perusing Potts of the Legare Street Pottses—screamed: "Goddamnit, Ina, shut the hell up and behave!" and shoved her back down in her chair. I couldn't believe it. One night on call, and a Southern gentleman had become a sadist.

"Hi, Potts, how'd it go last night?"

Raising his head, with tears in his eyes, he said, "How'd it go? Terrible. The Fat Man said to me 'Don't worry, the Privates know the new terns are here, and they're only admitting emergencies.' So what happened? I get five and a half emergencies."

"What's a half?"

"A transfer from another service to medicine. I asked the Fat Man about that, too, and he said, 'Since you only get half credit for the admission, you only do half an exam.'"

"Which half?"

"You do whichever half you want. With these patients, Roy, I'd suggest the top."

Ina rose again, and as Potts pushed her back down in the chair, the Fat Man and Chuck arrived, and Fats said, "I see you went ahead against my advice and hydrated Ina, eh?"

"Yessir," said Potts sheepishly. "I hydrated her, and you were right, she got violent. She acted psychotic, so I gave her an antipsychotic, Thorazine."

"You gave her what?" asked Fats.

"Thorazine."

Fats burst into laughter. Big juicy laughs rolled down from his eyes to his cheeks to his chins to his bellies, and he said, "Thorazine! That's why she's acting like a chimp. Her blood pressure can't be more than sixty. Get a cuff. Potts, you're terrific. First day of internship, and you try to kill a gomere with Thorazine. I've heard of the militant South, but this is the limit."

"I wasn't trying to kill her—"

"Blood pressure fifty-five systolic," said Levy, the BMS.

"Get her head down in her bed," said Fats. "Get some blood into it." As Levy and the nurse carried Ina to her room, the Fat Man informed us that Thorazine in gomers lowers the blood pressure so that the higher human levels don't get perfused. "Ina was struggling to get up so she could lie down. You almost did her in."

"But last night she went crazy—"

"Sundowning," said Fats. "Happens all the time with gomers in the House. They don't have much sensory input to begin with, and when the sun goes down, it gets dark, they go bananas. Come on, let's do the cardflip, eh? Thorazine? I love it."

The Fat Man did the cardflip, beginning with the five and a half admissions that had turned Potts into a sadist. Again, like the day before, most of what I'd learned at the BMS about medicine either was irrelevant or wrong. Thus, for a dehydrated Ina, hydration made her worse. The treatment for depression was to order a barium enema, and the treatment for Potts's third admission, a man with pain in his abdomen but who "knew all of you doctors are Nazis but I'm not quite sure just yet which one of you is Himmler," was not a barium enema and bowel run, but what the Fat Man called a "TURF TO PSY-CHIATRY."

"What's a TURF?" asked Potts.

"To TURF is to get rid of, to get off your service and onto another, or out of the House altogether. Key concept. It's the main form of treatment in medicine. Just call up psychiatry, tell them about the Nazi stuff, don't mention the gut pain, and presto—TURF TO PSYCHIATRY." Ripping up the index card containing the Nazi-seeker and throwing the bits over his shoulder, the Fat Man said, "The TURF, I love it. Let's go. Next?"

Potts presented his last admission, a man of our age who'd been playing baseball with his son, and who, while trying to beat out a hard screaming line drive, had dropped down in the base path unconscious.

"What do you think it is?" asked Fats.

"Intracranial bleed," said Potts. "He's in rough shape."

"He's gonna die," said Fats. "Do you want him to have the benefit of a neurosurgical procedure first?"

"I've already arranged it."

"Great," said Fats, ripping up the man our age and sowing him on the floor. "Potts, you're doing great—a TURF TO NEUROSURG. Two TURFS outa three patients."

Potts and I looked at each other. We felt sad that someone our age who'd been playing ball with his six-year-old son on one of the super twilights of summer was now a vegetable with a head full of blood, about to have his skull cracked by the surgeons.

"Sure it's sad," said Fats, "but there's nothing we can do. The ones our age are the ones who die. Period. The kind of diseases we get, no medico-surgico-bullshitology can cure. Next?"

"Well, the next is the worst," said Potts in a husky voice.

"What's that?"

"The Czech, the Yellow Man, Lazlow. Last night about ten o'clock he had a convulsion, and no matter what I did, he wouldn't stop convulsing. I tried everything. His liver function tests late last night were off the scale. He . . ." Potts looked at Chuck and me, and then, ashamed, looked down into his lap and said, "He's got fulminant necrotic hepatitis. I transferred him to the isolation ward on the other service. He's not my patient—our patient—anymore."

Fats asked Potts in a kind voice if he'd given the Yellow Man steroids. Potts said that he'd thought about it, but had not.

"Why didn't you tell me the lab results? Why didn't you ask me for help?" asked Fats.

"Well I . . . I thought I ought to be able to make the decision alone."

A somber quiet floated down over us, the quiet of sadness and grief. Fats reached over and put his thick arm around Potts's shoulder and said, "I know how shitty you feel. There's no feeling like it in the world. If you don't feel it at least once, Potts, you'll never be a good doc. It's all right. Steroids never help anyway. So he's TURFED to 6-North, eh? Tell you what: after breakfast, since we've got so many TURFS, I'll demonstrate the electric gomer bed."

On the way to the electric gomer bed, whatever that was, Potts, despondent, turned to Chuck and said, "You were right, I should have given him the roids. He's gonna die for sure."

"Wouldn't have helped him none," said Chuck, "he was too far gone."

"I feel so bad," said Potts, "I want Otis."

"Who's Otis?" I asked.

"My dog. I want my dog."

The Fat Man gathered us around the electric gomer bed containing my patient, Mr. Rokitansky. Fats explained how the goal of the tern was to have as few patients as possible. This was opposite the goal of the Privates, the Slurpers, and the House Administration. Since, according to LAW NUMBER ONE: GOMERS DON'T DIE, the gomers would not be leaving the tern's service by way of death, the tern had to find other ways to TURF them. The delivery of medical care consisted of a patient coming in and being TURFED out. It was the concept of the revolving door. The problem with the TURF was that the patient might BOUNCE, i.e., get TURFED back. For example, a gomer who was TURFED TO UROLOGY because he couldn't urinate past his swollen prostate might BOUNCE back to medicine after the urology intern with his filiform probes and flexible followers had managed to produce a total body septicemia, requiring medical care. The secret of the professional TURF that did not BOUNCE, said the Fat Man, was the BUFF.

We asked what was a BUFF.

"Like BUFFING a car," said Fats. "You gotta BUFF the gomers, so that when you TURF them elsewhere, they don't BOUNCE back. Because you gotta always remember: you're not the only one trying to TURF. Every tern and resident in the House of God is lying awake at night thinking about how to BUFF and TURF these gomers somewhere else. Gath, the surgical resident downstairs, is probably giving his terns the same lecture at this very moment, about how to produce heart attacks in gomers to TURF TO MEDICINE. But one of the key medical tools to TURF gomers elsewhere is the electric gomer bed. I'll demonstrate on Mr. Rokitansky. Mr. R., how you doing today?"

PURRTY GUD.

"Good. We're going on a little trip, OK?"

PURRTY GUD.

"Good. Now, the first thing to notice is that the electric gomer bed has side rails. They don't matter. LAW NUMBER TWO: —repeat after me—GOMERS GO TO GROUND."

Responsively we repeated: GOMERS GO TO GROUND.

"Side rails up, side rails down," Fats said, "no matter how securely restrained, no matter how demented, no matter how seemingly incapacitated, GOMERS GO TO GROUND. The next thing about the gomer bed is this foot pedal. Gomers don't have good blood pressures, and when, like Ina, they stop perfusing the newer parts of their brains, they go crazy, start yelling, and try to GO TO GROUND. In the middle of the night, when you get called for the fact that your gomer now has a blood pressure the same as an amoeba, you kick this pedal. Basic, like knowing C major. OK, Maxine, take the blood pressure for a baseline reading."

"Seventy over forty," said Maxine.

"Good," said Fats, and kicked the pedal. The electric gomer bed roared into action. In less than thirty seconds Mr. Rokitansky was virtually upside down on his noggin, his feet pointing at forty-five degrees and his head jammed against the headboard, down below at the other end.

"Blood pressure, Max? Mr. Rokitansky, how ya doin'?"

Although Mr. Rokitansky didn't look like he was doing too good, as Maxine tried to read his BP—blood pressure—from his nearly vertical arm, he said:

PURRTY GUD.

A trouper.

"One hundred and ninety over one hundred," said Maxine.

"This position," said Fats, "is called Trendelenberg. You can get any blood pressure you want out of your gomer, depending on how much Trendelenberg you order. The reverse of Trendelenberg is what?"

Nobody knew.

"Reverse Trendelenberg," said Fats. "Since most gomers have trouble making a BP, you don't put a gomer in reverse too often."

Next the Fat Man showed us how to get just the head of the bed up, for pulmonary edema; the foot of the bed up, for stasis ulcers of the foot; the middle of the bed up, for disorders of the middle. Finally, after he'd done everything with the gomer bed but twist it into a pretzel, using Rokitansky for the holes, he became solemn and said in an excited voice, "I've saved the most important control for last. This button controls the height. Mr. Rokitansky, are you ready?"

PURRTY GUD.

"Good, 'cause here we go," and pushing the button, which sent the bed going down, Fats said, "This is the up-down button and we are going down. Given LAW NUMBER TWO, which is . . . "

"GOMERS GO TO GROUND," we said automatically.

". . . the only way to prevent them from hurting themselves is to have the mattresses on the floor. The nurses hate this position 'cause they have to go around searching for the bedpans on their hands and knees. We tried it last year and it didn't work—the traffic in bedpans went down and the place started to smell like the cattle yards in Topeka. However, now we are going up." Fats shouted out, "Going up!" pushed the button, and Rokitansky began to rise. During the smooth journey Fats called out, "Vacuum cleaners, ladies' lingerie, appliances, toys," and finally, when Rokitansky was five feet off the ground, chest-level with us all, the Fat Man said, "This is one of the most important positions. From this height, if a gomer goes to ground it is an automatic intertrochanteric fracture of a hip, and a TURF TO ORTHOPEDICS. This height," said Fats, beaming, "is called 'The Orthopedic.' The penultimate. And now, the ultimate." Again Fats hit the button, and Mr. Rokitansky floated on up, coming to rest at the level of our heads. "This height is called 'The Neurosurgical.' Going to ground from here results in the TURF TO NEUROSURGERY. And from there, they rarely BOUNCE back. Thank you, gentlemen, see you at lunch."

"Wait," said Levy, the BMS. "You're being cruel to Mr. Rokitansky."

"Whaddaya mean? Mr. Rokitansky, how are you doin'?"

PURRTY GUD.

"But he always says that."

"Oh, yeah? Hey, Mr. Rokitansky, hey, you up there, you got anything else you want to tell us?"

We waited with bated breath. From the Neurosurgical Height the words floated down to us: YEAH.

'What?"

KEEP THE LOWDOWN LOW.

"Gentlemen, thank you again. You will find that if you push the down button, Mr. Rokitansky will come down. Lunch."

"Of course he wasn't serious," said Potts. "No one could be that sadistic. It was a perverted way to try to cheer me up."

"I think he was," I said. "I think he meant it."

"That's crazy," said Potts. "You mean he wants us to use that bed to get old people to break their hips? That's sick."

"What do you think, Chuck?"

"Who knows, man, who knows?"

Potts and I sat at lunch, watching the Fat Man shovel food into his mouth. Chuck, on call that night, had been called away to admit his first patients. All Potts could talk about was how he should have hit the Yellow Man with steroids, and how he wanted to be with Otis, his dog. I felt more confused

59

than scared, puzzled by the Fat Man's version of "the delivery of medical care." We were joined by the three terns on another ward, 6-North. Supported by Eat My Dust Eddie and Hyper Hooper was the Runt, with that same shot-out-of-a-cannon look as Potts. Chuck had seen the Runt earlier in the day and had told me how nervous the Runt was: "Man, he's goin' around with a big gigantic box of Vay-li-um tablets, and about every five minutes he's walkin' around and poppin' one into his mouth." Harold "the Runt" Runtsky had been a friend of mine through the four years at the BMS. A short, stocky product of two red-hot psychoanalysts, the Runt seemed to have had something analyzed out of him, and although he was as smart as anyone in the class, he'd been left shy and quiet, with a little too much slack in his strings, a reactive rather than an active guy, his raucous laugh usually being at someone else's jokes. The Runt had trouble standing up to women sexually. Saddled all through BMS with a roommate who was the most promiscuous guy in the class and who allowed him at times to peek through the keyhole at what was going on, the Runt had gotten into "two-dimensional" sex, magazines and movies. After much prodding, shortly before the internship he'd begun a relationship with an intellectual poet named June. The poems were sexless, asensual, bone-dry.

The Runt looked defused. His mustache drooped. As he sat down, he took out a pillbox, put a pill on his hamburger, and munched it down. When I asked what it was, he said, "Valium, Vitamin V. I've never been so nervous in my life."

"Were you on call last night?"

"Nope. Tonight. Hooper was on call last night."

When I asked Hooper how it had been, he got that same gleam in his eye that he'd gotten at the B-M Deli when the Pearl told the story about doing the autopsy in secret, and he giggled and said, "Great, just great. Two deaths. One permission for the postmortem. Watched it myself this morning. Fantastic."

"Does the Valium help?" Potts asked the Runt.

"It makes me feel kinda sleepy, but I feel pretty unflappable. I'm writing orders for it for all my patients."

"What?" I asked. "You're putting them on Valium too?"

"Why not? They're all very nervous, having me as their doc. By the way, Potts, thanks a lot for that transfer last night, the Yellow Man," said the Runt sarcastically. "Terrific."

"I'm sorry," said Potts, "I should have given him the steroids. Has he stopped convulsing?"

"Nope. Not yet."

I got beeped to go back to the ward, and as I left I asked Eat My Dust how it was going for him.

"How's it going? Compared to California, it sucks."

When the Rokitansky girls asked to speak with me again, I felt grand. Their hearing aids turned up full blast, they asked for the latest bulletin from "our brother's doctor." I felt like I was in command, like I had something to give. They hung on my every word. When my beeper called me away, they said they were sorry they'd bothered me and that I must have more important things to do, and as I left them to go down to my first Outpatient Clinic, I felt a real thrill. When I stepped into the elevator, people looked at me, tried to read my name tag, knowing I was a doc. I was proud of my stethoscope, of the blood on my sleeve. The Fat Man was a burnt-out case. Being a doc was a thrill. You could do things for people. They had faith in you. You couldn't let them down. Rokitansky would get well.

Cocky, seduced by the illusion of somehow getting Rokitansky to regenerate his brain, I entered the Outpatient Clinic. Chuck and I had our Clinics on the same day, and, side by side, listened as the Clinic was explained. We'd be functioning just like General Practitioners, except we wouldn't get paid. We each were given an office, to use once every two weeks. The final seduction was when they presented each of us with our cards:

ROY G. BASCH, M.D. OUTPATIENT CLINIC, HOUSE OF GOD.

Bolstered by pride, pretending to know what I was doing, I waded through my first Clinic. Too poor to afford a House Private, Clinic patients would turn out to be of two types: fifty-two-year-old husbandless black mothers with high blood pressure, and seventy-two-year-old husbandless Jewish LOLs in

NAD with high blood pressure. I would hardly ever see a male, and to see someone below the age of fifty-two, except for "mental disturbance" or venereal disease, would be publishable. My first very own patient was a LOL in NAD in need of a checkup and a prescription for a new artificial breast and padded bra with fillable pockets. Who knew how to write a prescription? Not me. She wrote it, I signed it, and, grateful, she left. Next was a Portuguese woman who wanted me to do something about her corns. Who knew about corns? I toyed with the idea of writing her a prescription for an artificial foot and a padded shoe with fillable socks, but then I remembered the Fat Man and TURFED her to Podiatry. The next LOL in NAD was seventy-five, Jewish, and came in with her upper eyelids Scotch-taped to her forehead. Reading her old chart, I found out that this was a case of "drooping lids of unknown etiology" and that her previous Clinic tern had TURFED her to Ophthalmology, where the resident had told her to "tape them up or I operate" and she'd chosen the tape and had been TURFED back to Medicine. This was a BOUNCE.

"Oh, I love meeting all you nice young doctors," she said.

"How long have you had this tape on your lids?"

"Eight years. How much longer do I have to wear it?"

"What happens if you take it off?"

"My eyelids fall down."

I wrote her a prescription for more tape. She grasped my hand and began to chatter about how glad she was to have me as her doctor. It was hard for me to listen because her taped-up lids made her eyes bulge out like a monster of the deep, and the only thing that stopped her life story from pouring out was that the nurse brought in my next patient, the last of the afternoon. This was a hypertensive black woman of fifty-four named Mae, with no chief complaint except "my joints hurt when I play basketball with my kids" and a request for a pelvic exam. When she was up in the stirrups Mae started spouting Jehovah's Witness gospel, and after she got dressed, chattering all the while a mixture of religion, family history, and history of her previous terns at the House Clinic, she spewed out some Witness pamphlets and left. These women loved coming to the doctor. I walked into Chuck's office and found him with a LOL in NAD too. He was doing something I'd never seen done before in medicine, something with a tape measure and a breast.

"Well, you see, man, this lady says her breast is growing."

"Just one of them?"

"Right. So I thought I'd better measure and see if it gets any bigger in the next two weeks."

Back on the ward, I felt grand. I was excited, thrilled at being a doctor. Having been a red-hot in my academic career, there was no reason not to be a House red-hot too. Hadn't the Pearl himself, earlier in the day, congratulated me on the way I'd cleaned out his patient for the bowel run? Feeling Dr. Kildarish, I sat in the warm sunlight of the nursing station. Looking into the room across the hallway, I saw Molly, perky transparent Molly, bending over the bed, fiddling with the sheet. She kept her legs straight, so her miniskirt rode up her thighs, and with a final reach over to the far side of the bed, she hiked the hem up over her ass, showering me with the rainbow-and-flower pattern of her little-girl panties, snug against the firm full gluteal folds that formed an awning over the juicy female thing that grew up there. I could feel a half-chub mumbling and squirming in my whites.

"That's the straight bendover." It was the Fat Man. He sat down beside me, unrolling the *Journal*.

"Huh?"

"That nursing maneuver, where they bend from the waist and flash their ass. Called the Straight Bendover Nursing Maneuver. Learn it in nursing school. What are you going to do about TURFING Sophie? She's settling in, and I'm warning you, she's really getting Putzeled this time. She could be here for months."

"Putzeled?"

"Bob Putzel, her Private, remember? He uses the standard method: admit the LOL in NAD, do a test, produce a complication, do another test to diagnose the complication, get another complication, and so on until they're gomertose and non-TURFABLE. Do you want that nice LOL in NAD to become an Ina Goober? Nip it in the bud. Do something now. You gotta get her to leave."

"How?"

"Do a painful procedure. She doesn't like painful procedures."

"I can't think of anything that's indicated."

"Oh. Well, she has a headache, and her noon temp is a degree high. No matter that it's almost a hundred Fahrenheit up here and all the temps are a degree high, no matter, 'cause the chart is BUFFED with a recorded noon temp a degree high. Oh, and she has a stiff neck too. So: headache, fever, stiff neck; diagnosis?"

"Meningitis."

"Procedure?"

"Lumbar puncture, LP. But she doesn't really have meningitis."

"She might. If you don't LP her, you might miss it, like Potts missed with Mellow Yellow. And don't worry about hurting Sophie, she's tough. A Gray Panther. Get Molly to help." Looking in the paper, Fats mumbled, "The Dow Jones is up, baby, up. Good. Good climate for the Invention now, for sure."

"For what?"

"The Invention, the Invention! The Great American Medical Invention!"

With the Dow Jones rising up over America's colorful ass, how could I not enjoy doing an LP on Sophie? Molly had never before assisted at an LP and was glad to help. Together we walked into Sophie's room. Levy the Lost, my BMS, was sitting on Sophie's bed Putzeling her hand, "taking a history." He was still at the beginning, asking her "What brought you to the hospital?"

"What brought me? Dr. Putzel, in his white Continental."

I stopped Levy, and instructed Molly in how to hold Sophie curled up in a fetal position on her side, exposing her back to me. As Molly bent down over Sophie, grabbing her behind the knees and neck, arms spread apart like Christ on the Cross, I noticed that the two top buttons of her ruffled blouse were undone, and I was staring into an enticing cleft between Molly's breasts, bubbling up out of lacy bra cups. She noticed me noticing, and said, smiling, "Go ahead." How bizarre, the contrast between these two women. I had an urge to slip my penis into Molly's cleft. Potts popped his head in, and asked us if we knew where a Bible could be found.

"A Bible? What on earth for?" asked Molly.

"For pronouncing a patient dead," said Potts, vanishing again.

I tried to recall how to do an LP. At BMS I had been particularly bad at these, and to do an LP on an old person was more difficult, for the ligaments in between the vertebrae are calcified, like guano on an old rock. And then there was the fat. Fat is death to a tern. All the anatomical landmarks get obliterated in fat, and as I tried to locate Sophie's midline, with my ill-fitting rubber gloves and the rolling fat, it was impossible. I thought I had it, and as I put the needle in, Sophie screamed and leaped, and as I advanced the needle further, she yelped and leaped again. Molly's hair came loose, a blond cascade over Sophie's old and sweaty torso. Every time I looked into Molly's cleavage I got aroused, and every time Levy said something I got mad and wanted to slug him, and every time I advanced the needle Sophie leaped up in pain. I began to sweat. I tried another spot on Sophie's fat back. No luck. Another. Nothing. I noticed that blood was coming out of the spinal needle, so I knew it wasn't where it was supposed to be. Where was it? Lubricated by the sweat, my glasses fell off and contaminated the sterile field. Molly let go at the same time, Sophie uncoiled and looked like she was about to GO TO GROUND from just below the Orthopedic Height but we caught her in time. Embarrassed, my cockiness splattered in sweat all over Sophie, I told Levy to stop smirking and get the Fat Man. Fats came in, in two shakes had Molly expose herself and Sophie's porcine back, and, humming a TV commercial that sounded like "I wish I were an Oscar Weiner weiner," with a smooth and effortless Sam Snead stroke sliced through the fat and popped into the subarachnoid space. I was amazed at his virtuosity. We watched the clear spinal fluid drip out. Fats took me aside, and like a coach put his arm around my shoulders and whispered:

"You were way off the midline. You hit either kidney or gut. Pray kidney, 'cause if it's gut, it's Infection City, and she may suffer the ultimate TURF, to Pathology."

"Pathology?"

"The morgue. No BOUNCE. But I think it worked. Listen."

"I WANT TO GO HOME I WANT TO GO HOME I WANT TO . . . "

I began to feel scared that I had started an infection that would send Sophie home for good. As if in confirmation, from the next bed, behind the curtain, Potts was dealing with his first death. His patient, the young father who'd dropped on the first-base line the day before, had died. Potts had been called to pronounce the patient dead, as required by law. We peeked through the curtain: Potts was standing at the foot of the bed, his BMS beside him holding a Bible, on which rested Potts's hand. His other hand was raised toward the body, which was lying there as white as a corpse, which was what it was. As we watched, Potts intoned:

"By the power vested in me by this great state and nation I hereby pronounce you, Elliot Reginald Needleman, dead."

Molly, snuggling up to me so that her left breast brushed my arm, asked, "Is that really necessary?" and I said I didn't know, and I asked Fats, who said, "Of course not. The only federal regulation is that you take the two pennies out of your loafers and put them over the dead man's eyes."

Potts, decimated, sat with us at the nursing station. Slurring his words, his eyes bloodshot, he said, "He's dead. Maybe I shoulda shipped him to surgery sooner. I shoulda done something. But I was so tired when he came in, I couldn't even think."

"You did all you could," I said. "He popped an aneurysm, nothing would have helped. The surgeons refused to operate."

"Yeah, they said it was too late. If I had moved faster, maybe—"

"Enough of that," said the Fat Man. "Potts, you listen to me. There's a LAW you've gotta learn, LAW NUMBER FOUR: THE PATIENT IS THE ONE WITH THE DISEASE. Understand?"

Before he had a chance to understand, we were interrupted by the Chief Resident, the Fish. He had a concerned look on his face. It turned out that both Needleman and the Yellow Man were not Private patients, but House patients, and the Fish was partially responsible.

"Liver disease is a special interest of mine," said the Fish, "I've recently had the opportunity to review the world literature on fulminant necrotic hepatitis. Why, the case of Lazlow would make a very interesting research project. Perhaps the House Staff would wish at some point to undertake such a project?"

No one said he wanted to undertake such a project.

"However, both the Leggo and I feel, Dr. Potts, that you waited too long without giving steroids. Do you understand?"

Stabbed, Potts, said, "Yes, you're right. I understand."

"I'm on my way to an impromptu colloquium on Lazlow. We've brought in the Australian, the world's expert on this disease. It does not look good. You waited too long. Oh, and one more thing," said the Fish, looking at Chuck's dirty whites and unbuttoned shirt without a tie, "the way you dress, Chuck. Not professional. Not enough for the House. Clean whites here, and a tie. Understand?"

"Fine, fine," said Chuck.

"And you, Roy," said the Fish, pointing to the cigarette I'd just lit up, "enjoy that, because it will prove to be three minutes off your life."

I saw red. The Fish slid off down the corridor to the colloquium. A morbid silence coated us. The Fat Man broke it, spitting out, "Jerk! Now, just remember this, Potts, if you want to end up like that jerk, you'll believe him. If not, you'll listen to me: THE PATIENT IS THE ONE WITH THE DISEASE."

"Are you really going to dress better?" I asked Chuck.

"'Course not, man, 'course not. In Memphis, we don't even wear neckties to funerals. Man, these gomers are sumphin' else. None of my four admissions so far believes I'm really their doctor. They all think I'm the hep."

"Hep?"

"H-e-l-p. Hep. The colored hep. See you later."

Staring out the window, Potts muttered to himself something about how he should have given the Yellow Man the roids, but the Fat Man stopped him, saying, "Potts, go home."

"Home? Charleston? You know, right now my brother—he's in construction—he's probably lying out in a hammock on Pawley's Island, sipping a fizz. Or maybe upcountry, where it's all green and cool. I never should have left. The Fish is right in what he said, but if this was the South, he never would have said it. Not like that. My mother has a word for him: 'common.' Guess I made my choice, though didn't I? Well, I will go home. Thank God Otis is at home."

"Where's your wife?"

"She's on call tonight at the MBH. It'll be just Otis and me. That's just fine, 'cause he loves me, too. He'll be lying there on the bed with his balls up in the air, snoring. It'll be good to go home to him. See you tomorrow."

We watched Potts stumble on down the hallway. He came to the colloquium, outside the room containing the Yellow Man. Without looking in, as if ashamed, Potts slunk past them and out the door.

"This is crazy," I said to the Fat Man, "this internship is nothing like what I thought it would be. What do we do for these patients anyway? They either die or we BUFF and TURF them to some other part of the House."

"That's not crazy, that's modern medicine."

"I don't believe it. Not yet."

"Of course you don't. You'd be crazy to. It's only your second day. Wait till tomorrow, when you and me are on call together. Well, I'm going home. Pray for the Dow Jones, Basch, pray the fucker stays on up."

Who cared?

I finished my work and walked down the corridor toward the elevator. The crowd around the Australian expert was breaking up, and out of it rolled the Runt. He looked a lot worse. I asked him what was going on, and he said, "The Australian said we should do an exchange transfusion, where you take all the old blood out and replace it with new."

"That never works. The blood still has to go through the liver, and there is no liver. He's going to die."

"Yeah, that's what they all said too, but since he's young and was walking around yesterday, they think it's worth a try. They said I had to do it, tonight, and I'm scared stiff."

Screams came from the room. The Yellow Man was flopping up and down on the bed like a hooked tuna, screaming. A member of Housekeeping ambled up, pushing two huge carts

68

laden with linen, gowns, operating-room garb, and large polyethylene bags labeled "Danger—Contaminated." The head
nurse told the Runt that the blood would be ready in half an
hour and that there was only one nurse to assist, since the others were scared of sticking themselves with a needle and
catching the fatal disease. They refused to work in the room.
The Runt and I watched the nurse walk away, and watched
Housekeeping, whistling, disappear into the down elevator.
The Runt looked up at me with terror in his eyes, and then put
his head on my shoulder and cried. I didn't know what to do. I
would have volunteered to help, but I was scared of catching
whatever bad thing it was that had you walking around chatting up the Tit one day and convulsing like a hooked tuna the
next.

"Do one thing for me," said the Runt. "If I die, take the
money in my trust fund and donate it to the BMS. Make a prize
for the member of the class who first realizes the insanity of
this business and drops out to do something else."

I helped him on with his sterile operating-room garb, his
gloves, face mask, hat. Like an astronaut, he launched himself
with an awkward shuffle into the room, up to the bed, and
started the procedure. The bags of fresh blood began to arrive.
With a lump in my throat I walked out, down the corridor. The
cries, smells, bizarre sights riddled my head like bullets in a
nightmare war. Even though I hadn't touched the Yellow Man,
I went to the bathroom and gave myself a long surgical scrub. I
felt terrible. I liked the Runt, and he was going to poke himself
with a contaminated needle, catch this liver-ripping hepatitis,
turn yellow, flip like a gaffed fish, and die. And for what?

As if in a tankful of water, I listened to Berry while I read my
father's latest letter:

> . . . By now you must be in the middle of your work and it
> will settle down to a routine. I know that there is so much to
> learn and you will be immersed in it. Medicine is a great profes-
> sion and it is a wonderful thing to be able to heal the sick. I
> played eighteen on Saturday in the heat and it was made bear-
> able by a gallon of iced tea and a birdie on number . . .

Unlike my father, Berry was not as interested in preserving an illusion of medicine as she was in understanding my experience. She asked me what it had been like, and although I tried to tell her, I realized that it had not been like anything, and I could not.

"But what made it so hard? The fatigue?"

"Nope. I think what made it hard was the gomers and the Fat Man."

"Tell me about it, love."

I told her how I couldn't decide whether or not what the Fat Man taught about medicine was crazy. The more I saw, the more sense the Fat Man made. I had begun to think I was crazy for thinking he was crazy. As an example, I told Berry about the gomers and about how we'd laughed at Ina in her Rams helmet socking Potts with her purse.

"Calling old people gomers sounds like a defense."

"Gomers aren't just old people. The Fat Man says he loves old people and I believe him, because he gets tears in his eyes when he talks about his grandmother and her matzoh balls that you eat sitting on ladders scraping them off the ceiling."

"Laughing at this Ina is sick."

"It does seem sick right now, but it didn't then."

"Why did you laugh at her?"

"I don't know. It was hilarious at the time."

"I'd like to understand. Try again."

"Nope. I can't."

"Try to snap out of it, Roy, please—"

"No! I don't want to think about it anymore."

I shut up. She got mad. She couldn't have known that all I wanted then was to be taken care of. Things had moved fast. Two days, and already, like swimming in a strong current, I'd looked up and found my life an eternity farther downstream, the near bank far gone. A rift had opened. Up until then, Berry and I had been in the same world, outside the House of God. Now, for me, the world was inside the House, with the Yellow Man my age and the Runt both about to crump, with the dead father my age who'd popped an aneurysm playing baseball, with the Privates, the Slurpers, and the gomers. And with Molly. Molly knew what a gomer was, and why we'd laughed.

With Molly, so far, there had been no talk, there'd been only the straight bendovers, the clefts and the round full hollows, the red nails and blue lids and panties splashed with flowers and rainbows, and the laughter amidst the gomers and the dead. Molly was the promise of a breast against an arm. Molly was recess.

Yet Molly was recess from much that I loved. I didn't want to laugh at patients. If it really were as hopeless as the Fat Man said, I'd give up now. I didn't like this rift with Berry, and so, thinking to myself that the Fat Man really was bananas after all and that, somehow, if I believed him I'd lose Berry, I said, "You're right. It's sick to laugh at the old people. I'm sorry." For an instant I saw myself as a real doc rushing in and saving lives, and Berry and I sighed together and snuggled together and got undressed together and were together in love together tight and warm-wet, and that portending rift sealed over again.

She slept. I lay awake, afraid of my tomorrow, my upcoming first night on call.

5

When I went to wake up Chuck the next morning, he looked wrecked: his afro smushed down over one side of his head, his face scarred from the wrinkles of the sheets, the white of one eye red, and the other eye swollen shut.

"What happened to your eye?"

"Bugbite. Bugfuckinbite, right in my eye. There's some fierce kind of bug in this on-call room."

"Your other eye looks terrible too."

"Man, you should see it from this side. I called Housekeeping for some clean sheets, but you know how it is. I never answered calls neither, before those postcards started arrivin'. There's only one way to handle Housekeeping, man, and I'm gonna do it."

"What's that?"

"Love. The boss of bedmaking is named Hazel. She's a big Cuban woman. I know I could love her."

In the cardflip, Potts asked Chuck how it had gone.

"Great. Six admissions, the youngest seventy-four."

"What time did you get to sleep?"

"Midnight."

Amazed, Potts asked, "How? How'd you ever get the write-ups done?"

"Easy, man, shitty write-ups, man, shitty write-ups."

"Key concept," said the Fat Man, "to think that you're doing a shitty job. If you resign yourself to doing a shitty job, you go

72

ahead and get the job done, and since we're all in the ninety-ninth percentile of interns, at one of the best ternships in the world, what you do turns out to be a terrific job, a superlative job. Don't forget that four out of every ten interns in America can't speak English."

"So it wasn't so bad, Chuck?" I asked hopefully.

"Bad? Oh, it was bad. Man, last night I was used."

My worst warning was the Runt. As I'd walked into the House that morning, deflated by the transition from the bright and healthy July to the diseased neon and a-seasonal stink of the corridor, I'd passed the room of the Yellow Man. Outside it were the bags marked "Danger—Contaminated," now full of bloodstained sheets, towels, scrub suits, and equipment. The room was covered with blood. A special-duty nurse, wrapped like a spacewoman in sterile clothes, was sitting as far from the body as possible, reading *Better Homes and Gardens.* The Yellow Man lay still, absolutely still. The Runt was nowhere to be seen.

It wasn't until lunch that I was to see him. He was cigar-ash gray. Eat My Dust Eddie and Hyper Hooper led him to the lunch table like a dog on a leash. As he put his tray down, we noticed there was nothing on it but silverware. No one pointed that out.

"I'm going to die," said the Runt, taking out his pillbox.

"You are not going to die," said Hooper. "You are never going to die."

The Runt told us about the exchange transfusion, about taking the old blood out of one vein and putting the new blood into another: "Things were going pretty well, and then, I'd taken a needle out of the groin and was about to put it into the last bag of blood, and that porpoise, Celia the nurse, well, she held up this other needle from the Yellow Man's belly and . . . stuck it in my hand."

There was a dead silence. The Runt was going to die.

"All of a sudden I felt faint. I saw my life ebb past me. Celia said Gee I'm sorry and I said Aw shucks it's all right it just means I'm going to die and Mellow Yellow's twenty-one and I'm twenty-seven and I've already lived six more years than him and I've spent my last night doing something I knew was completely worthless and we'll die together, him and me, but it's OK, Celia." The Runt paused, and then screamed, "HEAR ME, CELIA? IT'S OK! I went to bed at four A.M. and I was sure I'd never wake up."

"But the incubation period is four to six months."

"So? So in four months one of you will exchange-transfuse me."

"It's all my fault," said Potts. "I shoulda hit him with steroids."

After the others had left, the Runt turned to me and said he had a confession to make: "It's about my third admission last night. In the middle of all this crap with the Yellow Man, this guy comes into the Emergency Room and I . . . I couldn't handle it. I offered him five dollars if he'd go home. He took it and left."

Prodded by my fear of its arrival, my time to be left alone on call arrived. Potts signed out his patients to me and went home to Otis. Scared, I sat at the nursing station, watching the sad sun die. I thought of Berry, and wished I was with her, doing things that young ones like us were supposed to be doing, while we still had our health. My fear mushroomed. Chuck came up, signed out his patients and asked me, "Hey, man, notice anything different?"

I did not.

"My beeper, man, it's off. They can't get me now."

I watched him walk down the long corridor. I wanted to call out to him, "Don't go, don't leave me alone here," but I did not. I felt so lonesome I wanted to cry. The Fat Man, earlier in the afternoon, as I'd gotten more and more nervous, had tried to reassure me, telling me that I was lucky, that he'd be on call with me all night.

"Besides," he'd said, "tonight's a great night, it's *The Wizard of Oz* and blintzes."

"The Wizard of Oz and Blintzes?" I asked. "What's that?"

"You know, the tornado, the yellow brick road, and that terrific Tin Man trying to get into Dorothy's pants. Great flick. And at the ten-o'clock meal, blintzes. We'll have a ball."

That hadn't helped me much. As I tended to the chaos of the ward, handling the now-hydrated and violent Ina Goober and tending to the feverish Sophie, who by now was so out of it from the LP that she'd attacked Putzel, I almost trembled with fear of what was to come. And then, when my time came, I choked. I was on the toilet and from six flights down, in her communications bunker, the page operator scored a direct hit: DR. BASCH CALL EMERGENCY WARD FOR AN ADMIS- SION, DR. BASCH . . . Someone was dying in the E.W. and they wanted me? Didn't they know not to come into a teaching hospital in the first week of July? They wouldn't see a doctor, they would see me. What did I know? I panicked. Olaf's Potato started to zing through my mind again, and, heart pounding, I sought out the Fat Man, who was in the TV room immersed in · *The Wizard of Oz.* Nibbling at a salami, he was singing along with the flick: "Because because because because because of the wonderful things he does. We're off to see the Wizard, the wonderful Wizard of Ozzz . . . "

It was difficult to interrupt him. I thought it peculiar that he'd take an interest in something as playful as *Oz*, but I soon found out that his interest was, like many of his interests, per- verted:

"Do it," Fats muttered, "do it to Dorothy with the oil can. Spin her around on your hat, Ray, spin her around on your hat."

"I've got something to tell you," I said.

"Shoot."

"There's a patient, an admission, in the Emergency Ward."

"Good. Go see her. You're a doctor now, remember? Doctors see patients. Do it, Ray Bolger, do it to her STAT!"

"Yeah, I know," I squeaked, "but I . . . you see, someone's going to be dying down there, and I . . ."

Taking his eyes off the tube, Fats looked at me and said in a kind voice, "Oh, I see. Scared, huh?"

I nodded and told him that all I could think of was Olaf's big potato.

"Right. OK, so you're scared. Who isn't, his first night on call? Even I was scared too. Let's go. We gotta hurry. We've only got half an hour till the ten-o'clock meal. What nursing home is she from?"

"I don't know," I said as we walked to the elevator.

"You don't know? Damn. They've probably already sold her bed, so we won't be able to TURF her back there. One of the true medical emergencies, when the nursing home sells the gomere's bed."

"How do you know it will be a gomere?"

"The odds, just playing the odds."

The elevator opened, and there was the 6-North tern, Eat My Dust Eddie, standing with a stretcher on which was piled his very own first E.W. admission: three hundred pounds of flesh, naked but for dirty underpants, huge herniations of his abdominal wall, a great medicine ball of a head with little slots for eyes, nose, and mouth, and a bald skull covered with purplish crisscrossing neurosurgical scars so it looked like a box of Purina dog chow. And all of it was convulsing.

"Roy," said Eat My Dust, "meet Max."

"Hi, Max," I said.

"HI JON HI JON HI JON," said Max.

"Max perseverates," said E.M.D. "They unhooked his frontal lobe."

"Parkinson's disease for sixty-three years," said Fats, "a House record. Max comes in when his bowels get blocked. See that intestine pushing its way out through the scars in his belly? Those lumps?"

We did.

"If you X-ray it, you'll find it's feces. Last time Max was here, it took nine weeks to clean him out, and the only thing that finally worked was a small-handed female Japanese cellist who was also a BMS student, equipped with special long-armed gynecological gloves, and promised the internship of her choice if she would disimpact Max manually. Wanna hear 'Fix the lump'?"

We did.

"Max," said Fats, "what do you want us to do?"

"FIX THE LUMP FIX THE LUMP FIX THE LUMP," said Max.

Eat My Dust Eddie and his BMS put their shoulders to the wheels of the stretcher, and Max, gathering momentum, rolled off into the neon sunset. Yoked together, the three looked like they were trudging around a ring of the mountain of Purgatory. Coming back to my senses as we rode the elevator down, I asked the Fat Man how come he seemed to know all the patients, like Max, Ina, and Mr. Rokitansky.

"There is a finite number of House gomers," said Fats, "and since GOMERS DON'T DIE, they rotate through the House several times a year. It's almost as if they get their yearly schedules in July, just like us. You get to know them by their particular shrieks. But what diseases does your gomere have?"

"I don't know. I haven't seen her yet."

"Doesn't matter. Pick an organ, any organ."

I fell silent, so scared that I was having trouble thinking of an organ.

"What is this? Where did they get you from? On quota? Is there affirmative action for Jews? What lies inside the chest cavity and beats?"

"The heart."

"Good. So the gomere has congestive heart failure. What else?"

"The lungs."

"Terrific. You're really cooking now. Pneumonia. Your gomere has CHF and pneumonia, she's septic from her indwelling catheter, refuses to eat, wants to die, is demented, and has an unobtainable BP. What's the first thing—the crucial thing—to do?"

I thought of the diagnosis of septic shock, and suggested an LP.

"Nope. That's BMS textbook. Forget textbook. I am your textbook. Nothing you learned at the BMS will help you tonight. Listen—key concept—LAW NUMBER FIVE: PLACEMENT COMES FIRST."

"I think that's going a little too far. I mean, you're making all kinds of assumptions about this person. You're treating a human being like a piece of baggage."

"Oh? I'm crass, cruel, and cynical again, am I? I don't feel anything for the ill. Well, I do. I cry at movies. I've spent twenty-seven Passovers being pampered by the sweetest grandma any Brooklyn boy ever had. But a gomere in the House of God is something else. You'll find out for yourself tonight."

77

We stood at the nursing station of the E.W. Several others were sitting there: Howard Grinspoon, who was the new tern on call in the E.W.; and two policemen. Howard I'd known from the BMS. He was blessed with two traits which were to prove to be so useful to him in medicine: unawareness of self, and unawareness of others. Not smart, Howard had slurped his way through BMS and into the House by doing something with urine, either putting urine through computers or running computers on urine. This had endeared him to that other man of little urine, the Leggo. A plodder and a planner, Howard was also into using IBM computer cards to aid in medical decision-making. By the start of the ternship, he already had developed a terrific bedside manner, to hide his rampant indecisiveness. Although Howard wanted to "present the case" to Fats and me, Fats ignored him, focusing on the policemen. One policeman was huge, barrel-shaped, with red hair growing out of and into most of the slitty features on his fat red face. The other policeman was a matchstick, decked out, facially, in white of skin and black of hair, with vigilant eyes and a large and worrisome mouth filled with many disparate teeth.

"I'm Sergeant Gilheeny," said the red, barrel-shaped one, "Finton Gilheeny, and this is Officer Quick. Dr. Roy G. Basch, we wish you hello and Shalom."

"You don't look Jewish," I said.

"You don't have to be Jewish to love a hot pumpernickel bagel, and besides, the Jews and the Irish are similar in one respect."

"What respect is that?"

"In their respect for the family unit, and the concomitant fucked-up nature of their lives."

Howard, irritated at being ignored, tried to tell us again about my admission. The Fat Man silenced him at once.

"But you don't know anything about her," said Howard.

"Tell me her shriek, and I'll know it all."

"Her what?"

"Her shriek. Whatever sound she makes."

"Well," said Howard, "she does shriek. She makes a ROODLE."

"Anna O.," said Fats. "Hebrew House for the Incurables. This admission will be approximately number eighty-six. You start with a hundred sixty milligrams of the diuretic Lasix and you go up from there."

"How'd you know all that?" asked Howard.

Ignoring him, Fats turned to the policemen and said, "It's obvious that Howard has failed to do the most important things in the case. I trust that you two gentlemen have?"

"Even in our role as policemen who patrol the city and environs of the House of God and often sit and chat and drink coffee with the brilliant young medicos," said Gilheeny, "we do sometimes intervene in emergency patient care."

"We are men of the law," said Quick, "and we followed the House LAW: PLACEMENT COMES FIRST, and called the Hebrew House. Alas, during the ambulance ride here, Anna O.'s bed was sold."

"Too bad," said the Fat Man. "Well, at least Anna O. is a great one to learn on. She's taught countless House terns medicine. Roy, go see her. You've got twenty minutes till the ten-o'clock meal. I'll wait here and jabber with our friends the cops."

"Magnificent!" said the redheaded policeman, beaming a grand sunny smile, "for twenty minutes of Fat Man chat is a gift horse we shall look everywhere but in the mouth."

I asked Gilheeny why he and Quick were so well-informed about this medical emergency, and his reply puzzled me:

"Would we be policemen if we were not?"

I left the Fat Man and the two policemen huddling together, intensifying their chatter. I went to the door of room 116, and once again I felt alone and afraid. Taking a deep breath, I went in. The walls were covered with green tile, and the bright neon light glittered off the stainless-steel equipment. It was as if I had stepped into a tomb, for there was no doubt that here, somehow, I was in touch with that poor thing, death. In the center of the room was a stretcher. In the center of the stretcher was Anna O. She lay motionless, her knees bent up toward the ceiling, her shoulders curved around toward her knees, so that her head, unsupported and rigid, almost touched her thighs. From the side she looked like the letter W. Was she dead? I called to her. No answer. I felt for a pulse. No pulse. Heart-beat? None. Breath? No. She was dead. How fitting, that in her death her entire body should have hooked around in mimicry of her persecuted Jewish nose. I felt relieved that she was dead, that the pressure to care for her was off. I saw her little tuft of white hair, and I remembered my grandmother lying in her coffin, and I was filled with sadness for that loss. A lump formed in my midsection, tugged at the tip of my heart, and pulled itself up into my throat. I felt that strange sensation of gritty warmth that comes just before tears. My lower lip curled down. To control myself, I sat.

The Fat Man rushed in and said, "All right, Basch, blintzes and . . . hey, what's the matter with you?"

"She's dead."

"Who's dead?"

"This poor woman. Anna O."

"Baloney. Have you lost your mind?"

I said nothing to this. Perhaps I had lost my mind and the strange policemen and the gomere were all a hallucination. Sensing my sadness, the Fat Man sat down next to me.

"Have I steered you wrong so far?"

"You're too cynical, but whatever you say seems to be true. Even though it's crazy."

"Exactly. So listen to me, and I'll tell you when to cry, 'cause there are times during this ternship when you'll have to cry, and if you don't cry then, you'll jump off this building and they'll scrape you up from the parking lot and drip you into a plastic bag. You'll wind up a bagful of goo. Get it?"

I said I did.

"But I'm telling you that now is not the time, 'cause this Anna O. is a true gomere, and LAW NUMBER ONE: GOMERS DON'T DIE."

"But she's dead. Just look at her."

"Oh, she looks dead, sure. I'll give you that."

"She is dead. I called to her and felt for a pulse and listened for a heartbeat and looked for a breath. Nothing. Dead."

"With Anna, you need the reverse stethoscope technique. Watch."

The Fat Man took off his stethoscope, plugged the earpiece

into Anna O.'s ears, and then, using the bell like a megaphone, shouted into it: "Cochlea come in, cochlea come in, do you read me, cochlea come . . ."

Suddenly the room exploded. Anna O. was rocketing up and down on the stretcher, shrieking at great pitch and intensity: ROODLE ROODLE ROOOOOO . . . DLE!

The Fat Man plucked his stethoscope from her ears, snatched my hand, and pulled me out of the room. The shrieks echoed through the E.W., and Howard, at the nursing station, stared at us. Seeing him, Fats yelled: "Cardiac arrest! Room 116!" and as Howard jumped up and came running, the Fat Man, laughing, pulled me into the elevator and punched the cafeteria button. Beaming, he said, "Repeat after me: GOMERS DON'T DIE."

"GOMERS DON'T DIE."

"You betcha. Let's eat."

Few things could have been more disgusting than watching the Fat Man shovel day-old blintzes into his mouth, talking all the time about things as different as the porno motif in *Oz*, the virtues of the foul food we were eating, and finally, when he and I were left alone, his prospects in what he still would refer to only as the Great American Medical Invention. I drifted off, and was soon with Berry on a June beach, filled with love's excitement, of possibility shared. Capability Brown. English landscapes. Eye within eye, sea salt on our caressing lips—

"Basch, cut it out. You stay there much longer, and when you come back to this shithole, you'll snap."

How had he known? What had they done to me, putting me with this madman?

"I'm not crazy," said Fats, "it's just that I spell out what every other doc feels, but most squash down and let eat away at their guts. Last year I lost weight. Me! So I said to myself, 'Not your gastric mucosa, Fats baby, not for what they're paying you. No ulcer for you.' And here I am." Sated, he mellowed, and went on, "Look, Roy, these gomers have a terrific talent: they teach us medicine. You and I are going down there and, with my help, Anna O. is going to teach you more useful medical procedures in one hour than you could learn from a fragile young patient in a week. LAW NUMBER SIX: THERE IS NO

BODY CAVITY THAT CANNOT BE REACHED WITH A NUMBER-FOURTEEN NEEDLE AND A GOOD STRONG ARM. You learn on the gomers, so that when some young person comes in to the House of God dying . . ."

My heart skipped a beat.

" . . . you know what to do, you do good, and you save them. That part of it's exciting. Wait'll you feel the thrill of sticking a needle blindly into a chest to make a diagnosis, to save someone young. I'm telling you, it's fantastic. Let's go."

We did. With the Fat Man's guidance, I learned how to tap a chest, tap a knee, put in lines, do an LP properly, and many other invasive procedures. He was right. As I got better with the needle, I began to feel good, more confident, and the possibility that I might become a competent doc glowed inside me. Fear began to leave me, and when I realized what was happening, I felt, deep inside, a blush, a rush, a thrill.

"All right," said Fats, "so much for diagnosis. Now, treatment. What do we do for her heart failure? How much Lasix?"

Who knew? BMS had taught me nothing about the empirics of treatment.

"LAW NUMBER SEVEN: AGE + BUN = LASIX DOSE."

This was nonsense. Although the BUN—Blood Urea Nitrogen—was an indirect measure of heart failure, it was clear that Fats was playing another joke, and I said, "That equation is nonsense."

"Of course it is. And it works every time. Anna is ninety-five and her BUN is eighty. A hundred and seventy-five milligrams. Twenty-five to grow on, and it's an even two hundred. Do what you like, but she'll start to piss only when you get to two hundred. Oh, and remember, Basch, BUFF her chart. Litigation is nasty, so put a good shiny BUFF on Anna O.'s chart."

"OK," I said, "but do I have to get her out of heart failure before I start her bowel run?"

"Bowel run? Are you nuts? She's not a private patient, she's your patient. There's no bowel run on her."

Feeling grateful, feeling glad that this medical wizard was with me, I said, "You know what you are, Fats?"

"What?"

"You're a great American."

"And with luck, soon a rich one. Bedtime for Fats. Remember, Roy, *primum non nocere,* and *hasta la vista* muthafucka."

Of course he was right. As I wrote up my admissions from the day, BUFFING the charts, I tried lower doses of Lasix on Anna, and nothing happened. I sat at the nursing station listening to the cooings of the gomers punctuated by the BLEEP BLEEP of the cardiac monitors. It had a soothing lullaby quality:

BLEEP BLEEP, FIX THE LUMP: BLEEP BLEEP, ROODLE ROODLE:

GO AVAY, ROODLE ROODLE: FIX THE LUMP, BLEEP BLEEP:

BLEEP BLEEP . . .

Les Brown and his gomer band of renown serenading me as I awaited Anna O.'s pee. At 175 she trickled, and at 200 she gushed. It was crazy. Nevertheless, seeing the urine, like a new father, my chest puffed with pride. I announced the event to Molly.

"Golly, Roy, that's terrific. You're going to get that nice old lady back on her feet. Great. Have a good night's sleep. I'll be here. We'll take care of things together. I've got a lot of confidence in you. Happy Fourth of July."

I looked at my watch. It was two A.M. on the magnificent Fourth. Feeling good, feeling proud and competent, I walked down the empty corridor to the on-call room. Power trip. I was in charge of all this. I felt a chill go through me, like the intern in the book. Far-out.

The bed was unmade, and I couldn't find any surgical pajamas and Levy the Lost BMS was snoring in the top bunk, but I was so tired, who cared? As I headed toward my dreams, listening to the BLEEP BLEEP, I mused on cardiac arrests, and as my mind covered all I knew about cardiac arrests, I was soon left with all I didn't know. I started to worry. I couldn't sleep, because any minute I might be called to an arrest, and what would I do? I felt a nudge, and there was Molly. She put a finger to her lips to signal silence. She sat on the bottom bunk and took off her white nursing shoes and pulled down her white pantyhose and bikini panties. She lifted the covers and said something about not wanting to get her uniform wrinkled and sat cross-legged on top of me. She unbuttoned her front and bent over and kissed me full on the lips, and as I put my palm round her glassy ass her perfume—

There was a tap on my shoulder. Perfume. I turned my head toward the tap and found myself looking straight up into Molly's thighs as she squatted down to awaken me. Damn, it had been a dream, but this was not. It really was going to happen. She put her hand on my shoulder. Jesus, but wasn't she going to leap into the sack with me after all.

I was wrong. It was about a patient, one of Little Otto's cardiac cases who refused to lie quietly in her restraints. Trying to hide the stiff screaming crowd living it up in my white pants, I stumbled out into the corridor, blinking in the glare, and followed that pert bouncing ass to the patient's room. There was an explosion. We ran in to find the woman, having GONE TO GROUND, standing naked in the middle of her room, screaming obscenities at her own reflection in the mirror. She picked up an IV bottle, screamed, "There! There! That old woman in the mirror!" and hurled the bottle at her reflection, smashing the mirror to bits. When she saw me she knelt in the broken glass, grabbed my knees, and said, "Please, mister, please don't send me home." It was pathetic. She smelled stale. We tried to cool her off. We roped her back into restraints.

This was the first of a series of explosions, to mark the Fourth. When I called Little Otto to tell him that his patient was living it up, Otto exploded, accusing me of "worrying my patient with your inept attention. She's a nice woman and you must have upset her. Leave her alone." Next, the elevator door opened, and exploding out of yet another ring of Hell, out rolled Eat My Dust and his BMS, wheeling yet another human carcass to the far end of the hall. This one was a bony mollusk of a man, with a red knobby protuberance popping out of his skull, sitting as rigid as a corpse, chanting:
RUGGALA RUGGALA RUGGALA RUGG,
RUGGALA RUGGALA RUGGALA GUGG . . .
"This is my fourth admission," said Eddie, "and it means

that you're next up. You should see what they're cooking up in the E.W. now."

Next up? Inconceivable. I went back to bed, and I fell asleep, until my finger, celebrating the Fourth on its own, exploded in pain. I screamed at the top of my voice, bringing Levy down from the top bunk and Molly in from the ward, pushing those fun thighs into my puss.

"Something bit me!" I shrieked.

"Honest, Dr. Basch," said Levy, "I swear it wasn't me."

My finger started to swell. The pain was excruciating.

"I was going to call you anyway," said Molly. "There's another admission for you in the E.W."

"Oh, no. I can't stand another gomer tonight."

"Not a gomer. Fifty, and sick. He's a doctor himself."

Fighting panic, I went to the E.W. I read the chart: Dr. Sanders. Fifty-one. Black. On the House of God Staff. Previous history of parotid and pituitary tumors with horrible complications. Came in this time with chest pain, increasing weight loss, lethargy, difficulty breathing. Should I call the Fat Man? No, I'd see him myself first. I walked into the room.

Dr. Sanders lay flat on the stretcher, a black man looking twenty years older than he was. He tried to shake my hand, but he was too weak. I took his hand and told him my name.

"Glad to have you as my doctor," he said.

Moved by his helplessness, his weak hand still lying trustfully in mine, I felt sad for him. "Tell me what happened."

He did. At first I was so nervous I could barely listen. Sensing this, he said, "Don't worry, you'll do all right. Just forget I'm a doctor. I'm putting myself in your hands. I was where you are once, right here, years ago. I was the first Nigro intern in the House. They called us 'Nigroes' then."

Gradually, thinking of what the Fat Man had taught me, I began to feel more confident, more wide-awake, nervous, but excited. I liked this man. He was asking me to take care of him, and I would do my best. I went to work, and when the X ray showed fluid in the chest cavity, and I knew I'd better tap it to see what it was, I decided I'd page the Fat Man. Just as he arrived, I put together the findings and realized that the most likely diagnosis was malignancy. I got a sick feeling in my gut. The Fat Man, a jolly green blimp in his surgical pajamas, floated in, and with a few words with Dr. Sanders established a marvelous rapport. A warmth filled the room, a trust, a plea to help, a promise to try. It was what medicine might be. I tapped the chest. Since I'd practiced on Anna O., it was easy. The Fat Man was right: with the gomers you risked and learned, so when you had to perform, you did. And I realized that the reason the House Slurpers tolerated the Fat Man's bizarre ways was that he was a terrific doc. The mirror image of Putzel. I finished the tap, and Dr. Sanders, breathing more easily, said, "You be sure to tell me what the cytology of that fluid is, all right? No matter what it shows."

"Nothing will be definite for a few days," I said.

"Well, you tell me in a few days. If it's malignant, I've got to make some plans. I've got a brother in West Virginia; our father left us some land. I've been putting off a fishing trip with him much too long."

Outside the room, chills running up and down my spine as I thought of what might be in the test tubes of fluid in my pocket, I listened to the Fat Man ask, "Did you see his face?"

"What about it?"

"Remember it. It's the face of a dying man. Good night."

"Hey, wait. I figured it out—the reason they let you screw around the way you do is that you're good."

"Good? Nah, not just good. Very good. Even great. Night-night."

I wheeled Dr. Sanders back up to the ward and went back to bed just as the dawn was exploding the hot nasty night. The frenetic surgeons were just beginning their morning rounds, getting ready for a day of doing nice civic things like sewing people's hands back on people's arms, and the first shifts of Housekeeping were boogeying along in the House bowels. I pulled on my socks to go to the Fat Man's cardflip, and realized that I felt like socks: sweaty, stale, smelly, stiff, worn a day longer than I should have been. From the cardflip on, things began to melt, meld, and blur, and by lunchtime I was so woozy that Chuck and Potts had to lead me through the cafeteria line to the table and the only thing I'd put on my tray was a big glass of iced coffee. I was so ataxic that when I tried to sit I banged my shin on the table leg, stumbled, and spilled the iced coffee all over my whites. It felt cool dripping through my crotch. It felt far off, somewhere else. That afternoon the Leggo was holding Chief's Rounds with our team. He came down the hallway wearing his usual butcher-length white coat with that long stethoscope wending its way across his chest and down and tucked into his pants, and he was whistling "Daisy, Daisy, give me your answer troooo." As he examined the patient, I had an urge to shove Levy into the Leggo so that both would tumble into bed with the gomer who was being saved at all costs, and I fantasized that "Leggo" was somehow cryptographic for "Let my gomers go," and I pictured the Leggo leading the gomers out of the peaceful land of death into the bondage of prolonged pitiful suffering life, legging it through the Sinai wolfing down the unleavened bread and singing "Daisy, Daisy, give me your answer trooo."

Chaos. The blur blurred. I didn't think I would make it through the day. The nurse came up to me and said that my only Italian patient, nicknamed Boom Boom, who had no cardiac disease, was having chest pain. I walked into the room, where the family of eight were chattering away in Italian. I took an EKG, which was normal, and then, a showman with an audience of eight, decided to use the Fat Man's reverse stethoscope technique. I plugged Boom Boom in, and yelled into the megaphone: "Cochlea come in! Cochlea come in! Do you read me, cochlea . . ." Boom Boom opened her eyes, shrieked, jumped, put her fist to her chest in the classic sign of cardiac pain, stopped breathing, and turned blue. I realized that I and eight Italians were witnessing a cardiac arrest. I thumped Boom Boom on the chest, which produced another shriek, signifying life. Trying to assure the family that this whole thing had been routine, I ushered them out and called an arrest code. The first to arrive was Housekeeping, for some reason carrying a bunch of lilies; next came a Pakistani anesthesiologist. With the ring of the Italian delegation in my ears, I felt like I was at the United Nations. Others arrived, but Boom

Boom was now doing OK. Fats looked over the new EKG and said, "Roy, this is the greatest day of this woman's life, 'cause she's finally had a bona fide heart attack."

I tried to pursuade the intensive-care resident to take her off my service, but taking one look and saying, "Are you for real?" he refused the TURF. Sheepishly, trying to avoid the family, I slunk down the hallway. The Fat Man pointed out a valuable House LAW, NUMBER EIGHT: THEY CAN ALWAYS HURT YOU MORE. I finished my work for the day, and, woozy, paged Potts, to sign out to him for the night. I asked him how it was going.

"Bad. Ina's on some kind of rampage, stealing shoes and pissing in them. I never should have given her the Valium."

"You gave her Valium?"

"Yeah. To try to control her violence. Worked with the Runt, so I thought I'd try it on her. Made her worse."

Walking to the elevator with the Fat Man, I said, "You know, I think these gomers are trying to hurt me."

"Of course they are. They try to hurt everyone."

"What difference does that make? I never did anything to hurt them, and they're trying to hurt me."

"Exactly, that's modern medicine."

"You're crazy."

"You have to be crazy to do this."

"But if this is all there is, I can't take it. No way."

"Of course you can, Roy. Trash your illusions, and the world will beat a pathway to your door."

And he was gone. I waited for Berry to pick me up outside the House. When she saw me, her face twisted in disgust.

"Roy! You're green! Phew! Stinky! Green and stinky! What happened?"

"They got me."

"Got you?"

"Yeah. They killed me."

"Who did?"

"The gomers. But the Fat Man just told me that they hurt everybody and that's modern medicine so I don't know what to think anymore. He said to trash my illusions and the world would beat a pathway to my door."

88

"That sounds bizarre."

"That's what I said too, but now I'm not so sure."

"I could make you feel better," said Berry.

"Just tuck me in."

"What?"

"Just put me in my bed and tuck me in."

"But today's your birthday. We're going out to dinner, re-member?"

"I forgot."

"Your own birthday and you forgot?"

"Yup. I'm green and stinky, and just tuck me in."

She tucked me in, and green and smelly as I was said she loved me all the same and I said I loved her too but it was a lie because they had destroyed something in me and it was some lush thing that had to do with love and I was asleep before she closed the door.

The phone went off, and out of it came two-part harmony: "Happy birthday to you, happy birthday to you, happy birthday dear Roy-oiy, happy birthday to you." My birthday, forgotten, then remembered, then forgotten again. My parents. My father said, "I hope that you're not too tired and it must be great to have patients of your very own at last," and I knew he thought modern medicine was the greatest invention since the high-speed dental drill, and as I hung up I thought of Dr. Sanders, who would die, and of the gomers, who would not, and I tried to figure out what was illusion and what was not. I had expected, just like in the *How I Saved the World Without Dirtying My Whites* book, to have been rushing in and saving people at the last moments, and here I had been observing a wrecked Southerner being socked in the puss by a gomere wearing a ram-horned football helmet, all the time being told by a fat wizard who was a wonderful doc and also something phantasmagorical like either a madman or a genius that doing nothing except BUFFING and TURFING was the essence of the delivery of medical care. If there had been the feeling of power in the empty corridor at night and in the crowded elevator during the day, there had also been the awesome powerlessness in the face of the gomers and the helpless incurable young. Sure there had been the clean whites, and the clean white of Putzel's Continental, but the clean whites had gotten spewed with vomit and blood and piss and shit, and the dirty sheets had bred bugs that went right for the finger and the eye, and Putzel was a jerk. In months, Dr. Sanders would be dead. If I knew that I were to die in months, would I spend my time like this? Nope. My mortal healthy body, my ridiculous diseased life. Waiting for the hard screaming line-drive ball, for the aneurysm straining in my brain stem to pop and squirt blood all over my cortex, draining it dry. And now there was no way out. I'd become a tern in the stinky tern in the green house in the House of God.

6

At the end of three weeks, the Fat Man was TURFED out of the House of God to do a rotation at one of the neighboring community hospitals, what he had called one of "The Mt. St. Elsewheres." Although he would still be the resident on call with me every third night, in his fat wake came the new ward resident, the woman named Jo, whose pop had just leaped to his death off a bridge. Like so many of us in medicine, Jo was a victim of success. Growing up short and wiry, plain and tough, in adolescence Jo had ignored her mother's invitations to come out as a deb and had concentrated instead on biology, dissecting rather than attending balls. She first became a victim of success when she successfully annihilated her twin brother by getting into Radcliffe while he went off to some beer-swilling football factory in the Midwest, a trombonist in the marching band. Her academic performance continued to accelerate through college, rocketing her into BMS at a barely pubescent age, her meteoric rise halted only slightly by her mother's all-American involutional psychotic break, which had had the effect of reducing her pop to a quivering jellylike mass. The disintegration of her family had intensified her medical achievement, as if by learning how to do a stellar rectal exam she could detect her family's psychological cancer. And so Jo had come to the House of God, and had become its most ruthless and competitive resident.

From the first day that Jo stood before us, feet apart and

hands on hips like the captain of a ship and said, "Welcome aboard," it was clear that she was so different from the Fat Man that she would be a threat to all he'd taught us. A short, trim woman with clipped black hair, a jutting jaw, and dark circles under her eyes, she wore a white skirt and a white jacket, and in a special holster fastened to her belt was a two-inch-thick black ring notebook filled with her own transcription of the three-thousand-page *Principles of Internal Medicine*. If it wasn't in her head, it was on her hip. She spoke strangely, in a monotone devoid of feeling. If it wasn't fact, she didn't handle it. She recognized no humor. "Sorry I couldn't be here when I was scheduled to," she said to Chuck and Potts and me and the BMSs that first day, "but I had personal reasons for being away."

"Yes, we heard," said Potts. "How are things now?"

"They're fine. These things do happen. I took it in stride. I'm glad to be back at work to get my mind off it. I know you had the Fat Man for the first three weeks, and I want you to know that I do things differently. Do things my way and we'll get along swell. There's nothing sloppy about the way I run a ward. No loose ends. OK, gang, let's go make rounds. Get the chart rack, eh?"

Delighted, Levy the Lost leaped up to get the chart rack.

"With Fats," I said, "we sat here for rounds. It was relaxing and efficient—"

"And sloppy. I see every patient every day. There's no excuse for not seeing every patient every day. You'll soon find out that the more you do in medicine, the better care you give. I do as much as possible. It takes a little longer, but it's worth it. Oh, by the way, that means that rounds will start earlier—six-thirty. Got it? Swell. I run a tight ship. No slop. My career interest is cardiology. I've got an NIH Fellowship next year. We'll be listening to a lot of hearts. But listen: if there are any complaints, I want to hear 'em. Out in the open, got it? OK, gang, let's cast off."

There was no way that Chuck or I would show up for rounds an hour earlier than we had been showing up for rounds. We followed Jo as she marched out of the room with that fanaticism known only to an overachiever, one who lives with the eternal fear that some lurking underachiever will, in a flash of brilliance, achieve more. As we wheeled the chart rack into and out of the room of every one of the forty-five patients on the ward, with Jo examining each one and then shooting off a lecture from the transcription holstered on her hip, telling each of the terns what he had forgotten to do, I felt a growing apprehension. How could we survive her? She went against everything Fats had taught. She would work us into the ground.

We came to the room containing Anna O. Looking through the chart, Jo went in and examined Anna, despite the Wing of Zock jackhammers, focusing on Anna's heart. As Jo listened and poked and prodded, Anna grew more and more resentful and cried out:

ROODLE ROODLE ROOOOO-DLE!

After she'd finished, Jo asked me what the most important part of Anna's care was.

Thinking of the Fat Man's LAWS, I said, "Placement."

"What?"

"PLACEMENT COMES FIRST."

"Who taught you that?"

"The Fat Man."

"That is baloney," said Jo. "This woman is suffering from a severe senile dementia. She's oriented neither to place, time, nor person, all she says is ROODLE, she's incontinent, and confused. There are several treatable causes for dementia, one of which is operable brain tumor. We've got to work it up completely. Let me tell you about it."

Jo shot off a lecture on the treatable causes of dementia, filled with obscure neuroanatomical references that brought back to me a story I'd heard about her and an anatomy exam at the BMS. The exam had been impossible, the average score forty-two, and Jo had made ninety-nine. The one question she'd missed was to "identify the Circle of Polgi," which turned out to be a trick question, the said Circle being the traffic island situated just outside the front door of the BMS dorm. Jo's lecture on Anna was crisp, complete, coherent, and cohesive. She finished, looking as if she'd just had a satisfying bowel movement.

"Start ordering the tests," said Jo to me, "we're really going to work this up. Completely. No one's going to be able to say that we do sloppy work."

"But the Fat Man said that Anna O. is always like this, and that in a ninety-five-year-old, dementia is normal."

"Dementia's never normal," said Jo, "never."

"Maybe not," I said, "but the Fat Man said that the way to treat her is to do nothing except try like hell to find a new bed at the nursing home."

"I never do nothing. I'm a doctor, I deliver medical care."

"The Fat Man said that for gomers, doing nothing is the delivery of medical care. If you do something, he said, you make everything worse. Like Potts hydrating Ina Goober—she's never recovered from that."

"And you believed him?" asked Jo.

"Well, it seems to be working with Anna," I said.

"You listen to me, smartass," said Jo, amazed and threatened. "One—the Fat Man is nuts; two—if you don't believe me, ask anyone else in the House; three—that's why they wouldn't let him start with the new terns; four—I'm the captain of this ship, and I deliver medical care, which, for your information, means not doing nothing, but doing something. In fact, doing everything you can, see?"

"Sort of. But Fats said that was the worst—"

"Stop! I don't want to hear it. Do the work-up for treatable causes of dementia: LP, brain scan, bloodwork, skull films. Do it all, and then if it's negative, then talk to me about placement. Ridiculous. All right, gang, let's shove off and move on. Next?"

We sailed through Rokitansky, Sophie, Ina with her football helmet that Jo removed, the sick Dr. Sanders, and all the rest, almost all of whom wound up with some hitherto undetected cardiac disease, Jo's specialty. We finished just outside the door of the Yellow Man, at the border of the domain of 6-North. Even though he was not our patient, Jo had to have a look at him. Coming out, she turned to Potts and said, "I heard about this case. Fulminant necrotic hepatitis. Fatal unless you catch it early and use steroids. Let me tell you about it."

She blasted off with her lecture on the disease, oblivious to the pain on Potts's face. She finished, said she would photo-copy references for us, and left to tell the Fish and the Leggo, on their rounds, about our rounds. Somehow she'd managed to deflate each of us. She'd left something in the air, something tight and heavy and gray, a stomach churning in the leap down toward the water from the bridge.

"Well, she sure is something else than Fats," said Chuck.

"I miss him already," I said.

"Seems like everybody knows about the Yellow Man," said Potts.

"Do you think I should do the dementia work-up on Anna O.?"

"Don't look like you got much choice, man."

"The Fat Man was never wrong, not once," I said.

"I don't think there's anybody in the whole worl' who knows more about the gomers than Fats," said Chuck. "He was a cool dude about these gomers. Be cool, Roy, be cool."

Prodded by my fear of missing something and being haunted by it as Potts was haunted by the Yellow Man, in the first weeks with Jo I did what she suggested. I ordered every test I could think of on every patient I had, and I wrote down everything in the charts. With Jo's help, I even wrote down references, in footnotes. The charts soon looked terrific, BUFFED to a fine shine. The House Slurpers like the Fish and the Leggo took a look at the shiny BUFFED charts and their faces lit up with fine and shiny smiles. BUFF the chart, you automatically BUFF the Slurpers. Not only that, but I soon found out that the more tests I ordered, the more complications there were, the longer the House kept the patients, and the more money the Privates collected. BUFF the chart, you automatically BUFF the Privates. Jo was right: the more you did, the more you BUFFED the doctors.

The hooker was the patients, especially the gomers. About the gomers Jo was dead wrong. The more I did, the worse they got. Anna O. had started out on Jo's service in perfect electrolyte balance, with each organ system working as perfectly as an 1878 model could. This, to my mind, included the brain, for wasn't dementia a fail-safe and soothing oblivion of the machine to its own decay? From being on the verge of a TURF back to the Hebrew House for the Incurables, as Anna knocked around the House of God in the steaming weeks of August, getting a skull film here and an LP there, she got worse, much worse. Given the stress of the dementia work-up, every organ system crumpled: in a domino progression the injection of radioactive dye for her brain scan shut down her kidneys, and the dye study of her kidneys overloaded her heart, and the medication for her heart made her vomit, which altered her electrolyte balance in a life-threatening way, which increased her dementia and shut down her bowel, which made her eligible for the bowel run, the cleanout for which dehydrated her and really shut down her tormented kidneys, which led to infection, the need for dialysis, and big-time complications of these big-time diseases. She and I both became exhausted, and she became very sick. Like the Yellow Man, she went through a phase of convulsing like a hooked tuna, and then went through a phase that was even more awesome, lying in bed deathly still, perhaps dying. I felt sad, for by this time, I liked her. I didn't know what to do. I began to spend a good deal of time sitting with Anna, thinking. The Fat Man was on call with me every third night as backup resident, and one night, searching for me to go to the ten-o'clock meal, he found me with Anna, watching her trying to die.

"What the hell are you doing?" he asked.

I told him.

"Anna was on her way back to the Hebrew House, what happened—wait, don't tell me. Jo decided to go all-out on her dementia, right?"

"Right. She looks like she's going to die."

"The only way she'll die is if you murder her by doing what Jo says."

"Yeah, but how can I do otherwise, with Jo breathing down my neck?"

"Easy. Do nothing with Anna, and hide it from Jo."

"Hide it from Jo?"

"Sure. Continue the work-up in purely imaginary terms, BUFF the chart with the imaginary results of the imaginary tests, Anna will recover to her demented state, the work-up will show no treatable cause for it, and everybody's happy. Nothing to it."

"I'm not sure it's ethical."

"Is it ethical to murder this sweet gomere with your work-up?"

There was nothing I could say.

"Well, then, there you are. Let's eat."

During the ten-o'clock meal I asked Fats about Jo. He became somber and said that Jo was terribly depressed. He thought of her as he thought of the Fish and the Leggo and many other Slurpers: terrific medical texts lacking in common sense. They all shared the belief that disease was some wild and hairy monster to be locked up in the neat medical grids of differential diagnosis and treatment. All it took was a little superhuman effort and all would be well. Jo had dedicated her whole life to that effort, and she had little energy for anything else. Her whole life, Fats said, was medicine:

"It's real sad, and everybody knows it. Jo's been preparing for this moment as ward resident for years, and now it's arrived and she's bound to make a hash out of it. She needs these patients so badly to fill up the emptiness of her life that she comes in on Sundays and on her nights off. She never feels needed except when she imagines that her terns or her patients need her, which they don't, because she's such a *klutz* when it comes to practical medicine and human contact. The most important treatment for Anna O. would be to find her lost eyeglasses. Jo should go into research, but she knows that if she did, it would confirm what everybody else knows already—she can't deal with people."

Thinking of Berry, I said, "You sound like a male chauvinist."

"Me?" asked Fats, genuinely surprised. "How?"

"You're saying women like Jo make lousy doctors because they're women."

"Nope. I'm saying women like Jo make lousy people because they're doctors, just like some men do. The profession is a disease. It doesn't care what sex you are. It can trap us, any of us, and it's pretty clear that it's trapped Jo. It's awful. You should see her apartment—it's like no one lives there. She's been there over a year, and she still hasn't unpacked her stereo."

We sat in the gloom of Jo's trapped life, each chewing on it, until, finally, it went down, and Fats, brightening again, said, "Hey, did I ever tell you about this dream of mine, the Invention?"

"Nope."

"Dr. Jung's Anal Mirror: the Great American Medical Invention."

"Dr. Jung's Anal Mirror? What the hell is that?"

"Don't you remember in medical school during the gastroenterology course they told you to 'examine your own anus with the aid of a small mirror'?"

"Yeah."

"Were you able to do it?"

"Nope."

"Of course you weren't. It's impossible. But not with the aid of Dr. Jung's. Anyone can examine his or her very own anus in the comfort and privacy of the home."

"What the hell is it?" I asked, caught up in the joke.

He showed me what it was. On a napkin he drew a complex and intricate combination of two reflecting mirrors and a large focusing lens all fastened together on adjustable stainless-steel rods. He drew the pathways of the light rays from the anus to the eyeballs and back, splitting it into colorful rainbows and sophisticated spectra which he elaborated with multivariate complex equations and graphs. Finishing, he said, "Do you know how many Americans each day have painful bowel movements and blood on their toilet paper or in the bowl? Millions."

"Why just Americans?" I joked. "Why not the world?"

"Exactly. The only problem is translation. If it's millions in America, it's billions in the world. The anus is a great curiosity to almost all mankind. Everyone would like to see it, but no one can. Like darkest Africa before the missionaries. The Congo of the body."

The hairs on the back of my neck tingled as I started to think that this might not be a joke, and I said, "You're joking."

98

The Fat Man did not reply.

"This is the most ridiculous idea I've ever heard."

"It's not. And besides, that's always what they say about great inventions. It's like those vaginal mirrors that gynecologists are passing out—oh, by the way, you can adjust the Anal Mirror to look in there too—women are using the vaginal mirrors to get to know their vaginas. This is a unisex device. GET TO KNOW YOUR ASSHOLE." Spreading his hands apart as if reading a bumper sticker or a marquee, Fats said, "ASSHOLES ARE BEAUTIFUL. FREE THE ASSHOLES. The potential in human and financial terms is immense. Big fortoona."

"This is outrageous."

"That's just why it will sell."

"But it's a joke, right? You didn't actually make an anal mirror?"

The Fat Man looked distractedly out into thin air.

Feeling queasy, I said, "Come off it, Fats," and I pleaded with him to tell me the truth. It was so preposterous that it might just be real, and over the past ten years whenever I'd estimated what was fantasy in America—from Jack Ruby's blasting Lee Harvey Oswald's guts all over the insides of the TV tubes of America, to the brown paper bags of money delivered to Spiro Agnew in his vice-presidential chambers—I'd been wrong, dead wrong, and had always underestimated, falling far short of the absurd, which had inevitably turned out to be the real. "Come on, Fats," I shouted, "tell me the goddamn truth! Do you mean it or don't you?"

"Do I?" Fats seemed to awaken from his reverie, and composing himself, said, "Oh, of course I don't, do I? I mean, no one would think seriously of anything as crazy as that, would they? Just remember, Basch, about Anna and the other gomers: BUFF the charts, and hide it from Jo. See you later."

I tried it. I decided to go all out on Anna O. and do my best to do nothing. Teetering on that barren precipice above the long leap down to death, Anna was put into a holding pattern governed by LAW NUMBER ONE: GOMERS DON'T DIE. Finally, one day, as I passed by her room I heard a healthy demented ROODLE! and my heart swung around on its apex with pride and I knew that Anna was back and that I had proved scienterrifically that, just as Fats had said, to do nothing for the gomers was to do something, and the more conscientiously I did nothing the better they got, and I resolved that from that time on I would do more nothing on the gomers than any other tern in the House of God. Somehow I'd find a way to hide my doing nothing from Jo.

It still wasn't clear how Jo's orthodox medical approach would work on those who the Fat Man had said could die, the nongomers, the young. As the sweaty green and smelly summer months wore us out, as America frolicked in the news given it by a small-time White House bureaucrat named Butterfield who revealed that Nixon had gotten so excited about being President that he'd installed a tape system to record every single immortal presidential word, which immortal words he was trying like hell via some ruse called "executive privilege" to keep from Sirica and Cox, Chuck and I gave ourselves up, during the day, to Jo's fanaticism about the dying young, letting her show us how to do everything to these nongomertose patients, always. During the day we'd slog along with her, using her as a live textbook, and also, since she found it impossible to let us do things on our own, by feigning incompetence, using her to do anything distasteful, like disimpactions. I'd told Chuck and Potts about the Fat Man's analysis of Jo, and so at first we held ourselves in check, walking around her as if she were a fragile house of cards. We hid our contempt of her from her, and Chuck and I hid our doing nothing on the gomers from her. I slogged through the long, dull, duplicitous days with Jo, keeping Fats alive inside me until, every third night, he and I were together again on call. Remembering his saying about himself, "I spell out what every other doc feels, but most squash down and let eat away at their guts." I studied Jo to detect the symptoms of her ulcer, and studied the Fish for his big ulcer and the Leggo for his giant ulcer. Looming more and more clearly so as almost to be touchable, with me was always that comforting fat presence, just past the edges of my sight.

While I had Fats, and Chuck had himself—which seemed, given his having endured worse than the gomers, to have been enough—Potts didn't have much, and was having a helluva time. Having been burned by not telling Fats about the liver functions of the Yellow Man, Potts was reluctant to hide data from Jo. Jo was always on call with Potts, and so every night for Potts was the same as every day, with Jo niggling at him to "feed the cat," to do everything for all forty-five patients, always. Even if he'd wanted to try doing nothing on a gomer or two, Potts would not have been able to conceal it, for Jo, in her inability to trust anyone else, more or less took over Potts's service, running it for him. Like an overeager BMS trying to make an A, Jo would stay up the whole night writing obscure referenced discussions of the "fascinating cases" in the charts, each BLEEP and shriek and nurse's question echoing off the lonely tile walls making Jo feel real full and needed as she never felt full and needed outside the House of God.

And so Potts was in rough shape. Thanks to Jo's aggressive treatment of the gomers, they got worse and never got TURFED, and the dying young took longer to die, and Potts's service swelled, so that out of the forty-five patients, he had twenty-five. Jo's increasing his work meant that on his nights on call he didn't sleep, and that he had to work harder and longer to stay afloat during the days. While Chuck and I, often being off duty the same nights, got to be better and better friends, Potts never could do things with us outside the House, and he became more and more quiet and withdrawn. His wife, titillated on the rack of her surgical internship at Man's Best Hospital, MBH, where she was on call at least every other night, had virtually disappeared from his life. We watched Potts sink, and the deeper he sank, the more out of our reach he became. His dog began to pine.

During a late-August thunderstorm, the Yellow Man began to scream, and from the look on Potts's face when he heard the screams, it was as if his own liver was screaming in pain and affront. Coincidentally, another liver disease had presented itself to Potts: Lazarus was a middle-aged janitor who'd had the bad sense and good fortune to hold night jobs all his life, which allowed him to sit and destroy his liver with cheap booze. Lazarus' liver disease was not classy, it was just the standard sure-death brand of cirrhosis seen sucking the end of bottles wrapped in paper bags on every street corner of the world. Lazarus was going to die and was trying hard to do so. Jo and Potts stood in his way. Their efforts began on the plane of the heroic, and soon became, even in the House of God, legendary. From time to time Chuck and I would try to make Potts feel better about Lazarus, talking about how sad it was that he had cirrhosis and was dying.

"Yeah," said Potts, "the fuckin' liver gets me every time."

"Why don't you just let him die?" I asked.

"Jo says he's gonna make it."

"Make what, man, a new liver?" asked Chuck.

"Jo says I have to go all-out on him, do everything."

"Is that what you want to do?" I asked.

"No. There's no cure for cirrhosis, and besides, I'll tell you something: Lazarus told me, the last time he was conscious, that he wanted to be dead. He was in so much agony he begged me to let him die. That last bleed from his esophagus, where he was drowning in his own blood, scared him to death. I want to just let him die, but I'm afraid to tell that to Jo."

"Man, you heard her. She wants to hear our complaints."

"That's right," said Potts, "she did say 'any complaints, out in the open.' I'm going to tell her about not keeping him alive."

Thinking that Jo would bring up the Yellow Man, I said, "Don't tell her. She'll blast you to bits."

"She wants to hear," said Potts, "she said she wanted to hear."

"She doesn't want to hear," I said. "No way."

"I want to hear 'em," Jo had said, "out in the open, got it?"

"She wants to hear 'em, she said she did," said Potts.

"She doesn't. You tell her, and she'll blast you to bits."

Potts told her that he didn't think that she was asking him to do the right thing by keeping Lazarus alive, and Jo blasted him to bits. As an example of Potts's failings, Jo cited the Yellow Man.

7

Having been pushed around for five steaming weeks with
Jo, Chuck and I had learned a lot. One of our main skills was
how to put a terrific BUFF on any chart to satisfy Jo, who could
thus satisfy the Fish, who could thus satisfy the Leggo, who
could thus satisfy whomever he had to satisfy. In addition,
Chuck and I had learned to hide what we were actually doing
with the gomers from Jo, since what we were actually doing was doing nothing, more intensely than any other terns in
the House. Time and again, reading about our prodigious
efforts on the gomers in their charts and then seeing how well
the actual gomers were doing, Jo would turn to Chuck and me
with pride and say, "Good job. By God, that's a damn good job.
I told you that the Fat Man was nuts about patient care, didn't
I?"

Without realizing it, Chuck and I were hanging ourselves.
On our rounds with Jo, our charts looked so terrifically
BUFFED that when Jo on her rounds with the Fish displayed
them to him, and when the Fish on his rounds with the Leggo
displayed them to him, all were amazed. This was it: the delivery of medical care. These footnotes! These cures! And so the
Leggo decided that Chuck and I should be rewarded.

"How will they be rewarded?" the Fish asked the Leggo.

"We'll give them the greatest reward any intern could
wish," said the Leggo. "When I was an intern, we used to fight
to get the toughest cases, to show our Chief what we could do.

That will be their reward, to let them show me what they can do. We'll give them the toughies. Tell them that."

"We'll give them the toughies," said the Fish to Jo.

"They're giving you the toughies," said Jo to us.

"The toughies?" I asked. "What are they?"

"The toughest admissions to the House."

"What? Why?"

"Yeah, man, what all did we do wrong?"

"That's just it," said Jo, "Nothing. It's the Leggo's way of saying thanks, to challenge you with the toughies. I think it's great. You should see the cases we're going to get now."

Soon we saw the cases we were going to get then. They were the worst. They were the House of God disasters, mostly young men and women with horrible diseases just past cure and just our side of death, diseases with rotting names like leukemia, melanoma, hepatoma, lymphoma, carcinoma, and all the other horrendomas for which there was no cure in this world or in any other. And so Chuck and I hung ourselves, and created, in 6-South, the toughest ward in the House. Without realizing it, without choosing it, and in fact choosing the opposite at every turn, we had to learn to handle the worst disease the House could dish up. We sweated and we cursed and we hated it, but we used each other—him using me for the facts and the numbers and me using him for the nuts and bolts—and we risked, and we learned. Given the increasing concentration of the dying young, the number of bowel runs for headache decreased, and the traffic in gomers went down, with Rokitansky getting sent back to his nursing home and Sophie getting driven back to her house in Putzel's Continental. Ina and Anna, the residua of our mistakenly aggressive approach, were still on the ward, slowly returning to their cradling dementia. Dr. Sanders turned out to have Hodgkin's disease, advanced and incurable, and had been started on chemotherapy and sent home to arrange his last fishing trip with his brother in West Virginia. The Yellow Man lay in his bed, flat and still, as withered as the first yellowing leaf of the fall.

When Chuck and I found out how much we each loved basketball, we began playing every chance we got. Two out of every three nights Chuck and I would be off call together, and we'd help each other finish our work, evade Jo, sign out to Potts, shove our black bags into our lockers and take out our jointly owned regulation basketball and our black low-cut sneakers, which, as we laced them, sent hot memories of the times before the big games racing through us, change into our green surgical scrub suits, jog down the corridor of the House and out into the street with that "school's out!" feeling that we'd known for a quarter of a century. At the public playground, if it was just the two of us we'd go one-on-one, caught up in that electric moment of making the slick move that would fake your best friend out of his jock. At times, in pickup games, we'd play on the same team, and we'd have that thrill of playing together with just the right blend of dazzle and unselfishness, playing against a strange mixture of strabismic Jewish BMSs and tough ghetto kids, running and yelling and breathing hard and worrying about chest pain meaning heart attack, throwing sharp elbows and playing dirty under the boards and getting into all-out screaming arguments with fifteen-year-olds about disputed calls, the elbows in fact thrown at Jo and the Fish and the Leggo and the deaths and diseases and wasted healthy moments spent cooped up in the House of God. Afterward we'd go to bars or to Chuck's apartment, which looked, with its garish furniture, like a TV commercial, and we'd sit and drink bourbon and beer and watch the ballgame or, with the tube sound off and stereo playing Chicago soul, watch a movie. We began to understand each other. Turned into ten-year-olds by the pressures of the House, we became friends as only ten-year-olds can, and one day something happened that made me realize what I'd always suspected: my new friend's studied indifference was only and all an act.

Chuck and I found ourselves in a basketball game with some BMSs who thought they were hot-shit ballplayers. With the same kind of ferocious competitiveness that had gotten them into the BMS, these guys started to play rough—hand-checking, fouling, calling us for the slightest foul and disputing calls as if they were making an A in surgery if they won. Chuck's opponent was the worst, the kind of kid whose arrogance had oozed through the umbilical cord and breast and had always been the part of him that his mother loved, the kind of kid whom everybody hated and who played for the fans and not for the game, even when there weren't any fans to play for. Every time Chuck had the ball, this kid would foul him, and every shot the kid took, he'd call a foul on Chuck. Despite the fact that Chuck was taking a beating, he never called a foul. Finally, on one outrageous call that even had his own team telling the wiseass to "just play ball, Ernie, all right?" Ernie said to Chuck, "Hey if you didn't foul me, why don't you say so?" and all Chuck said was, "Fine, fine, let's play," and he handed over the ball.

Something in that "Fine, fine" was ominous, and from then on Chuck began to play. He'd stay outside and bomb for hoops, and he'd take Ernie inside and overpower him despite the fouls, and he'd fake the shot from outside and slip past, and he'd fake the drive and stop and pop, and as he did all this, scoring point after point, wise Ernie got madder and madder and fouled more and more, but it had about as much effect as a fly on a racehorse. It became a ballet of strength and smarts and finesse. The game turned into a one-on-one, played out in a raging intense silence. Chuck made a fool of Ernie until finally somebody said it had gotten too dark to see the rim. Chuck asked Ernie for our ball, and Ernie threw it into some bushes. A hush fell. I wanted to smash Ernie in the teeth. Chuck said, "Well, Roy, I guess I better go get our ball, now that we won this game," and, smiling, arms around each other's sweaty shoulders, proud of winning, we left. Later, drinking with him, I said, "Damn, you are some ballplayer. Did you play in college?"

"Yup. Small College All-American, my senior year. First team."

"Well, I found you out," I said. "Your indifference is all an act. You care about everything you do."

" 'Course it is, man, 'Course I care."

"Well, why do you pretend that you don't?"

"On the street, it's the only way to be. If'n you let on what you are and who you are and what you got and how someone can use you, you get yourself used worse. Like Potts with Jo. I may be painin', man, but nobody's gonna know it. Being cool is the only way of stayin' alive."

"Amazing. Where I come from, it's just the opposite—you keep showing your pain so that people will lay off you. What do you think about that?"

"What do I think? I think, fine, man, fine."

On those rare days when Potts came out to play ball, it was embarrassing. He was clumsy and shy, scared of hurting someone and scared of standing out. Open for a shot, he'd pass. In a dispute, the other guy was right. He rarely yelled. As the maples began to do their reddening, as the touch-football games sprouted on the browning fields and as the dawn dew got more and more chill, Potts got worse and worse. Left out of Chuck's and my lives, left for weeks on end by his wife, worried about his golden retriever's growing whine, hounded by the Yellow Man and by Jo, Potts became scared of taking any risks. Since the only way to learn medicine was to take risks in those hard times when you were alone with your patient, Potts had trouble learning. Ashamed and afraid, in the computer rotation handed us on our first day, Potts moved on to his next assignment and left our ward.

His replacement was the Runt. On the day of his arrival, Chuck and I were sitting at the nursing station, our feet up, drinking ginger ale from large House ice buckets. Knowing how nervous he would be, Chuck and I had filled a syringe with Valium and taped it under his name on the blackboard, with a prescription: "to be injected into right buttock upon arrival." The blackboard was the standard way that the House Privates communicated with the terns about their patients. Under my name was an insignia:

***
MVI
***

This cryptic insignia had begun to appear throughout the House. It was always the same, always only associated with my name, and no one knew who was writing it. Recently it had become known that it stood for Most Valuable Intern. The rumor was that there was a competition among the interns, sponsored by the Fish and the Leggo, for this award, the ***MVI***. Since this insignia was associated only with my name, people began to address me as "the ***MVI***" and often I was greeted with "here comes the ***MVI***." I asked the Fish whether I really was the front-runner for the ***MVI***. He said he hadn't known there was an award. I told him that I'd heard the Leggo say that there was an award and that it was "part of the special tradition of the House." I then asked the Leggo, who said he hadn't known there was an award, and I told him that I'd heard the Fish say that there was and that it was "part of the special tradition of the House." I began to protest to the Fish that I didn't enjoy having my name plastered with ***MVI*** all over the House, and the Fish said he'd get House Security on the case, and for the past few days I'd glimpsed a bouncer dressed in fake West Point peering out from a corner, hoping to catch whoever was putting up ***MVI*** under my name.

And yet the ones most irritated by the ***MVI*** were the Privates, and of the Privates the most irritated of all was Little Otto Kreinberg, the Private whose name still rang no bell in Stockholm. Since Otto wouldn't talk to the terns, and since the blackboard was the only way of communicating with the terns, and since the ***MVI*** left no room for communication, it drove Little Otto wild. As Chuck and I sat, we watched Otto march in, curse, erase the ***MVI***, write a note to me, and depart. Almost as soon as he was gone, when the bouncer's back was turned, there appeared under my name on the blackboard:

As the insignias continued to multiply, gnomes like Otto spent a greater and greater amount of time manning the erasers. And when the erasers disappeared, Little Otto got big in anger. As Otto got angrier, I got more and more angry with the Fish and the Leggo, protesting the abuse of my name. With my protests, they employed more and more bouncers to peer around more and more corners, and with all this attention given to the award, the other terns began to protest to the Fish and the Leggo that Basch, who spent so much time sitting with low-cut black-sneakered feet up drinking ginger ale could not possibly be the front-runner for the ***MVI***, which award may not have existed at all, ever, anywhere, except on the blackboards of the House.

"Hombre?"

"Hey, hey, Hazel," said Chuck. "Come on in, gurl."

Hazel from Housekeeping stood in the doorway. I'd seen her pushing mops and emptying trash, but I'd never seen her look like this: she wore tight white tights and a green uniform stretched tautly over her chest so that the buttons were tugging at the fabric, which parted to reveal enticing bits of black breast in white bra. Her face was marvelous: ruby-red lipstick on black lip, light-brown afro on head, mascara, eye shadow, false lashes, and a carnival of bangles. Her tongue lay like a cushion on the couch of her mouth. Her teeth were moonstones.

"You got your hot water and clean sheets, Chuck?"

"Great, Hazel, just great, gurl. Thanks."

"And your car? Maybe it needs some fixing?"

"Oh, yeah, Hazel, my car's not runnin' well. Needs a lotta work. Gotta get my car fixed for sure, soon. See, my front end needs some looking at. Yeah that's it, my front end."

"Front end? Ho! You bad boy! And when do you want to put your car in the garage?"

"Well, let's see—tomorrow, gurl, how about tomorrow?"

"Ok," said Hazel, giggling. "Tomorrow. Front end? Ba' boy. *Adíos.*"

I was astounded. I'd known that Chuck had been interested in Hazel, but I'd had no idea that things had progressed this far. Even after the Cuban Firecracker had left, her afterburner—afterimage—seemed to remain in the air around us, real hot and red.

"But Hazel's not a Spanish name," I said.

"Well, man, you know how it is. That's not her name."

"What's her name?"

"Jesulita. And we ain't talkin' no auto mechanics, neither."

Jesulita. And that was the other thing that had started to happen: the sexualization of the ternship. Without realizing it, perniciously, hand in hand with our growing competence and rising resentment at the way we were being drilled by Jo and the Slurpers, we had begun to, almost without knowing it, as Chuck said, "get it on" with those erotic ones of the House of God.

I thought about Molly, a beautiful woman who happened to have been disappointed in romantic love and who happened to have made an A in the straight bendover in her Catholic nursing school and about how I'd begun to get involved. It had started innocently enough with my finding her in tears one day at the nursing station, and when I'd asked her why, she'd said that she was scared she was going to die because she had this mole on her thigh—her upper thigh—that had started to grow, and I said Let me have a look and so we went into the on-call room like naughty kids and on the lower bunk bed she pulled down her pantyhose and let me have a look and Christ it was a marvelous thigh and of course I saw those wonderful garden-flowered panties on that bulging blond *mons* but sure enough it was a bad black mole and she was gonna die. But I didn't know anything about moles, and so I pretended to be a big shot and used my "Dr. Basch" title to get her to the derm clinic that morning, and the resident in derm slobbered all over himself because he would get to look at her *mons* and panties instead of the usual excoriated psoriatic lesions of the gomers and he took a little biopsy of it and within twenty-four hours he told her it was just a mole and completely benign and she was not going to die. Being saved from death by me made her grateful, and she had invited me to dinner. Dinner was a terrible casserole and I had tried to get her into bed that night but had managed only to get into her bed with her and with my hands on her almost little-girl breasts and long nipples and to hear the NO NO NO without the final scrumptious YES and to hear also the religious IF I GAVE YOU THAT I'LL HAVE GIVEN YOU EVERYTHING and so that was where the damn thing stood so far, perched erotically amidst the gomers and yet on that age-old and tantalizing ledge called the affair, the new lover versus the steady, the only one who could understand the pull to the lover being the steady, and yet to tell the steady before she found out would wreck it all. Inside the House of God Berry did not seem to exist, and even outside, when I was with Molly she didn't seem to exist either. And so it had become clear to Chuck and me that one way to survive was sexually. This was terribly puzzling and threatening to our sexual dud of a resident, Jo, for the only time she had dropped much below the top of the class at BMS had been in "Medical Aspects of Human Sexuality." Her limbic was out to lunch. Our trump card with Jo could always be sex.

When the Runt showed up, he was so nervous—from having spent eight weeks with a Double O Resident named Mad Dog and with Hyper Hooper and Eat My Dust Eddie, from having heard about "the toughies" awaiting him on our ward, from living with the fear that he was gonna die from being stuck with a needle from the Yellow Man's groin, and also from his intellectual poet June, who was furious at him for spending time away from her—he was so nervous that he seemed to be flying, living three inches above the floor. His hair was frazzled and his mustache seemed to be alive, and he tugged first at one end and then at the other. Chuck and I tried to talk him down, but it was no use, and so we called for Molly to get the syringe of Valium.

"OK, man," said Chuck, "pull down your pants."

"Here? Are you crazy?"

"Go ahead," I said, "we've got things all ready for you."

The Runt pulled down his pants and bent over the nursing-station desk. In walked Molly, with a friend of hers, a nurse from the MICU—Medical Intensive Care Unit—named Angel. Angel was red-headed, buxom, Irish, with wraparound muscular thighs and a creamy complexion. Working in Intensive Care, the Death Row of the House, was rumored to have intensified her sexuality, and it was said that year after year Angel gave intensive care not only to the sick, but also to the male tern. This talent, perhaps apocryphal, had at any rate yet to be experienced by anyone in our group.

"Molly," I said, "I'd like you to meet the new tern, the Runt."

"Pleased to meet you," said Molly. "This is Angel."

111

Craning his neck around, the Runt blushed, his *bulbococ-cygeals* tightened, causing his *testes* to leap up in his *scrotum* like startled fish in an electrified pond, and he said, "Pleased to meet you. I . . . I've never met anyone in this position before. It's their idea, not mine."

"Oh it's"—gesturing up toward the thin air—"nothing new for a"—gesturing toward herself—"nurse," said Angel.

How strange that Angel had difficulty putting words together without gesturing, but it must have had something to do with her nervousness at meeting the Runt from the rear. Angel seemed to be having a hard time resisting the impulse to go to the Runt and run her creamy hands over his leering lumpy rump, his cheeks, his testicles, even the crenellations of his anus, why not? We settled on Angel delivering the dose of Valium, which she did with professional skill, finishing by planting a kiss on the spot. The nurses left, and we asked the Runt how he felt and he said fine and in love with Angel but that he was still scared stiff about starting with the toughies on the ward.

"Man, there's nothing to worry about," said Chuck. "Even though you inherit Potts's disasters, you inherit Towl too."

"Who is Towl?"

"Towl? Towl, boy, you get in here stat!" yelled Chuck. "Towl is the best damn BMS you ever saw."

He was. In he walked: four feet tall with thick black glasses and thick black skin, with a voice gruff as a drill sergeant's and a vocabulary that was short and tough like him. The words Towl knew, he slurred, and his main gift was action, not talk. He was a locomotive. A locomotive from Georgia.

"Towl," said Chuck, "this is the Runt. He's gonna be your new tern, starting tomorrow."

"Rhhmmmmm rhmmmm hi the Runt," growled Towl.

"Boy," said Chuck, "you gotta run the Runt's service, just like you did Potts's. OK? Now, you tell him about it."

"Rhhmmmmm rhmmmm twenty-two patients: eleven gomers, five sickees, and six turkeys who nevah shoulda been heah in the foist place. All in all, nine of 'em are on da rolla coasta."

"Rolla coasta?"

"Right," said Towl, making a motion with his hand like a

112

car on a roller coaster, up and down, up and down, and finally up and flying out into space.

"He means TURFED out of the House," I said.

"But what about the sickees?" asked the Runt. "I'd better start seeing them right away?"

"Rhhmmmmm rhmmmm, nope. You don't have to. Ah takes care of 'em. I nevah lets the new tern touch 'em, not till I'm sure he knows what he's on about."

"But you can't write orders," said the Runt.

"Oh, I can write 'em, I jes cain't sign 'em. Go home, Runt, and come on back in tamarra. Well, gotta go finish mah shit on the ward so I can take off early. So long, Runt. Tamarra."

Despite our preparations, Jo and ward 6-South began to destroy the Runt. Jo, on call with him, took up where Mad Dog had left off, making the Runt feel that he never could do enough and that he never should do anything without first consulting her. Afraid to risk, the Runt didn't learn. Jo's aggressive approach to the gomers soon created for the Runt the sickest, most pitiful service on the ward. The Runt was completely disorganized, and, worse, if a patient did poorly, he thought it was his fault. If Lazarus bled, it was his fault. If a birdlike woman with intransigent bowels hadn't had a bowel movement, it was his fault. He began spending more time talking to his patients, and formed such an attachment to one old man that whenever the Runt showed up, the old fellow would grasp his hand, start to cry, kiss his hand, say that the Runt was his only friend, and when the Runt would try to leave, the old fellow would kiss his hand again, start to cry, and offer him, over and over, the same present, a used bowtie. Despite Chuck, Towl, and me, the Runt was being eaten up by guilt. We'd seen it happen to Potts, and we didn't want it to happen again. Chuck and I decided that if the Runt could only get something going with Angel, he might gain some confidence. His poet, fed up with his being too preoccupied with medicine to read her runes, now demanded that he sleep out on the living-room couch. Yet the Runt was too unsure of himself to ask Angel out.

"Why don't you ask her out?" I'd ask. "Don't you like her?"

"Like her? I'm nuts about her. I dream about her. She's beautiful. She's the kind of woman my mother would never let me go out with. She's what I watched my roommate Norman screw for four years at BMS. A centerfold."

"So why don't you ask her out?"

"I'm scared she won't like me and say no."

"So what? What have you got to lose?"

"The possibility—if she says no—that she might have said yes. Whatever I do, I don't want to lose that possibility."

"Look, man," said Chuck, "you know unless you get your dick moving a little faster, you never gonna learn medicine at all."

"What the hell does that have to do with it?"

"Who knows, man, who knows?"

And instead of asking her out, the Runt kept floundering in guilt on the ward and kept tossing and turning fitfully on the couch in the living room of the poet and kept going to the funerals of his dead young patients and kept letting Jo lop a bit off his schlong daily by telling him what he'd failed to do, and on top of all that, at his poet's suggestion, she being deep into the anal sadistic stages of her psychoanalysis, the Runt followed the path of cure that had warped his organ in the first place in his hyperanalyzed family and went back to the therapist he'd had throughout BMS to work out the torment he'd felt from his promiscuous roommate, Norman, who had had an electric organ and played only one song: "If You Knew Suzie Like I Know Suzie"; that song because all of his girlfriends were named Suzie and each was oh so delighted when she knocked on Norman's door and he leaped to his organ, yelled, "Come on in, Suzie," and in the words of each Suzie, "played my song."

One horrendously hot and steamy night I was on call, and the Runt, working late, refused to leave a patient of his who was in serious trouble. I urged the Runt to go home, and then I urged him to call up Angel and ask her out, and he would do neither. Towl had gone home and so the Runt was at a loss about what to do with his patients, a particular problem being Risenshein, a LOL in NAD whose bone marrow had been wiped out by our cytotoxic agents and had failed to regenerate blood cells, which meant that she was bound to die. The Runt kept asking me what to do with her. Since I was busy with my admissions and with keeping track of the decompensating ward of "toughies," I blew my cool and said, "Get out of here, damnit! I'll take care of things. Go home!"

"I don't want to go home. June's at home. If I go back there, we'll get into some argument about her anal sadism."

"So long," I said, walking off.

"Where are you going?"

"To the bathroom," I said, "I've got the flu." I retreated to the sanctuary of the toilet, wrapped in the latest graffiti: WAS ST. FRANCIS ASSISI?

"What should I do?" wailed the Runt outside the door.

"Call up Angel."

"I'm afraid. Why should I call her, anyway?" Receiving no answer, he struggled with the silence, and said, "All right. Damn! I almost forgot—I'm late for therapy. I'll call her when I get back."

"Nope. Call her now, and don't come back. I'm on call here, see?"

So he finally called her and asked her out and rushed off to talk it all over with the therapist, whom he was paying fifty an hour to take the starch out of his penis. I sat at the nursing station, worn out by a nagging influenza that had me shitting on the hour, and overcome with gloom at the work I had to do. The sun was setting over the changing leaves, and even though it was a boiling-hot Indian-summer night, I knew that soon the days would turn crisp and clear and bright, football weather, when you huddled with a sweatered woman under a blanket and got drunk to avoid getting cold and kissed her lips and shivered . . .

"Mrs. Biles is back from her cardiac catheterization," said my BMS, Bruce Levy the Lost. "The cath fellows wrote in the chart that 'Mrs. Biles had excessive bleeding from the site of needle puncture in the groin.' I'd better work it up, Dr. Basch. She might have a bleeding disorder."

Mrs. Biles had no bleeding disorder. The cath boys always wrote "excessive bleeding" to BUFF the charts in case of litigation. In fact, Mrs. Biles, Little Otto's patient, didn't even have cardiac disease at all, but—as everyone including Otto

115

knew—bursitis. Little Otto was after the big bucks. Bruce
Levy, the BMS, was after playing the invent-an-obscure-dis-
ease-to-make-an-A-in-medicine game. Who was I to stand in
his way?

"Sounds interesting, Bruce. How ya gonna work it up?"

Bruce rattled off several blood tests he was about to order.

"Wait a sec," said Jo, who'd been on her way out but who
had stopped back in to make sure all was OK before she went
back out to where she was just another lonely single woman
and not an admiral of the gomers in the House of God. "Those
tests cost a fortune. What evidence do you have that she has a
bleeding disorder? For example, did you ask her if she suffers
from nosebleeds?"

"Hey, great idea!" said Bruce, and ripped off down the hall
to ask. Returning, he said, "Yeah, she suffers from nosebleeds.
Great!"

"Wait a sec," I said, "everybody will say that when you ask,
right?"

"Yeah, right," said Brucie, looking crestfallen.

"Did you ask her if she bleeds after tooth extraction?" asked
Jo.

"Hey, terrific idea!" said Bruce, and ran out again. "Yup,
she bleeds like crazy after tooth extractions."

"Brucie, everyone bleeds like crazy after extractions," I said.

"Damnit, Dr. Basch, you're right," said the BMS, and he
looked sad, since to become an intern in the BMS system he
had to make an A, and to do that he had to make a disease so
he could make a cure and make a lecture, and he saw his grade
fluttering down toward low C and his internship moving west
of the Hudson River.

"Say, Brucie," I said nonchalantly, "what about bruising?"

"Bruising? Hey, fantastic idea—"

"WAIT! Save yourself a trip. She's gonna say yes, that she
bruises easily, right?"

"Right, Dr. Basch. Who wouldn't say that?"

"No one," I said. "But how can you test it out for sure?"

"I don't know," said Brucie, his fist furrowing his brow.

"Too bad," I said. "Bleeding disorders are fascinating."

All of a sudden Brucie lit up, shouted, "I got it!" and ran

down the hallway, and a few seconds later there echoed back up to us a scream YEEE-OWWWW! and in a moment Brucie was back, grinning from ear to ear, and he said, "Well, I did it," and reached for the hematology slips.

"You did it? You did what?" asked Jo, eyes popping.

"I bruised her."

"WHAT? YOU DID WHAT?"

"Just like you suggested, Jo, I bruised Mrs. Biles. Punched her in the arm. You were right, I shouldn't have gone ahead with this expensive work-up until I'd bruised her with my own two hands."

Just before the Runt returned from his therapy, a forty-two-year-old patient of his had a cardiac arrest, and as the Runt came down the hallway, he was passed by the intubated patient being wheeled to the MICU by Eat My Dust Eddie, the tern on rotation here. The Runt looked horrified and said, "I'm sure it was something I did wrong."

"Don't be silly," I said, "it's a good TURF. Now, get out of here—you'll be late for your date with Thunder Thighs."

"I'm not going."

"You are. Think of those red pubic hairs."

"I can't. I better go see Mrs. Risenshein. I feel terrible that these young patients are all dying."

"LAW NUMBER FOUR: THE PATIENT IS THE ONE WITH THE DISEASE. Get the hell out of here," I said, pushing him out the door. "Scram."

"I'll call you from the Chinese restaurant."

"Call me from the saddle or don't call me at all."

"But why? Why?" he screamed, his foot jamming the door like a salesman. "Why am I doing this?"

"Because it's limp."

"Because what's limp?"

"The whole goddamn shooting gallery. So long."

He left. As usual, all hell broke loose on the ward, mostly with the Runt's patients. The Runt had learned to be aggressive with the gomers and cautious with the dying young, and since Chuck and I had begun to believe the Fat Man's idea that the reverse was the essence of medical care, the Runt's patients were disasters, and the first part of each night on call

117

had to be spent BUFFING the Runt's service, in secret, hidden from Jo, the Runt, and the charts. Surreptitiously I'd slip into the room containing the young asthmatic who would die without the steroids that the Runt was afraid to give her and BAM BAM hit her with a big secret dose that would get her through the night; next it would be his nice leukemic lady, whom Towl was keeping alive, and secretly I'd transfuse her six more units of platelets without which she'd bleed out before sunrise; and the final horrendoma was Lazarus, the alcoholic janitor, who was always in shock, always infected, and whom the Runt was always treating with homeopathic doses of meds for fear of doing something bad. Each day, Lazarus made a determined effort to die, usually by bleeding out, from nose or lip or gut or balls, and each night Chuck or I in a clandestine and almost religious operation would BUFF the shit out of him for his next day's thrilling adventures with a tern who was limp and unstrung and scared to death of doing anything active, anything active at all. That night I remembered that I'd forgotten what the Runt had told me just before he'd left the first time, when I'd asked him if he'd tapped the infection in Lazarus' ascitic belly:

"He's all right," the Runt had said, looking away.

"Wait a sec," I'd said, "did you tap his belly or not?"

"Nope."

"Jesus Christ! Why the hell not?"

"I never learned how. You need to use a big needle and I . . . I was scared I'd hurt him."

Limp. Cursing, I went into Lazarus' room, where he was dying again in earnest, and since I'd been in this situation with him every other night on call, I knew what to do, and got busy raising him up yet again. Molly came up and said I had a phone call. It was the Runt.

"How's Mrs. Risenshein?" he asked.

"Fine, but Lazarus just started to go down the tubes," I said, telling myself I won't yell at him for not having tapped his belly.

"I should have tapped his belly."

"Where are you?"

"Chinatown. But how's Lazarus?"

118

"What did you have?"

"Lo mein, moo goo gai pan, and a lotta rice, but how is he?"

"Sounds delicious, he went down the tubes," I said.

"Oh, no! I'm coming in!"

"But I saved him."

"Hey, great!"

"Hang on," I said, watching Molly gesture from Lazarus' room, "he's trying to go down the tubes again."

"I'm coming in!"

"What are you doing after dinner?"

"I thought I'd take her back to my place."

"What? With June there, are you nuts?"

"Why not?"

"Never mind. I gotta go, but listen, whatever you do, do not take her back to your place. Go to her place. Remember: FAKE HIGH, GO LOW. So long."

For some reason, admission diagnoses in the House of God ran in spurts: three cardiac, two renal, four pulmonary. That hot and dismal night, the disease matched the oppression—it was cancer night at the House. First it was a little tailor named Saul. As I read his chart in the E.W., Howard—the tern who seemed to love every aspect of the ternship and whom I hated for that—bubbling with excitement at "really being a doc," told me that Saul had pneumonia. The blood smear told me that Saul had acute leukemia, his pneumonia being part of his generalized sepsis because his white cells didn't work. Saul knew he was sick, although he didn't know yet how sick, and when I wheeled him to X Ray for his chest film, I asked him if he could stand up by himself.

"Stand up? I could peech a full game," said Saul, and fell down. I propped him up, this little bony just-young-enough-to-die old man, whom I'd just told he had leukemia. As I left him to himself in front of the X-ray beam, his boxer shorts fell down.

"Saul," I said, "you're losing your shorts."

"Yeh. So? Here I'm losing my life, and you tell me I'm losing my shorts?"

I was moved. He was all of our grandfathers. With the laconic resignation of a Diasporic Jew he was watching the latest

Nazi—leukemia—force him from his only real home, his life. Leukemia was the epitome of my helplessness, for the treatment was to bomb the bone marrow with cell poisons called cytotoxins until it looked, under the microscope, like Hiroshima, all black, empty, and scorched. And then you waited to see whether the marrow regenerated any healthy cells, or the same old cancer. Since there was a period of time when there were no blood cells—no whites to fight infection and no reds to carry oxygen and no platelets to stop bleeding—to deliver care was to fight the infection and transfuse red cells for oxygen and platelets to control bleeding, all the time creating more bleeding and anemia by drawing blood for countless tests. Terrific. I'd gone through it with Dr. Sanders, and I hated it. The start of this horrific treatment was to inject modified rat poison, nicknamed the Red Death for its color and the way it eroded your skin if you splashed it around, directly into Saul's veins. Thinking "so long, marrow," I did so, brimming with disgust.

The second E.W. admission: Jimmy the name, cancer the game. Young enough to die for sure. Howard, smiling, chubby, smoking his chubby pipe like a TV doc, presented the case to me: pneumonia, and Howard thought he might have leukemia. One look at Jimmy's chest X Ray showed that Howie had missed a homungus lung cancer that would kill Jimmy pretty quick. As I worked on him in the E.W., trying to shoo away the hovering Howie, I heard Hooper battling a gomere behind the next curtain. The gomere, his third admission of the night, was trying to kick him in the nuts. I asked Hooper how it was going.

"Terrible. MOR, Roy, MOR."

"MOR?"

"Marriage On Rocks. We're both doing everything we can—joined a California-style sauna where they whip you with hot eucalyptus leaves and give you some aquanude group psychotherapy—but I don't think it's going to work. The little woman is mad as hell that I'm here all the time, and that I'm into death."

"You're into death?"

"Who isn't? It's where we're all headed, you know."

120

"I can't deny that, but I guess I just don't get the charge out of it that you do. I'm sorry about the MOR," I said, wondering if my R—for Relationship—would get to the point of ROR during the internship.

"Doesn't matter," said the hyperactive tern, "no kids. In California, being married two years means you've hit the median. Hey, I got a question for you: do you think it's legal to have this woman sign her own postmortem permission slip along with her insurance voucher?"

"It's probably legal, but I'm not sure it's ethical."

"Great," said Hooper, "another post coming up. In Sausalito nobody's heard of ethics. Hey, thanks. I didn't want to stay married to that bitch anyway. You should see what I've got simmering down in the morgue."

"In the morgue?"

"A female pathology resident from Israel. Dynamite. Grooves on thanatos, like me. Romeo and Juliet, man, so long."

I sat in the E.W. nursing station thinking about how the Leggo and the Fish had blessed our ward with "the toughies," the dying young, like Jimmy, like my friend Dr. Sanders, out there on his last fishing trip before his last autumn—

"That's tough to do, to face the dying and the dead."

I looked up. It was one of the policemen, the fat one, Gilheeny.

"Strength of character," said the other one, Quick, "it doesn't grow on trees."

"Nor can one buy it in any store," said the redhead. "It's the toilet training that does it, I do believe. So said Freud and Cohen."

"Where did an Irish cop learn about Freud?" I asked.

"Where? Why, here, man, here, from spending the last twenty years here, five nights a week, in trialogues of discussion with fine young overeducated men like you. Better than night school, more broad and useful. And we get paid to attend."

"Not only that," said Quick, "but all the different viewpoints contribute. Over twenty years one learns a good deal. Currently a surgeon named Gath brings us the news from the

Southern Rim, and with Cohen we are in the middle of a gold mine of psychoanalytical thought."

"Who is Cohen?"

"A sophisticated, jocular, and unrestrained resident in psychiatry," said Quick. "A textbook in himself."

"You must make his acquaintance," said Gilheeny. Twitching his red eyebrows so that they coerced the rest of his fat face into a gap-toothed smile, he went on, "We can hardly wait to hear from a Rhodes Scholar like yourself, a man with high qualities of body and mind, with experience gleaned from corners of the round globe, like England, France, and the Emerald Isle, which I have visited only twice."

"A textbook in yourself," said Quick.

Upstairs, I had just finished working Jimmy over, putting in lines and tubes and starting to treat his untreatable diseases, when Mrs. Risenshein arrested and I was surprised to hear myself cursing under my breath as I resuscitated her, "I wish she would die so I could just go to sleep," and I was shocked when I realized that I'd just wished a human being dead so I could go to sleep. Animal. Eat My Dust rolled up from the MICU to take Risenshein away and I asked how he was.

"Glad you asked. It's going just great. Here, Bob," he said, nodding to his BMS, "wheel this stretcher on down to the Unit, will you, pal? Keep pumping the oxygen and keep the lines open, I'm just going up to floor eight for a minute to jump off and kill myself."

He left, and Molly—clean and pretty and sexy and off duty—left, and I was desolate watching her go. I should have been going with her. The Runt called back again.

"How's Lazarus?" he asked.

"Stable. Where are you?"

"At Angel's. I'm scared. How's Risenshein?"

"There's nothing to be scared about. Risenshein's had a cardiac arrest and is in the MICU."

"Oh, no! I'm coming in right away!"

"You do and I'll kill you. Put Angel on."

"Hri, Roy," said a healthy drunk voice, "I'm"—gesture—"drunk."

"Fine. Listen, Angel, I'm worried about the Runt. He's not

122

going to make it unless he gets some confidence in himself. He's a great guy, but he needs some confidence. Chuck and I are really concerned—suicide—that's how concerned we are."

"Sruicide!" Gesture. "Wow! WhatcanIdo?"

I told Angel exactly what she could do to prevent the Runt's suicide.

"Sruicide!" Gesture. "You mean he's freee?"

"Not yet, Angie. Right now, he's still a bird in a cage. Open it up, Angel, set him free, let him fly."

"Flyfly his"—gesture—"fly bye-bye," and the phone went dead.

Hot, sweaty, with the dried sweat salt like sand on my eyelids, with my flu declaring itself in malaise, photophobia, myalgia, nausea, and diarrhea, cursing being in the House while Molly was out and Berry was out—where and with whom?—and while the Runt was getting seduced out of "sruicide," I tried to finish my write-up of young and soon-to-be-dead Jimmy. Chubby, grinning, puffing his pipe, Howard appeared.

"What the hell are you doing up here?"

"Oh, I just thought I'd do some follow-up on Jimmy. Great case. Guess he's had it, huh? Oh, and I wanted to ask you about that nurse in the MICU, Angel. Very fine girl, and I thought I might ask her out."

I watched him puff his pipe, and, hating him because his happy life even in the House was a puff on his pipe, I said, "Oh, so you haven't heard about the Runt and Angel?"

"No. You don't mean—"

"Exactly. At this very moment. And, Howard, listen carefully: you should see what she does with her mouth."

"With her . . . her what?"

"Her mouth," I said, knowing that by morning Howard would have puffed what Angel did with her mouth all over God's House. "See, she takes her lips and she puts them around his—"

"Well, I don't want to hear about that, and I'm glad you warned me before I asked her out. But I want to know why when I took Jimmy's blood pressure just now it was only forty systolic."

123

"It's what?" I said, rushing into Jimmy's room, where I found that it was forty systolic and Jimmy was trying to die right away. I panicked. I didn't know where to start, to save him. I looked at Howard leaning casually against the doorway lighting his pipe and smiling, and I said, "Howard, help me with this."

"Oh, yes? And what might I do?"

I didn't know what he might do or what I might do either, but then I thought of the Fat Man and I said, "Page the Fat Man, stat."

"Oh? Do you think you need him? No, you can handle it, Roy. Besides, they say you can't become a real doctor without killing a few patients at the least."

"Do something to help me," I said, trying to think clearly.

"What might I do?"

The Fat Man arrived, puffing from the race up the stairs, and sensing my panic, ordered me to take my own pulse. As I did so, he began to get Jimmy organized so he would not die right then. Fats attacked Jimmy with that fantastic smooth expertise of his, and you could almost hear the click click click of each essential procedure. Fats chattered as he worked, addressing comments to us all, including the nurse and a woman named Gracie from Dietary and Food Services who somehow at that late hour had been with him—in bed?!—

"What's wrong with Jimmy?" asked Fats, putting in a big needle.

"Cancer of the lung," I said.

"Christ," said Fats, "and he's young enough to die."

"If I were you, I'd try laetrile," said Gracie from Dietary and Food Services.

"Try what?" asked Fats, stopping trying to save Jimmy.

"Laetrile. A cure for cancer," said Gracie.

"A what for what?" shot out Fats, standing up stock-still.

"The Mexicans have found that an extract from apricot pits, called laetrile, can cure cancer. Controversial, but—"

"But worth a big fortoona," said Fats, eyes aglitter. "Hey, listen, I gotta hear more about this, Roy," he said, starting to leave.

"Fats, wait!" I said. "Don't leave me yet!"

"Did you hear what Gracie said, Roy? A cure for cancer. Come on, Gracie, I want you to tell me more."

"It's bullshit," I said. "There's no cure for cancer, it's a hoax."

"It's not," said Gracie from Dietary and Food indignantly, "it worked on my cousin's husband. He was dying and now he's fine."

"Dying and now he's fine," said Fats, and then, walking toward the door, he murmured, as if in a trance, "dying and now he's fine."

"Please Fats," I said, "don't leave me alone yet," as Jimmy began once again to die and I began once again to panic.

"Why not?" asked Fats, puzzled.

"I'm scared."

"Still? You still need some help?"

"Yes, I do,"

"Well, then, you're going to get it. Let's get to work."

We got to work, but soon I realized that Fats had slipped away, and I was left alone with Jimmy and Howie and Maxine, the night nurse. And then I knew that Fats's slipping away and leaving me in charge meant that he knew I could handle it, and I felt a warm rush go through me. I could handle it, and although all I wanted to do was to beat the shit out of Howard, I worked on Jimmy until it was clear that he needed to be breathed by a respirator, which meant a TURF to the SICU— Surgical Intensive Care Unit—and as I watched the cheery sadistic surgical resident wheel Jimmy off, Jimmy, who by now was surrounded by so much tubing that he looked like a meat ball in the middle of a plate of spaghetti, I felt great relief, and I heard Howard say, "Impressive, Roy, impressive job on a tough case," and he left and I was filled to my eyeballs with hate.

With the sweat dripping from my brow onto Jimmy's chart and the flu dripping through every muscle and bowel villus in my body, I finished my write-up and sent the Bruiser along with it to the SICU. I sat for a moment musing: Well, this has been the worst night of my life, but now it's over, and now I can go to sleep. They can't get me now. Through the open window came that comforting smell of fresh rain on hot asphalt. The nurse came in and said, "Mr. Lazarus has just had a bowel movement that is all blood."

"Hey, that's really funny, Maxine. You got a great sense of humor."

"No, I'm serious. The bed is solid blood."

They wanted me to go on, and I could not. The world became the world just before the head-on crash. It could not be what it was. "I can't do anything more tonight," I heard myself say. "I'll see you in the morning."

"Look, Roy, don't you understand? He's just bled out a gallon of blood. He's lying in it. You're the doctor, and you have to do something for him."

Filled with hate, trying to get rid of thoughts that Lazarus wanted to die and I wanted him to die and I had to break my ass to stop him from dying, I went into his room and was face to face with black putrid sticky wet blood. On autopilot, I went to work. My last clear memory was putting a naso-gastric tube down into Lazarus' stomach and having the bloody vomit spew up and out and all over me, as Lazarus rolled his death-defying eyes.

Just after Lazarus, just before dawn, Dr. Sanders came back in, bald from the chemotherapy, infected and bleeding, having had to cut short his fishing trip.

"I'm glad you'll be taking care of me again," he said weakly.

"So am I," I said, wondering if this admission would be his last, and realizing how attached to him I felt.

"Just remember: no whispering behind my back, Roy. And as for heroic measures—we'll talk about that, together."

I put him in the same room with Saul the leukemic tailor, thinking that while Sanders would die, Saul might be just old enough to survive. How crazy was that? As I lay down in my spewed clothes for my hour's sleep, I found myself wondering where Molly was, more than where Berry was, and wondered if that meant that it was the beginning of the ROR—Romance On Rocks—and then I thought with pleasure of the phone call I'd gotten at about one A.M. from June, the Runt's poet, wondering if I knew where he was, and I chuckled at that and composed a letter in my head to give the Runt in the morning: "Congratulations on your *bravo* three-dimensional night of

126

love. You are herewith charged with rape. Red pubic hairs, I might warn you, will stand up in court." But then I realized that, Goddamn! the Runt was seeing what Angel did with her mouth while I still hadn't gotten past Molly's long nipples, and then finally I recalled that no one yet knew what Angel did with her mouth because I'd just made that up to torment that optimist Howard, who knew that being a doc really was the cat's balls after all. And I realized that they could never hurt me more than they had just hurt me that night, and that out of chaos like this had to come confidence and skill. Something had happened when I was with Saul and Jimmy and Lazarus and Dr. Sanders, and I didn't know for sure what, but I knew that from taking the risks and learning and remembering Fats, I had pinned down my terror and exploded it to bits. From that night on, I might be everything else, but I'd never again be panicked in the House of God. It was a thrilling thought—almost like in the intern novels and in the inside of Howard's skull and in my father's letters—until I realized with alarm that I hadn't learned how to save anyone at all, not Dr. Sanders or Lazarus or Jimmy or Saul or Anna O., and that what I was thrilled about was learning how to save myself.

8

By mid-September, according to Jo's schedule, neither I nor any other tern was supposed to have learned how to save himself. That next morning, as the warmth of the fading summer percolated up through the crisp air, as the clear cirrus football weather blew into the ward through the skeleton of the Wing of Zock rising higher and higher like jail bars over our windows, I showed up for rounds a half-hour late, and I was the first tern there. Jo was furious, and when, an hour late, Chuck ambled in, wearing yet again the same dirty whites with the same fly open and the same no necktie, Jo exploded, saying, "I told you, Chuck, that rounds start at six-thirty. Got it?"

"Fine, fine."

"Where have you been?"

"Oh, well, I been getting my car fixed."

Just as rounds ended, in flew the Runt. His hair was frazzled, his belt undone, his shirt was hanging out, his stethoscope dragged from his back pocket, and he had a big smile plastered over his carnival of a face. He was sizzling.

"Are you sick?" asked Jo.

"Hell, no. I feel grrr-ate!"

"Where have you been?"

"I've been fucking my eyes out," said the Runt, and then, roaring, clapped a hand on each of Chuck's and my shoulders, and with an idiotic rolla coasta of a grin, yelped.

"You've been what?" asked Jo.

128

"Fucking. Copulating. You know, vasodilation of the penile veins, it gets hard and the male sticks it into—"

"That's inappropriate—"

"Hey, Jo," said the Runt, looking to us for support, and then, ignoring her fragility, "go fuck yourself, huh?"

With that Chuck and I knew we had created a monster and felt real good about it, but Chuck pointed out that it was sort of like watching your mother-in-law drive your new Cadillac off a cliff, because we knew that Jo would not go fuck herself but would go talk to the Fish, who would go talk to the Leggo, who would get us back but good, since the essence of any hierarchy is retaliation. Jo led the rest of rounds in silence, until we got to the admission named Jimmy, who'd been TURFED to the SICU. Jo insisted we go see him, and as our caravan turned up the hall, Jo got excited about the case, and unable to contain herself any longer, blurted out, "Hey, Roy, that sounds like a really great admission."

Without thinking, remembering how Jimmy's decompensation had strung me out, as if from somewhere else than me, although I knew it did come from some bilious region within me, I heard myself create a new LAW—NUMBER NINE: THE ONLY GOOD ADMISSION IS A DEAD ADMISSION, which stopped Jo in her tracks, the same way that, a few minutes later, when Chuck and the Runt and I were poodling around the SICU while Jo macerated Jimmy, we were stopped in our tracks when we saw, rigged up in an orthopedic apparatus, the remains of a human. Bandaged head to toe, it was clear that the patient had collided with something and that the point of impact had been his testicles. They were cantaloupe, even honeydew. Here we had an aberrant Hell's Angel who, on his Harley Hawg, had smashed head-on into a tree. A sign on the end of his bed read: IT TAKES BALLS TO RIDE A HARLEY.

None of us could have imagined what an ace auto mechanic Angel was until we heard from the Runt how, even the first time, she had fixed his compact car: "Well, I was so upset at what was happening last night, I couldn't even talk straight by the time I got to her apartment. I don't know what you said to her on the phone, Roy, but when she hung up, things were a lot easier. She poured me a drink, but all I could think of was

Lazarus and Risenshein and the graffiti above the urinal at the Chinese restaurant: STAND CLOSER, IT'S SHORTER THAN YOU THINK. Well, anyway, she asked if I'd like to watch TV and I said sure. We were sitting on the couch, and I didn't know if she liked me, and then all of a sudden she's sort of leaning her boob against me and her red hair is unpinned and down to her scapula and I start to feel better. And she says It's kind of uncomfortable in here, why don't we watch inside, and unplugs the TV and carries it into the bedroom. I couldn't believe it. I start to nuzzle her neck and she says Clothes are such a hassle, and she takes off her sweater and her skirt. Well. She starts to make husky noises and since she's taken off her sweater, I take off her bra. Ha! Perfect! Big soft tits! Ha! I pull off her panties," said the Runt, pulling off Angel's panties right before our eyes in the middle of the nursing station, "and she pulls off my pants. Incredible!"

"What about her pubic hair?" I asked.

"Bright red!" said the Runt with a wild look in his eyes. "Perfect! Ha! Well, then I kind of hesitated when I go to put it in, and I think of Lazarus dying and all and it . . . well, it dies too."

"Damn!" said Chuck.

"But she's right there with her hand, and it raises right back up, and when I get it in, she's wet and ready, not like June or all the others my mother always liked. The first time I was a little off, and I came too soon, but before I knew it she had her hand between my legs and we're at it again. Ha! Hahaaa! Twenty-three minutes. I timed it. And then when she was reaching orgasm she said something like This is terrii—fick! and her words were like a whip spurring me on. Bells rang and the earth shook. Yippeee! And then the next time—"

Chuck and I looked at each other.

"—she was sort of lying there with her back to me, and I thought she was asleep, but no, she kind of reached around and started pulling on my penis and the next thing I know she had kind of maneuvered it in and we were at it again, and I think that was the time that did it. Yee-ow!"

"Did what?"

"Did what you guys said it would—made me a doc. We

went on and on, her moaning and calling out things, and me
sweating and grunting, and just before we came, she started
saying, at first in a whisper and then louder and then screaming it out so I was worried that someone might hear, DOCTOR
RUNTSKY DOCTOR RUNTSKY DOCTOR RUNT—SKEEE!
and when it was over, lying there, she snuggled up to me and
sighed this wonderful satisfied sigh and said, Runt, you are a
great doc, g'night, and the last thing I saw this morning was
the sunlight on those fiery red pubic hairs. Ha! I owe it all to
you. There's nothing I won't try now, nothing!"

"Damn," said Chuck, "Runt, you've become completely un-
nervous."

"Right. I can't wait to tell that dry bitch June it's all over.
Poetry? Ha! That ain't poetry, this is. You know what's coming
next?"

Neither Chuck nor I knew what was coming next.

"I'm gonna taste her pubic hair, 'cause I know in my heart
that it's strawberry red. Roy, I just want to say thanks. Thanks
for taking over my service last night, for helping me out, and
for kicking me out of the House and into bed with Angel."

Such was the first installment of the Runt's relating to us,
blow by blow, his love affair with Angel. While Chuck and I at
first felt a little uncomfortable listening to the intimate details
the morning after each thrilling episode, we didn't feel so bad
that we couldn't listen, and we realized that the Runt was going through a healthy stage of development that we'd both
passed about ten years before. Besides that, it was unctuous
steamy stuff. In gratitude, we taught the Runt medicine, and
each of us, with a growing sense of camaraderie, helped each
other do the work of the House of God.

Shortly after the Runt's first auto repair, Chuck's true great-
ness came out. First it was Lazarus. Chuck and I, in an effort to
lighten the Runt's load, had flipped a coin for Lazarus, and
he'd become Chuck's patient. One day on rounds we stopped
outside the room Lazarus had occupied since July. Screams
came from it. A fresh gomer was in the Lazarus memorial bed.

"What happened to Mr. Lazarus?" asked Jo.

"Oh, he's daid," said Chuck.

"Dead? What happened?"

"Dunno, gurl, dunno. Guess he died."

"Potts and I and the Runt and I kept him alive for the past three months, and then the first night he was on your service he died? What's going on?"

"Wish I knew."

"Did you get the postmortem?"

"Nope."

"Why not?"

"Who knows, gurl, who knows?"

That same day, at Chuck's insistence, we stopped outside the room containing the woman who was to make Chuck famous throughout the House. "Now, this is the most amazin' thing," said Chuck, "I was called down to the E.W. to see this whale. She'd been seen already by Howard, by Mad Dog, and by Putzel. She was lyin' there, not breathin' worth shit, and nobody could figure out why not. Well, I went in there and did my exam. I say to myself, Not breathin, eh? Hmm. Better have a look in her mouth. I opened it up and looked in. Damn! I say, what's that big ole green thing in there? So I put on about four pairs of gloves and I reach on back down in there, and this is what I foun'."

He took out a specimen jar in which was a large sprout of broccoli.

"Broccoli!" said the Bruiser, with one of his rare correct answers.

"Nuthin' but," said Chuck. "Howard, Mad Dog, Putzel— none of them dudes bothered to look in the ole lady's mouth."

"The Broccoli Lady," I said. "A save!"

"No foolin'. Y'all come in an' see her."

The Broccoli Lady was huge, gomertose, and smelly. Except for an occasional spasmodic shiver of her chest, she still wasn't breathing and she didn't look like she was doing too great.

"Doin' great, ain't she?" asked Chuck.

"A real save," said the Runt.

"What are you doing for her?" asked Jo.

"What am I doing for her? Why, I got her on a low-broccoli diet, gurl, what else?"

From that time on, the House looked at Chuck not as a dumb

black admitted on quota, but as a smart tern. As he and I and even the Runt became competent, we began to realize that since no one else would want to do what we terns were forced to do, we were becoming indispensable. The House needed us. The House thought it needed us to do something for the gomers and for the dying young.

What the House really needed us for was to do nothing for the gomers and to bear the helplessness of caring for the dying young. As autumn flared, as it looked more and more like both Agnew and Nixon would get thrown into the slammer at the same time, we struggled to hide our doing nothing from our ferret, Jo. Rounds became a *bravura* performance in duplicity, with us trying to recall what imaginary test we'd written down, what imaginary complications had ensued, what imaginary treatment for the imaginary complications had been initiated, and what the imaginary response to all this had been, and all the time working like hell on trying to get the gomer placed. It was such a great strain on us that occasionally things would break down. One day, faltering under Jo's demanding why I hadn't ordered a four-A.M. temperature to work up Anna O.'s imaginary fever, I blurted out another new LAW—NUMBER TEN: IF YOU DON'T TAKE A TEMPERATURE, YOU CAN'T FIND A FEVER, and I'd begun to catalogue the other things that you might not do, to not produce something you might not treat, such as, instead of TEMPERATURE and FEVER, substituting EKG and CARDIAC ARRYTHMIA, and I'd gotten as far as CHEST X RAY and PNEUMONIA before Chuck and the Runt collared me and ushered me out of Jo's grasp.

To ease the strain, Chuck and I spent more and more time with our feet up drinking ginger ale in the nursing station, doing nothing. Although the Runt was somewhat calmer, he was still too tense to sit with us. Towl, his BMS, was not, and filling a ginger-ale container, Towl groaned and put his feet up.

"Towl, I want to ask you about Enid," said the Runt. "She's still not cleaned out for her bowel run."

"Rrhhmmmmm rhmmmm, Ah know. So wut?"

"So what should I do? I gotta get her cleaned out, and no

133

matter what I do, without eating anything she keeps gaining weight and hasn't had a bowel movement for the past three weeks. Her daughter says she hasn't unloaded spontaneously for eight years. It's amazing—she turns water into shit."

"Rrhhmmmmm rhmmmm, Ah know. Why you wanna do the bowel run?"

"Because that's why she's here."

"Yeah, but I mean, is she really havin' the bowel run, or are we jus' pretendin' she's havin the bowel run? Ever since I toined her over to you, I caint keep her straight."

Sheepishly the Runt admitted that Enid's Private, Putzel, wanted the bowel run done, and the Runt was really trying to do it.

"Rrhhmmmmm rhmmmm, well, then, give her milk and 'lasses, down her mouth and up her direcshum hole, the both at once."

"Milk and 'lasses?"

"Right. Milk and mo-lasses. Both ends. She gonna explode."

Inevitably, during our ginger-ale rounds, like a floorwalker, the Fish would appear. He walked up and, avoiding our eyes, asked, "Hey, guys, how's it going?" and then, without waiting to hear how it was going, said, "You know, don't you, that that looks unprofessional."

"Fine, fine," said Chuck, lifting his feet down off the counter.

To irritate the Fish, I lit a cigarette.

"I hear from Jo that you've been coming in late."

"Oh, yeah," said Chuck. "Well, the thing is my car. Keeps breakin' down and I gotta keep takin' it to the garage."

"Oh, well, that's different. Got a good mechanic? You could use mine if you like. Get the damn thing fixed right once and for all, so you don't have to worry about it. Yes, and another thing: your spelling is atrocious. We'll go over a few of your write-ups together, OK?"

"Fine, fine."

"But there's one thing I don't understand," I said. "I can't figure out if I drink 'cause I pee or I pee 'cause I drink."

"Stop drinking and see what happens."

"I tried that. I get thirsty."

"Perhaps you have Addison's disease," said the Fish, and his attention shifted to my cigarette until he couldn't stand it any longer and said, "I don't understand how, knowing what you know about lung cancer, you continue to smoke. Maybe you don't inhale?"

I did not inhale, and so I said, "I inhale."

"Why do you do it?"

"It feels good."

"If everyone did what feels good, where would we all be?"

"Feeling good."

"You're too loose," said the Fish, "I don't know how you do such good work, being that loose. Enjoy that cigarette, Dr. Basch, for it's three more minutes off your life."

Just then Little Otto marched in, went to the blackboard to leave a note for me, saw the space taken up with a fresh ripe

***
MVI
***

let out a sharp bark which turned all our heads toward him, and finding no eraser handy, spat on the board and wiped the thing off with his sleeve, snarling.

"Now, that's just the kind of thing I resent," I said to the Fish, "having that damn ***MVI*** smeared all over the House under my name. Your kinky bouncers haven't done anything. Can't you stop it?"

"I tried," said the Fish, "but it didn't do any good. The damn thing may all be a practical joke anyway."

"That's not what I heard. I heard that the prize for the ***MVI*** is a free trip for two to Atlantic City for the AMA meetings in June, with you and the Leggo."

"I didn't hear that," said the Fish, beginning to leave.

"Damn!" said Chuck. "Man, would you look at that!"

The Fish and I and Towl and Little Otto looked at that, which was, somehow, under my name on the blackboard, in all the colors of the rainbow, that neat yet ornate insignia:

135

***
*** ROY G. BASCH ***
***
*** MVI ***
***

Later that week the Leggo and the Fish called a B-M Deli luncheon to announce another award, which we were to nickname the Black Crow. Since this was the first time all the terns had been gathered together since July the first, we greeted each other warmly and with relief. Everything had happened. Most of us had learned enough medicine to worry less about saving patients and more about saving ourselves. Although some of our ways of saving ourselves were beginning to seem bizarre, they weren't so far-out, yet, as to be dangerous or intolerable. Looking around the room, hearing the simmering jokes and laughter and chatter that from time to time popped its lid and boiled over into a happy roar, I realized how much we'd grown to care about each other. We were developing a code of caring, helping each other leave early, not fucking each other over, tolerating each other's nuttiness, and listening to each other's groans. Each life was being twisted, branded. We were sharing something big and murderous and grand. Sensing that, I felt close to tears. We were becoming doctors.

Eat My Dust Eddie, being run ragged in the deathhouse, the MICU, looked awful, and was talking about his previous night on call: "I was admitting my sixth cardiac arrest and I got this call from the E.W.—Hooper, it was you—saying that there was a guy down there who'd arrested and you were thinking of sending him to me if he survived. I hung up the phone, got down on my knees, and prayed: Please, God, kill that guy! I was on my knees, I mean ON MY KNEES!"

"He died," said Hooper. "Jo was the resident, and she wanted to keep pumping his chest, but I said, 'As far as I'm concerned, this guy was dead ten minutes ago,' and I left."

"Hooper, you're a great man," said EMD. "I feel like kissing you."

"Kiss me you can, kiss me if you like, but all I know is that if a human disaster like that had shown up in Sausalito, he'd have had to sign his own postmortem permission slip to be admitted at all."

"I think that's a bit crass," said Howie, grinning.

"Stay out of Sausalito when you're having your cardiac arrest."

Potts came in, late, made a thin sandwich, and sat down, and I was reminded that the Yellow Man had yet to die. Potts was haunted by him, linked with him, and whenever we saw Potts, we saw the Yellow Man. Potts was becoming more withdrawn. He hadn't come out for our touch-football game. He was a tree with a limb ripped off, the pulp a harsh raw white. No one ever mentioned the Yellow Man to him. Or to the Runt. But if the Runt was infected, at least he'd have done some snazzy dirty things with Angel before he died. I asked Potts how he was.

"I don't know. OK, I guess. Otis loves the fall, the leaves. I keep thinking I'm not doing a good job here, you know."

"You're all doing a good job," said the Leggo, standing before us, "but you as a group have not been getting enough postmortem permissions. It's hard to describe the importance of the autopsy. Why, the autopsy is the heart—no, the flower, the red rose—of medicine. Yes, the great Virchow, the Father of Pathology, performed twenty-five thousand autopsies with his own two hands. It's crucial to our understanding of disease. For instance, that Czech, nicknamed—what was he called, Dr. Fishberg?"

"Not *was* called, sir, *is* called. The Yellow Man, sir."

"Yes, take the Yellow Man . . . "

The Leggo went on to take the Yellow Man, stressing how important it would be for us to get the post when he died, and as he spoke, each word seemed to rip into poor quiet Potts.

"When I was an intern," said the Leggo cheerily, "we got seventy-five percent post permissions. Of course, in those days we did the autopsies ourselves, but you know something, we didn't mind. Because we were helping to advance the science of medicine."

The Leggo said that the terns were not getting enough postmortem permissions, and since he knew "how hard it is to approach the family for permission in their hour of need," he thought of "a way to raise the incentive: an award. The award will go to the intern with the most postmortem permissions for the year. The prize will be a free trip for two to Atlantic City for the AMA in June, with Dr. Fishberg and myself."

There was dead silence. No one knew what to say, until Howie, puffing and smiling, said, "Damn good idea, Chief, but maybe it should be a trip to the American Pathological instead."

"I don't think it should be the most posts," I said, sure that the Leggo was joking, "I mean, after all, wouldn't that put a premium on death? The tern with the most deaths would probably win, and that would make us lay off treatment, or, even worse, kill off patients to win the prize."

"Yeah," said Eddie, "why not make it a percentage of deaths?"

The Leggo and the Fish didn't laugh, and as the meeting broke up, no one was sure whether they'd been serious or not.

"Of course they're serious," said Hyper Hooper, "and I'm gonna win it. The Black Crow! Atlantic City, here I come. Saltwater taffy, strolling along the boardwalk." He grinned, and started to sing to us: "Under the bo-o-orrdwalk, down by the seee-eeee . . . "

And so if they were serious the Black Crow Award came into being, at least as much being as the ***MVI***. Hyper Hooper, the tern who got off on death, really got off, and we others, who still didn't like death and were repulsed even more by autopsies, felt that once again the odds were getting stacked against the living, and that we had to work even harder to protect the poor unsuspecting patients who came, trusting, into the House of God oblivious to that incentive for their deaths and posts, the Black Crow. Hooper didn't waste any time, for the next afternoon as I was dictating a discharge summary, from the next cubicle I heard his familiar voice: "The patient was admitted in good health except for a urinary-tract infection . . . "

I went on dictating, but tuned back in a few seconds later:

". . . the temperature rose to 107 and a resistant strain of *Pseudomonas* grew out of the spinal-fluid culture . . ."

Spinal fluid? I thought it had started in the urinary tract?

". . . the intern was called to see the patient and found her unresponsive. She expired three hours later. Permission for the postmortem was obtained. Yahoo! This is H. Hooper, M.D."

As he was rushing out I caught his arm and asked him what had happened, and he said, "The usual, Death City. And I got the post. Atlantic City, here I come, Black Crow, Black Pants, and all."

"But she came in healthy."

"Yeah, and then she boxed, and I get credit for the post. The Black Crow's gotta go. So long."

"That award's a joke. They couldn't mean it."

"It's no joke. Autopsies are the flower—no, the red rose—of medicine. The Leggo wants more posts so he looks good."

"To whom?"

"Who cares? With that awful birthmark, he'll try any cosmetic procedure. Hey, I gotta go. The little woman and I are going to the Eucalyptus Room again tonight. Trying to float the M off the R. *Ciao!*"

And so the intern first out of the starting blocks for the Black Crow Award sped off down the hallway, out of the House of God, with that same glitter in his eye that the Fat Man had had over his food and his Invention and that Chuck and I had seen in the Runt's eye when he talked pornographically about Thunder Thighs, and the same glitter that Chuck had had when he'd made mincemeat of Ernie on the court or talked about Hazel, and the same glitter that I had whenever I thought of Molly.

Whenever I thought of Molly, I thought of her bendovers and her lacy underwear and the tears that she'd shed when she knew she was going to die when she pulled down her panties to show me the mole on her thigh. Whenever I thought of Molly, something rolled over in my pants and I felt younger than I was, and I got a glitter in my eye and I thought about my first love, and that bittersweet chaos of fumbling with hooks and belts and zippers and parents on couches on front seats on back seats on movie seats on rocks and everywhere except on beds. I imagined Molly as young and innocent and fun.

139

Young and innocent? How could I have known that that preceding figment had been brought to me through the courtesy of my imagination? Feeling guilty about trying to seduce this young and innocent fun, I tried my hardest to seduce her. In the House, I would touch her, when we worked together, putting a hand on her shoulder, on her hip. She would brush my arm with her breast, she would leave her dress unbuttoned, and in addition to the bendover, she showed more of her repertoire, including what Fats had called the "flash sitdown," where in the instant between the sit down and the leg cross, there's the flash of the fantasy triangle, the French panty bulging out over the downy *mons* like a spinnaker before the soft blond and hairy trade winds. Even though, medically, I knew all about these organs, and had my hands in diseased ones all the time, still, knowing, I wanted it, and since it was imagined and healthy and young and fresh and blond and downy soft and pungent, I wanted it all the more.

So finally she asked me to go out with her and some other nurses, and we went to this bar where the rock music blasts off only the ossicles of those, like me, over thirty, and leaves unshaken the under-thirty, who want the volume turned up, and then she taught me to do a dance I'd never heard of to music I'd never heard of, and then we went back to her apartment she shared with a toothpick of a nurse named Nancy, and Molly asked me if I'd ever seen her place before and I lied and said No and she started to show me and we wandered in on Nancy undressing and Molly said, I was showing him the place, and Nancy, remembering that I'd been there before, said, He's seen the place before, and Molly looked me in the eye and I gulped and said, Yup, I've seen the place before, and she said, Well, let me show you my bedroom.

Delight delight. She showed me her bedroom with her little-girl trinkets, furry toys and an alive furry kitten and Halloween masks and temple bells from the Far East and a make-up kit with backstage-type light bulbs and the usual prints and strewn panty hose and bras and then in a fit of romance I feared I was too old for, we embrace, and I fumble with her bra hooks and then I get caught up in things so I don't notice what I'm fumbling and after a little bit of protest from her with my mouth all over her long nipples and my hand on her own furry thing we are kind of wrassling, she gets on top of me, in the middle of a NO she says OOPS and in I slip, and she shows me her secret, which is that she fucks not like a young innocent little girl but like a moaning Byzantine courtesan, all gold and warm oil and myrrh.

"Now you know my weakness," Molly said the next day in the middle of the nursing station, holding a Fleet's enema in her hand like a pistol.

"What is it?" I asked.

"I'm very physical."

"How is that a weakness?"

"It just is."

"Not if you can handle it."

"What do you mean handle a weakness?"

"You wouldn't call it a weakness in me, would you?" I asked.

"That's different, you're a man."

"You're not going all sexist on me, are you?"

"No."

"Then it's not a weakness in you any more than it is in me. You're just going to have to learn how to handle it."

"Yeah," she said in a way that confused me, since I couldn't tell if she were concerned or not, "I guess I just will."

Only later, when it became obvious that both of us loved the sex and, in a loose way, each other as much as we did, when the moaning *mons* had moved out of the little-girl bedroom into the on-call bunk bed whenever I could get rid of the Bruiser, and then moved into the ward bathroom for a five-minute one sitting on the can, and even, late one night, crooned to by the gomer band of renown, moved to a darkened corner of the ward standing up with our orgasms racing against the appearance of the patrolling night supervisor, only then did Molly—who called the feeling of making love the feeling of having a centipede walk through wearing gold cleats—only then did she tell me that she didn't give a damn about my having another woman, a steady woman, that she had been hurt by "involvement" and hurt by the nuns with their spiritual whips and that what she was "into" was "freedom in relationships," which I thought was terrific and too good to be true until I wondered whether someone else with the old gold cleats was hearing those chuckles and moans and glittering rainbows of orgasms when I was with my long love, Berry.

Berry must have suspected something was up. She'd remarked on my changed mood, on how suspicious I'd become of her, accusing her of going to bed with other men when I was on call in the House. She must have known that my jealousy came from my guilt, my fury from my jealousy of who was with her or with Molly when I was not. Things became strained, although at first the least strain was the emotional one. I was having a fantastic time making love to two women on the same day, enjoying the way that I could separate which aching muscle group went with which woman's moves. The real strain was how to hide Molly from Berry. What contortions I went through, as Molly began to come to my place, to hide her traces—her hair on the pillow, her spoor on the sheets, her hairpin on the bureau, her earring left on the bathroom shelf, her perfume in the air. I began to spend all my time doing laundry. I dreaded the ringing of my phone. Yet I couldn't tell Berry. I cared too much. I was too ashamed. I had too much to lose.

Berry and I had thought that we might try living together, but when we found out that my being on call turned me into a snarling bear, we'd decided that it was not a good idea. We'd also decided that we'd not see each other the night after my night on call, because all we did was bicker and bitch. That left only one night in three, the night that I was supposedly not exhausted. With our contact decreased, with Molly zinging through my *rectus abdominus* and ball-tingling *cremaster* muscle groups, with Berry the Clinical Psychologist off into mind and with me off into body, we began to drift apart. I began to think her cat hated me.

We tried hard to enjoy the fall. We went to a football game, but instead of the bright cheeriness I remembered from going to football games in college, the day turned cold and wet and somber, filling us both with the dread of winter. Exhausted, more or less in silence, skin catching on the rough edges of our love, we dragged back to my apartment, and Berry, feeling woozy with the flu, curled up in my bed with her cat. A safe warm fetal ball, she slept. Her cat, eyes closed to me, purred. She snored. I felt so much in love with her, with protecting her from the flu and the world and my fury and guilt, that I was filled with joy. But as my joy for what had been and could be showed itself, my sadness for what had happened to us crushed it. What a terrific turd I was.

She awoke, we talked. We talked about the gomers and about how furious Jo and the Fish and the Leggo were making me, and about how Berry couldn't possibly understand.

"You know what your problem is?" she asked.

"What?"

"You've got no role models. You can't look up to any of them."

"What about the Fat Man?"

"He's sick."

"He's not," I said, starting to get angry. "Besides there's Chuck and the Runt and Hooper and Eat My Dust. And Potts."

"Oh, sure, there's the camaraderie, and you're right, the only reason men go to war is to die with their buddies, but it seems to me that what's happening to you is the total institutionalization of the internship, à la Goffman."

"What did you say?" I asked as evenly as possible, swallowing my rage at her high-ass theory of my pain.

She started to repeat it, and seeing that the words weren't registering, said, "Never mind."

"Why never mind?"

"Because you could care less. Damnit, Roy, you've gotten so concrete. You won't talk about anything except the internship."

Feeling swamped with words, I found myself shouting like sewerman Ralph Cramden on TV, "Goddamnit, I don't want to think, 'cause when I do, I think of the disgusting things I do every day and it's so awful I want to kill myself. Get it?"

"You imagine that talking about your feelings would destroy you?"

"Yeah."

"That's a fantasy."

143

"A what?"

"A fantasy. Why don't you get some help?"

"Help?"

"Therapy."

We fought. She probably knew we were fighting about Dr. Sanders' long dying and about the illusion in my father's letters and about my plethora of absent role models and the blossoming idea that the gomers were not our patients but our adversaries, and most of all we were fighting over the guilt that I felt for having Molly in a dark corner of the ward standing up, this Molly, who, like me, wouldn't stop and think and feel either, because if she ruminated on what she felt about enemas and emesis basins, she'd lose faith even in her centipede and want to kill herself too. Our fight was not the violent, howling, barking fight that keeps alive vestiges of love, but that tired, distant, silent fight where the fighters are afraid to punch for fear the punch will kill. So this is it, I thought dully, four months into the internship and I've become an animal, a moss-brained moose who did not and could not and would not think and talk, and it's come like an exhausted cancerous animal to my always love, my buddy Berry, and me—yes it's come to us: Relationship On Rocks, ROR.

9

"Fats?" I blurted out in amazement.

"The Today Show!" said the Runt, eyes popping.

"The Today Show?" I yelled.

"Fats!" said the Runt.

My mind did a swan dive.

"But did you actually see him on *The Today Show?*" I asked.

"Nope," said the Runt, "but somebody said they saw him disguised as Dr. Jung, and Barbara Walters was interviewing him about some crazy thing called—"

"The Anal Mirror. I know all about it."

"They say Barbara was giggling all the time. Hey, Roy, you wanna hear what she does with her mouth?"

"Barbara Walters?"

"No, Angel. See, she takes her lips and wraps them around my—"

"Later," I said. "First I want to find Fats."

I knew I'd find him eating, for it was lunchtime, and although he'd been farmed out to the Mt. St. Elsewhere, he'd made some special deal—as he always made some special deal—with Gracie from Dietary and Food which allowed him to eat in the House of God for free. With my stomach flip-flopping, I sat down with this Gargantua of medicine.

"What a delicious rumor," said Fats, laughing. "I wish it

145

was true. I sometimes daydream about a spot interview with Cronkite on the CBS nightly news."

"Why Cronkite?" I asked, reeling from the bizarreness of fatherly Walter Cronkite springing Dr. Jung's Anal Mirror on millions of great Americans expecting only war and jowly Nixon.

"Supposedly he has an anal fissure. Much of the disease in the world is reflected in the anus, you know, and I keep thinking that, somehow, packaged right, the reflection of the diseased anus could make me rich. Just think: if there was an Anal Mirror, and if Nixon owned one, every day he'd get a good look at exactly what he was. It's just the money, you know. I just want to be rich before Socialized Medicine kills me off. It's like what Isaac Singer said."

"Singer the writer?"

"No, Singer the sewing machine. He said, 'I don't give a damn for the invention, it's the dimes I'm after.' But listen, Basch, that laetrile idea the other night was dynamite. There's money there."

"Laetrile? It's a hoax. Worthless. A placebo."

"So what's wrong with placebos? Don't you know about the placebo effect?"

"Of course I do."

"Well, there you are. Placebos can relieve the pain of angina. If you're cooling from cancer, placebos are hot stuff. Like dyspareunia."

"How?" I asked, my mind spinning around the simile.

"You know what they say: It's better to have dyspareuned than never to have pareuned at all."

"You're crazy."

"Imagine: we get the laetrile from apricot pits from Mexico, by bartering the Anal Mirrors for apricots."

"You'd try to sell Dr. Jung's Anal Mirror to the Mexicans?"

"Of course not Dr. Jung's. Dr. Cortez' Anal Mirror. Lotta diarrhea in Mexico. You know how a Mexican knows he's hungry?"

"How?"

"His asshole stops burning. Ha! But we'd have to be careful in Mexico—might get sued for malpractice."

146

"Why is that?"

"Well, even though we'd translate the warning into Spanish, there's always the danger that some jerk would use the Anal Mirror outdoors on a bright sunny day, and you know what happens then?"

"Nope."

"Well, the lens concentrates the sunlight and it bounces back through the two mirrors and WHOOSH you get one flaming asshole, I'll tell you. Suit City. Demand their money back and all the rest."

"And where would the money for all this come from?"

"From the raffle and the research project."

"What raffle and what research project?"

"Well, at the Mt. St. E., I'm thinking of running a raffle, like they did in a Vegas hospital. If you're scheduled for surgery on Monday, and if you come in on Friday instead of Sunday night, you get free tickets to a raffle for a cruise. That way the Mt. St. E. fills its beds and I get a cut. If you win the raffle but die in surgery, the cruise goes to your estate."

"And what about the research project?"

"I'd rather not say. It would come out of your tax dollar, and it's completely illegal."

"How's that?"

"My next rotation is the VA Hospital. Everybody knows how crooked the old VA is, eh? Big-time Watergate-style graft. Graft City."

"This is all fantasy, right?" I asked, thinking of what Berry might say. "To feed your idling mind? I mean, you wouldn't do any of this, would you, Fats?"

After a pause that sent a shiver through me, he said, "Money is not shit. It is nothing to be ashamed of. This great country has a long and glorious history of graft and corruption and exploitation. Just think of what we've done to whole continents and entire little countries chock full of underdeveloped little people we've treated like rodents, let alone what we do to individuals. Why should I—or we—hold back? Did that anti-Semite Henry Ford hold back? Did Spiro Agnew? Did Joe McCarthy or Joe DiMaggio—you know the Yankee Clipper is hocking instant coffee on TV these days—or Marilyn Monroe hold back from letting any subway grate in the world blow up her flimsy dress and whistle around her frigid genitalia? Did Norman Mailer ever, on anything? Did the CIA or the FB-fuck-ing-I? The hell they did, Basch, the hell they did. You just gotta do it, flush it, and pick up the money you get for it."

"For fraud?"

"For dreaming the American Dream. In this case, the American Medical Dream."

The Runt and Chuck sat down with us, and the Runt, like a TV serial that you couldn't turn off, rolled out the latest thrilling episode of *Thuunnnn-der Thighs:* "She was her usual voracious self. We were watching TV, she rubbed the inside of my thigh, the news finished, she took off all her clothes, she walked into the bedroom. She didn't want to mess around with a lot of foreplay, and the first time, she said something—it got me so turned on I was short-circuiting left and right."

"Well, man, what'd she say?"

"I'm not sure, but I know it had the word 'cunt' in it. She's a gold mine. I'd been poring over her body quite a bit, and it was getting to the point where she was going to have to do some poring over mine. I'd been nibbling at her *labia*—they're fine and thin, like puppy dog's ears—and since I've had this fantasy that she was knocked up in high school and had a kid, I was trying to get in there to have a good look for an episiotomy scar, but I got too close, and my eyeballs got all steamed up. Ha! We were really building up to something big—we were in this crazy contortion sort of the Reverse Dog with her sort of sitting on my face like my old roommate Norman's women used to do to him and she was bending over fiddling with my cock and then I did it. I sort of gave her one big slurrp and gently nudged her head down between my legs and I'm telling you she . . . went . . ."

We all stopped chewing.

". . . bananas!"

"Bananas?" asked Fats, jaw slack.

"Very bananas," said the Runt. "HA! It was animal. We were all over the bed. She was moving around on my face and I could feel her teeth on the base of my dork. Wow! Those girls my mom liked, they'd scream whenever my pants would get lumpy at the sock hop. And do you know what she said this time, when I was inside her?"

We did not know what Angel'd said with the Runt's penis inside her.

"She said, 'Oh, Dr. Runtsky, you're soooo big!'" and the Runt did look kind of big, sitting there before our eyes. "This morning she handed me a toothbrush, and when I went to the bathroom, mine was the third toothbrush in the rack."

The Fat Man had stopped eating at about the time that Thunder Thighs had put her lips on the Runt's penis, and staring at him as if he were loony, Fats said, "What the hell's been going on with you guys up there anyway?"

So we told him. We told him about Chuck and Hazel and about me and Molly and about how the Runt with the help of Towl and Thunder was getting bigger. We told him about the Golden Age, where we were legendary in our ability to care for "the toughies" and legendary in our liaisons, which, because of Hazel, had produced clean sheets and bug-free bedding and, because of Molly, had produced snappy instant nursing care. We told him how we were as high as the golden leaves riding the crests of the October maples, falling through the gestating skeleton of the Wing of Zock.

"There's only one thing missing," I said, "placement. We still can't get the gomers placed. Anna and Ina are still there."

"No problem," said Fats, "placement is as easy as pie. Who's responsible for placing the gomers?"

"The Social Service."

"Yup. The Sociable Cervix. The third toothbrush means that Angel doesn't mind sharing, so why should you? You guys gotta scrog the Sociable Cervix. Oh, and remember: if you want to scrog the librarian, you gotta talk about Shakespeare. So long, and good luck."

Well, of course it was brilliance. Each ward had a Sociable Cervix, whose responsibility it was to get the gomers placed. It was an impossible job. No one wanted the poor gomers. The nursing homes would say the gomer was too well and didn't need them, and the families would say that the gomer was too sick and needed a nursing home, and the House Privates would say the gomer was way too sick and needed the House of God Blue Cross care, and the terns would say we couldn't stand having Broccoli Ladies who blasted us for keeping them alive, and would the Cervix kindly get them the hell out. The gomers offered no opinion.

The Cervix was the pimp. It was made up of two types of women: the first was young and energetic and idealistic, working out the guilt of separating from her parents and abandoning her grandparents, all the time jockeying for Mr. Right, who had to have a stethoscope in his pocket; the second was menopausal, divorced, abandoned by kids like the first, not energetic but empathic and tearful, cynical and masochistic, working out the upcoming old age and all the time searching for a second or third Mr. Right, who had to have something nonstethoscopic in his pants. The younger Cervix for us was Rosalie Cohen, a young woman who had that pizza-faced look of severe adolescent acne, the kind that never responded to anything. She had the habit of opening her blouse down past Thursday, as a decoy from her pitted face. The older, or Head Cervix, was Selma, whose nose was big and bent. Billing and cooing with Selma would be more bill than coo, perhaps earning the tern a punctured eyeball, and yet from the neck down Selma was good. Struggling against the life force as it swept by her, Selma was sexy and suffused with the *form fruste* of the more-liberated-than-my-children syndrome that was ravaging America in the seventies, producing the pot-smoking mama, and the daughter wailing, "Pass me the joint, Mother, please." Selma fell right into my lap: "I attended that grand rounds where you made those points about keeping the patients in the House too long, Dr. Basch, and I want to tell you, the way you handled the flak was terrific."

Chuck looked at me and then at the Runt, who looked at him and then at me, and I looked at Chuck and then back at Selma, who went on: "For thirty years I've been trying to learn to express my anger like that, and you've already got it. I wish you could show me how. And let me tell you, a lot of psychotherapists—the best in town—have tried and failed."

Smiling seductively, heart sinking, I knew that I was the one.

The next morning, Chuck was first to arrive at Jo's rounds, a half-hour late. An hour later I straggled in, and sometime later, in rolled the Runt. When we had shaken off the foaming Jo, I told Chuck and the Runt how I'd gone over to Selma's that night, how we'd started listening to hard rock, how Selma had started to talk about her loneliness and her burdenous nose and how, after a drink and a joint, Selma had told me she wanted me to stay. Cringing at the way she reminded me of my mom, I'd thought of my obligation to my buddies and prepared for the worst, and when Selma rheostatted down the lights and took off her bra, I was shocked.

"Bad, huh? Man, we'll never get these gomers placed."

"Nope. Not bad. Good. Great! Her breasts are beautiful. Vintage Ava Gardner, made in 1916 and still dynamite."

"Well, man, how does she do it?"

"I asked her. Premarin."

"Premarin? Premarin!"

"Premarin. Estrogen supplements. Total-body female hormone. It's like making love to purified molecular woman. Stupendous!"

During all this, the Runt had been silent, but as I finished, he burst out with his story, which was that he'd spent the night with Rosalie Cohen, which prompted Chuck to grimace and say, "You did it with that ugly-bugly? Yecch!"

"It was grr-ate!" said the Runt, beaming his maniac smile.

"The Man Who Scrogged Rosalie Cohen," I said. "Chuck, we have created a monster."

"Man, what was it like to wake up to ole Rosalie?"

"Well," said the Runt, "I did try hard not to look on her face."

The gomers began to get placed. The true Golden Age had arrived. From the Leggo to the Bruiser, no one in the hierarchy could understand how the nursing-home beds seemed to open at a touch for ward 6-South, and only for ward 6-South. Gomers as close to legal death as possible were described by our Cervix as being "of excellent rehabilitation potential" and were admitted to the homes the day the beds fell free. Incontinent gomers who were shitting all over the ward were described as "continent of feces and urine" and, shitting on the ambulance stretcher and shitting on the down elevator and shitting in the hallway leading to the ambulance and shitting through the wailing ambulance ride, came to rest to shit their way to immortality in the nursing home of their family's choice, in homes like the New Masada, their bodies stacked floor by floor in order of morbidity, those imagined closest to death put on the topmost floors, imagined closest to heaven. Anna and Ina had been around for four months, and so it was sad to see them go, but if they sensed our waving good-bye, they answered only with ROODLE and GO AVAY. Heaving and smelly, the Broccoli Lady left too, and the exodus went on and on.

As the gomers left, the ward filled up with more toughies, and every once in a while one of these dying young would be saved. One day, in Saul the leukemic tailor's latest bone-marrow biopsy, like a rash of crocuses in the charred fields of Hiroshima, normal white cells sprouted.

"What?" I said, peering through the microscope at these millions of flowers that meant that Saul might live, "a remission! Look!"

"Damn! Somethin' else!" said Chuck, looking.

"Rrhhmmmmm rhmmmm, now, ain't that some fine shit!"

"It's wonderful!" I said, realizing how I'd kept myself from hoping anything for Saul, given the odds against these buddings, these buds, and I ran up to his room, and panting, yelled at him, "Saul, you've got a remission!"

"Sounds bad," he said, "first leukemia, now remission. Oiy."

"No—remission means cure. A miracle! You're not going to die."

"I'm not? What do you mean I'm not going to die?"

"Not now you're not, no."

The bruised little man stopped, still. He let go of his banter, he looked me in the eye, he slumped down on his bed. "Oh . . . I'm not going to die now, I mean right now?"

"No, Saul, you're not. You're going to live."

"Oh . . . Oh, thank God, thank . . ." and he grabbed me and put his head on my shoulder and with all those centuries and years of never daring to hope, he sobbed, and his thin body trembled against me like a child's. "So? So some more of

152

this wife of mine, eh? Oh, it's good, it's real good. Thank God—mind you, Dr. Basch, till now, for me, He hasn't done so much, but this . . . this is life . . . this is a new baby, born . . ."

We were so happy. The whole world was curable and sexual and fun, and we were high, we were red-hots at the bosoms and nipples and bangles and thighs of the House of God. It was as comforting as had been the trucks rumbling down the cobblestone hill in the Bronx lulling me to sleep as a child when we stayed at my Aunt Lil's, and it was all so easy and it was all so damn much fun.

It wasn't easy and it was not fun. Our crooked Veep resigned and honest Jerry Ford started right in bashing those helicopter doors with his head. On the Sunday after Nixon's Saturday Night Massacre, when he tried to stop people trying to get rid of him by getting rid of them, I awoke to a blaring late-fall day leaved with all the leafy colors, glad to be alive, until I entered the living death of the House of God for the next thirty-six hours. Sundays in the House always made me feel like a punished kid, locked inside and looking out. Jo, the outsider, spent her life looking in, and, reluctant to entrust her ward to sex fiends and maniacs like us, she'd always come in on her day off, Sunday, to help.

Jo had invited me to dinner the previous week. Her apartment was motel-cool. The stereo was still not unpacked. There were no plants. The dining-room table had had to be cleared of journals and texts. Struggling stiffly through dinner, we sat and talked. I became immersed in her loneliness. When she talked about how hard it was to be a woman in medicine, to meet men outside the field, what could I say? She wanted to try hard to understand us, even be friends with us. She didn't like the tension on the ward. Choosing me because I was the oldest, seemingly the leader, she asked me what I thought was getting in the way.

"You've got to trust us more," I said. "Loosen up. It's no crime not to do everything for every patient always, is it?"

Nervously she said, "No, it's not. I know that, but it's hard for me to accept it."

"Try."

153

"What can I do?"

"Well, I guess one thing would be not to come in when I'm on call next Sunday. That would be a good start."

"Right. I'll try. Thanks, Roy, thanks a lot."

On that Sunday, Jo was in the House of God earlier than me. Trying to restrain myself, I said, "You had to come in?"

"I tried not to, Roy, believe me I tried. But I'm studying for Boards, and I can only study so much. Besides, you might need some help."

I realized I was trapped. Enraged, I couldn't tell her, for fear it would send her hurtling down off a bridge. Even with her terns tormenting her with their sexual carnival, each hint of which hurt her, making her feel more and more left out, her only happiness was inside the medical hierarchy inside the House, where she could kill herself by doing superdedicated medical stunts.

The combination of Jo, the Bruiser, and my first admission . brought me to my knees. The admission? Henry was a twenty-three-year-old with no workable kidneys, who'd been sent from one of the Mt. St. Elsewheres after they'd parlayed his renal disease into an infected dry dribbling uremic mass of flesh just this side of the grave. Henry was also retarded. To save Henry, I had to be able to understand the chart sent in from the Mt. St. E. It was lightly photocopied, unnumbered, and written by a Foreign Medical Graduate and I could not read it. The Bruiser came in and tried to help by reading some of the chart out loud. I told him that this was not a BMS case and to scram, and, leaving, he asked, "What's he got?"

"Microdeckia," I said.

"What's that?"

"Look it up."

He left, and once again I tried to read the chart and I could not. I looked out the window at the autumn. A young couple was having a leaf fight, the leaves sticking to their white Irish sweaters. I got tears in my eyes. I was all choked up with what I was missing, the second cup of coffee in bed with the woman and the Sunday *Times*, the ache in the lungs from the icy morning air. Jo came in and asked me to "present the case." I blew. I forgot everything and screamed at her that if she stayed one more minute, I was leaving. I shouted at her, all kinds of dark green things about her, her emotional problems, her hunger to be on the inside. I stood up, towering over her, and I yelled until I was bright blue and tears were on my cheeks, and I didn't stop until I'd chased the little twirp of a victim of success out the door, down the elevator, and out of the House of God.

I went back to the notes on Fast Henry. I sat there and cried. It was a balancing act, and I slammed my fist down on the desk over and over, bashing away at the world. I could not go on. I thought what I'd thought as a kid, playing Superman: if I did my best, I couldn't be wrong. I went on. I went to see Fast Henry, a gray young fellow with a retarded look, a voice that leaped from bass to falsetto every other word, and his hair parted down the middle like Wrong Way Corrigan. I asked him how he was doing and he said, "Doc, if I died tomorrow I'd be the happiest man alive," and somehow that helped me and I went to work on him. The other help that miserable day was the Bruiser, who single-handedly destroyed Jo's ward. He'd started to work up the second admission, a young woman with black lace undies, suffering from ulcerative colitis. Although the Bruiser was excited at the blood and mucus he found on his finger on rectal exam and was all hot to sigmoidoscope her that day and go to the library to "read like crazy about stool," he was embarrassed by the erotic part of the exam. Unfortunately, the patient took a liking to the Bruiser and, naked head to toe, got the message to him that she was turned on, enjoying his exam. When the Bruiser got that message, he freaked, ran away, and came to me quivering.

"I've never seen a woman naked before, and never a young female patient. They didn't teach us about this. Oh, I'm so ashamed."

"Ashamed? What the hell did you do to her?"

"Nothing. I'm ashamed of the unprofessional thoughts in my heart."

He was so upset that he refused to continue to work her up until he'd talked it over with his analyst, and so I let him continue to work on Mrs. Biles, the woman with the fake heart disease, whom he'd bruised earlier in her House stay. At one A.M. the Bruiser stood before me and said, "Well, I've just finished hypnotizing Mrs. Biles."

"You did what to whom?" I asked nonchalantly.

"Mrs. Biles. I hypnotized her to take away her cardiac pain."

"No fooling. Does Dr. Kreinberg know?"

"Nope. Didn't tell him yet."

"Hey, I'm sure he'd like to know. Why don't you give him a buzz?"

"Now?" asked Bruiser. "It's one in the morning."

"So? He likes hearing new developments on his patients."

The Bruiser called Little Otto Kreinberg:

"Hello, Dr. Kreinberg, this is Dr. Levy . . . Bruce Levy . . . No, you're right I'm not really a doctor, I'm a BMS but . . . right . . . well, I've gotten in the habit of calling myself Dr. Levy . . . Oh, yeah, I wanted to tell you I've just finished hypnotizing Mrs. Biles for her angi— . . . hypnotizing . . . h-y-p-n-o . . . right, like a magician, and she . . . for her anxiety and I . . . yes? . . . sure . . . oh . . . ohhhhh . . . but it's an accepted . . . OK, sorry, yes, I'll awaken her from her trance right away, sir, good-bye."

Looking sheepish, Bruiser started to slink out, and I asked him if he'd do me a favor.

"Yeah?" he asked, thinking he might redeem himself.

"I've been busy all day and I haven't had a chance to go to the toilet. Could you go for me? A number two. I've done a number one."

"You can't treat me like this. Besides, I looked up 'microdeckia,' and there's no such thing."

"Microdeckia? Sure—'not playing with a full deck.' Night."

I went to bed. Molly was night nurse, and all our efforts to get to bed had been frustrated, first by the Bruiser, then by the gomers. But now the Bruiser was in the library and I'd BUFFED the gomers for the night, and I sat on the on-call bed, naked, awaiting my nurse. Hazel had BUFFED the sheets, and next to the House of God pillow was a doll made from rubber tubing and gauze pads with a note pinned to it: "Roy the noisy boy, Molly the jolly girl; am coming in if you're my toy and not too busy for a whirl. Call me." Finally!

In delicious anticipation I found myself looking out the window at the nursing-school dorm. In one of the rooms a nurse was undressing. She took off her uniform and then made that wonderful motion of hyperextending the elbows around her back to undo her bra. Just as Molly walked in, she let them fly. Fine, fine. I was a time bomb. Molly sat on the bed and I showed her what I was watching. I unbuttoned her dress and unhooked her bra and caught her little-girl breasts by their longing nipples. All over me, her dress was off her pantyhose were off her bikinis were off and she was going off. I thought of the Englishman's idea of perfection, when he, his alarm, and his mistress all go off at the same time, and just before we got that firm fun thing into her hollow funnelly thing, she stopped and in between her little gasps of pleasure said, "Did I ever show you what the nuns teach nurses to do when a patient gets an erection?"

"Nope."

"The nuns said to slap it and it would go down."

"Do you want it to go down?"

"No, I want it to go up me and fuck me."

And we started doing that more and more and more and more, and just as we were about to go off, there was an incredible CRASH that rocked the bed and my beeper lady fired again and she wanted me right away, but Molly wanted me more right away, saying, Jesus Christ Almighty oh finish it off ah ahhh ahhhhhh!

The CRASH had come when the Bruiser, in trying to make up for all he'd done wrong that day, had decided to help me out by using the TURF-tool, the electric gomer bed to TURF Mrs. Biles, the bruised and hypnotized Little Otto'd Mrs. Biles, elsewhere. He'd chosen the Orthopedic Height, and it looked from the right-angle bend in Mrs. Biles's left trochanter that she'd broken her hip.

"I did it for you, Dr. Basch," said the Bruiser proudly, smiling. "I've already paged ORTHO."

"Bruiser, it's hard for me to tell you this: I appreciate what you did, but that gomer-bed thing was a joke."

"A what?"

"A joke. The Fat Man was joking."

"Oh, God. Oh, my God. I think I've made a terrible mistake. I'd better go and phone Dr. Kreinberg right away."

"Bruiser?"

"Yes?"

"Call your analyst first."

Many of the dying young died. Jimmy, in the SICU with the BALLS TO RIDE A HARLEY guy, was treated with the standard ratbane used to wipe out cancerous bone marrow, and, bald and infected and bruised and bleeding, he died. Fast Henry, who in fact also had a cancer, got his wish to be the happiest man alive one tomorrow when he died, and many other young ones died. When I asked Chuck, "Hey, how come the ones our age die?" he said, "Dunno, but we sure are leading a great life, ain't we?" Everyone knew that eventually the Yellow Man would die, and all that time Dr. Sanders had been dying.

Dr. Sanders had been dying a long time. Bald and infected, quiet and cachectic, he was getting his life in order. We were friends. He was dying with a calm strength, as if his dying were part of his life. I was beginning to love him. I began to avoid going into his room.

"I understand," he said, "it's the hardest thing we ever do, to be a doctor for the dying."

Talking about medicine, I told him with bitterness about my growing cynicism about what I could do, and he said, "No, we don't cure. I never bought that either. I went through the same cynicism—all that training, and then this helplessness. And yet, in spite of all our doubt, we can give something. Not cure, no. What sustains us is when we find a way to be compassionate, to love. And the most loving thing we do is to be with a patient, like you are being with me."

I tried to sit with him. I watched Molly take care to clip his fingernails and toenails so he wouldn't scratch himself and bleed or get infected. I watched everyone keep sterile around his bed. I watched Jo treat him like "a case," and I watched his oncologist chatter to him with perfect objectivity about his impending death, and all the time I hoped against hope that when he died, he would die neat.

His death was a mess. I was called in the middle of the night, and found him, despite massive platelet transfusions that had been dissolved by the cytotoxic rat poison in his system, bleeding out. Barely conscious when I got to him, his blood pressure almost nothing, he had trickles of geranium-red blood dripping from both nostrils and from the corners of his bloated bruised mouth, and I knew that he was bleeding from every little ruptured capillary in his gut. He was only conscious enough to say, "Help me, please help me."

I realized that there was nothing I could do to help him except what he'd said was the only thing a doctor could do, be with him. I took his head in my lap and sponged away the blood and looked into his sightless eyes and said, "I'm here," and I think he knew that I was.

"Help me, help me."

More blood trickled out, and I wiped it away and said, "I'm here," and I just cried. In silence, so as not to scare him, I wept.

"Hi, Roy boy, how's it going, anyway?"

Howard was in the doorway, filling it with his asinine grin and his pipe smoke, and I hissed at him, "Get out of here."

Sitting down in the chair across the room, he puffed and said, "Looks bad for Dr. Sanders, doesn't it? Gosh, it's tough."

"Get the hell out of here. Now!"

"You don't mind if I watch, do you? Follow-up, you know. It's tough in the E.W., because you don't get any follow-up on the patients you admit. I always like follow-up. Sense of completion. Ending. Learn a lot."

"Get outta here, Howard, please."

"Help me."

The blood ran. My lap was wet with it. The eyes were glazing.

"I'm here," and I hugged him.

"You gonna get the post?" asked Howard.

I wanted to leap up and kill him, but I couldn't—I wouldn't leave Dr. Sanders until he left me. I begged Howard to leave, and he smiled and said how hard it was to have someone dying whom you cared about, and he puffed his pipe and stayed.

"Help."

So I tried to obliterate Howard and as I was wetted with Dr. Sanders' thin blood I found myself wanting only to be able to kill Dr. Sanders with something painless and neat instead of being with him in my helplessness.

"Help me, God, this is awf . . ."

I tried to think of good things, of a woman in a punt on the willowed Cherwell at Oxford, trailing her finger in the leafy stream, but all I could think of was the day's headlines, the sixteen-year-old girl who'd run away to see the world and who was found off a Florida beach naked folded up in a weighted traveling case, and a beaten child wheeled into a courtroom curled up in a fetal position in a crib, who was a vegetable and who "was not going to get any better" and the surgeon said that when he'd first gotten to the child he didn't even know what he was looking at because it was a mass of rotten flesh, days old, and on the abused child's back, burned into his flesh and scabbed over, were the letters: I-C-R-Y.

When I looked back down into my lap, Dr. Sanders was dead. Much of the eighty-percent blood-water that had been him was drained out onto me.

I held his head in my lap until his sick killer blood had oozed out of his heart and brain and into his gut and skin and all the places it should never have been, and, refusing to clot, had flowed out of all the open holes in his body, the last his laxing anus. I held his hairless head in my lap and in my arms until the flow stopped. I laid him back in his bed and covered him gently with his sheet and I wept. He was the first patient whom I'd loved who'd died. I went to the nursing station. The way I put my feet down, one in front of the other, made me think of a chronic schizophrenic I'd seen, a former Ziegfeld Girl who'd been at an asylum since the Follies, and who, each day, rain or shine, would trudge across the meadow with a determined and precise step in an unerring and clean straight line that would have brought joy to a surveyor's heart, CLOMP CLOMP CLOMP, going nowhere, empty inside.

"Dr. Sanders is dead," I said, sitting down.

"That's too bad. Did you get the postmortem?" asked Jo.

"What?"

"I said, did you get the postmortem?"

I had a vision of lifting the little prodigy up by her thin shoulders, shaking her until her brain splattered against her shell of skull and she convulsed, kneeing her in the guts until I'd wrecked her ovaries from ever spitting out another egg, and then heaving her through the sixth-floor window so she'd splatter and have to be sucked up by noisy, powerful sucking-up machines and become a bag of goo, picked over and strained by Hyper Hooper's Israeli Pathology Resident in the morgue. But Jo was pitiful, and so I gritted my teeth and just said, "No."

"Why not?"

"I didn't want to."

"That's not good enough," said Jo.

"I didn't want to see his body ripped to shreds in the morgue."

"I don't understand what you're saying."

"I loved him too much to see his body ripped apart downstairs."

"That kind of talk has no place in modern medicine."

"So don't listen," I said, beginning to lose control.

"The postmortem is important," said Jo. "It's the flower of the science of medicine. I'll call the next of kin myself."

"Don't you dare!" I screamed. "I'll kill you if you do!"

"How do you think we're able to deliver such precise medical care to those entrusted to us?" asked Jo.

"That's bullshit, that we deliver medical care at all," I said.

"Have you gone mad? This ward—my ward—is looked up to in the House for being the most efficient and having the most success with placement and handling the toughies with skill. My ward is a legend. Damnit," said Jo, jutting her jaw, "I want that post."

"Jo. Go fuck yourself."

"I'll have to report this to the Fish and the Leggo. I won't have sentimentality ruining my ward. My ward has become a legend in its own time."

"Do you know why it's become a legend? You don't want to hear."

"Of course I want to hear, even though I know why already."

So I told her. I started by telling her about how Chuck and I had, after our original empirical test on Anna O., become fanatics at doing nothing and had lied to Jo about it, making up all forms of imaginary tests and BUFFING the charts. I told her how in modified form we'd done the same with the dying young, who went ahead and died, but died without the hassle, pain, and prolongation of suffering that their care might otherwise have produced. The final thing I told her about was placement.

"Placement picked up because the Social Service liked me and I did such a good job running my ward," said Jo anxiously.

"Jo, everybody hates you and the only reason that placement picked up is that the Runt and I are fucking Rosalie Cohen and Selma respectively. Not to mention the clean sheets."

"What about the clean sheets?"

"Chuck has been fucking Hazel from Housekeeping."

"I don't believe you. No one would do this to me."

"Everyone would if they could, but your terns are in a privileged position."

"You just think you're above it all," said Jo, "Better than everyone else, like you don't have to stoop down to get postmortems. You're afraid of the dirty side of medicine, right?"

"No, sir," I said.

"You mean you're not afraid of the dirty side of medicine?" asked the Leggo, his eyes running up and down my bloody whites.

"No, sir, to my knowledge I am not."

Clad in his butcher-length white coat and with stethoscope, as always, wending its way down into God knows where, he was standing looking out the window, holding my *curriculum vitae* in his hand. He looked lonesome. Like Nixon must have looked. I stood in front of his large desk. Diplomas buzzed me from all directions, and I was mesmerized by a model of the urinary tract, filled with colored water and driven by an electric motor, bubbling red urine through everything at a healthy clip. My mind was empty of everything but how Dr. Sanders had become a bag of blood—squishy, bloated, and dead.

"You know," said the Leggo, waving my C.V. around in the air, "you look great on paper, Roy. When I punched your name into the computer to match you for this internship, I was happy. I thought you could be a leader of the interns and of the residents, and even, someday, Chief Resident."

"Yes, sir, I understand."

162

"Say, you've never been in the military, have you?"

"No, sir."

"Yes, I knew that, because that's why you call me 'sir.' 'Sir' is the military form of address, do you see?"

"I don't get it."

"People who have been in the military never call me 'sir.' "

"Oh? Why not?"

"I don't know why not. Do you?"

"No, I don't. Except it seems to fit."

"It's the strangest thing. I mean, you'd think it would be the other way around, right?"

"What does it mean?"

"I don't know, do you?"

"No. It's the strangest thing. Sir."

"Yes, it's the strangest . . . "

As he trailed off out the window, I fantasized about him: his life had been lived with the vow never to be as cold as his own pop, and yet, like Jo, the Leggo had become a victim of success, had slurped his way up, and had become so cold that his own son must already be in treatment to work out his revulsion for his cold pop and his longing for his cold pop to be as warm and loving as his pop's pop, his grandpop. The Leggo had spent his whole life living for that electric moment in medicine when a concept cleared away the stench of a disease, and when this concept would be warmly applauded, as his cold pop never had applauded him. The Leggo was hell-bent on producing these electric moments in medicine. He thought that by being a kind of Van der Graaf generator in the House of God, he could get his boys to love him.

"You know, Roy, at the other hospital, the City, my boys loved me. They always—do you understand always—my boys always loved me before, we shared some terrific moments together, but here at the House . . ."

"Yes, sir?"

"Do you know why they don't?"

"Perhaps it has something to do with your attitude toward medicine, especially toward the gomers."

"The what?"

"The chronically ill, demented, geriatric-nursing-home

population, sir. Your idea seems to be that the more you do for them, the better they get."

"Right. They have diseases, and by God we treat them: aggressively, objectively, completely, and we never give up."

"Well, that's just it. I've been taught that the treatment for them is to do nothing. The more you do, the worse they get."

"What? Who taught you that?"

"The Fat Man."

The words plowed two furrows in the dry man's brow, and he said, "Surely you don't believe the Fat Man, do you?"

"Well, at first I did think it was crazy, but then I tried it out for myself, and, surprisingly, it worked. When I tried it your way—Jo's way—they developed incredible complications. I'm not sure yet, but I think the Fat Man had a point. He's nobody's fool. Sir."

"I don't understand. The Fat Man taught you that to deliver no medical care is the most important thing you can do?"

"The Fat Man said that that was the delivery of medical care."

"What? To do nothing?"

"That's something."

"Ward 6-South is the best ward in the House, and you mean to tell me it's from doing nothing?"

"That's doing something. We do as much nothing as we can without Jo finding out about it."

"Even placement?"

"That's another story."

"Yes, well, there are enough stories for today," said the Leggo, perplexed and haunted by the Fat Man, whom he'd thought he'd farmed out to the Mt. St. E. "So all this looseness that Jo talks about—IF YOU DON'T TAKE A TEMPERATURE YOU CAN'T FIND A FEVER—that's really trying your hardest to do something by doing nothing, right?"

"Right. *Primum non nocere* with modifications," I said.

"Primum non . . . But then why do doctors do anything at all?"

"The Fat Man says to produce complications."

"Why do doctors want to produce complications?"

"To make money."

The word "money" hit the Leggo hard, and he was reminded of something else, and said, "That reminds me: Dr. Otto Kreinberg said that you're abusing his patients: bruising them, hypnotizing them, raising their beds to dangerous heights. He's quite a little guy, Otto, was in line for the Nobel, years ago. What about that?"

"Oh, that wasn't me, sir, that was Bruce Levy."

"But he's your BMS."

"So?"

"So, damnit, you're responsible for him, just like Jo is responsible for you and Dr. Fishberg is responsible for her and I'm responsible for him. Levy is your responsibility, understand? Talk to him. Straighten him out."

Thinking that I'd better not ask the Leggo to whom he was responsible, I said, "Well, I tried to do that, sir, but I failed. Levy said that I couldn't take responsibility for his actions and that he had to take responsibility for them himself."

"What? That goes against all I've just said."

"I know, sir, but he's in psychoanalysis and that's what his analyst keeps telling him and he keeps telling me," and I found myself wondering who—when both Agnew and Nixon got thrown into the slammer at the same time—who would take responsibility for the rich pageantry that was America.

"And you're telling me you believe what the Fat Man said?"

"I'm not sure, sir. I've only been an intern four months."

"Good. Because if everyone felt the way he does, there wouldn't be any internists at all."

"Exactly, sir. There'd be no need. Fats says that that's why internists do so much, to keep medicine in demand. Otherwise we'd all be surgeons or podiatrists. Or lawyers."

"Nonsense. If he were right, why in the world would sensible men like me and all the other Chiefs believe in medicine? Eh?"

"Well," I said, seeing Dr. Sanders oozing his blood from his nostrils into my lap, "what else can we do? We can't just walk away."

"Right, my boy, right! We cure, do you hear, we cure!"

165

"Four months here, and I haven't cured anyone yet. And I don't know anyone who's cured anyone yet, either. Best so far is one remission."

There was an ugly pause. The Leggo turned back to the window, took a few deep breaths to blow the Fat Man from his nose and oropharynx and lungs, and, satisfied that he'd proved something, turned to me again: "Dr. Sanders died, and you didn't get the post, why not? Did he ask you not to have a post done on him? Sometimes people—even physicians—are squeamish."

"No. He said I could do a post if I wanted."

"Why didn't you?"

"I didn't want to see his body ripped to shreds downstairs."

"I don't understand."

"I loved him too much to have his body dissected."

"Oh. Well, you don't think I did too? You know Walter and I were buddies? First Nigro in the House. We were interns together. Gosh did we have times. Those electric moments in medicine, you know? When a warm thrill goes right on through you. Fine man. And with all of that," said the Leggo, turning to me with a papal humility, "with all of that, let me ask you, do you think I'd be afraid to get the post?"

"No, sir, I don't think so. I think you would get the post."

"Damn right I would, Basch, damn right I would."

"Can I say something, sir?"

"Of course, my boy, shoot."

"Are you sure you can take it?"

"I didn't get where I am by not taking it. Fire away."

"That's why your boys don't love you."

We loved them, and since I was leaving ward 6-South in a week to start my new assignment in the Emergency Ward, we decided that the only thing to do, given the third toothbrush, was to show them our love, and to do it in the bastards' House. And so Chuck and I and that four-dimensional sex fiend the Runt—who by that time was assaulting everything in skirts, including a pubescent Physical Therapist with the face of a chubby eight-year-old and the body of a chubby fifteen, whom he enticed by ordering PT six times a day on his gomers and whom he fondled amidst the parallel bars and artificial limbs while she was distracted by trying to teach his gomers to walk—ruminated on how in the world we could show three big women like Angel and Molly and Hazel and maybe even another big woman like Selma how much we loved them and how we appreciated their part in making us into dynamite terns on a dynamite ward of the House.

It was colorful and it was illicit. In an on-call room of the House where we were not supposed to be, the Runt and I awaited the others. Halfway snickered on bourbon and beer, dressed in a House nightie with a wig to make me look like a gomer, I lay on the bottom bunk while the Runt babbled about pubescence and hooked me up to a cardiac monitor. As the monitor flashed its green BLEEP into the red-lighted room, I thought that all we'd need was a yellow blinker and Chuck would think he was back home on a street corner in Memphis. When I'd told Berry that Dr. Sanders had died, she'd asked, Where is he? and I'd said, He's only in us, and I'd thought of how his life had fluttered round me like a butterfly in dying autumn, chilled, beating against my lashes, frantic, calling me to still the birth of winter. What had been in my father's latest letter?

. . . Winter is coming and you are undoubtably becoming accustomed to the hours and the stresses. You have a great opportunity to learn medicine and start dealing with people . . .

There was a knock at the door, and then two more, which was our code. There, in nursing uniform, were Angel and Molly. I watched Thunder Thighs throw her arms around the Runt and kiss him. He seemed embarrassed, and she said, "Hi"—gesture toward the Runt—"the Runt. Howthehellareya?"

"Hello, Angie Wangie," said the Runt shyly.

Angie Wangie took his hand and put it under her skirt, cupping it around her stormy ass. The Runt looked at Molly, wondering how she would take this openness. Molly went behind him and started to kiss his neck and run her hands up and down his front between his clavicular notch and his crotch. In a gomer falsetto I wailed HALP NURSE HALP NURSE HALP

167

and they came to me. They flung back the curtain covering the lower bunk and bent over me, and the fronts of both their dresses were open, showing four elastical fantastical breasts in a sea froth of lace with two clefts in between. Oh, to nuzzle there, to lay my angry grieving head nuzzling in there and nuzzle and guzzle like a thirsty dumb horse muzzling water. To suck. One two three four nipples. When I tried to do that they pushed me back down and decided that I was a gomer and that since GOMERS GO TO GROUND I needed to be restrained, and they began to work hard to do it.

. . . You will look back on this period of hard work and the experience will stay with you for life, for who else but man would do it? . . .

Restrained, struggling, I was to be given an alcohol sponge bath. I struggled enough to rip open Molly's dress almost to her waist, and I reveled, as they pushed me down again, in her glossy yet transparent French bra that flowed like silk over iced nipples, the kind of bra that lets breasts jiggle as they stroll down the Champs Elysées so the horny Americans can gape. Asking how long were her nipples, I began to be a gomer with an erection. They started to sponge me, with Angel discreetly covering my risen rod and my happily bounding balls. I saw both the Runt and Angel ogling Molly's breasts, and I thought that the third toothbrush might just be Molly's, why not? The stimulation was intense—tied down, helpless, with two half-naked women bathing my hot in vaporous alcoholic cool that rolled me back toward the fevers of childhood. My BLEEPS rose like a skyrocket to about 110, and with my impending explosion the Runt dragged Angel away.

Heaven. Molly sponged me up and down, kissing me lightly but not letting me out of the restraints, and every time she came near I'd make a motion to get at her, and my BLEEPS went to 130. She passed the damp sponge up and down against the *corpus spongiosum*, the erectile tissue on the underside of my penis, and then began to nibble and nip and *nosh* and suck, cradling my testes like eggs in a velvet glove. I begged her to let me out of the restraints, but she kept giving me these little bites and fondles. Well, that was it. Up and down and bites and boobs, and just before I blasted off she slipped out of her dress, took down her panties, straddled my face, her lips on my penis again. My olfactory lobe seized up and our machine, spewing camshafts hubcaps and racheted gears slammed out into the wild blUE YONDERRR!!

    . . . Political news is overwhelming with Nixon a maniac liar and I hope he will get it but good . . .

We lay with each other until the bleeper had detumesced down onto the scale and was breathing a bit easier, and then she got up. She kissed me and slipped out through the curtain. She came back and I asked her to let me out of the restraints now for Chrissakes. Saying nothing, she started back in on my cock and soon it wasn't weeping anymore but standing up straight singing a good Old Testament-fashioned Maccabean Army Song and she straddled me and took the tip of it and put it against that midget helmsman in her rowboat, her clitoris. Electric sparks slashed the dark and her snuggling *labiae* embraced me and let me squishy-squish on in. At that point I decided, Oh, what the hell, if I'm going to be a gomer, except for my *putz* I'll be a gomer, and I relaxed. She moved around on me slowly, rhythmically, as only women, laced into their rhythms, can move, and then, starting to go off, bent down to me.

  "Angel?"

  "Roy."

  "Roy!"

  "Angel."

    . . . Hope you are your usual self and not working too hard . . .

  "I thought I'd"—gesture toward sky—"thank you for"—gesture toward curtain—"sending me"—gesture toward floor—"the Runt."

So she did, by moving up and down and making little noises that I didn't hear too well and as she sat up and grabbed the springs of the underside of the top bunk she said with ges-

169

tures more than with words how this was like making love on a night train in Europe, and she bounced around like a kid in a jungle gym, and then she stopped.

"What's the matter?" I asked.

"I think there's someone"—gesture toward heaven—"up there."

We listened, and sure enough there was:

"Oh, Jesu Jesu Chuckie HAAY-ZUUUU—"

Thunder Thighs untied me, and as soon as my arms and legs were free I wrapped every one of them around her with me inside her and outside her all at once and then like a gomer who'd gotten the Ponce de Léon Rejuvenation Treatment—a Fat Man scenario?—I rolled her over on her back and really started doing what a crude person might call fuck and as I bashed away like a Léon I thought of smashing the Leggo in the nose and then Angel started groaning and saying something that sounded, without gestures, like Fuck my cunt baby fuck my cunt and the BLEEPS shot off the scale again and my coronary arteries got all pinched and protesting and BAM BAM BAMMmmmm there it was again.

. . . Hope you are well and we will get to see you soon . . .

Later, with all of us more or less huddled and humming nice tunes and Chuck singing "There's a moone out too-night" while we hummed the "Dooo-wahhs" there was a knock on the door.

"A raid!" screamed Hazel.

But there were two more knocks, and there was Selma, who said, "Sorry I'm late, kids," and joined in.

Things melded. I remember seeing the Runt cuddling in Selma's lap, and also Molly and Angel and Selma snuggling together, and as I floated in a sea of friendly genitalia feeling this and poking that, I thought that the third toothbrush could have been male or female and that these women were more liberated than any of us and more fun, and right at the end we all remarked upon what a nice party and sang in a sort of tickertape *dulcissimo:*

WHAT A GRAND GOOD-BYE, TO THAT COLORFUL GUY
THE SEXUAL ***MVI***, DOCTOR ROY G. BASCH.

10

". . . floozy."

"Huh?" I asked.

"Roy, don't you ever listen to me?"

It was Berry. Where were we, who knew? I was eating an oyster. I hoped I was in France, in Bordeaux, eating a Marenne oyster, or in England, in London, eating a Wheeler's oyster, but feared that I was in the United States, eating a Long Island oyster, fearing America because America contained the House of God, and most of the time the House of God contained me, and the times I was out of the House were more unbearable now, for their succulence, than the times I was in. I said to Berry that I did ever listen to her.

"I saw Judy the other day, and she said that whenever she sees you out with anyone else, it's with some floozy."

An American floozy, an American oyster.

"What the hell," I said, "they're American oysters, aren't they?"

"What?" asked Berry, looking at me strangely, and then, realizing I was elsewhere, turning sympathetic eyes on me, saying, "Roy, you've developed loose associations."

"Not only that, but according to Judy, I've got floozies, too."

"It's all right," said Berry, putting the tines of her fork through the juiciest part of an oyster, "I understand. It's all primary-process stuff."

"What's primary process?"

"Infantile pleasure. The pleasure principle. The floozies, the

171

oysters, even me—any pleasures at all, and all pleasures at once. It's all pre-Oedipal, a regression from the Oedipal struggle with your father for your mother, to earlier, infantile concerns. I just hope there's enough of the secondary-process Roy left to include me in his narcissism. Otherwise, it's curtains for us, for sure. See?"

"Not really," I said, wondering if she meant that she knew about Molly. Should I bring that up? Things with Berry had reached an uneasy equilibrium bound by what she called "limits," and floating on an unspoken shared acceptance of the other one's freedom, for now. I wouldn't say anything. Why should I?

"Where do you work next? What's your next rotation?"

"Next rotation?" I asked, seeing myself as an asteroid, rotating around Venus. "The Emergency Ward, tomorrow. From November first until New Year's Day."

"What will that be like?"

At that, my mind turned back to England, to one of the heightened moments in my formless "loitering years" at Oxford. That first summer of Mary Quant's miniskirt, I was idling on a busy street corner when suddenly there was a flurry and then the WEE-AWW of an ambulance approaching. The world stopped, curious and apprehensive, as the ambulance raced by, giving each of us a glimpse of the drama inside. Life or death. Chilling. And I'd thought, "Wouldn't it be great to be the one at the end of the ambulance ride?" That thought had turned me around and had gotten me back to America with its oysters and Mollys and BMSs. And Houses of Gods. Although that thought remained intact, to Berry's question I could only say, "In the E.W., I don't think they can hurt you as bad."

"Poor Roy, afraid to hope. Go ahead, have as many as you want."

With each new Watergate bombshell, Americans were realizing that Nixon's "Operation Candor" was one terrific lie. On the day that Leon Jaworski was appointed special prosecutor to replace Archibald Cox, just about the time that Ron Ziegler was rejecting Kissinger's suggestion that Nixon make a speech of contrition by saying "Contrition is bullshit," I entered the

House through the E.W. automatic doors. The waiting room was empty but for a sharp-eyed old buzzard standing in one corner rocking, a bulging shopping bag at his feet. Good. Only one patient to see. The stillness of the circular tiled E.W. was peaceful but ominous. A happy buzz, sprinkled with laughter, was coming from the central nursing station, where several people sat: the Head Nurse, named Dini; a black nurse named Sylvia; two surgeons, the uppermore, the resident, a gum-chewing Alabama native named Gath, and the lowermore, the intern, named Elihu, a tall beak-nosed Sephardic Jew with a frizzy Isro-Afro, rumored to be the worst surgical intern in the history of the House.

Gilheeny and Quick, the two policemen, also sat, and as they saw me come in, the redhead boomed out, "Welcome! Welcome to this little bit of Ireland in the heart of the Hebrew House. Your track record for the naughty upstairs ward has preceded you, and we know that you will amuse all of us with stories of passion in the long chill nights to come."

"Am I about to hear another story about the Irish and the Jews?"

"And with the High Holy Days just past, I heard a wonderful tale," said Gilheeny, "a story about the Irish maid coming to work in the Jewish household, do you know?"

I did not.

"Ha! Well, this fine Irish woman sought employment at this Jewish household about the time of the Rosh Hashonah, the New Year, and asked the doorman what the employment in the house was like. Well, said your man, it's all right, my darlin', and they celebrate all the holidays, for instance during the New Year there's a large family dinner, and the head of the household gets up in front of them all, and in gratitude blows the *shofar.* So your woman the maid's eyes light up and she says, He blows the chauffeur! Ach, mon, but they do treat the help well here, now, don't they?"

When the laughter had died down, I asked whether the patient with the shopping bag in the waiting room was surgical or medical.

"Patient? What patient?" asked Dini.

"Oh, he means Abe," said Flash, the E.W. orderly. Flash was

a dwarfish young man with a harelip and a scar that started at his lip and disappeared down into parts unknown. He looked as if he had suffered severe chromosomal damage as a child. "That ain't no patient, that's Crazy Abe. He lives out there, that's all."

"He lives in the waiting room?"

"More or less," said Dini. "His family gave big bucks to the House years ago when they died off, and now he doesn't have a home, so we let him stay here. He's OK, except that he doesn't like the waiting room to get too crowded, and he goes a little apeshit around Christmas."

How kind, to let a poor old man live in the waiting room. The two policemen, their tour of duty over for the night, arose to leave.

"Being policemen of the night," said Quick, "spending much of the dark cold night in this light warm room drinking coffee, safe from the dangers of the night, when our shifts coincide, we will meet again. Good morning and God bless."

Leaving, Gilheeny said, "Soon you will meet the resident in psychiatry, Cohen. A Freudian."

"A textbook in himself," said Quick as the door closed behind them.

Dini took me and Elihu on a tour of the premises. Although she was attractive, there was something disturbing about her. What was it? Her eyes. Her eyes were hard blank disks showing nothing in back of them. She had worked this beachhead for twelve years. She showed us the different rooms: gynecology, surgery, medicine, and then, last, room 116, which she affectionately called "The Grenade Room."

"Dubler named it, years ago. Grenade Room Dubler. The worst of the screaming gomers get put there. One night, with three of them in there, Dubler called us around, took a grenade from his pocket, opened the door, pulled the pin, tossed in the grenade, and waited for the explosion."

Elihu and I looked at each other, incredulous.

"Relax," said Dini, "it was a dud grenade."

We returned to the nursing station, where there were many clipboards containing the names and complaints of many patients. Having had a hearty breakfast and a second cup of coffee, the "emergencies" had begun to amble in. The waiting room was full. Crazy Abe, feeling crowded, was getting more agitated. There was no telling what would happen when Abe got really agitated. Gath had gone to the front line to triage those crowding Abe. The nurses had turned the people into patients in their hospital costumes, had taken their vital signs, and were once again sitting down. Dini turned her hard blank disks toward Elihu and me and said, "So you're all set now. Do it." Elihu and I went to do it.

I stood outside the gynecology room and read my first clipboard: Princess Hope, sixteen, black, pain in the stomach. I went blank, like during the first weeks of the ternship. What did I know about pain in the stomach? I'd had pain in my stomach, yes, but in a woman it's different: too many organs, and the same pain can stand for a decomposing tuna sandwich or a decomposing ectopic pregnancy that will kill in half an hour. I paused outside the door.

"Go on in there," yelled Sylvia, "she ain't got nuthin'."

I went in. Nine times out of ten in that room it would be small-time: V.D., vagitch, urinary, or tuna. This time, I thought it was big-time: appendicitis. I went back out to the nursing station and Sylvia said, "If you take that long with one, you'll only see about ten a day, and Abe will kill you."

"I think she's got appendicitis."

"Damn! Would you listen to this? Get me my scalpel, honey."

Hearing the word "scalpel," Gath was at my elbow. Eager yet skeptical, he listened to my diagnosis, and walked into the room. Nervous about my reputation, I retreated to the toilet. After a few minutes an Alabama-cracker voice outside the door yelled:

"Basch, boah? Hey, boah, you in theah?"

"Yes."

"Can we'all come in theah, boah?"

"What for?"

"To congratulate you. In the opinion of Dr. Dwayne Gath, surgical resident in this E.W., we got a keeper. Hotcha!"

"What's a keeper?"

"Keeper? 'Pendix. You go in theah with the steel blade, find

175

'er, and keep 'er. Listen heah: THE ONLY WAY TO HEAL IS WITH COLD STEEL. Basch, you gave some hungry surgeon a chance to cut, and A CHANCE TO CUT IS A CHANCE TO CURE. We gonner cut on ole Princess, quicker'n yesterday."

Wiping the sweat off my brow, I opened the bathroom door to the beaming eyes of a Good Ole Boy who'd just given a surgical buddy of his a chance to cut on human flesh.

Feeling better, I began to see other patients. I began to get bogged down with the lonely horrendomas, the LOLs in NAD and the gomers with multisystem disease, often the severity of which, according to textbooks, was "incompatible with life." I began poring over them, doing things I'd done on the wards— taking a history, doing a physical, putting in IVs, feeding tubes, Foley catheters, beginning to treat, to start them on their way back to dementia. After I'd seen about three of them, I came back to the nursing station to find the clipboards wrist-deep on my desk. I was overcome with a sense of futility. I saw no way that I would be able to dent the collection of bodies. How could I take care of all of them? How could I survive?

"You wanna survive here?" asked Dini, pulling me aside.

"Yes."

"Good. Two rules: one, treat only the life-threatening emergencies; two, everything else, TURF. You know TURF?"

"Yes, the Fat Man taught me."

"Oh? Great. So you're all set. Like he says, 'BUFF 'n' TURF.' It's not easy to separate emergencies from turkeys, especially in the Holiday Season, and it's even harder to TURF so they don't BOUNCE. It's an art. If they're not emergencies, we don't handle 'em. Now, get back in there and BUFF 'n' TURF like crazy!"

What a relief. Familiar Fat Man ground. These bodies, seeking rest, would get none here. They'd either get TURFED back out to the street, TURFED up into the wards, or, if dead, TURFED down to the morgue. The most grotesque screaming gomer might arrive, and I could attack the case with the calm assurance that soon he would be TURFED elsewhere. A mind-boggling thought: the delivery of medical care consisted of BUFFING and TURFING the seeker of care somewhere else.

The revolving door, with that eternally revolving door always waiting in the end.

The task was to separate disease from hypochondria. With the waiting room jammed with lonely, hungry bodies seeking a warm place to spend the winter night, complete with clean linen, good food, and the attention of a spanking fresh round-assed nurse and a real doctor, to MEET 'EM AND STREET 'EM was not easy. Having had years of experience with the House of God, many of the alleged ill had developed sophisticated methods to get in. I'd been a tern for less than six months; they'd been getting admitted to the House for up to ninety years. All it would take, often, was to have fooled one tern, years before, and thus to have documentation in the old chart, for with the increased threat of litigation, none of us could ignore documented disease. Using the local library, these people had BUFFED their own charts, and knew more about their diseases than me. A particular symptom of a given documented old disease could be revved up on any given night, and the sufferer admitted to be hugged and suckled at the bazooms of the House of God.

I began to work through the multiglomerate experienced ill. At one point, as I was BUFFING a gomer, I felt a tap on the back of my leg, low down. I turned and saw Chuck and the Runt, kneeling on the tile floor, looking up at me like cocker-spaniel pups in the window of a pet shop. The Fat Man stood behind them.

"Don't tell me," I said, "let me guess what you're on."

They told me anyway. They were on their knees.

"Man, do you know why?" asked Chuck.

"Because the last twelve weeks," said the Runt, "Howard has been in the E.W., and he's so scared of missing something by sending the patient back home that he admits them all. He's a SIEVE."

"A SIEVE?" I asked.

"Right," said Fats, "he lets everyone through. At Bellevue half the ones Howie admitted would have been TURFED out by the receptionist. Or they would have been too embarrassed to come in. New Yorkers have some pride, especially when it comes to degradation. Howie's been letting through six admissions per tern per day. These poor boys are on their knees. They were your friends, remember?"

"They still are," I said. "What can I do?"

"Man," said Chuck, "be a WALL. Don't let anyone in."

"In New York once," said Fats, "we had a contest to see how long the medical service could go without an admission. Thirty-seven hours. You shoulda seen what we sent outta there. Roy, help them. Be a WALL."

"You can count on me," I said, and watched them leave.

Later that afternoon I was sitting at the nursing station, musing on SIEVES AND WALLS . . .

"There's a cardiac case in the car!"

A woman stood inside the automatic doors, screaming. My first thought was that she was crazy, my second was why would a cardiac case be in a car and not an ambulance and that she was joking, and then I panicked. Before I could move, Gath and the nurses were running out the door to the car, wheeling a crash cart. By the time I was standing, they had slammed the guy on the chest, were breathing him and pumping his chest, Gath was sticking an IV into the big vessels in his neck, and all were barreling into the major-medical emergency room. Shaking, I flashed on a LAW: AT A CARDIAC ARREST THE FIRST PROCEDURE IS TO TAKE YOUR OWN PULSE. That helped, and I went into the room. He was a youngish man, coated with the pale blue-white skin of the dead. Gath was threading the line into the heart, Dini was taking a blood pressure, Flash was breathing him, and Sylvia was starting the EKG. I was standing there with my finger up my ass, woozy. And then the concept of the EKG saved me. As soon as I saw the little pink strip of paper with its blue-lined grid, I started to function. He no longer was a man five years older than me who was going to die, he was "a patient with an anterior MI having runs of V Tach which were compromising his pulmonary circulation and extending his MI. He became a series of concepts and numbers that might just respond to the right treatment. His rhythm fed into my head and CLICK out came a slogan LIVE BETTER ELECTRICALLY and I said, "Let's defibrillate him," and we did. He went into normal sinus rhythm, the deathly blue of his lips turned pink, he regained consciousness, the MICU resident came down, he was TURFED there, and I sat down again, shaking all over.

"Not bad for your first," said Dini clinically.

"I was panicked," I said, "and I don't understand it. I mean, I've been at lots of arrests before."

"On the wards," she said, "it's different. Up there, you have information about the patient and you know what to expect. Down here, all you've got is the body barreling through those doors. It's all fresh, not preprocessed. That's why I love it."

"You love it?"

"Yeah. It's a real thrill to have anything at all come through those doors and to be able to handle it. You better go talk to his wife. It's easier when they make it. Talk to her, and then you'll be all set."

Covered in vomit and blood, I walked out of the room into which the wife had seen her husband disappear, dying. She had a hungry, pleading look in her eyes, trying to read what I was about to say. Alive or dead? When I told her he was alive and in the MICU, she burst into tears. She grabbed my shoulders and hugged me and sobbed, thanking me for saving his life. Choked up, I looked past her and saw Abe, who'd stopped rocking and was staring at us with a laser-sharp buzzing beam in his eye. I went back through the automatic doors, imagining those times I'd have to say, "He's dead." I didn't tell her that if she'd waited another five minutes I'd have had to say that. End of the ambulance ride was exactly what it was.

Things were going well. I continued to wade through the unprocessed nonemergent, trying to be a good WALL. In the early evening, Gath sat down next to me and said, "Hey, boah, got sumpin' for ya. A sooprise. Close your eyes and hold out youah hand. Want ya to guess what it is."

I felt a wet, soft, smooth, wormy thing nestled in the palm of my hand, and guessed, "A skinny hot dog?"

"Nope. A keeper."

I opened my eyes, and sure enough it was nothing but, and Gath said, "A hot one, ready to pop. OPERATIONS ARE GOOD FOR PEOPLE, heah? And for he'pin' me, dahlin, I'm gonna he'p you. Jes call, y'heah?"

179

This was new. To have a good time in the House of God? To look forward to whatever flowed through the doors. To save a life? Two lives? I felt proud. The burden of treating the intractable, untreatable, unplaceable, unwanted, had been replaced by the fantasy of being a real doctor, dealing with real disease. Before midnight, waiting for my replacement, Eat My Dust Eddie, I was sitting in the nursing station talking to the two policemen, who'd stopped in for their first cup of coffee before braving the terror of the night.

"You have been vomited upon," said Gilheeny.

"Your baptism under fire," said Quick, "if you will excuse a metaphor from Roman Catholicism."

"It's been enough to snap my socks, that's for sure."

The night nurse came up with a final request. Pointing to a worried couple standing inside the doors, she said that they had been told that their daughter had been brought to the House, an overdose.

"There was no overdose who came in here," I said.

"I know, I checked, but you'd better go talk to them."

I did. Well-off, Jewish, he an engineer and she a housewife, they were concerned about their daughter, a student at the women's college across the street. I told them I'd call MBH—Man's Best Hospital—to check if she'd been taken there. I did so. MBH checked. Yes, she had been brought in: dead on arrival.

The two policemen looked at me. Again I felt choked up. I went back to the parents, not knowing what to say. "She was taken to the MBH. You'd better go there."

"Thank God," said the woman. "Sheldon, let's go."

"OK. Thanks, doc. Maybe, when she's better, they can transfer her back here. This is our hospital, if you know what I mean."

"Yeah," I said, unable to tell it to them straight, "maybe they can."

I went back to the nursing station and sat, feeling guilty about my cowardice, and thinking of the people I'd known who'd been alive and who now were dead, whatever that was.

"How hard to deal honestly with death," said Gilheeny.

"Harder than the hard elbow of a gomere," said Quick.

The House of God

"And yet that hardness brings out the softness in us all," said the redhead, "the soul in us that makes us cry at births and weddings and wakes and those sad times when the pebbles of the gravedigger dance upon the coffin lid. Sure, and it makes us more human. Yes, this emergency room is not a mean bad place, now, is it?"

"Not a mean bad place at all," said Quick.

Eat My Dust arrived, to the policeman's booming "Welcome!" I said good night and walked out through the waiting room. Crazy Abe stopped rocking and pinned me with his gaze, buzzing with electric current.

"Are you Jewish?" he asked.

"Yes I am."

"So far you did good. Watch out driving it's slippery with rain good night."

He was right, about the good job, the Jewishness, the rain, the slipperiness. How could I not be glad? I felt human. For the first time I had spent a human sixteen hours in the House of God.

11

Pitch-black, sweat-wet and foaming, the two matched horses struggled in the mire of the coal mine, searching for firm footing on the ramp leading out. I jumped down into the pool and unhitched them, and as they scrambled up and out, gobs of wet black muck sprayed down all around me, one landing with a SMACK on the exposed portion of my neck. Disgusted, I reached to wipe it away—

"OWW! Roy, you hit me in the eye. I was kissing you awake."

Berry. I'd hit her in the eye. Where were we? In her car, in my hometown. I said, "I'm sorry. I didn't know where I was."

"We're here. I came as far as I could on your directions. You've got to show me how to get to your house. Look—it's snowed here. Isn't it terrific? The first snowfall of the year."

It was terrific. Black of tree limb snuggling up to white of snow, all clouded in the gray of moist November. Thanksgiving. That was it. Despite our growling ROR, Berry and I were going to my house for Thanksgiving. She'd picked me up that morning at the door of the House E.W., after I'd worked all night, and had driven us to my home, in the Siberianoid Provinces of upper New York State. The tundra. Whaling town, whoretown, bartown, churchtown, it had reached its peak in population just before the American Revolution, and was now supported by two cement plants that nightly covered it in cement dust, the cement workers supporting the whores, bars,

182

churches, Lions, Elks, Mooses, and all the other remnants of man's bestiality to man.

"Your town is so quaint," said Berry.

"Buying condoms wasn't easy."

"What made your father move up here from the City?"

I remembered my father telling me how he'd struggled to make it as a dentist in the City after the war, he and my mother sleeping on the rollaway that doubled, during the day, as the waiting-room couch, and I remembered my mother telling me how pleased he was, after the first day in his office in this small town, when he came home like a kid with a new toy holding eighty-five dollars in cash in his hand and, remembering how he loved golf, I said, "Money, fear, and golf."

"Fear?"

"Yeah. Of being a nothing in the City."

Halfway up the main street, as I struggled with the confusion brought on by the Chamber of Commerce desecrating the memories of my youth by switching the buildings around so I didn't know what went with what anymore or which place I'd had my first beer or my first kiss or the first time I'd gotten the shit beat outta me by the Italians for going out with their sister even though their sister had wanted to go out with me, I saw a sign in the second-floor window of an old building, the snow falling to hide the peeling paint:

DENTIST.

My father's sign. Twenty-seven years there. Wanted to be a medical doctor, and the Jewish quota in the thirties in the City med schools had fucked him over. He and his generation had built the Houses of Gods, to ensure, to assure. Sad to see, that little sign. Tears came to my eyes. How much easier it was for me to feel sad, and show it, when I wasn't with them, with him cheerily whistling "Some Enchanted Evening" and restlessly swinging his arms back and forth and trying to live his dreams through me.

And so no tears came to my eyes when I saw them at home. Seeing me with Berry immediately raised everyone's hopes for my marriage. Despite my mother's reputation for breaking up relationships—the most blatant example being a Thanksgiving years before when, after dinner, she'd announced to my spinster cousin's beau that "Now it's time for you and me to talk turkey, Roger," and she'd stayed locked up in the den with him for an hour, and after she got through with him no one ever saw Roger again—she started right in on me. I was forced by fatigue to take a nap, and I excused myself from all their questions and lapsed into vivid daytime dreams. I awoke from that deep sleep that has you cheek to cheek with your own drool on the pillow, and at dinner my mind was still coated with sleep. I'd been up all night in the E.W. too often the past several nights, trying to deal with the ocean of humanity rolling and surging under my eyes. My mother resented my having taken a nap and my being tired, but Berry's being there diluted my mother's raging attention, and the yell level stayed at *mezzo*.

After dinner, things began looking up. The 18½-minute gap on the latest White House tape had just been revealed, and what pleasure it gave us all! Four generations of Baschs buzzed with the news of the Rose Mary Reach. Spurred on by the news photos of Rose Mary Woods spread-eagled between the foot pedal of her tape recorder and the phone behind her as if awaiting a quick roll in the hay with Nixon, we laughed and chortled together that now, finally, Nixon was going to get his. Good for us! Good for America! From the very tiniest Basch, my brother's four-year-old daughter, who was learning to play with her toy phone by picking it up and spread-eagling herself and screaming RO-MARY REACH RO-MARY REACH, through my brother, who seemed to despise Nixon even more than the rest of us, past my father, who was interested in the technical aspects of the erasure, foreshadowing the panel of experts who would show, beyond shadow of a doubt, that "there were four to nine consecutive manual erasures" and who'd conclude that "the event could not have happened by accident," and finally, to my grandfather, the only one of his generation left, who smiled a wise smile and said only, "After all these years, to see this, is a wonderful thing."

During a lull in the conversation my grandfather stood up and said to me, "Well, now, Doctor, now I get free advice. Let's go."

We went into my room and sat down, and he said, "Nah, I don' wanna talk with you about advice," and he pulled his chair up opposite me and leaned over the way old men do, and I remembered his wife, perenially sitting in back of him, an echo over his shoulder, now dead.

"So you know," he said, "you're the oldest grandchild, and I remember the day you were born. I hoid the news in Saratoga. I was president of the Italian American Grocers of Manhattan. We had our convention dere dat year."

"A Jew as president of the Italian American Grocers?"

"Yeh. The whole t'ing was Jews. You're an educated man, I'm asking you—would you buy from an Italian? They bought their spaghetti from us. After Polish and Yiddish, next I loined Italian. Den English. Basch's Italian American Grocery, that was me, then. I got 'black hand' letters from the Mafia, the woiks. Even in Kolomea in Poland, we were grocers. My father made all his money during the War with Japan: he bought up hides, and people said to him you're crazy what you buying these hides for, and he said never mind, and when war came, they needed them hides."

"What for?"

"Boots for the soldiers. To get to Japan. Ah, my healt's not too bad—a little trouble with the legs. But I want to know if I got something bad, 'cause dese days, dey can cure. I knew dis Italian—Ninth Avenue, nice boy. Oiy did dey cut him—a scar here to here, and here to here. But den, he ran around like a chicken. Not like some people—a little growt, and what do they say? Too busy, too busy. And den bang, dead. I'll fight like hell to live." He paused, and moved closer, until his knees almost touched mine and I could see the little clouds of cataract smothering his eyes. "Dat goil of yours she's a nice goil, isn't she?"

"Yes, she is."

"So what are you waiting? You don't got another one, do you?"

I tried not to let on that I had another one.

"So why wait? Be a *mensch!* I never waited. Sure, you couldn't wait den, but you know your grandma never wanted to marry me, never? You know what I did? I got a gun, and held it to her head, and I said, Geiger, marry me or I kill you. How about dat, eh?"

We chuckled, but then he got sad and said, "You know, in all dem years with her, I never went with another woman, never. Believe me, chances I had. In Saratoga. Chances plenty."

I felt bad about what I was doing with Molly.

"You're a smart fella. You see people from these Noising Homes all the time, in your hospital, right? Dey bring dem dere?"

"Yes, Gramp, they do."

"I never wanted to leave Magaw Place, never. I had my Club, my friends. When Grandma died, your father forced me to leave, to dis Home. A man like me in a place like dat. Sure, it's not bad in some ways—people to play poker, the shul right dere, it's all right."

"It's safe too," I said, remembering how he'd gotten mugged.

"Safe? What do I care safe? No, dat don't worry me. Never did. It's no good. The noise—we're in the flight path to Kennedy, would you believe? Dey treat you worse den a dog! All I did, all my life, and now dis. People die every day. It's a terrible, terrible . . ."

He started to cry. I felt desperate.

"It's a bad t'ing, dis. Who visits? Talk to your father, tell him I don't want to stay dere like an animal. He'll listen to you. I loved Magaw Place. I'm not a baby, I could have stayed there myself. You remember Magaw Place?"

"Sure, Gramp," I said, my mind filled with plush purple couches in a dark vestibule and the creaking metal-slatted elevator and then the childhood thrill of running down the long peculiar-smelling corridor toward Gram and Gramp's door, which would be thrown open and filled with their embraces. "Sure."

"And your father forced me to move out. So talk to him—dere's still time for me to move from dat home. Here—a little *gelt* from me, for your office, Dr. Basch."

I took the ten-dollar bill, and sat there as he got up. I knew how terrible it was. My father, adrift with the question of how to handle a single elderly parent, had found his solution in the standard middle-class ethos: "ship them to the gomer homes." Cattle in boxcars. I was mad. At the time he'd done it, I'd asked him why, and all he'd say was, "It's the best thing for him, he can't live there alone. The home is nice. We saw it. There are a lot of things there for him to do, and they take care of them there pretty good." How much my grandfather had gone through, and how little was left for him now. He would turn into a gomer. I knew, even better than him, where the ride from the nursing home would end. An ominous thought came to me: as he began to get demented, I'd visit him in the home, a syringeful of cyanide like a bar of candy in my pocket. He wouldn't be a gomer, no.

We rejoined the others. Things were cheery and bright. My mother, sensing my ambivalence about medicine, marched out a story: "You're never satisfied, Roy. You're like my great-uncle Thaler, my father's father's brother. The whole Thaler family were merchants in Russia—solid steady work, selling cloth, food, I think they even had the whiskey license in the town. But my great-uncle wanted to be a sculptor. Sculptor? Who ever heard of that? They laughed. They told him to be like all the rest. And then once, in the dead of night, he snuck into the barn, stole the best horse, and rode away, and no one ever saw or heard from him again."

Several hours later Berry deposited me again outside the doors of the E.W. of the House. As I entered the waiting room at midnight and said hello to Abe, I gave thanks that during Thanksgiving with my family I'd been able to get some sleep.

The policemen were sitting at the nursing station, as if awaiting my midnight arrival, and Gilheeny boomed out his opener: "Happy holiday greetings to you, Dr. Roy, and I expect that in the lap of your family, with your girlfriend in the lovely red Volvo, you have had a wonderful time."

I found myself relieved that they were there. I asked whether they'd had a good Thanksgiving as well.

"Red is a fine color," said the bushy redhead. "There is a continuity to the unconscious processes, at home, at play, at work, according to Freud and resident Cohen, and the continuity of the red of the Thanksgiving cranberry and the potential red of human bloodshed we observe nightly on our beat is pleasing to our senses."

"This Cohen is talking to you about the unconscious?" I asked.

"As Freud discovered and as Cohen points out," said Quick, "the process of free association is liberating, enabling the darkness of the child-policeman to light up with the understanding of the adult. See this lead billy club?"

I saw it.

"The crack of this lead stick on the elbow is a more sure and fail-safe blow, much to the consternation of those writing TV thrillers," said Quick. "To crack an elbow with the understanding of the childhood unconscious is almost free of guilt."

"We have only Cohen to thank," said Gilheeny, "for teaching the technique of the free association."

"Cohen and that master of the Jewish race, Freud. And we have high hopes for you, Roy, for like a racehorse, your track record is among the best."

"You are a man who looks great on paper," twitched Gilheeny, "humane yet athletic. The Rhodes will of 1903 says, I do believe, to choose 'the best men for the world's fight,' does it not?"

We were interrupted by a shriek from the Grenade Room:
GO AVAY GO AVAY GO AVAY . . .

My heart sank. A room-116 gomere. Even to put on the semblance of a BUFF before TURFING upstairs was, at that point, too much.

" 'Do not presume,' " said Gilheeny, " 'one of the thieves was killed; do not despair, one of the thieves was saved.' "

"Augustine, of course," said Quick.

"Where the hell did you learn that?" I blurted out, without thinking, and then blushed at the implication that these policemen were just two dumb lunky Irishmen.

"Our source for this was a remarkable firebrand of a minuscule Jew. A veritable Herzl," said Gilheeny, ignoring my rudeness.

"His name will be familiar, it is inscribed in the hearts of all, and above the lintel of room 116, the room named after him."

"Grenade Room Dubler?" I asked.

"The complete intern. Dubler knew all the fundamentals and tricky shortcuts that made him a medical wizard. Without question, in our knowledge of twenty years in God's House, Dubler was the best."

"Well, I'd like to hear about him, but I've got to go see that gomere," I said, picking up my bag to go, yet wanting to hear more about this enticing and eccentric Dubler.

"No need, man," said Gilheeny, putting a fat hand on mine, "no need. We all know her—Ina Goober, an archetype, and we have already put on as much of a BUFF as we could. She is with your pal Chuck at this very moment."

"You treated her?" I asked in some amazement.

"She is beyond treatment. She needs nothing but a new nursing-home bed, as hers has been sold. There is no need for you to see her, for she is virtually on her elevator ride up."

They were right. Chuck came out of room 116, put his bag down on the desk, and said, "Hey, Roy, how you doin'? Great case, eh?"

"Terrific. How'd it go with her?"

"Just great. She thought I was Jackson, the black tern she had last year. Not only that, she sees LeRoy in Outpatient Clinic, and she thinks I'm him too."

"LeRoy is another person of the black skin color?" asked Quick.

"No foolin.' So she has us all, and she gets us all confused. That's OK, man, 'cause I never did meet a gomer who could tell two black doctors apart. You know how it is. So long. An' be a WALL."

"Before we hit the beat tonight," said Gilheeny, "there is time to tell one further story of Grenade Room Dubler. After making ties of axial friendship with us, in repayment for the transfer of knowledge from his brain to ours on an encyclopedic range of subjects, Quick and myself offered to educate your man Dubler in the more pornographic side of our beat. He became excited in the sexual anticipation, and one night we picked him up at midnight at these very doors, telling him that we had arranged for him to do all manner of dirty things with a 'woman of the night,' if you get my meaning?"

"The great Gilheeny was at the wheel, and I was in the shotgun seat," said Quick, "and Dubler in the back, when in the area called the Strip, amidst the sailors and the seamen, we stopped the car and let an acquaintance of ours, one Lulu, jump into the back seat with Dubler. Lulu was the epitome of hot sex and cheap thrills."

"Instructing Dubler beforehand that he could do anything he wanted with Lulu and that the rearview mirror was not to be used by us, we turned on the radio and drove randomly about, our eyeballs blinking back at the bright lights."

"Dubler and Lulu began to go at it," said Quick. "His hand went to a breast, which responded in banner fashion. After much hesitation, the New Jersey Grenade bolstered up the courage to slip a hot hand up under a high skirt. Up and up and up the thigh it went, as we watched in the rearview mirror."

"Suddenly it hit something hard," said Gilheeny, "hard and long, in the shape of an erect male organ of the XY-chromosome species."

"There was a sharp explosion from the little Grenade. We stopped the car, Lulu jumped out one side, Dubler out the other. It was days before we could cease to do the only human thing, laugh."

"Dubler forgave us, but slowly."

"And only after we suggested that this had been part of our education of him, since we are, in some sense, textbooks, of a different sort, in ourselves."

"For what is learning if not the exchange of ideas?" asked the redhead cheerily. "Now we must go. For your willing ear and prospectus of what you might teach us, we will make sure, on your eight-hour shift, that we take all drunks, accidents, gunshots, and abusive hookers away from the House of God and across town to the E.W. at Man's Best Hospital, MBH. You should have an easy night, and good night."

"Why do you hang out here instead of at the MBH?" I asked. "And why are you being so nice to me?"

"Man's Best Hospital is not a friendly place. It is filled with overachievers lacking in the human quality of humor. In an instant it would commit a Crazy Abe. As a Jew, you know it is filled with red-hot and serious Gentiles. As Catholic policemen, we know it is filled with red-hot and serious Protestants. The odd Jewish tern there is a discredit to his roots. We know, for example, that Grenade Room Dubler, as well as yourself, were rejected by MBH for internship slots, in spite of your highest qualities on paper and in the flesh, and each rejected because of your 'attitude.'"

"How do you know that much about me?" I called after them as they were disappearing through the automatic doors, thinking that only the computer that matched me for my tern-ship knew that I'd listed the MBH ahead of the House of God, and had gotten turned down there. The computer matching was renowned for its secrecy. "How come you're so sure?"

Gently, wafting back through the whoosh of the closing doors and settling on an imaginary hook in the air as gracefully as a magician's silk scarf, came their reply:

"Would we be policemen if we were not?"

12

Santas were everywhere, punctuating the real world of wel-
fare and mugging with commas of fantasy and remembrance.
There was a Salvation Army Santa, a militant clanging his bell
in front of the mandatory tubercular trombonist; there was a
rich Rubensian *pasha* of a Santa in a chauffeured Caddy at
rush hour; there was even a Santa, a schizoid-looking Santa
but a Santa nonetheless, riding a chilly elephant through the
park. And of course there was a Santa in the House of God,
spritzing joy amidst the horror and the pain.

The best Santa was the Fat Man. To his gaggle of outpatients
in his Clinic, he was a Fat Messiah. Given his brusque manner
and raucous laugh, it was a surprise to me to find out how
much his patients loved him. One afternoon before Christmas,
I was walking with him to our Clinics.

"Sure they love me," said Fats, "doesn't everyone? All my
life—except for the ones who were jealous—everyone has always loved me. You know the kid in the center of the kids on
the playground? The kid whose house the others come over
to? Fats in Flatbush, always. So now it's kids we call 'patients.' Same thing. They all love me. It's great!"

"As crass and as cynical as you are?"

"Who said? And so what?"

"So why do they love you?"

"That's why: I'm straight with 'em and I make 'em laugh at
themselves. Instead of the Leggo's grim self-righteousness or

192

Putzel's whimpering hand-holding that makes them feel like they're about to die, I make them feel like they're still part of life, part of some grand nutty scheme instead of alone with their diseases, which, most of the time and especially in the Clinic, don't hardly exist at all. With me, they feel they're still part of the human race."

"But what about your sarcasm?"

"So who isn't sarcastic? Docs are no different from anyone else, they just pretend they're different, to feel big. Jesus, I'm worried about this research project, though—you know my trouble?"

"No, what?"

"Conscience. Would you believe it? Even ripping off the federal government at the VA Hospital makes me shiver. It's loony. I'm only making forty percent of what I could. It's awful."

"Too bad," I said, and then, as we approached the Clinic, I felt that sinking feeling of having to deal with these husbandless hypertensive LOLs in NAD with their asinine demands for my care, and I groaned.

"What's the matter?" asked Fats.

"I don't know if I can stand trying to figure out what to do for these women in my Clinic."

"Do? You mean you try to do something?"

"Sure, don't you?"

"Hardly ever. I do my best nothing right in my Clinic. Wait—don't go in there yet," he said, and pulled me aside, hiding behind the door. "See that crowd there?"

I did. There was a crowd of people in the waiting room, a mélange looking like a bar mitzvah at the United Nations.

"My outpatients. I do nothing medical for them, and they love me. You know how much booze, hot merchandise, and food there's gonna be in that crowd as Hannukah and Christmas presents for me? And all because I don't do a goddamn medical thing."

"You're telling me again that the cure is worse than the disease?"

"Nope. I'm telling you that the cure is the disease. The main source of illness in this world is the doctor's own illness: his

193

compulsion to try to cure and his fraudulent belief that he can. It ain't easy to do nothing, now that society is telling everyone that the body is fundamentally flawed and about to self-destruct. People are afraid they're on the verge of death all the time, and that they'd better get their 'routine physical' right away. Physicals! How much have you ever learned from a physical?"

"Not too much," I said, realizing that this was true.

"Of course not. People expect perfect health. It's a brand-spanking-new Madison Avenue expectation. It's our job to tell them that imperfect health is and always has been perfect health, and that most of the things that go wrong with their bodies we can't do much about. So maybe we do make diagnoses; big deal. We hardly ever cure."

"I don't know about that."

"Whaddaya mean? Have you cured anyone yet? In six months?"

"One remission."

"Terrific. We cure ourselves, and that's it. Well, let's go. You're gonna lose me in that crowd, Basch, so MEEE-RYY CHRISTMAS and always watch out for where you stick your finger next."

Puzzled once again and feeling that he'd shaken my brain like he usually did and that he was probably right, I stood there for a moment and watched him approach his crowd. When they saw Fats, they shrieked with delight and engulfed him. Many of them had been coming to him every week for a year and a half, and almost all of them knew each other. They were one big happy family, with this fat doctor as its head. Smiles were smiled, presents were presented, and Fats sat down in the middle of the waiting room and enjoyed himself. Occasionally he'd take a kiddie on his knee and ask what he wanted for Christmas. I was touched. Here was what medicine could be: human to human. Like all our battered dreams. Sadly I went into my office, a kid not invited to play at the Fat Man's house.

And yet, having been primed by the Fat Man, I was surprised to find my Clinic being fun. Relieved to think that my compulsion to try to cure was the only real disease in my pa-

194

tients, I sat back and let them, as people, bring me into their lives. What a difference! My basketball-playing arthritic black woman, when I ignored her aching knees and asked about her kids, opened up, chatted happily, and brought her kids in to meet me. When she left, for the first time she forgot to leave a Jehovah's Witness pamphlet. Many of my other patients brought me gifts: my LOL in NAD with the taped-up eyelids brought me her niece, a knockout *sabra* with a tanned face and shoulders like a fullback and a smile as enticing as a Jaffa orange; my artificial breast brought a bottle of whiskey, and my Portuguese artificial foot brought me a bottle of wine. These gifts were for "helping" them. The only way I'd helped them was by not TURFING them elsewhere. That was it: with the delivery of medical care this swiftly revolving door, with every doc on the planet frantic to BUFF and TURF elsewhere, these people had gotten expert at finding a static center and hanging on. They could spot a Fat Man a mile away. These people didn't give a damn about their diseases or "cures"; what they wanted was what anyone wanted: the hand in their hand, the sense that their doctor could care.

I did. I brought my patients to the Fat Man's affair.

In the E.W. as well, the jolt of feeling human refused to fizzle. I felt good, proud of my skills, excited. I didn't resent going to work, and outside the House, I could bear to think about inside the House. Sitting in the E.W. was like sitting on a bench in the Louvre: a human tapestry, ever unraveling under my eyes. Like Paris, the E.W. was a place unlimited in time: I'd leave it, and it would go on without me until I returned. An immense, humbling eternity of disease. With the luxury of the TURF, I began to live the fantasy "doctor" of my father's letters, competent to handle whatever unraveled at the end of the ambulance ride and came at me through those doors.

One Saturday afternoon before Christmas, in the lull before the Saturday-night storm, Gath and I sat at the nursing station. Crazy Abe had disappeared for two nights, and everyone was a little discouraged about his absence. The nurses were snappier, and even Flash, the orderly, used old parts of his brain, in irritation. Heavy wet snow had fallen, and I'd already treated the first of several expected myocardial infarctions, as the middle-aged out-of-shape suburban fathers shoveled their driveways clear. I told Gath that he looked kind of down, and he said, "Yeah, I am. It's Elihu—he don't know his ass from his elbow, so I'm supervisin' all his work. Suturin'. A man of my skills, suturin'. But if I let Elihu loose, it'd be a slaughterhouse down here. It'd be like when we had the old Chief of Surgery, Frannie. You know what they said about him?"

"What?"

"Killed mo' Jews than Hitler. Ah we're not gettin' the big stuff in heah anymo'. No gunshots, accidents, it's all belly pain, suturin', and twats. Makes me sick."

The nurse handed us each a clipboard. Gath glanced down, and wearily covering his eyes with his hand, said, "You know what's on heah, boy? A twat. A sick twat. I may be a racist 'Bama cracker, but for Chrissakes, Lord, give me some big stuff fo a change. All this sick twat is ruinin' this po' boy's sex life."

On my own clipboard was a thirty-three-year-old white toothpick brought in from the streets outside the public library where he'd gone to use the toilet. Zalman was six-four and weighed in at eighty-two. Looking concentration-campish, he was all buttock, rib, and jaw, too listless to do anything but talk: he didn't want to eat meat because animal souls transmigrated like humans, he was an unemployed philosopher, the world was full of incompetence, his typical dinner was a single seedless grape. Fascinating. TURF to psychiatry. My call to the psych resident was interrupted by my second snow-shoveling MI, about to die. Gath and Elihu and I trundled him back to life.

During the time it had taken to save the snow shoveler, the clipboards had piled up. The first nonswimmers, caught in the incoming Saturday-night tide. As I picked up some charts and headed back into the rooms, I was stopped by a balding guy my age, dressed in jeans and a black turtleneck.

"Dr. Basch, I'm Jeff Cohen, psych resident. I've just said hello to your anorexic, Zalman."

"Glad to meet you. The policemen have told me a lot about you. Yeah, Zalman—he's incredible. He needs your services."

"Tell me about him," Cohen said, sitting down, interested.

"I don't have time right now," I said.

"OK, later. We want him, but not yet. We don't touch patients until they're cleared medically. We never touch patients physically."

"You don't? Never? You never touch bodies?"

"You're surprised. No physical contact—it inflames the transference. Well, I see you're hassled, and I'm on my way upstairs to do some reading. Let's talk about him later, if you've got the time. Male anorexics are rare, and fascinating. Just page me, OK? See you later."

I watched him go. He was different: he listened. In the House of God, like in other Jewish houses, when someone talked, no one listened. I got the feeling Cohen had been interested in what I had to say. Like the Fat Man, but without the Fat Man's cynicism. And he was interested in his patients! I could see that: Zalman's bones were nowhere near as interesting as his story. Even I had listened, enthralled. And Cohen had time to read while on call? Far-fucking-out.

I reentered the revving-up Saturday night. A young woman was brought in from a party, over her boyfriend's shoulder, not breathing, turning blue. In a twinkling—PRESTO—Gath and I metamorphosized her from a Dead on Arrival overdose to a puking hysterical underdose, TURFED to Jeff Cohen. As I attended a Santa with acid indigestion, I saw Gath coaxing a young man farther inside the doors. The young man stopped and stood there, peering at us suspiciously from under a pair of pink silk women's panties he was wearing on his head. Cohen reappeared and tried to talk with him, but gave up, and when I asked him what was going on, he said, "Paranoid homosexual panic; stay away from him. Tincture of time. We wait." Cohen started in on a "Jesus Christ" and I went to see a "Son of Charlie Chaplin" who had intractable headache and demanded codeine and whom I TURFED back out to the street. I began to realize how many of these people needed Cohen more than they needed me. During a break, as I watched Elihu using what he called "the standard method" of awakening a Pantagruelian drunk Norwegian—shoving ice cubes against his balls—the nurse said there was a man I'd better see right away, his blood pressure being "patent pending over 150."

"Patent pending over 150? What the hell's that?"

"At the top of the scale where the mercury ends, the machine says 'patent pending.' The highest it goes."

A new House record. The Norwegian awoke from his stupor, screamed YOU BASTARD YOU KISS MY ROYAL NORWEGIAN ASS, and began to chase Elihu around the nursing station. Gath and I hoped he would catch him. I went and saw the man with the patent-pending blood pressure. He was a fat black guy with a nervous look in his eyes, swollen ankles, wet lungs, and a terrible headache. He let me put in an IV and when I informed him that at any moment his brain-stem arteries could explode, he agreed to come into the House. He then ripped out my IV, and spurting blood, said that first he had to "take care of some business" involving a silver Cadillac and two women, and ambled out. Claiming the House record for the highest blood pressure TURFED to the street did not harm my reputation as a WALL.

Toward eleven, something marvelous happened: a run of erotica. One of the few true pleasures of doctoring, when, with the excuse of a medical degree I could move past the fantasy of mentally undressing sexy women, and really do it. I started with a Persian princess and ended with a lonely oral collegian who, unable to choose between her father and her boyfriend, had suddenly developed difficulty swallowing, which obtained for her on this lonely Saturday night one young Jewish doctor, making bona fide medico-erotic contact with her mouth tongue tonsillar pillars naso-oro-pharynx neck throat clavicle rib cage breast even nipple, why not?

The most remarkable woman was Danish. Glittering white of tooth, blond of hair, blond of eyelash, which meant blond of pubic hair, pink of chill winter cheek, blue fjord of eye, she was dressed in a slinky gold wraparound which left one shoulder bare, two nipples poking. And a partridge in a pear tree. Her chief complaint: "crick in my neck, going around to my breast." Delight delight. I joked, flirted, asked the history of this crick and this breast. I had to decide whether or not to have her undress for me. I hesitated. The tension rose. In the silence she looked at me quizzically. Now I'd really blown it. I blushed, but said, "I'd better have a better look. Would you mind changing into this hospital gown?"

She looked me in the eye, and paused, and I thought, Oh, no, big trouble, now I've done it, she's gonna report me to somebody, and I saw tomorrow's headline: NORWEGIAN SAILOR SLAYS TERN IN HOUSE OF GOD—*CRIME DE PAS-SION* ALLEGED BY STATUESQUE DANE.

"But of course," she said, smiling a blue blond smile.

She knew and was going to play along! I went to the other side of the curtain, where there was another young woman, with a nurse, and I asked what the trouble was, and the nurse said, "Overdose of dog food."

"Oh?" I asked cockily. "And what's the usual dose of dog food?"

I started to examine the dog food, who presented a different erotic aspect: drowsy, stripped unashamedly to the waist, she was vomiting. As I put my stethoscope on her chest, something in the mirror between the curtains caught my eye: I could see into the other cubicle, where the Dane was undressing. Carefully, delicately, she unhooked her clinging gold dress and unwrapped it. She sat there on the stretcher, naked but for her gold panties, and then she stretched out her arms in a yawn. The pounding in my temporal arteries seemed to echo off the tile walls. She shivered in the chill, and hugged herself. Her nipples were tense brown buttons in the smooth silk flow of her breasts. Just before she reached for the House nightie, she looked down at her nipples, a child looking at two exciting toys, and with a feather-down touch gave each nipple a slow circular caress, the slow circular movement of a pelvis, of a thigh. Well, at that touch everything—her nipples, my *putz*, the House stethoscope—leaped up ensemble like hungry Jews at the last prayer of the fast of Yom Kippur. Suffused with a lover's anticipation, I prolonged the dog-food exam and then walked into the room containing the Dane and found myself ridiculously asking, "How are they?"

"They?"

"The pains in the neck?"

"Oh, yes. The same."

199

"Let me undo this," I said, untying her House nightie and dropping it to her waist. "Let me examine you."

As I let myself enjoy her, my hands and head wandered. I felt the sexual attraction bubbling up around us, reflecting prismatic elastic soap bubbles of erotica floating around us, glistening and gliding, straining and popping, all in an act of love. My palm on her pink cheek, testing the pain when the *trapezius* contracts; her hand on my forearm, holding as I checked the rotator cuff, feeling the lovely soft hollow of the *deltoid* insertion, for bursitic pain. My fingers on her ribs, her breast, yes, even brushing those erect itching nipples, for how could I avoid? Was it ethical to pick her up? Norman, the Runt's roommate at BMS, had picked up a premarin widow named—what else—Suzie in some E.W. one spring and had come away with a season box at the ballpark.

"Dr. Basch," she said as I reluctantly finished, and watching her cover her breasts again, told her to take two aspirin and wanted to tell her to call me in the morning, "can I ask you something?"

ANYTHING. PERHAPS THAT NEAT YOUNG KIPPER IN MY PANTS.

"Is it hard for you to see so much . . . disease all the time?"

"Yes, it is," I said, struggling with how to ask her out.

"You're attracted to me, I can tell."

WELL, YA FOUND ME OUT!

"And I like you. You have good hands: gentle, but strong."

IT'S FINALLY GONNA HAPPEN LIKE IN THE BOOKS.

"What a shame I'm flying to Copenhagen tomorrow, yes?"

OWWWwww.

"Wal, rump buddie, how'd ya like 'em, eh?" asked Gath, sitting down with me at the nursing station.

"Incredible. What a run of luck, eh?"

"Luck, hell. I was out theah triagin'—above the waist to you, below the waist to Elihu. All this greeny creamy twat cain't hurt his sex life none, can it? Hot damn! Would you look at that—Crazy Abe came back! Abie baby is back!"

He was. With that electric glint in his eye, Abe waved to us from just inside the automatic doors. Flash ran up and hugged him, and the spirits of the nurses lifted. What a wonderful night! When a lost old man finds his way out of the wilderness into the House of God, who could not be glad?

Before midnight, I was sitting with the policemen. Cohen joined us, filling out the data on a young schizophrenic who had come in comatose, having inhaled the contents of an aerosol can of Ban spray deodorant.

"Hello, Dr. Jeffrey Cohen," blared Gilheeny, and then, turning to me, said, "You will forgive us focusing on Cohen, but we must take advantage of his being on call only once per seven nights. A much more human schedule than yours, Dr. Basch, proving Dr. Cohen's wisdom in choosing psychiatry, and proving the maxim of Dr. Cohen's hometown: 'You can take the boy out of South Philadelphia, but you can never take South Philadelphia out of the boy.' "

Stunned by the idea of being on call once in seven nights, I listened as Gilheeny asked Cohen, "What remarkable depth of the human mind have you plunged tonight? And what is your total idea about our young schizoid inhaling the Ban?"

"Problems of closeness," said Cohen, "define schizophrenia. All of us, as Freud noted, suffer egodystonic neurotic conflicts."

"As you have told us," said Quick, "you never outgrow your need for neurosis."

"True," said Cohen, "but the schizophrenic's struggles are much earlier, pregenital, centering around personal boundaries—how close to get to someone before being consumed. I gave him some Stelazine."

"And as for the suicidal motive for the Ban?" asked Gilheeny.

"Easy," said Cohen, "BAN TAKES THE WORRY OUT OF BEING CLOSE."

"It would not be a bad thing," said Quick, "for the entire police force to come to you, Dr. Cohen, for a large group therapy."

"We've heard all about the police," said Cohen, winking at me, "buncha queers."

"Oh, Dr. Cohen!" said Quick. "You can't generalize like that."

"The thing is," said Gilheeny, "is that we live in constant fear of our lives. It makes the blood pressure elevate like an Arabian geyser, and the tension headaches we get would knock the balls off a bull with the twist in the maxillary sinuses themselves."

"I have to confess," said Quick, "that I have developed a strange passion for bendy, kinky plastic straws. And when my wife yelled at me the other night, I told her to 'bite a fart.' What is wrong with me?"

"See?" said Cohen, turning to me again, eyes twinkling. "Just like I told you: homosexuals, the lot."

Eat My Dust Eddie arrived to relieve me. I'd had such a great time, I didn't want to go. In the waiting room I was met by Abe, who ventured out of his corner, in which was to be found, in addition to his shopping bag, the young man with the pink silk women's panties on his head, who was scanning me with suspicion.

"Are you glad I came back?" asked Abe.

"Yes, I am."

"So far you did good. I made a friend, over there in the corner. You know sometimes it can get lonely in this room on the slow nights but I don't like it too crowded neither. That guy's strange but he's a friend. Won't talk to anyone but me so he's my friend. My friend. Be careful driving it's slippery with snow good night."

I was filled with hope. The sixteen hours had been the way it was supposed to, in the novels, in the texts. It had been a textbook. In itself.

Glitter and glide. Under the colored lights, the spangled couple swirled and sparkled in patterns stored and practiced, and now effortlessly performed. Her costume was minuscule, the straps holding sequined breast cups and crotchpiece hidden by the darkness of the ice rink. Gliding on big strong legs around and around, in intricate figures to enhance the sexual ballet. And then, for the finale, he lifted her high up and carried her in a final glide around the ice-white, the spotlights slicing off her skate blades, man and woman motionless, a climax as smooth and as violent as the ice. As often happened, I was caught in a detail: his thumb, dimpling her gluteal fold, stretching sensitive nerve endings in the *labia*, the clit—

"Ooohh! Isn't it fantastic, Roy?"

Reflexively, before I knew which woman it was, I said, "Yup."

"It's so—you know—exciting and neat and clean."

It was Molly where were we the Ice Follies.

"You know," she said, slipping her hand under my sweater, briefly rubbing upward toward my chest and then unhesitatingly diving down, deep deep down to where I was lumpily grumpily half-chubbing along, "this really turns me on. Like Angel says to the Runt: 'It makes me hot to trot.' I got you a Christmas present. It's at my apartment. Let's go."

It was definitely Molly and the Follies. The skating couple finished their particular ice folly with a spin and a sudden stop, slashing the ice, the woman ending up spread-eagled, her glittering sequined genitalia winking at me. As we left, I thought of the gynecology room of the E.W., of all those women's legs wishboned apart, of the gray-drab perineum of the gomeres. Molly led me out through the slushstorm that coated the city from November through March, and back to her house, where she couldn't undo my pants fast enough, and when some snow dropped from her hat onto my inflating *glans* and I yelped and shivered all over, she laughed and said, Oh, Oscar needs to be warmed up, doesn't he? and did just that with her mouth—where did these nurses get these gymnastic hungry mouths? I began to get more wild, and with my thoughts crumbling around me I asked about my penis having just been christened Oscar and she said, It's cute—I named my breasts, from when I first got them. Look. Taking off her sweater and unhooking her bra, she marched them out and pointed out that the one on the right, slightly larger, was named Toni, and the one on the left, slightly pinker, was named Sue. Well, that did it. I twirled Toni and I sucked Sue and the visions of the gray gomere twats and the diseased white and black and native American and under- and overprivileged twats were replaced by fuzzy blond Danish twats and a neat little clit writhing in those spangeled gluteal folds. Hot, we did trot.

The Follies had been a matinee, and I had to go directly

from Molly to the E.W. for an eight-to-eight night shift. I tickled Toni and slobbered Sue until Molly awoke, and as she saw me leaving she said, "Oh, Roy, wait, I forgot to give you your Christmas present," and she leaped up, hanging Toni lower than Sue, and bounced over to her dresser, and as I marveled at the genius of creation to make such a warm, pink-tittied, and soft-twatted thing as woman, she handed me a little box wrapped up in little-kid wrapping. I opened it, and there, to my astonishment, was a tiepin, in silver, which said:

***
MVI
***

"I got the letters and soldered them myself," said Molly. "You really are the ***MVI***, to me. You know, I think you're the smartest person I ever met—a genius. You must think I'm awfully dumb. I don't care, though, I just appreciate the time we're together."

The perfect gift. Strong feelings clashed in my head, from my grandfather asking me about another woman, to how much I did care about Molly, and I asked her, "Don't you think I'm a real bastard for having Berry and seeing you?"

"Nope. I really don't, Roy."

"It's incredible," I said, "you're so beautiful and so sexy and so much . . . fun and so free it's just hard to believe. I didn't know someone like you could really exist. I care about you a whole lot."

"Well, I kinda love you, Roy, even if you do see me as some dumb nurse and that's all."

"You're not some dumb nurse."

"Nope, I'm not. I'm just a fed-up Catholic who's had it up the kazootie with the nuns, and I'm making up for lost time. And now I'm gonna play."

"I'm not a bastard to you?"

"Oh, Roy boy, stop it. You and I are just going to have fun, OK?"

Well, sure it was OK, I guessed, and I gathered her up into my arms and kissed her and Toni and Sue and that hot moist and hairy thing whose name I hadn't caught who could

204

squeeze Oscar as only twenty percent of vaginal vaults can, and she kissed me and we kissed everybody, and with warmth and kisses and the tiepin and everything getting aroused all over again and saying good-bye, it was a miracle that I and big Oscar could walk at all, much less walk out, into the slush-storm and down to the House of good old God.

And wasn't it on just such a night that my great-great-uncle Thaler, denied the chance to be a sculptor, had snuck into the barn, stolen the best horse, and ridden away, never to be seen or heard from again?

13

But that was it. That night shift was the fulcrum of my stay in the E.W. The fun was over. The abuse had begun.

It started when I walked through the waiting room and saw Abe rocking in his corner, alone, a pair of silk women's panties on his head. He was abusing those waiting, and they were beginning to abuse him back. When he saw me he stopped, looked at me as if he didn't know me, and demanded:

"Are you a Jew?"

"Yes, I am."

"You know the problem with you Jews is you're circumcised."

The nurses were upset at Abe's regression, and were trying to convince Cohen to do something to prevent the inevitable, Abe's rehospitalization at the State Facility. Cohen seemed on edge. The policemen were not expected until midnight. Flash had taken his vacation, hitchhiking out to some godforsaken hole in the dull belly of the country to be ravaged by his retardate agrarian kin.

I went to see an abusive drunk who said, "I was hit by a pushcart in the garment district and I've got a problem with my legs."

"When were you hit?"

"Six years ago."

"It's not an emergency. Come back to the Clinic Monday."

He wouldn't leave, and I called Gath, and together we tried

to convince him to leave, but instead he began to unwrap his right leg, saying, "Here, just look at this, eh?" As the yellow bloodstained rags began to unwind, my stomach turned, and Gath screamed, "DON'T TAKE THAT OFF!"

"Why not?" asked the drunk gleefully. "You're doctors. Look."

The pus-yellow rags slipped away, and we were faced with the most foul-smelling, ugly, oozing ulcers down to bone that either of us had ever seen. I felt sick. Gath went red and livid, sticking his face smack up against the drunk's and yelling, "YOU HAD TO DO THAT, DIDN'T YOU, YOU BASTARD!"

From there things went downhill. All joined in the chorale of abuse. Underdoses, overdoses, drunks, psychopaths, whores, V.D., and vagitch, providing me with the pleasure of sitting between the gynecology stirrups, looking down the diseased barrel of the Holiday world. My attempts at sleep were constantly interrupted. At three A.M. I saw a suburban housewife brought in by her husband.

"I can't stand up straight," she said, leaning.

"How long have you had this problem?" I asked, sleepy-eyed.

"Three months."

"Then why did you come in tonight?"

"It's worse tonight. See, I can stand like this," she said, leaning, "but I can't stand like this," she said, standing up straight.

"You are standing like that," I pointed out.

"I know, but I prefer to stand like this."

I TURFED her out and she abused me some, and left. At four-thirty I was awakened by a refrain of OIY OIY OIY and I knew that a medical admission had arrived. The nurse handed me the clipboard, saying, "Don't worry, it's hopeless: end-stage breast cancer, metastatic throughout pelvis, abdomen, and spine." It was awful. A scoliotic wreck of a woman, bent into an ungodly shape, demented from the spread of the cancer to her brain, fighting like an animal in pain against my doing anything for her. Two sisters hovered, demanding I do everything. The disease was disgusting and painful. These sisters were irritating in their absurd hope. This was no live thing, no hope. This was death. This was despair, that rare

207

look into the mirror at first wrinkle, at first graying, at gray. This was the bottomless panic at the lost smooth cheek of childhood, at no longer being young. I was angry at this woman because this, the beginning of her end, meant work for me. Sick at heart, I admitted her. The sun rose on this pivotal night shift of mine, and to me the sun seemed defective, a second, a lightweight and tired speck at the edge of a vast unseen interstellar black. On the way out of the E.W. I was the recipient of Abe's abuse, heaped like shit on my head. Suspicious and angry, I felt the world too depleted to wash away my bitterness. A child's rocking horse was rotting in the snow. For all I knew, the first cells of a cancer were budding in my bladder. My own crab, lost on a winter-dusk shore, scuttling among the lifeless debris, asearch with timeless confidence in my ultimate ebb, for food.

"Stand up, Roy." someone said harshly, shaking me. "Royoy . . ."

It was Berry. All around me were well-dressed people, standing up, and Berry said, "Come on, Roy, it's the Hallelujah Chorus, stand up."

I stood up where was I Symphony Hall. I was listening to that penultimate grenade, *The Messiah*, as performed by the lonely and ratchet-voiced members of the Handel Society. Another matinee. As usual with any activity outside the House of God, *The Messiah* had put me right to sleep. FOR THE LORD GOD OMNIPOTENT REIGNETH! HALLELUJAH! Sing it, boys. How could you know that He doesn't seem to reigneth much in the House of God E.W. AND HE SHALL REIGN FOREVER AND EVER. FOREVER! AND EVER! HALLELUJAH! HALLELUJAH! It wasn't a bad grenade, this *Messiah*, really. I looked around at the audience, stretching from the giant double organ onstage, back in row on row of creaky benches. Many gomers and gomeres, especially toward the front. Tufts of gray, hyperemic flesh over sallow cheek. GOMERES DON'T DIE! HALLELUJAH! HALLELUJAH! FOREVER! THEY LIVE FOREVER! The price of the seats had the rich gomers in front, the kids in the rear. Berry and I were halfway to being rich gomers.

"Roy, sit down. Now you sit, see?"

Some sharp-toothed woman let out with a menstrual I KNOW THAT MY REDEEMER LIVETH and Berry and I left. Our feet got soaked in the slushy snow, and I said, "I feel sick. I can't seem to get this heaviness out of my chest, and I don't know what to do."

"It sounds congested," said Berry.

"Yeah, what do you think I should do? I don't even cough."

"That's your trouble. You're not coughing. You need something to break it up. A tussive."

"You think so? I never thought of that. What do you suggest?"

"Roy, what is this? You're the doctor, not me."

"You're right. I never thought of that."

"Dissociation. You're dissociating yourself from everything. You must be really depressed."

"Didn't I tell you? The policemen say I've become paranoid. They've seen it happen to interns before. It comes from working in the E.W."

"I thought you liked the E.W."

"I used to. It had been fun. It wasn't all gomers. There were people whose lives I saved, I actually saved."

"What happened?"

"I got competent to handle the big stuff, and the other stuff is just one abusive person after another. It shits. Addicts trying to dupe you for dope, drunks, the poor, the clap, the lonelies—I hate 'em all. I don't trust anyone. It comes from being vomited on and spit at and yelled at and conned. Everyone's out to get me to do something for them, for their fake disease. The first thing I look for now is how they're trying to take me for a ride. It's paranoia, see?"

"Paranoia's OK," said Berry, "it's just a more primitive defense. If you think someone's watching you, you think you're not alone. It keeps the desperation of loneliness out of your mind. And the rage. You're so depressed, Roy, you've been so far down lately, it's horrible to see. You've changed."

At that I got tears in my eyes. The gap between what was human, with this smart, caring woman, and what was inhuman, with the gomers and the abusers, became too much. Choked

209

up, I hung my head, and found myself blurting out that I had something to tell her and that I was screwing around with a nurse. I awaited the explosion.

"You don't think I knew that?" asked Berry.

"You did?" I said, surprised.

"Sure. Floozies and oysters and all the rest, remember? I know you pretty well. It's all right with me, Roy. As long as it goes both ways."

"It is? You mean that?"

"Yeah," she said, and then, looking me square in the eye she went on, "with the internship wrecking you, we can't keep on just as we were. That's been obvious for months. We'll keep this love going, Roy, I'm going to fight for it. Just remember, though—your freedom means my freedom too. OK, buddy?"

Crunching down the jealousy, I said, "Sure, buddy . . . sure, love," and I hugged her and kissed her, and with tears in my eyes I said, "There's only a week to go in the E.W., and I'm really worried what's going to happen. I might not make it. I'm scared that one of these nights, with nobody else around, when someone starts to abuse me, I'm going to lose control and beat the shit out of some poor bastard."

"Let me warn you, Roy: in psychiatry, this week coming up, the one between Christmas and New Year's, is the worst. It's a week of death. Be careful, get ready. It's going to be terrible."

"A Holocaust."

"Exactly. Savage."

"How am I going to survive?"

"How? Maybe like in the camps: survive to bear witness, to record the ones who didn't survive."

Later, after the fury of sex had given way to the tenderness of a caress, I began to talk about Gilheeny, Quick, and Cohen. I started to laugh, Berry started to laugh, and soon the bed, the room, the world itself was one gigantic mouth and tongue and tooth engaged in one ellipsoid laugh, and Berry said, "They sound incredibly bizarre. I mean, they really talk like that? Like textbooks? How did they get that way?"

"They say it's from hanging around the House E.W. for twenty years and talking to smart guys like me. They've absorbed every tern's liberal-arts education for the last twenty years."

"You love them, don't you?"

"Yeah, they're great. They're keeping me going."

"And you're puzzled and interested by Cohen."

"Yeah. You know what he told me—he never touches bodies. If I didn't have to touch 'em, I'd like listening too, what the hell."

"You mean he doesn't blow into his stethoscope at the gomers?"

"He doesn't own a stethoscope. He wears jeans to work."

"Well, how does he communicate with the gomers?"

"He doesn't."

"He doesn't?" Berry asked in a tantalizing tone.

"Damn! He doesn't. Maybe I should be a shrink!"

Well, at that, peals of laughter rang out again. A resident in psychiatry, a psychiatrist? No gomers, no rotting twats, no vagitch, no itchy blotchy penises, no leg ulcers, no rectals, not much on-call. Just the old chit-fuckin'-chat. That's what most of them needed anyway, these ones sucking on doctors for what doctors couldn't give. I could throw away my stethoscope and wear a pair of jeans to work.

Berry and I got dressed to go to the Leggo's Christmas party. She put on slinky black, and I, since I had to report to the E.W. at midnight, House white. Berry, excited at meeting the Fish and the Leggo, said, "I'm anxious to see how much of what you've told me is transference."

"What's transference?"

"The distortion of the real relationship by unconscious forces. Maybe you hate the Fish and the Leggo because they remind you of your father."

"I love my father."

"How about your mother?"

"The Fish and the Leggo remind me of a gutsy woman who keeps kosher?"

The party was at the Leggo's house, on the edge of the suburbs. A grand circular drive led up to a regal mansion. There was money in urine. We were greeted in the foyer by the Leg-

SAMUEL SHEM, M.D.

go, whose eyes went immediately to my House name tag and
to Berry's boobs. When I said Hello, sir, the horny little guy
looked puzzled, and I knew he was trying to remember whether or not I'd ever been in the military. In the hour before I went
to the E.W. I decided I'd try to drink as many champagnes as I
could, and soon I was bubbly and high, and stood there when
Chuck arrived. He was dressed in his dirty whites, having
come directly from ward 6-South, and was covered in the usual ward excretia. The Leggo gave Chuck a big Oh, hello there,
uh . . . and then, searching out the name tag, he said
. . . uh . . . Charles. Er, have you been at work? and Chuck
said, Naw, I always look like this, Chief, you know how it is.

The party went on. The Leggo's wife was about as sexy as a
catheter. The talk was, on the part of the doctors, all medicine,
and on the part of the spouses, mostly women, all about how
hard medicine was on them. Chuck and I fell in love with a
woman and couldn't figure out why. As I got more loaded, it
seemed that Berry's face was getting more and more incredulous. She met the Leggo, she met the Fish. After forty minutes
she came up to us and said she was leaving. I'd never seen her
so ripped, and Chuck and I asked her why.

"You two are drunk," she said, "and I can see why. I'd get
drunk too if I had to deal with these *schmucks*. It's not transference, it's obsessive-compulsive neurosis. You spill something, they have an attack of diarrhea. No wonder doctors have
the highest rate of suicide, divorce, addiction, alcoholism, and
premature death. And probably premature ejaculation too. In
two hours here, nobody asked me anything about me. It's as if
I were only an appendix to you."

A keeper, I thought to myself.

"Roy, I've never had a more degrading time. You know what
these people are? Cocksuckers. So long."

Kissing each of us on the cheek, she got her coat and left. After as many bubblies as we could get down, Chuck and I drove
back to the House.

"Damn, that Berry's sumthin' else."

"Yeah, she's great. Hey, try and stay on the road, huh? You
know, she's worried about you."

"Well, man, what all is she worried about?"

212

I was drunk enough to tell him. I told him how she'd noticed that he'd gotten so much fatter, so out of shape. How he
wolfed down his food, how he'd stopped caring about his
body, and how much he was beginning to drink.

"No foolin'. I used to be in great shape, and look at the mess
I'm in now. Pitiful, man, pitiful."

"She says it's anger, that all of us are so pissed off we're beginning to do strange things. With you, she says it's all oral.
She's worried that you're turning into an alcoholic."

He parked the car like an alcoholic, orthogonally to the
House white lines. We got out and in unspoken defiance peed
on the House lot. The two clouds of steam were a comfort.

"So Berry's a little worried about me, huh?" asked Chuck.

"Yup. More than a little. Hey, I'm worried about you too."

"Well, Roy, tell you a little secret: so am I, man, so am I."

The alarm went off. I separated myself from the hothouse
under the covers with Berry. I groaned. Potts's father had died
and Potts had left for the funeral in Charleston and Eat My
Dust Eddie was covering the ward for Potts and I had to cover
for Eddie in the E.W., a twenty-four-hour shift. The morning
was so cold that despite my bundling, when my ass hit the
seat of the car the chill made me shake and chatter, and as I
shivered my way down to the House, I thought about Wayne
Potts.

The strange thing about Potts was that he wasn't acting
strange. Perhaps he'd grown more quiet, more withdrawn.
One night I'd found him sitting in the nursing station with a
dazed look on his face, like that of a child at a funeral. "Oh, hi,
Roy," he'd said. "You know, I just went to see the Yellow Man
and I could have sworn he looked right at me and knew me,
but then, when I looked again, he was the same as ever, eyes
closed, comatose."

Potts plodded along. With his wife having multiple orgasms
of power as an MBH surgical intern, Potts spent a lot of time
alone. We'd get together, and I'd grown to like him. His Southern roots resonated with my love of the rootedness of England,
of Oxford with its cameo pieces of strawberries and cream and
champagne served on the smooth lawns in the fifteenth-centu-

ry courtyards. We became friends partly through a shared contempt for the competitive Slurpers of the North, and a shared longing for permanence, for a solid past. We'd sit at his house talking and listening to blues and gospel, Potts's favorite ballad being Mississippi John Hurt, on dying:

When my earthly trials are over, cast my body down in the sea;
save all the undertaker's bills, let the mermaids flirt with me.

One day we'd talked about how we'd gotten into medicine.
"Well, I remember one summer at Pawley's Island, I was about twelve. Mother had kicked Daddy out, and that summer my brother and my mother and me went to the shore. One day I spilled hot oil all over my hand, burned it real bad, and Mother rushed me back into Charleston to our family doc. His office was just these two big old rooms all mahogany-paneled with brass knobs and fixtures, apothecary drawers, urns, you know? He dressed my burn and said, 'Boy, you like fishin', don't you?' 'Yessir.' 'What do you like to cetch, boy?' 'Sea bass and bluefish, sir.' 'Are the bluefish runnin' yet?' 'No, sir.' 'Well, you see if we don't have you back fishin' by the time those bluefish are runnin,' eh?' So I went to him every couple of days for him to change the dressing. He used some special ointment on it, and I remember once, after a week or so, he said to me, 'Well, I've run outta that ointment, and I called up the company that makes it, New Jersey, but they say that some government bureau has banned its use in human beings, 'cause it harmed some white mice. Now, there ain't nothing wrong with that ointment, boy, and I know, 'cause I've been using it for almost twenty years. So what I did was go out to my farm and get some I've been using on my horses. Works on them, reckon it's gonna keep right on workin' on you.' Well, of course it did, and I healed up fine. I was catching bluefish that summer, just like he said. I drifted into hanging around with him, doing things on his rounds with him. The things I saw! Wherever he went, people opened their doors to him. He'd be up all night in a Negro shack delivering twins, and then his next call'd be at the grandest house on the East Battery, washing himself with their scented soap and served chickory coffee

by the butler on the Bahamas porch, the sea breeze from Fort Sumter mixing with the honeysuckle from the garden in back. I did a lot with him, saw a lot, and wanted more than anything to be like him."

"What happened to him?"

"Oh, he's still there. He's waiting for me to finish up here and come on down and join him for a while, till he retires and I take over. I suppose it could be as soon as next year."

"Sounds great. Is that what you want to do?"

"Yeah, but I guess it's just a dream."

"Why just a dream?"

"It's not the kind of medicine I'm learning here, is it? I wouldn't know one end of a twin delivery from another. And my wife doesn't want to move away from the surgery program at the MBH. She doesn't want to move to the South at all."

At the Leggo's party, Berry had asked me which one was Potts, and I'd pointed him out. He was the only one without a name tag, and Berry asked me why that was.

"He lost it."

"He didn't get another?"

"Nope."

"Doesn't sound too healthy. Unless he's being flamboyant."

"Potts flamboyant? No way."

"It doesn't sound like he cares too much about himself."

"You're much too analytic," I said, getting irritated.

"Maybe, but I'd worry about him, Roy."

"Thank you for your expert diagnosis. I'm not losing any sleep over Potts."

I had been wrong. One night I'd found myself lying awake thinking about him. I thought of his disappointments: his wife, his too-academic internship, his withering dream of going home to Charleston to be a doc there, his sad dog. I began to feel nervous. A few days before, Potts and I had been watching the Crimson Tide of Alabama roll over Georgia Tech on his TV in his bedroom. Next to his bed was a revolver, an unholstered loaded forty-four.

I parked in the House lot and hurried toward the E.W. When I'd told Potts over the phone that I was sorry about his father's death, he'd said, "I'm not. He died in the gutter after a fight

215

with some other drunk. I figured it would end this way. I feel kinda relieved."

"Relieved?"

"Yeah. You've got to understand, Roy: for years he used to walk into my bedroom when he thought I was asleep, and stand there in the dark staring at me. And every once in a while I'd see a glint of light off the barrel of the revolver he carried in his hand. I'm just going to the funeral to see Mother. Sorry you've got to cover for me. I'll make it up to you."

And so it was a bone-chilling Sunday in the middle of the dead week between Christmas and New Year's, and I expected, in my twenty-four-hour shift, few major traumas and more the small stuff trying to get into God's House for the warmth. How shortsighted, to think that on that Sunday I'd see only the products of that Sunday. Two thousand years previously Christ had bit the dust, hundreds of years ago some Renaissance red hot had thought up hospitals, fifty years ago some Jewish red hot had thought up the House, two months ago God had reincarnated winter, a few days ago some TV programmer had switched off a spine-tingling pro-football game to put on a rerun of that Teutonic grenade *Heidi*, elevating male blood pressures across the land, and one night ago, two crucial events had taken place: first, in the interest of "educating the public," there'd been a TV show on "the signs of heart attack"; second, it had been a Saturday night in a city gone sour. They were gonna get me. The question was how, and how bad.

Even at eight A.M. the waiting room was full, mostly female, mostly black. Crazy Abe, jumping up and down amidst these women, screamed at me YOUR PROBLEM IS YOUR CIRCUMSISED YOUR PROB . . . At the nursing station, things were out of whack. Howard Greenspoon, looking pale, was sitting with Gath, Elihu, Cohen, and the two policemen, and Howie was drinking a cup of coffee, something I'd never before seen him do, since his IBM cards showed a positive correlation between cups of coffee and cancer of the bladder. Howie was telling the crowd what had happened:

"I went into the bathroom on the second floor an hour ago, and I was in the toilet, and a guy opened the door, poked a shotgun in, and demanded my money. I gave him three bucks, and then I did a really stupid thing—I gave him my college ring. How could I? I loved that class ring, I really did. He didn't even ask me for it, and I offered it to him. Why? WHY?"

"Remarkable," said Gilheeny, "but better it gone and you here than vice versa."

Howie left, but the policemen stayed on, and Quick, explaining, said, "It is a season of terror, and we have been asked to serve another eight hours, until four P.M. Sixteen hundred in the military convention, is it not, Naval Officer Gath?"

"Aye aye, mutha," said Gath. "I shore wish we'd get some of that big stuff in heah, instead of all this vagitch. I feel so mean I could go bear huntin' with a whip."

"A remarkable statement, and no less so than the night just past," said Gilheeny, "when Quick and I were summoned on police radio to a naked bar for an alleged shooting. We entered, the music stopped, all heads turned to us. The Law. Silence. 'Too calm,' I whispered to Quick as we watched the barkeep slowly mop the floor and deny any shooting in his establishment. Then Quick supplied the clue."

"The slop the barman mopped was red. Beer is not red, and yet red blood is," said Quick.

"I then spotted three men sitting too close together against the wall, and commanded them to move. They did, and the man in the middle fell over, dead. Such was their surprise that we refrained from having to 'stick them' with our lead nightsticks, thus avoiding many months of work with Cohen around the gnawing question of guilt. A dangerous time."

"The raw red time when words give way to acts," said Quick.

"We must all take care," said the redhead. "With luck we shall see you again at sixteen hundred in the fine post meridian. Good-bye."

They were gone, and fear and gloom coated my mind. The charts were already piling up, the main themes being anxious men who'd seen the TV special on "How to Have a Heart Attack" and women with Sunday-morning belly pain. Picking up a chart, I ventured into the crotch of the day, my head ringing with the words COMPASSION and HATRED. There was no "big stuff," there was no humor, there was only the clear translation of black rage into, as Cohen put it, "the body ego." The main translation was into the abdomino-genito region, and I heard the chief complaint of "pain in my stomach" over and over again, until there were quarts of urine to be looked at, tens of pelvic exams to do, and do carefully, for every once in a while there could be a "keeper."

With one particular woman came disaster. Having done the total work-up, and finding nothing, I'd gone back into the room to tell her I could find nothing wrong with her that I could treat. She accepted that, and began to put on her clothes, but her boyfriend did not, and said, "Hey, wait a minute, man. You mean to tell me you're not going to do anything for her? Nothing?"

"I can't find anything I can treat."

"Listen, dude, my woman is in pain, real pain, and I want you to give her something for it."

"I don't know what's causing her pain, and I don't want to give her anything, because if it gets worse, I want to know about it, and have her come back. I don't want to mask what's going on."

"Damn you, look at her, she's suffering. Now, you gotta give her something for her pain."

I said I would not. I went back to the nursing station to write up my findings. The boyfriend pursued me, and although the woman was embarrassed and stood near the door wanting to leave, he would not, and began to use the crowded E.W. as a forum: "Goddamn you, I knew we wouldn't get any help here. You just want her to suffer, 'cause you enjoy it. You honkies don't give a shit, as long as we get the hell out."

My temper rose, and I felt that warm limbic flush creeping about my ears, my neck. I wanted to jump the counter and beat the shit out of him, or have him beat the shit out of me. He couldn't have known that I shared his sense of being a victim, his sense of despair about the wrecking of black women by forces out of control, his frustration with disease, with life. I even had grown to share his paranoia. I couldn't tell him, and he couldn't hear. Paralyzed by rage, both of us, the same rage that put bullets into the Kennedys and King. I ground my teeth and said, "I told you all I can tell you. That's all." The nurses called House Security, who stood around flashing their fake West Point medallions until the man, tugged by the woman, left. I sat there shaking, drained. I couldn't write up the chart; my hand was trembling too much. I couldn't move.

"You're white as a sheet," said Cohen. "That guy really blasted you."

"I don't know how I can take twenty-three more hours of this."

"The secret is to decathect. Withdraw your libidinal investment in what you're doing. It's like putting on a space helmet, and going around on autopilot. Emotionally, you withdraw, so that you're not really there. Survival, eh?"

"Yeah. I wish I did have a space helmet."

"Not a real space helmet. Decathexis is an inner space helmet. Almost all jobs are decathected, you know why?"

"Why?"

" 'Cause all jobs are boring, except this one. Try it."

I donned my imaginary space helmet, put myself on autopilot, and decathected like crazy. I waded through gallons of urine and immersed myself in the steady stream of frightened men from sixteen to eighty-six who'd seen the TV show and whose chief complaint was "chest pain." This TV show had served the primary purpose of confusing the American male about anatomy, since none of the chest pain was chest pain, but stomach pain, arm pain, back pain, groin pain, and one valid pain, in a big toe, which turned out to be gout. Wading through these normal EKGs, I felt a deep contempt for "educating the public" about disease. Some TV Evangelist was trying to hock "heart attacks"; terns across the country were being broken. The only MI I did see that day was a man my age, Dead on Arrival. My age. And here I was spending my few remaining pre-MI years trying to deaden myself, to survive.

Midafternoon. Lull. Breathing a little easier inside my space helmet, thinking I might just make it. Suddenly the doors slammed open. I and Gath and Elihu were thrown into that surreal hyperacute time sense brought about by real disaster. Sirens blared, lights flashed, and there, carried by a priest on one side and Quick on the other, in came Gilheeny, sheet-white, the right side of his body all blood. We jumped up and in an instant were in the major-trauma room. Gilheeny was alive. In shock. As the nurse cut off his clothing and we put in the big lines and went over his vital parts—head heart lungs—we heard Quick, shaken, tell us what had happened:

"There was a robbery at an ice-cream shop. We chased the thief, and he turned on us and emptied a shotgun into Finton."

"Officer Quick," said Gath, "you bettah leave the room."

I felt hyperalive, and found myself doing five things at once. Despite my concentrating on Gilheeny, I felt amazed that on a Sunday afternoon of the coldest day of the year, not only should some bastard rob a store, an ice-cream store, but that it should be done armed, and with a shotgun? How much cash could there have been in an ice-cream store on a freezing Sunday afternoon in winter? As I looked at the bloody mess that was the right side of the policeman's body, I wanted to have the robber in the room, to beat the shit out of him.

Gilheeny was lucky. His leg might not work right ever again, but it didn't look like he was going to die. Gath, shaky as the rest of us, trying bravely to make a joke, told Gilheeny that OPERATIONS ARE GOOD FOR PEOPLE and that the redhead was about to have one. I sat with Gilheeny while he waited to go to the OR, making sure that nothing bad could happen. Quick came in, shaken, and sat down, and then in walked the priest and the biggest policeman I'd ever seen, with four stars on each shoulder, braids on his blue coat, a big gold badge, gray hair, and elegant orange tinty glasses.

"Top o' the mornin' to you, brave Sergeant Finton Gilheeny."

"Is it the Commissioner?"

"None other. The young doctor says that with the aid of an operation, with the usefulness of the scalpel being demonstrated, you will survive."

So this peculiar speech pattern comes from the very top. I wondered how many years the Commissioner had served in God's House.

"Dr. Basch, I believe that I now have no need of the last rites. If so, could the priest depart? He scares me in the memory of how close to heaven or that hot other place I came."

"And is there a message for the little woman, the wife?" asked the Commissioner as the priest left.

"Ah, yes. Don't call her, for you see, I told her always I would send someone by, and if you call her instead, she will think I am dead, and with the epileptic daughter and the wife continually having the nervous breakdowns, it would be a sorry mistake. So send someone by the house, sir, if you could."

"I will go myself. Oh—the robber has been caught. Yes," said the Commissioner, cracking his knuckles, "and after apprehending him, we asked him to 'step outside for a moment for a private interrogation,' if you catch my drift. A long and careful 'private interrogation,' for you are a dear policeman to us. Sure, and didn't I myself hit him with a few hard interrogations? Ah, well, all the best, boyo and I'm on my way to your wife and will soothe her with my boyish good looks and TV-cop mien. Good-bye, and for the young scholar here who saved your fine red life, SHALOM and God bless."

Savage, all of it, savage. Gilheeny went to his operation, and Quick sat with us the rest of the day, shocked and drained. Abe, who had witnessed most of these events, went apeshit. Despite Cohen's efforts, he kept screaming over and over I'M GONNA KILL THEM I'M GONNA KILL THEM and he was finally put in four-point restraints and carted off to the State Facility.

Day passed, night came. Gilheeny made it through. Quick went home. Abe was gone. I stumbled through the night and finally at about two A.M., just before falling into a deep sleep, I thought that that moment, a kind of ecstasy of escape, would have been the perfect time to die. Not dead, I was awakened at three. I tried to focus on the clipboard: Twenty-three-year-old married woman; chief complaint: I was walking home and I was raped. No. Come on, will you? It's ten below out there. I went and saw her: at eleven that night she'd been walking home from her friend's house, a man jumped out of a driveway, held a gun to her head, and raped her. She was in shock, dazed. She hadn't been able to go home to her husband. She'd sat in an all-night diner and finally had come into the House.

"Have you called your husband yet?"

"No . . . I'm too ashamed," she said, and she lifted her

head up for the first time and looked me in the eyes, and first her eyes were dry cold walls and then, to my relief, they broke apart into wet pieces, and she screamed, and screamed out sob after sob. I took her in my arms and let her cry, and I was crying too. After she'd quieted some, I asked for her husband's number, and after I did the workup for rape, I called him. He'd been worried stiff, and was glad she was not dead. He couldn't know, yet, that part of her had died. In a few minutes he was there. I sat in the nursing station as he went in to see her, and sat there as they came out to leave. She thanked me, and I watched them walk down the long tiled passage. He went to put his arm around her, but with a gesture that I knew was her disgust at the ruination of her body by a man, she pushed it aside. Separate, they walked out into the savageness. Disgust. Revulsion. That was how I felt—revolted, enraged, pushing the hand away, because the hand can't ever help, because it's a myth that the hand can touch the part that's dead.

The *finale* that night was an alcoholic homosexual addict with a potentially lethal overdose of something unknown. In white pants, white shoes, a white sailor outfit with a red kerchief and a white sailor hat, his fingernails painted white, he was comatose, near death. I thought of methadone, and gave him, IV, a narcotic antagonist. He came out of his coma and became abusive. He took a knife from his pocket. I thought he was going to come at me, but no. He grabbed the IV tubing and cut it. He stood up and walked to the automatic doors. To be sure I'd be able to save him if he'd started to go down the tubes, I'd put in a large-bore needle, and now the blood flowed easily out, dripping in big red globules onto the polished floor, and I said, "Look, at least let me take your IV out before you leave."

"Nope," he said, flashing the knife, "I'm not leaving. I want to bleed to death, right here on your floor. You see, I want to die."

"Oh, well, that's different," I said, and I called the Bouncers from House Security.

We sat there, afraid to jump him, watching as the red dots on the floor coalesced into blobs, small pools. He smeared the blood around with his cute white shoes. When it became a puddle, he splashed it at us, leaving lines of blood reaching out toward us like rays from a Mayan sacrificial sun. I'd ordered four pints of blood, typed and crossed, and Flash was waiting in the blood bank for my call, ready to rush the blood down. As I sat there engorged with despair, I tried to get the arms of my mind around the savageness of the day. I could not. I waited for him to faint.

Berry and I were in Our Nation's Capital, visiting Jerry and Phil, who'd been at Oxford with me as Rhodes Scholars. While I'd chosen the fanaticism of American med school, they'd chosen that of law. At present they were each clerking for Supreme Court Justices, an "internship" similar to mine. There were many parallels. The Chief Justices, like the House docs, were a mixed lot, some borderline incompetent, some alcoholic, some dummies, and a few just plain nonfolks like the Leggo and the Fish. Jerry and Phil were delegated the task of making the highest law of the land, just as I was the one dealing with the actual bodies and deaths. Their main job was to periodically wind up their particular Justice and "launch" him on a particular side of a decision that would affect millions of great Americans. In fact, they spent much of their time at the *de facto* "highest court," the basketball court on the top floor, directly above the slightly lower, *de jure* Supreme Court chambers. One of their main thrills was throwing elbows at a body-beautiful Commie-hunting Nixon Court appointee.

Despite my newfound penchant for viewing all persons as sick and despite their newfound penchant for viewing all persons as defendants, things went well for a while. Walking through the echoing marble Court, we laughed at various farces making the gossip columns, the choicest being the rumor that a reporter, using high-powered binoculars from a hidden vantage point on the bluffs over San Clemente, while watching Nixon and Bebe Rebozo walking along the beach in their dark suits, had seen the President stop, turn, and kiss Bebe squarely on the lips.

And yet neither friendship nor a weekend away from the House could contain my rage. Feeling free, more like a person, made the contrast even more painful. I carried my suspicion

SAMUEL SHEM, M.D.

and contempt with me. At one point Jerry and Phil were surprised at my vehemence, and at how far I'd moved, from English Socialist Left to Alabama Right à la Dwayne Gath. For some reason my friends' cynicism did not extend into the realms of paranoia. The trip turned sour, and on the plane back, Berry said, "You've got to be socialized all over again, Roy. No one can be that angry and be in this world with anyone else. Your friends are really worried about you."

"You're right," I said, thinking how every part of my life had suffered from my experience in the House of God, and how, from all the awful venerealia, even my sex life had curdled and quit.

Things got only worse. At the New Year's Eve party which I had to leave early because I had to report, for the last time, to the House E.W. at midnight, and at which I got pretty drunk, Berry blew up at me: "I hardly know you anymore, Roy. You're not like you were before."

"You were right about this time of year," I said, leaving. "It's sick, and it's crazy, and it sucks. So long."

I walked out the door into the bitter cold, through the frozen snow and over a snowbank turned black from the city dirt, to my car. That terrifying empty space between what was love and what is no more loomed large. I sat there disgusted, alone, the blue mercury arc lamps adding to the surreal night. Berry appeared, trying to pull me back to the human. She leaned in through the window, hugged me, kissed me, and wished me a Happy New Year, and said, "Look at it this way, the New Year means you're halfway through."

Feeling that I'd been cheated, promised a life and then saddled with death, I went into the E.W., drunk, searching for whoever it was who had cheated me. At precisely midnight, as the old year rolled over and showed its white underbelly and the new year starting sucking at its first black morning, a naked drunk celebrated by vomiting something awful into his lap. I sat at the nursing station surrounded by the futile attempts of the nurses to make a party out of the place. As I watched Elihu do a hip-swinging, clog-clacking campy rendition of the horah with Flash, I thought of "The Follies" at Treblinka. And then I thought about the pictures of the camps, taken by the Allies at liberation. The pictures showed emaciated men peering through the barbed wire, all eyes. Those eyes, those eyes. Hard blank disks. My eyes had become hard blank disks. Yet there was something in back of them, and, yes, that was the worst. The worst was that I had to live with what was in back of them, and what I had to live with, the rest of the world must never see, for it separated me from them, as it had just done with my former best friends and with my one long love, Berry. There was rage and rage and rage, coating all like crude oil coating gulls. They had hurt me, bad. For now, I had no faith in the others of the world. And the delivery of medical care? Farce. BUFF 'n TURF. Revolving door. I wasn't sitting at the end of the ambulance ride, no. There was no glamour in this. My first patient of the New Year was a five-year-old found in a clothes dryer, face bloodied. She had been hit by her pregnant mother, hit over and over with a bludgeon of pantyhose stuffed with shards of broken glass.

How could I survive?

14

I had high hopes that the Fat Man would save me.

Chubby, pumped up, bubbling with all the fresh optimism of a baby rocking in the cradle of the New Year, the Fat Man was back, ward resident in the House of God. During his long swing through the various Mt. St. Elsewheres and the Veterans Administration Hospital, I had missed him. Of course he had loomed large always, and in frantic times, his teachings had pulled me through. For months we had been in touch mostly through rumor. According to Fats, things were going great. Yet, the more I got to know him, the more contradictions there seemed to be. While laughing at a system that cherished Jo and the Fish and Little Otto and the Leggo, Fats seemed not only to be able to survive but also to use it for himself and even to enjoy it.

Among the rumors that had floated in from Fats's long road trip were several about Dr. Jung's Anal Mirror, including one that allegedly had *Esquire* publishing its listing of "The Ten Most Beautiful Assholes of the World." Yet whenever the Fat Man talked about his invention, it was always in the subjunctive tense, "would" and "could," not "will" and "can." Gregarious inside the House, when Fats left it, he disappeared. In spite of my offers, I never saw him outside. Although inside the House he was doing something erotic with Gracie from Dietary and Food, there was no word of female relationships outside. Ambitious, Fats wouldn't let women stand in his way. Even his goal in life, to "make a big fortoona," was complicated: whenever I'd ask him how it was going, he'd get a wistful look in his eye and say, "I'm just not crooked enough," and tell me that he'd passed up opportunities that would have made ten fortoonas in the past year alone. "If only I had the hearts and minds of the Watergate Boys," he'd sigh, "if only I was G. Gordon Liddy."

I knew for sure that he was going into a GI Fellowship, that he was the only graduate of Brooklyn College ever to make it to the House of God, and that he was the only true genius I'd ever met. Now, fat and snappy and with a small gold ring on a fat finger of a fat hand and a sparkling gold chain around a huge rubbery neck that barely existed at all, given the way the fat, sleek, black-haired head seemed to rest entirely upon the rolling mound of shoulder, now the Fat Man's good cheer seemed a strange contrast to the searing winter that held the city in its frozen tongs from January until the thaw. I knew from what other terns had said that this ward—ward 4-North—would be the worst. With Fats as our resident, I hoped that it would not be the worst.

"This ward will be the worst," said Fats, chalk in chubby fingers scrawling THE WORST on the blackboard of the on-call room. "This ward has taken fine young men and broken them." BROKEN THEM went up. "And yet, last year, I made it through, and this year, with me for these three months, you guys will make it through OK."

Hyper Hooper, one of the other terns, asked, "What makes this ward the worst?"

"Name it," said Fats.

"The patients?"

"The worst."

"The nurses?"

"Salli and Bonni—they both wear caps and tin nursing-school badges like meter maids—who say things to the gomers like, 'Now we eat our custard, sport.' The worst."

"The Visit?"

"The Fish."

The third tern, Eat My Dust Eddie, let out a long slow groan of despair. "I can't stand it," he said, "I can't stand having the

Fish. He's a gastroenterologist and I can't stand any more talk of shit."

"To hear you," said Fats, "you'd think no one ever shits in California." Then, getting serious, he leaned forward and said, "That reminds me—my Fellowship Application. I'm trying to get my GI Fellowship for July the first. The Leggo still hasn't written the crucial letter of recommendation. He says he's waiting to see how I run this ward. Don't screw me on that letter, hear? This is a 'Protect the Fat Man's Fellowship' ward rotation, see?"

"Where do you want to go for your fellowship?" asked Hooper.

"Where? L.A. Hollywood."

Eat My Dust groaned and covered his face with his hands.

" 'The Bowel Run of the Stars,' " said Fats, stars sparkling in his dark eyes.

Fats was into money. He'd grown up poor. His mother, during the High Holy Days, even though there wasn't anything to make soup from, had put pots of water on the stove to boil, so that if anyone dropped in, the illusion of soup would be there. Nourished by his family as being a true genius, he'd shot up like a Flatbush meteor, barreled through Brooklyn College in science, cutthroated through Einstein Med, and arrived at the best internship of the Best Medical School, the House of God. Now, as he said, he was "going all the way to the top," and it seemed that from Flatbush, the top was Hollywood: "Imagine doing a sigmoidoscopy on Groucho Marx?" he'd said, "on Mae West, on Fay Wray, on Kong! On all those stars who think that the colon is filled with cologne."

I tuned back in as Fats was saying, "This ward is a GI Man's Heaven, and even for a GI man, it's Hell. How are you terns going to survive?"

"By killing ourselves," said Eddie.

"Wrong," said Fats seriously, "you are not going to kill yourselves. You are my A Team, you all know what you're doing by now. You will survive by going with it."

"Going with it?" I asked.

"Right. Like in the card game: finesse, men, finesse."

Finesse? I drifted off, thinking that this was a little bit different from what Fats had said before. How would this ward be the worst? There would be no hiding our doing nothing from Fats, and after what I'd been through on the wards and in the E.W., there would be no doubts about my ability to handle just about anything. I guessed it would be the worst because the gomers would try to torment us by holding up their end of the delivery of medical care by camping in the House, and the Slurpers and the Privates would try to torment us as well, each in his own fail-safe way. It would be the worst precisely because there would be no duplicity or pretense, but only the eternal, almost ecological struggle to do revolving-door medicine the House of God way.

"Remember," said Fats, finishing, "if you don't do anything, they can't do anything to you. Believe it or not, guys, we're gonna have a ball. OK, now we're ready to go on out there. Let's break!"

We broke with all the enthusiasm of a high-school football team breaking from the locker room knowing they were going to get creamed and leaving their guts in the toilet bowls behind. Ward 4-North was yellow-tiled, smelly, and contorted like a gomer. We went from room to room, and in each there were four beds and on each bed was a horizontal human being who showed few signs of being a human being except being on a bed. No longer did I think it crazy or cruel to call these sad ones gomers. Yet part of me thought it was both crazy and cruel that I no longer thought so. In one male room a gomer was spasmodically tugging at his catheter and moaning something like PAZTRAMI PAZTRAMI PAZTRAAAH—MI and at that, Eat My Dust began making dog-vomiting noises in my ear. We went into the hallway and saw two more males, side by side, the only difference being their mouths, which were:

The Fat Man asked the BMSs—the terrified, eager, and idealistic BMSs—what the inspection of these two men would produce as diagnoses, and they had no idea. Fats said, "These are classic signs: the O SIGN on the left and the Q SIGN on the right. The O SIGN is reversible, but once they get to the Q SIGN, they never come back."

We proceeded down the corridor. Suddenly there they were: side by side in armchair recliners sat two patients, the same two patients Chuck and I had turned back from that first day, Harry the Horse (HEY DOC WAIT HEY DOC WAIT) and Jane Doe (OOOO-AYYY-EEEE-IYYY-UUUU). Still there! We stood in front of them, mesmerized.

"Come on, come on," said Fats, dragging us away down the corridor. "This is the worst, the Rose Room. This room has taken fine young men and broken them. There should be an antidepressant dispenser at the door. Always remember, when you leave the Rose Room and feel like killing yourself, remember that it is they of the Rose Room, and not you, who are ill. THE PATIENT IS THE ONE WITH THE DISEASE."

"Why is it called the Rose Room?" we asked.

"It is called the Rose Room because it invariably happens that the four female beds contain gomeres named Rose."

In hushed silence we stood in the middle of the dimly lit Rose Room. All was still, spectral, the four Roses horizontal, at peace, barely dimpling their swaddling sheets. It was all very nice, until the smell hit, and then it was disgusting. The smell was shit. I couldn't stand it. I left. From the corridor I could hear Fats continue to lecture. Out came EMD, gagging. Still Fats talked on. Out came Hyper Hooper, snorting. On and on Fats talked. The three fresh BMSs, holding to the fantasy that if they left the Rose Room before the Fat Man, their grade would plunge down toward that deadhouse, middle C, stayed. Fats droned on. Yelping and retching, handkerchiefs to their mouths, out ran the BMSs. As Fats rattled on to himself and to the gomertose Roses, the BMSs threw open a window and hung out their heads, and the burly construction workers who were riveting together the Wing of Zock pointed to them and laughed, and the laughter seemed to come from far away. I wished I could have been a robust hardhat, far from the smell of shit. Fats droned on to himself. The next one out, I mused, would be a Rose. Finally, out came our leader, asking, "What's the matter, guys?"

We told him the matter was the aroma.

"Yeah, well, you can learn a lot from that aroma. With luck, in three months you'll be able to stand in the middle of that room and give the four diagnoses as the different bowel odors smack your olfactory lobes. Why, just today there was a steatorrheac malabsorption, a bowel carcinoma, a superior mesenteric insufficiency giving rise to bowel ischemia and diarrhea, and last? . . . yes! Little packets of gas slipping past a long-standing fecal impaction."

"Hey, Fats," said Hooper, "how about having a box with postmortem permission slips here at the doorway of the Rose Room?"

"LAW NUMBER ONE: GOMERS DON'T DIE," said Fats.

"Hooper, what the hell is it with you and those posts?" I asked.

"The Black Crow Award," said Hooper.

"That was a joke," I said.

"It was not. The postmortem is the flower—no, the red rose—of medicine."

As Hooper went on down the corridor, I thought how happy he'd gotten, now that he'd lodged his M firmly OR, and now that he had his Israeli Path Resident doing autopsies for him on a "same-day" basis. Racing for the Black Crow, Hooper hated the seemingly immortal gomers, and sought out younger patients, the ones who could die. In particular, he cherished the upper socioeconomic young, who, according to a recent *J. Path.* article, were most likely to sign for their own posts. Occasionally someone would mention to Hooper that maybe he was a little too heavy into death, but he'd just smile his boyish California smile, hop up and down like a Mouseketeer, and say, "Hey, it's where we're all headed, right?" Death had become a lifeline for the perky little Sausalitan.

Fats had gone straight from the stench of the Rose Room to breakfast, and Eddie and I were left alone. He turned his tense eyes to me and said, "I can't take it—they're all gomers."

"It's a tremendous opportunity to utilize your twenty-six

years of education and maturity to procure the delivery of medical care for a needy geriatric population."

"They're all gomers, every one of them."

Neck and neck for the Black Crow with Hooper, Eddie had gotten deep into sadomasochism, in particular grooving on patients "hurting" him or on his "hurting" them. I tried to change the subject, and said, "Say, I hear your wife's having a baby."

"A what?"

"A baby. Your wife. Sarah, remember?"

"Yeah, the wife is having her baby. Soon."

"It's not just hers, it's yours too!" I shouted.

"Yeah. Say, did you see 'em? All gomers. If three of them were seen in California they'd close up the state. They smell, and I hate smells. Gomers and gomers and more gomers. And"—he looked at me with a puzzled and almost pleading expression and said, ". . . and gomers. I mean, do you know what I mean?"

"Yeah I do," I said. "Don't worry, we'll help each other through."

"I mean . . . gomers is all there is here is gomers."

"Sweetheart," I said, giving up, "it's Gomer City."

The Fish was remarkable. Hands in his pockets, head in the clouds, he was so bananas in his own way that almost every time you had a conversation with him you wanted to run and tell someone about it because it did strange things to your brain, as if someone had unrolled a few convolutions, and if it hadn't come from the Chief Resident you'd swear it had come from a lunatic. That first day as our Visit, he strolled up and was greeted by Fats in between Harry the Horse and Jane Doe and said, "Hi, guys, how's it going?" and avoided our eyes and didn't wait to hear how it had been going and said, "Let's see the patients, huh?"

"Welcome, Fish," said Fats. "We're both GI men, and is there ever good GI material here, eh?"

Jane Doe cut a long, drawn-out, liquid fart.

"What'd I tell you, Fish?" said Fats. "The Gee Eye Tract!"

"The GI Tract is a special interest of mine," said the Fish, "as is flatulence. I've recently had the opportunity to review the world literature on flatulence in liver disease. Why, flatulence in liver disease would make a very interesting research project. Perhaps the House Staff would be interested in undertaking such a research project?"

No one said he was interested.

"Let me ask you this," said the Fish, looking at Hooper. "What enzyme is missing in liver disease to produce flatulence?"

"I don't know," said Hooper.

"Good," said the Fish. "You know, it's so easy to answer a question. Why, quite often it's harder, here on rounds, to say frankly 'I don't know.' In some hospitals, like the MBH, it would be frowned on to say 'I don't know.' But I want the House of God to be the kind of place where an intern can be proud to say 'I don't know.' Good, Hooper. Eddie? What's the enzyme?"

"I don't know," said Eat My Dust.

"Roy?"

"I don't know," I said.

"Fats?" asked the Fish, with trepidation.

After a tense pause Fats said, "I don't know."

The Fish looked a little perturbed that everyone had said "I don't know," Jane Doe broke wind again, and the Fish, irritated, said, "I love the GI Tract as much as anyone, but it's not professional to have someone with that kind of looseness of bowel control sitting in the middle of the corridor. Too loose. Put her in her room."

"Oh, we can't do that," said Fats, "she gets real violent in her room. But don't worry, I'm working on something special to stop the farting. Part of the TBC."

"TBC? What's TBC?"

"Total Bowel Control. Part of the Research Project at the VA."

"Excuse me, Fish," said Eddie, "but maybe you could tell us the answer to that question about the enzyme?"

"Oh? Why, I don't know."

"You don't know either?" asked Eddie.

"Why, no, and I'm proud to say it. I was hoping one of you

would. But I'll say one thing: I'll know by tomorrow on rounds."

Since the placement of the gomers was hot stuff in Gomer City, so was the Sociable Cervix. Soon after our sexual carnival in the fall, my thing with Premarin Selma had cooled. On Social Service rounds that first day, both Selma and Rosalie Cohen were cordial but wary. I didn't mind. I was preoccupied by what I'd already seen of "the worst" ward, and I had a hard time concentrating on the meeting. I caught Eddie muttering something about "I looked up, and all I saw was gomers," and the nurses demanding we go over the three-part placement form, poring over questions like "Anointed: Yes No Date" and "Incontinence: Bladder Bowel Date of Last Enema." By the end of rounds I found myself zeroed in on a young blond guy with a terrific tan, sitting in a corner giving his forelock an occasional flick up out of his baby-blue eyes.

Later Hooper and Eddie and I were sitting in the on-call room, finding new ways to play with our stethoscopes without sucking on them outright. I raised the question: "Why are there only gomers on this ward?" Hooper and Eddie looked at each other, puzzled. No one knew.

"Why don't you dial HELP and find out?" Hooper suggested.

"Dial what?"

"H-E-L-P. The guy in the Blue Blazer. It's a new House concept: if you need help with anything, you dial HELP."

I dialed HELP and said, "Hello I need help . . . No, I'm not a patient, I'm on the opposing team, the doctors, and I need one of those Blue Blazers . . . Which? Damn! Yeah, floor four . . . 'Bye." I turned to the others and said, "Each floor has a Blazer of its very own, and ours is named Lionel."

"Amazing," said Eddie. "I wonder how much those jokers get paid?"

The Blue Blazer arrived. He was the same Blazer as in rounds, and he looked just as terrific as before. We welcomed him and invited him to sit down. With a dynamite aristocratic flick of the wrist and forelock, he did. He crossed his legs in a slick way that showed that here was a guy, finally, who really knew how to sit down and cross his legs.

A strange thing happened. We asked the Blazer all kinds of questions about what he and HELP was and did and how much HELP got paid, and "Why are there only gomers here on this ward?" Lionel answered each question in a sincere and soothing voice, and seemed to be a storehouse of information that he was glad to disseminate to us hardworking terns "without whom the House of God would fall like a house of cards." Yet each soothing answer was cotton candy, 'cause after it was, it wasn't. Lionel had said nothing. It was crucial to our survival in Gomer City that we get answers, since even if we TURFED every gomer out, if somehow each TURFED-out gomer was to be replaced with a fresh one, why the hell bother at all? We got angry, and our questions turned nasty. This did even less good, and just as the three of us were beginning to boil, in walked Fats. Sizing up the situation, he said a few soothing things to Lionel, who scurried out, and then Fats turned to us and asked, "What are you guys doing?"

We told him.

"So?" asked Fats, sitting down and smiling. "So what?"

"So the prick never did tell us what HELP did or how much they get paid. Where I come from, they pay help what they're worth, they pay 'em shit," said Eddie.

"Take it easy," said Fats. "Go with it. Getting pissed at jerks like that is useless."

"I want to know how come there are only gomers here," I said.

"Yeah? Well, so do I and so does everyone else, and you know what? You'll never find out. Why get angry, eh?"

"I'm not getting angry," I said, "I *am* angry."

"So? So what good does that do? Finesse, Basch, finesse."

Gracie from Dietary and Food poked her head into the room, carrying an IV bottle filled with yellow liquid, and holding it up, announced, "The extract is ready, dear."

"Hey, great," said Fats, "let's try her out."

We followed Fats and Gracie down the corridor, and we watched Gracie replace Jane Doe's IV bottle with the bottle of "the extract." Fats, using the reverse stethoscope technique, shouted into Jane's ears: "THIS WILL MAKE YOUR BOWELS STOP RUNNING, JANIE. THIS WILL BIND YOU UP!"

235

"What is this extract?" I asked.

"Oh, it's something I invented and Gracie prepared, and it's part of the TBC, part of the VA Research that's gonna make the fortoona."

"Fresh fruit is God's own cathartic," said Gracie, "and we hope that this is the opposite. It's completely organic. Like laetrile."

I asked Fats about this research at the VA, and he told me that some "shyster" there had gotten "a big government grant" to try out a new antibiotic on those eternal guinea pigs, the shell-shocked derelict vets. The Fat Man had contracted with the shyster to get a percentage for every vet he'd put on the antibiotic, and so Fats had put them all on it.

"How'd it work?" I asked, realizing as soon as I said it that it was a dumb question, since it hadn't been given to work on anything.

"Great," said Fats, "except for one thing: the side effect."

"Side effect?"

"Yeah, see, it wiped out the intestinal flora, and one of the latent intestinal viruses took over and produced an incredible diarrhea that nothing can control. Nothing yet, that is. So we've got high hopes for this extract, see?"

"Yeah, but what's a little diarrhea?" Hooper asked.

"A little diarrhea?" said Fats, eyes widening. "A little . . ." And he dissolved into laughter, jolly chubby gusts of laughter that got bigger and bigger until he was holding onto his gut as if it would break apart and slop all over the tile floor, and Gracie and I and Eddie and Hooper laughed, and with tears in his eyes Fats finally took us aside and said, "Not a little diarrhea, men, a big diarrhea. A big contagious diarrhea. This first half of TBC, this VA antibiotic, can produce a diarrhea in anyone's bowels. If I had known how bad the side effect would be, I never would have done it. That's why I gotta find the second half, the cure. You see, this diarrhea's the most contagious and uncontrollable son of a bitch in the whole wide GI world."

At the end of the day I went to sign out to EMD, who was on call. I asked how it was going.

"Compared to California, it sucks. My third admission is on her way. I'm already on my knees."

"Why?"

"She's on her way from Albany. Three hundred miles. In a taxi."

"In a taxi?"

"In a taxi. A totally demented wiped-out gomere who, according to the scouting report, has not urinated in weeks and is too demented to sign her informed consent for dialysis, who tormented her family to the point where they surreptitiously TURFED her into a slow-moving cab in Albany and who's been making her way here since noon. She's being sent here for dialysis."

"If she won't sign there, what makes them think she'd sign here?"

" 'Cause like you said: 'Sweetheart, here it's Gomer City.' She's gonna be a special private patient of the Leggo's. It's the greatest day of her life."

On my drive home, the sun wore that harsh steely look of tired midwinter, slashing and aslant, enraged at the gray of the ice. I felt cold, unsheltered, perplexed. I had high hopes that the Fat Man would save me, and yet here he was telling me not to get angry at the Blazer.

"He told me to cool it, and I don't feel like cooling it," I told Berry. "I mean, you're always telling me to express my feelings, and I worry that if I cool it I'll go nuts. How can I listen to both of you?"

"Maybe there's some common ground," said Berry. "But I can see how you'd be scared to try and survive there if you and he are at odds. What does he say about all the gomers?"

Realizing with sadness that now even Berry had been sucked into calling these pitiful old ones "gomers," I said, "He says he loves 'em."

"That's just being counterphobic. Secondary narcisissm."

"What's all that?"

"Counterphobic is when you do what you're most scared of doing, the guy who's afraid of heights becoming a bridge painter. Primary narcissism, like with Narcissus at the Pool, is when he tries to love himself, but he can't embrace his own reflection, and he fails. Secondary narcissism is where he embraces others, and they love him for it, and he loves himself even more. The Fat Man is embracing the gomers."

"He's embracing the gomers?"

"And everybody loves him for it."

. . . Everybody loves the doctor and I'm sure by now your patients do love you. Hope you are busy and know you are doing a terrific job. Watched the Knicks on cable TV and they prove that basketball is essentially a team game . . .

Fats had called us his "A Team." And yet what kind of team would it be if its ***MVI*** began questioning its coach?

15

"I want to eat," said Tina, the woman sent in the taxi.

"You can't eat," said Eat My Dust Eddie.

"I want to eat."

"You can't eat."

"Why can't I eat?"

"Your kidneys don't work."

"They do."

"They don't."

"They do."

"They don't. When was the last time you peed?"

"I don't remember."

"See? They don't."

"I want to eat."

"If your kidneys don't work, you can't eat! You're gonna sign up for dialysis and have a rotten life."

"Then I want to die."

"Now you are talkin', lady, now you are talkin'!" said EMD, and slipping past the Albany cabbie, who was trying to collect his two-hundred-dollar-plus-tip fare, Eddie and I left Tina and sat down to the Fat Man's cardflip.

"Card one," said Fats, "Golda M.?"

"Great case," said Eddie, "the Lady of the Lice. Seventy-nine-year-old admitted from the floor of her room; found grimacing like *The Exorcist* version of a Barbie Doll. Plum-sized lymph nodes all over her body, thinks she's on the T-line in St. Louis, and has lice."

"Lice?"

"Right. The creeping cooties. Nurses refuse to enter her room."

"OK," said Fats, "no problem. The way to TURF her is to find the cancer or find the allergy. We need skin tests: TB, monilia, strep, flyshit, egg foo yong, the works. One positive skin test explains the nodes, and it's a TURF back to the floor of her room."

"Putzel, her Private, says he won't let this poor old lady go back there. He demands that we find placement."

"Swell," said Fats, "I'll call Selma. Next? Sam Levin?"

"By the way," said EMD, "I didn't have a chance to tell Putzel about the cooties. He's in there now."

A creeping coup.

"Sam's an eighty-two-year-old demented derelict living alone in a rooming house, picked up by the police for loitering. When the cops asked him where he lived, he said 'Jerusalem,' and then he pretended to faint, so they TURFED him here. Severe diabetes. He's a well-known pervert. Chief complaint is, 'I'm hungry.'"

"Of course he's hungry," said Fats, "his diabetes is burning his own body for fuel. Lice and perversion? What are the Jews coming to?"

"To the Black Crow," said Hooper.

"Insulin City," said Fats. "Rough TURF. Next?"

"You should know," said Eddie, "that Sam Levin is a man who eats everything. Watch your food, Fats."

Fats got up and locked his locker, in which he kept a stash of food, including several prized Hebrew National salamis.

"Next is Fast Tina the Taxi Woman," said Eddie, "a private patient of the Leggo's." At that the cabbie started yelling about his fare, and Fats TURFED him to HELP. He left, cursing, and in walked Bonni and said to Eddie: "Your patient Tina Tokerman's IV bottle has run out. What do you want me to hang next?"

"Tina," said Eddie.

"That's inappropriate. Now, about the lice: it's not our job to delouse, it is the intern's."

"Crap," said EMD, "it's a nursing job, 'cause nurses already got lice."

"What?! Well! I'm calling my supervisor! And as for the lice, I'm dialing HELP! We're having problems in communication, good-bye."

"Anyway," Eddie went on, "there was Tina, and I thought, Hmm dementia, I'll go right for the money and invade. So first I did the LP."

"You did the LP first? Did you ask the Leggo before you did it?"

"Nope."

"A private patient of the Leggo's sent three hundred miles in a cab and you started with a painful invasive procedure without asking him first? Why?"

"Why? It was either her or me, that's why."

"Maybe she didn't mind it, right?" asked Fats.

"Oh, she minded it. She screamed bloody murder. And at three A.M. I heard some maniac whistling 'Daisy, Daisy, give me your answer troo.'"

"Daisy, Daisy . . . " said Fats, looking out the window into the face of a hardhat hanging like a spider from the rising web of the Wing of Zock. "It wasn't really the Leggo who came in at that hour. Why should he? I mean, there's no Wing of Tokerman, is there?"

"Tina was so mad she smashed me in the nose and I got that stinging feeling all up and down my face and tears in my eyes. I realized then that I needed a big CVP line in her internal jugular in her neck."

"You didn't put in a big CVP line, because you know that the Leggo hates them because they managed without them in his day and he can't understand them anyway, right?"

"Right, I didn't."

"Good, Eddie, good," said Fats.

"But I tried like hell to, and as I was trying, the Leggo came in and asked Tina, 'Is there anything wrong, dearie?' and Tina screamed out 'Yes! This needle in my neck!' and the Leggo turned to me and said 'We managed without those in my day. Take it out and come see me tomorrow morning.' And Tina refuses to sign for dialysis."

"Eddie," said Fats quietly, "don't do what you're doing. Believe me, it's not worth it to antagonize these guys. Go easy, it's better to go easy, see? Ah, it's a tough case: the only relief for her dementia is dialysis, but the thing that keeps her from signing for dialysis is her dementia. A real tough TURF."

"How about holding a pen in her hand and scribbling her name with it?" asked Hooper. "I do that to get my gomers to sign for posts."

"Well, stop doing that, it's illegal!" yelled Fats.

"No sweat," said Eddie, "when Tina realizes that at night, when I'm on call, she's totally at my mercy, she'll sign, Fats, she'll sign."

Later that morning, Hooper and Fats and I were sitting at the nursing station. Fats was into his *Wall Street Journal*, and Hooper and I were watching the flow. We were still chuckling at having seen Lionel from HELP, paged by the nurse, checking out the room numbers and then, with a spiffy straightening of his Blazer and forelock, entering the room of the Lady of the Lice, the room crawling with the crabs. Eddie had been called to the Leggo's office, and we had been worried, but we were relieved to see the Leggo come walking down the corridor with him, his arm around Eddie's shoulder. While we waited for the Fish so we could start rounds with our leggy Chief, Fats collared Eddie and rushed us all into the on-call room, locking the door behind us.

"All right, Eddie," said Fats, "you are in serious trouble."

"Whaddayamean? We had a nice chat. Go slow with Tina, was all he said. He even put his arm around me as we walked back down here."

"Exactly," said Fats, "that arm around you. Did you ever look closely at the anatomy of that arm? Fingers like a tree frog's, with suckers on the ends. Arachnodactyly, like a spider. Double joints at the knuckles, universal joints at the wrist, elbow, and shoulder. When the Leggo puts his arm around someone, often it's the end of a promising career. The last guy he put his arm around was Grenade Room Dubler, and do you know where he went for his Fellowship?"

"Nope."

"Neither does anyone else. I doubt if it was on the continental USA. The Leggo puts his arm around your shoulders and whispers in your ear something like 'Akron' or 'Utah' or 'Kuala Lumm-poore' and that's where you go. I don't want my Fellowship in the Gulag, get it?"

242

"Yours?" asked Eddie. "And what about mine? In Oncology."

"What? You? Cancer?"

"Natch. What could be better than a gomer with cancer?"

Chief's Rounds that day were introduced by the Fish, and the patient was one Moe, a tough truckdriver who'd had to wait in the freezing cold during the gas crisis to fill up his rig. He had a rare disease of the blood called cryoglobulinemia, where with cold the blood clots in small vessels, and Moe's big toe had turned as cold and white as a corpse on a slab in the morgue.

"What a great case!" cried the Leggo. "Let me ask a few questions."

To the first question, a real toughie he asked Hooper, Hooper said, "I don't know," and so the Leggo answered the toughie himself and gave a little lecture on it. To the next question, not a toughie, to Eddie, Eddie answered, "I don't know." The Leggo gave him the benefit of the doubt and gave a little lecture none of which was news to Eddie or to anyone else. The Fish and the Fat Man were getting apprehensive about what we were doing, and the tension rose as the Leggo turned to me and asked me an easy one that any *klutz* who read *Time* could answer. I paused, knit my brow, and said, "I . . . sir, I just don't know." The Leggo asked, "You say you don't know?"

"No, sir, I don't, and I'm proud to say it."

Startled and troubled, the Leggo said, "In my day, the House of God was the kind of place where on Chief's Rounds the intern would be embarrassed to say 'I don't know.' What is going on?"

"Well, sir, you see, the Fish said that he wanted the House to be the kind of place where we'd be proud to say 'I don't know,' and, damnit, Chief, we are."

"You are? The Fish said? He . . . never mind. Let's see Moe."

The Chief fairly burned with the excitement of getting at Moe the Toe's toe, and yet at Moe's bedside, for some strange reason, he went straight for Moe's liver, poodling around with it sensually. Finally the Leggo went for Moe the Toe's toe, and no one was sure exactly what happened next. The toe was white and cold, and the Leggo, communing with it as if it

could tell him about all the great dead toes of the past, inspect-
ed it, palpated it, pushed it around, and then, bending down,
did something to it with his mouth. Eight of us watched, and
there were to be eight different opinions of what the Leggo did
with Moe's toe. Some said look, some said blow, some said
suck. We watched, amazed, as the Leggo straightened up and,
kind of absentmindedly fondling the toe as if it were some
newfound friend, asked Moe the Toe how it felt and Moe said,
"Hey, not bad, buddy, but while you're at it could you try the
same thing a little higher up?"

"The Ten Commandments and Chicken?" I asked the Fat
Man later that night as we awaited our admissions and the ten-
o'clock meal.
    "Right. Charlton Heston, Jews squashed under rocks, and
then the House of God 'chicken with tire tracks.' And Teddy."
    "Who's Teddy?"
Teddy turned out to be one of the horde of patients who
loved Fats. A concentration-camp survivor, Teddy had been
brought into the House E.W. bleeding out from an ulcer one
night when Fats was on call. Fats had TURFED him to surgery,
and, losing half his stomach, Teddy was convinced that Fats
had saved his life. Teddy "owns a deli and is lonely so he
comes in when I'm on call, with a bag of food. I deck him out
in whites and a stethoscope, and he pretends he's a doctor.
Sweet guy, Teddy." Sure enough, as Fats and I and Humberto,
my Mexican-American BMS, sat down in the TV room to
watch the MGM lion begin to roar, in walked a thin, worried-
looking fellow in shabby black, in one hand a radio spewing a
melancholic Schumann, and in the other a big paper bag
splotched with grease. As Moses grew from being a baby bul-
rushing around the Italian extras to being a six-foot-three
Egyptian red-hot looking like Charlton Heston, Fats and I and
Teddy and Humberto ran the ward via the Bell Telephone System. Just about the time that God, playing doctor, handed
down the Ten Commandments, saying, "Take these two tablets and call me in the morning," Harry the Horse had chest
pain. I sent Humberto to take an EKG, and when he returned,
without looking at it Fats said it was "an ectopic nodal pace-

maker taking over from the sinus node and producing chest pain." He was right.

"Of course I'm right. Harry's Private, Little Otto, has worked out a method to keep Harry here indefinitely: whenever Harry's ready to be TURFED out, Otto tells him he's leaving, Harry wills his heart into that crazy rhythm with chest pain, and Otto tells him he's staying. Harry's the only man in history to have conscious control of his A-V node."

"The A-V node is never under conscious control," I said.

"For Harry the Horse, it is."

"So how do we get him to leave?"

"By telling him he can stay."

"But then he'll stay forever."

"So? So what? He's a *landsman*, a brother. Nice man."

"So you don't have to take care of him, I do," I said, irritated.

"He's no work for you. Let him stay. He loves it here. Who doesn't?"

"I do," said Teddy. "Here was the best six weeks of mine life."

As *The Ten Commandments* finished, we got a call for an admission from the E.W., and Fats gathered us to him and said, "Men, pray that this is our sleep ticket."

"What?" asked Teddy. "You need a ticket to sleep here?"

"We need an admission around eleven that's not too much work, so we can get to bed and the rotation doesn't hand us another admission at four A.M. Pray, men, pray, to Moses and Israel and Jesus Christ and the entire Mexican nation."

He heard. Bernard was a young eighty-three, not a gomer, and able to talk. He'd been transferred from MBH, the House's rival. Founded in Colonial times by the WASPs, the insemination of MBH by non-WASPs had taken place only mid-twentieth century with the token multidextrous Oriental surgeon, and, finally, with the token red-hot internal-medicine Jew. Yet MBH was still Brooks Brothers, while the House was still Garment District. For Jews at MBH the password was "Dress British, Think Yiddish." It was rare to get a TURF from the MBH to the House, and the Fat Man was curious: "Bernard, you went to the MBH, they did a great work-up, and you told them,

245

after they got done, you wanted to be transferred here. Why?"

"I rilly don't know," said Bernard.

"Was it the doctors there? The doctors you didn't like?"

"The doctus? Nah, the doctus I can't complain."

"The tests or the room?"

"The tests or the room? Vell, nah, about them I can't complain."

"The nurses? The food?" asked Fats, but Bernard shook his head no. Fats laughed and said, "Listen, Bernie, you went to the MBH, they did this great work-up, and when I asked you why you came to the House of God, all you tell me is, 'Nah I can't complain.' So why did you come here? Why, Bernie, why?"

"Vhy I come heah? Vell," said Bernie, "heah I can complain."

As I headed to bed on the ward, the night nurse came up to me and asked me to do her a favor. I wasn't in the mood, but asked what it was.

"That woman transferred from surgery yesterday, Mrs. Stein."

"Metastatic cancer," I said, "inoperable. What about it?"

"She knows that the surgeons opened her, took a look, and then just sewed her up."

"Yeah?"

"Well, she's asking what that means, and her Private won't tell her. I think that someone should tell her, that's all."

Not wanting to face it, I said, "It's her Private's job, not mine."

"Please," said the nurse, "she wants to know; someone has to—"

"Who's her Private?" asked Fats.

"Putzel."

"Oh. It's OK, Roy, I'll take care of it myself."

"You? Why?"

" 'Cause that worm Putzel will never tell her. I'm in charge of the ward, I'll take care of it. Go to sleep."

"But I thought you're telling me and Eddie not to make waves."

"Right. This is different—this woman needs to know."

I watched him enter her room and sit on the bed. The woman was forty. Thin and pale, she blended with the sheets. I pictured her spine X rays: riddled with cancer, a honeycomb of bone. If she moved too suddenly, she'd crack a vertebra, sever her spinal cord, paralyze herself. Her neck brace made her look more stoic than she was. In the midst of her waxy face, her eyes seemed immense. From the corridor I watched her ask Fats her question, and then search him for his answer. When he spoke, her eyes pooled with tears. I saw the Fat Man's hand reach out and, motherly, envelop hers. I couldn't watch. Despairing, I went to bed.

At four A.M. I was awakened for an admission. Cursing, I wobbled into the E.W. cubicle and found Saul the leukemic tailor, at whose remission in October we'd wept with joy. Saul was dying. As if enraged at the delay in its onrush to death, Saul's marrow had gone wild, spitting out deformed cancerous bone cells that left Saul delirious with fever, oozing blood, anemic, in pain, and, where the malignant white cells had failed to prevent the spread of his normal skin flora, his body coated with maggoty pustules of *staphlococcus*. Too weak to move, too mad to cry, gums swollen and tongue bruised, he shooed away his wife and motioned me to bend down to him, and whispered, "Dis is it, Dr. Basch, right? Dis is the end?"

"We can try for another remission," I said, not believing it.

"Don't talk to me remission. Dis is hell. Listen—I want you to finish me off."

"What?"

"Finish me off. I'm dead, so let me die. I didn't want no treatment—she forced me. I'm ready, you're my doctor, so give me something to finish me off, OK?"

"I can't do that, Saul."

"Crap. Remember Sanders? I was dere, next bed. I saw. Suffered? Terrible. Don't make me go like him. So? You want me to sign something, I sign. Do it."

"I can't, Saul, you know that."

"So find me someone who will."

"I promise you'll have no pain. That's the best I can do."

247

"Pain? What about pain inside, in my heart? What do I have to do, Dr. Basch," he said angrily, "beg? You don't want me to suffer like Sanders. You liked him too, I know."

I looked into his bloodshot eyes, the infection creeping over the lids toward the conjuctival vessels that were pale because there were so few red cells, and I wanted to say, No, I don't want you to suffer, Saul, I want you to die easy.

"Dere, see? It's a cinch. Please, finish me off."

As I continued to protest, remembering how Sanders had suffered and died, a horrible thought crossed my mind, horrible because for an instant it didn't seem horrible, like seeing a baby and thinking of putting an icepick through a fontanelle of its skull, the thought, Yes, Saul, I'll do it, I'll finish you off. I began to work like hell to save him.

I went back to the ward, and came to the room with Putzel's terminal-cancer woman. Fats was still there, playing cards, chatting. As I passed, something surprising happened in the game, a shout bubbled up, and both the players burst out laughing.

After the next morning's cardflip, when Fats had gone to eat and Hooper had gone to Path, EMD got a silly look on his face and told me that Lionel the Blazer had paged him to take a look at some "little red things" on his gorgeous pubis that itched like hell. Eddie asked me what to do, and I said, "Do? You're a doc, so do what docs do: examine him. Give me five minutes and do it in here."

I got the operator to page Fats and Hooper and Selma and the nurses and the Fish and Housekeeping to come STAT to Gomer City, and then I watched Lionel come up the hallway, look around cautiously, and enter the on-call room. I ran up to the group I'd paged and said, "Hey, I got paged to go into the on-call room, STAT!" and then the ten of us rushed into the room. Lionel was blue-blazered only from the waist up and was sitting on the table naked from the waist down, pawing through his brown pubic hair. Eat My Dust was sitting across from him, lost in contemplation. When Lionel saw us, he went red and started to explain. He realized that he didn't want to

explain and stopped, and blushed, and said, "It's about a medical problem."

"Crab lice," said Eddie, "Lionel's got the venereal crabs."

"Medical problem?" I said. "You know, we can't blame Lionel for this, no. We can only blame the system, the one that has
paramedical personnel seeking free medical advice. How often is it that here in the House one gets tapped on the shoulder
and hears, 'Hey, doc, I got this problem, you got a minute?'"

Lionel put on his spinnaker-patterned briefs and his classy
gray slacks and left. From that time on, whenever any of us ran
into Lionel we couldn't help but think of him in terms of his
unblazered, crab-infested prick.

"You shouldn't have done that, Basch," said the Fat Man,
walking out onto the ward with me.

"Why not?"

"'Cause with guys like the Blazers, you can't win: as soon as
you engage in the struggle, you lose. Lionel's boss, the flunky
Marvin, who assigns admissions, is gonna make life miserable
for you. Look, Roy, you're older than Hooper and Eddie, you
can step back a little, and roll with it. It's hard enough without
Blazers and Privates and Slurpers making it harder."

"Give in to those assholes?"

"I never said that."

"What's the alternative?" I asked, challenging him.

"Don't let them use you, Roy. Use them."

"How?"

"Like this," said Fats, sitting down across from Jane Doe
and taking out his stopwatch. "Observe." "Watch."

"What are you dong?"

"Using them. In ten minutes I'll explain."

"Look, I want to go home. I'm going to sign out to Hooper."

"Go ahead. Come back here in ten and I'll explain."

I went into the on-call room and signed out to Hooper, and
even though I knew he hadn't heard a word I'd said, I didn't
care, and I got up to go home. Hooper was reading the manual
I'd used at the beginning of the year, *How to Do It for the New
Intern*, the section on "How to Do a Chest Tap." I thought this
strange, since we were more than halfway through the year

and a chest tap was standard procedure. As we had gotten into the habit of helping each other out, even if it meant staying around a little longer, I asked Hooper if he needed help and he said, "You mean Lionel?" and I said, "No, me," and he said, "Nah, I'll just read this manual and then go tap Rose Budz's chest." I left him poring over the book and pointing his own finger at his own chest in the imaginary needle track he was going to take on Rose Budz. On the ward I rejoined Fats, who clicked off his watch, turned to me, and asked, "What didn't happen?"

"I don't know."

"Ten minutes, Basch, and Jane Doe didn't fart."

"So?"

"So her bowel is completely turned off, for the first time in House memory. That extract might just be the cure for that VA diarrhea. A good deed; a fortoona. Just what I and the world need. Use 'em, Basch, use 'em."

"Did you and the Fat Man get along any better?" asked Berry.

"Worse," I said, "not only does he love the gomers, but he's acting like a Boy Scout. He keeps telling us not to fight back, he makes me search the whole place for a demented ninety-seven-year-old's eyeglasses, and then he spends the whole night sitting up with a woman with terminal cancer after he's told her she's gonna die."

"He did that?"

"Yeah, why?"

"I never pictured him doing things like that. The way you described him, he seemed so cynical, so sick. Now I'm not sure."

"He's not cynical enough. He's turned into a patsy. It's almost like he's deserting me."

"He seems more reasonable now. You're the one who's acting sick."

"Thanks a lot."

"I'm concerned, Roy. This acting out is dangerous. Maybe the Fat Man is right: someone's gonna get burned."

I lay awake chewing on Berry's concern. It had been fun to

say "I don't know" to get the Fish, to get Lionel, to race around laughing and sarcastic, but there was a bud of bitterness in it that might blossom into savageness and make me sad enough to kill myself or mad enough to bite. I tried to get my worry in my hand, but I was a child grasping a sunbeam, opening my hand to find the light turned dark, the warmth gone. I drifted toward dream, finding myself ringside at a circus and seeing an elephant, yes, an elephant, and seeing a busty girl on a musty elephant puffing dusty sawdust under the roustabus-tybout and lusty really big and bustyredhot tent of a bighot top—WAIT!—with some alarm I realized that Hyper Hooper had been sitting in the on-call room reading my manual with his finger as his needle pointing—no, it couldn't have been, but yes it was—pointing in a straight shot right toward Rose Budz the LOL in NAD's heart.

16

"OK, Hooper, let's hear about the postmortem on Rose Budz. Let's hear what you with your one little needle shot have done."

Fats was flipping cards as we lay in the icy ventricle of dead February as it lay in the corpse of the year. There was no question that Eddie and Hooper and I were on our knees and that they were breaking us. Most of the House hierarchies hated us. Gomer City was turning out to be the worst. Far from taking care of it, it was beginning to take care of us.

"The post on Rose Budz confirmed what we thought from when they sectioned the needle I used," said Hooper in a tone of contrition mixed with a certain professional satisfaction. "I got spleen, lung, stomach, heart, and . . . and liver." Hooper paused, watching the Fat Man drum his fingers on the desk, and then went on, "In other words, Fats, all the organs you named the other day, plus a helping of liver and stomach as well. I think it's a new world record for most organs hit with a single needle shot."

"Liver? The liver's nowhere near where you went in."

I thought back to that day when Hyper Hooper had presented his attempt to tap the chest of Rose Budz, and had told us that "there had been a little bleeding." If a Californian isn't enthusiastic, it means a disaster has occurred, and Hooper meant that Rose was dying. He'd sent her to the MICU, and Fats, concerned and thinking malpractice, brought his Gomer City A Team to the MICU to see where the needle had gone in. The hole in Rose's chest was in the front, right over her heart. Fats had said, "Come on, Hooper, you didn't really put your needle in there, did you?" and Hooper had said, "Yup, that's what Roy's manual said, unless I had it upside down." Although Hooper had seemed a bit contrite when the Fat Man had said, "You never tap a chest from the front because things like the heart get in the way," Hooper had brightened right up and said, "It's OK, Fats, it's a great family for the post.

"I know there's usually no liver," said Hooper, "but it seems as how in this case there was an aberrant lobe."

"Messy TURF, Hooper, messy TURF," said Fats solemnly, slowly ripping Rose Budz to shreds. Again Hooper had managed to snatch defeat from the jaws of victory. Holding up another card, Fats called out, "Tina? Eddie?"

"Dead," said Eat My Dust.

"What?!" shouted Fats. "Tina too? How? Who killed her?"

"Not me," said Eddie, "all I did was get her to sign for dialysis. The Leggo's crack dialysis team did the rest."

Tina had died by being inadvertently murdered by a nurse in dialysis who'd mixed up the bottles. Instead of diluting Fast Tina's blood, the machine had concentrated it further, and all the water had been pulled out of Tina's body and her brain had shrunk and rattled around in her skull like a pea while the nurse sat and read *Cosmopolitan*. Tina's pea-brain had rattled and stretched until one of the arteries straining between her neck and thalamus burst and she had hemorrhaged to death.

"Sorry to say this, Hooper," said Eddie, "but since Tina was my patient, it's another postmortem for the kid."

"Stop!" said Fats. "Tina was the Leggo's patient. No post."

"But the Leggo loves posts. He called them the flower—"

"Not when they prove malpractice!" said Fats in a tone that would hear no answer, all the while ripping Tina's cards to pieces. "Next? Jane Doe?"

"Hey, doin' great," said Hooper. "I coulda sworn that today she sat up and gave me a big hello—"

"Never mind," said Fats, irritated. "That woman's never

253

given any intern a big hello and she's not gonna start with an intern like you, slobbering after her corpse. Any bowel activity yet?"

"Nope. No bowel sounds at all. Bowel might be dead. No nuthin' since you slipped her that 'extract' of yours last month."

"That stuff is dynamite," said Fats. "Keep running in the VA antibiotic, Hooper. We've got to turn her on again. Next."

We waded through all the rest and ended with the Lady of the Lice, and Fats asked Eat My Dust if he'd found the cancer or the allergy.

"Who knows?" said Eddie. "I'm OTC."

"OTC? What the hell's OTC?"

"Off The Case," said Eddie. "New concept."

"Stop it. Pull yourself together. You can't be OTC."

"Why not?"

"Because you're her doctor, that's why, get it?" said Fats, mopping his brow. "Jesus. Did you ever find the cancer or the allergy?"

"Nope," said Eddie's BMS, "the only thing we found was the sperm. Her last three urinalyses have come back 'sperm.'"

"Sperm? SPERM? In a demented seventy-nine-year-old gomere?"

"Sperm. We think it's from Sam Levin, your pervert with diabetes."

That morning, the Fish was taking us on a field trip. Hooper had gotten paged to see the Leggo, and while we waited for him, wondering whether the Leggo had paged Hooper to castigate him for killing poor Rose Budz or to congratulate him for obtaining Rose's tricky postmortem, Eddie and I continued to torment the Fish in our usual ways until, eyeing us suspiciously, he left to make final arrangements. When Hooper reappeared, the Fish loaded us into his station wagon for our field trip. On the way, he talked sincerely about Hooper killing Rose Budz: "You know, you can't possibly learn medicine without killing a few patients. Why, I myself have killed patients. Yes, every time I killed a patient, I learned a little something from it."

It was hard to believe that he was actually saying that, and I drifted off, imagining the Fish saying, "Killing patients is a special interest of mine. I have recently had the opportunity to review the world literature on killing patients. Why, it would make a very interesting research project . . . " and by the time I snapped out of it, we were in the office of the Pearl.

This was our second field trip. The Fish took us on field trips to get us out of the House, to minimize the damage we were doing to his Chief Residency year and his career. The first field trip had been a ghetto health center, where the Fish had seemed ill at ease. This was the opposite. The Pearl had risen up through the House Slurpers as easily as the Fish might have wished, and by this time had become the richest Private in the House, the city, perhaps the world. In his office all was automated and set to Muzak. The Muzak played *Fiddler on the Roof.* The place was jam-packed: LOLs in NAD getting their blood drawn humming in tune with SUNRISE SUNSET, waiting to move on around the corner where the tech and the LOL in NAD could hum TRADISHUNNNN as the EKG was done, and then, further along past the sign that said "This way to Annatevka," sure enough, there where the LOL in NAD had to give a urine sample wouldn't she be bathed in the rippling bittersweet strains of ANNATEVKA, the song about the Fiddler's lost home. Lastly, we and the LOLs in NAD got a personal guest appearance by the Pearl in his private office, where he sat perusing the computer-processed results of the tests. Muzak played IF I WERE A RICH MAN, and there, behind a dual flagholder in which were both Israel and the USA, sat Pearl, surrounded by original Chagalls and what looked like the original Hippocratic Oath. He was sweet and kind and generous and seemed like the best damn doc and he told us he was seeing an average of one hundred and nineteen LOLs in NAD per day. No gomers. On the ride back I calculated that the Pearl made my yearly intern's salary in two days. Turning to the Fat Mound next to me on the back seat, I said, "Fats, that was Money City."

"Of course. Even in the bowels of the nonstars, one can find the big fortoonas."

* * *

After the ten-o'clock meal I went to see Molly on floor six. She was mad at me for forgetting it was Valentine's Day and not getting her a gift. She yelled at me and I felt guilty because I did like her and I even found myself dreaming about her, which must have meant that I sort of loved her, and I really loved making love to her because she still moaned like a moist Mesopotamian every damn time. Theoretically I had just as much interest in her, and I still saw her as a short-skirted majorette from St. Mesopotamia High marching along throwing her tan kneecaps first at one curb and then at the other and masturbating the longest baton in the band between those far-flung thighs, producing MIs in the senile Legionnaires lining the route, but I had been bombed on Gomer City and my sexual stride had been broken. I knew I'd been screwing her partly to affirm life, and the uneasy thought occurred to me, syllogistically, that since now I was not screwing her much, did that mean I'd ceased affirming life? I listened to her telling me I was getting dull and acting thirty, and I realized that in some ways I was, because it seemed like such an effort to go out in the razored wind and blasting cold to see her, despite my desire when I was with her and my jealousy that maybe some other guy was wearing gold cleats and getting the hot oil and myrrh all over him. I began to warm to her, and see her as sexy and loving right then and there, and I reached out and put both my hands under her boobs all tight-lifted and beruffled in her cute nursing costume and I flashed on her blond pubic hair in which I'd nuzzled and laid my head and I levered her to me and kissed her and remembered the round-the-town movements of her hips and lips and we began to get as excited as we used to get in bed. I began to ask myself where that part of me that was willing to make the effort had gone, and I began to scheme about sleeping with her that night, but she pulled away and asked me to do her a favor, to check out a patient having agonal respirations.

"Agonal respirations mean death. Is he supposed to die?"

"That's just it: I'm not sure. He's got end-stage multiple myeloma and renal failure and he's been in coma for weeks, but Dr. Putzel has never told the family and there's an argument about his dialysis continuing and about when he's supposed to die. It's all confused."

I went and saw him. It was too much. Young man, gray and dying, filling the room with his stale ammonium breath. His human centers of respiration were dead and phylogenetically he was breathing like a stranded fish. I went back to Molly and said, "He'll be dead in fifteen minutes. He's not in any pain?"

"No. The Runt's been giving him morphine all night."

"Good." Overcome with tenderness because she and I were young and not dying but one day would die, filled to our gills with morphine if we were lucky, I said, "Go draw his curtain, love, and come sit down with me and talk."

The House of God found it difficult to let some young terminal guy die without pain, in peace. Even though Putzel and the Runt had agreed to let the Man With Agonal Respirations die that night, his kidney consult, a House red-hot Slurper named Mickey who'd been a football star in college, came along, went to see the Agonal Man, roared back to us and paged the Runt STAT. Mickey was foaming at the mouth, mad as hell that his "case" was dying. I mentioned the end-stage bone cancer, and Mickey said, "Yeah, but we've got an eight-grand dialysis shunt in his arm and every three days the dialysis team gets all his blood numbers smack back into line perfect." Knowing there was going to be a mess, I left. The Runt came out of the elevator, fuming, and ran down the long corridor, his stethoscope swinging side to side like an elephant's trunk. I thought of the bones in multiple myeloma: eaten away by the cancer until they're as brittle as Rice Krispies. In a few minutes the Man With Agonal Respirations would have a cardiac arrest. If Mickey tried to pump his chest, his bones would crunch into little bitty bits. Not even Mickey, seduced into the Leggo's philosophy of doing everything always for every patient forever, would dare call a cardiac arrest.

Mickey called a cardiac arrest. From all over the House, terns and residents stormed into the room to save the Man With Agonal Respirations from a painless peaceful death. I entered the room and saw an even bigger mess than I'd imagined: Mickey was pumping up and down on the chest and you could hear the brittle bones snap, crackle, and pop under his meaty hands: a Hindu anesthesiologist pumped oxygen at the head of the bed, looking over the mess with a compassionate disdain, perhaps thinking back to the dead beggars littering dawn in Bombay; Molly was in tears, trying to follow orders, with the Runt shouting, "Stop! Don't resuscitate him!" and Mickey cracking and crunching and shouting, "Go all-out! Every three days his blood numbers are perfect!"

And yet the most sickening part of it was when Howard, pipe clenched like a bit between his teeth, ran into the room, with a nervous smile decided to take charge, and just like the tern in the *How I Saved the World* book, shouted out, "Gotta get a big line into this guy, STAT!" grabbed a homungus big needle, saw a pulsating vessel in the forearm, which happened to be the surgically constructed, meticulously protected shunt between artery and vein, which was Mickey's dialysis team's pride and joy, and, eyes glittering with big-time-intern excitement, Howie rammed the needle home, destroying forever Mickey's continued attainment of perfection every three days. When Mickey saw this, he stopped crunching, his eyes got fierce as a linebacker's, and he went bananas, screaming, "That's my shunt! You asshole, that's my shunt! Eight grand to make it, and you wrecked my shunt!" That was it for me, and I left, thinking to myself, Well, at least they'll end it here and not transfer the Man With Agonal Respirations And Crushed Bones to the MICU.

They transferred him to the MICU, where Chuck was the tern on call. When I went to see Chuck, I saw the family outside the MICU, weeping as Mickey explained things to them. Chuck was drenched in blood, bent over the residual mess of the Man With Agonal Respirations, who now had no respirations at all except those generated by a respirator. Chuck looked up from the mess and said, "Hey, man, great case, eh?"

"How are you doing?"

"Pitiful. You know what Mickey said to me? 'Just keep him alive till tomorrow, for the family.' Sumthin' else."

"What the hell are we doing this for?"

"Money. Man, I want to be so rich! Black Fleetwood with gangster whitewalls and a funeral wreaff in the back winda."

We sat down in the staff room and nipped at Chuck's Jack Daniels. He leaned back in his chair and crooned his *falsetto* "There's a . . . moone out too-nahht . . " and as I listened, I thought about how our friendship was becoming as wispy as Chuck's dream of being a singer. Chuck had been having a terrible time adjusting to his new city, one reason being he couldn't figure out where the graft was. Stopped for speeding and using the standard Chicago practice of handing the cop his driver's license with a ten-dollar bill had gotten him a stern lecture about "bribing an officer of the law" and the maximum fine. Puzzled, displaced, he spent his time at home sleeping and eating and drinking and watching TV. His suffering showed in his waistline and his hangovers. I'd tried to talk with him about it, but he'd get that blank look on his face and say to me—to me!—"Fine, fine." Each of us was becoming more isolated. The more we needed support, the more shallow were our friendships; the more we needed sincerity, the more sarcastic we became. It had become an unwritten law among the terns: don't tell what you feel, 'cause if you show a crack, you'll shatter. We imagined that our feelings could ruin us, like the great silent film stars had been ruined by sound.

The Runt came into the room, apologizing to Chuck for TURFING the Man With Agonal Respirations, but Mickey stormed in and asked how the Man was.

"Oh, fine," said Chuck, "jes' fine."

"Right. He never should have gotten that morphine," said Mickey.

"He was terminal and in pain," said Runt, getting mad, "he—"

"Never mind. I'm leaving. Just keep him alive till morning."

"Till what time?" I asked nonchalantly.

"Till about eight-thirty, quarter to . . . " Mickey began, and then, realizing what a fool he looked, he stopped, cursed us, and left.

We sat, finishing the bottle, as the Runt drifted off into his thing, sex. Identifying him, isolating him from the trauma of the ternship and the hurt he felt inside, his sloshing around in genitalia at times got out of hand. At one point I'd found him on the phone, red in the face, screaming into the receiver: "No

I haven't been home for a while and I'm not going to tell you where I've been staying. It's none of your business." Capping the phone, the Runt had grinned his hall-of-mirrors grin and said it was his parents, and went on, "How's my analysis going? I quit . . . June? I quit her too . . . I know she's nice, Mother, that's why I quit her. I got a nurse now, a hot one you should see her . . . " I'd promised myself that if the Runt started to tell his mother what Angel did with her mouth, I'd grab the phone and take over. "Goddamnit, Mother, stop it! . . . All right, you wanna know what she does? Well, you should see what she does with her—"

"Hello, Dr. Runtsky?" I said, snatching the phone from the Runt. "This is your son's friend Roy Basch." Two doctors' voices said hello. "There's nothing to worry about, folks, Harold is doing just fine."

"He seems very angry at me," said Dr. Mrs. Runtsky.

"Yeah, well, it's just a little primary-process stuff," I said, thinking of Berry, "just a little regression. But what the hell, eh?"

"Yes," said the two analysts *en chorale*, "that must be it."

"I know this nurse, she's very nice. Don't worry. So long."

The Runt had been furious at me, saying, "I've been waiting to do that for ten years."

"You can't do that."

"Why not? They're my parents."

"That's why not, Runt, 'cause they're your parents."

"So?"

"So you can't go around telling your parents about some nurse sliding around on your face!" I'd screamed. "Christ Almighty, don't you use your higher cortical centers anymore at all?"

The Runt had become pure testosterone. Neither Chuck nor I wanted to hear the latest thunderous Harold Runtsky fuck, and so we started to leave. Before he left us, the Runt asked if we noticed anything different about him. "I'm not yellow," he said. "It's been over six months since I got stuck with the needle from the Yellow Man, and I'm not yellow. The incubation period's passed. I'm not going to die."

While it cheered me to think that Runt was not dying, except at the rate we all were dying, I thought of Potts and what a terrible time he was having. The Yellow Man was still in coma, neither alive nor dead. Potts had suffered one disappointment after another, the most recent being his having to handle his mother as she raged at his father's funeral. Last time I'd seen him, he'd said he was down, that he felt like he used to feel as a kid when his family closed up the Pawley's Island summerhouse for the winter, with his mother emptying his room of all the things he loved, and him looking back before leaving, at the bare floor, the sheet over his chair, his one-eyed doll propped up on the brass railings of his bed. Although he was contemptuous of the North, he was too polite to put his bitterness into words. He became more quiet. My questions, my invitations, seemed to echo in his empty rooms. He made it hard to be his friend.

Leaving Chuck in the MICU, I said, "Hey, you got a great voice. Not a good voice, Chuckie baby, a great, great voice."

"I know it. Be cool, Roy, be cool."

It was hard to be cool in Gomer City that night. The usual horrendous things had gone wrong with the gomers. At midnight I was hunched over a Rose Room Rose, slamming the bed with my fist and hissing I HATE THIS I HATE THIS over and over again. But it was Harry the Horse who did me in. Humberto and I had planned carefully: assuring Harry he could stay, we planned that night to zonk him with Valium and the next morning drive him to the nursing home ourselves. We had told no one of this, not even Fats. Early in the morning I was awakened by the nurse saying that Harry was in a crazy cardiac rhythm and having a chest pain and looking like he was dying and should she call a cardiac arrest? I yelled, awakening Humberto from the top bunk, shot to my feet, started to race out the door with Humberto following close behind, stopped suddenly so that Humberto slammed into me like a Keystone Kop, and said to him, "Stay here, amigo. At your stage of training you shouldn't see something like this." I raced to Harry's room, where he was saying HEY DOC WAIT and clutching his chest, and eye to eye with him I

261

screamed, "Who told you, Harry? Who told you you were going back to the home?" Knowing that now he could stay in the House, Harry said:

"P . . . P-p-p . . . Putzel."

"Putzel? Putzel's not your doctor, Harry. Little Otto is your doctor. You mean Dr. Kreinberg, right?"

"No . . . P-p-p-p . . . . Putzel."

Putzel? And so Harry had succeeded in infarcting just enough more of his ventricle to stay in Gomer City for another six weeks, which was two weeks longer than me or Eddie or Fats or Hooper, and so he'd have fresh new terns and residents whom he could fool much more easily because they probably would inform him when he was about to be TURFED out and he could go into his infarcting rhythm with plenty of time to spare. I had lost. Harry the Horse had won.

On the way back to bed I passed the room with Saul the leukemic tailor. My tormenting him with my attempt, against his will, for a second remission had made him much worse. Comatose, by most legal criteria he was dead. He would not recover and yet I could keep him alive for a long time. I looked at the pale form. I listened as the pebbles of phlegm ebbed and flowed in his waves of breath. He could no longer beg me to finish him off. His wife, suffering and spending their retirement income, had become bitter, saying to me, "Enough is enough. When will you let him die?" I could finish him off. I was tempted. It was impossible to shut out. I hurried past his doorway. I tried to sleep, but the phantasmagorical night whirled on, and by dawn so many things had happened to shatter me that I found myself standing at the elevator door waiting for it to come down so I could go up to Gomer City for the day's cardflip, enraged, and about to blow.

The elevator wasn't moving. I waited and bashed on the button and still it wasn't moving. All of a sudden I went kind of nuts. I started banging on the elevator door, kicking the polished metal at the bottom, and hammering the polished metal at the top and screaming COME ON DOWN, YOU BASTARD, COME ON DOWN. Part of me wondered what the hell I was doing, but still I kept banging and kicking and screaming like an acromegalic cretin in labor screaming at her fetus COME ON DOWN, YOU BASTARD, COME ON DOWN!

Luckily, Eat My Dust Eddie came along and guided me to the cardflip. When I asked him if he thought I'd gone off the deep end he said, "Deep end? Ha! Roy, I think you were giving that elevator just what the fucker always deserved!"

That morning at the cardflip, thinking of how Putzel had putzeled my discharge of Harry the Horse, I decided to counterattack, to start a rumor. I asked Eddie if he'd heard the rumor about how some tern had threatened to assassinate Putzel, to put a bullet through his brain, and Eddie said, "Hey, high-powered medicine! Just what the fucker always deserved!"

"Why a bullet?" asked Hyper Hooper. "Wire his sigmoidoscope: when he presses the starter button, it explodes!"

"Listen to me, you guys," said Fats, "you've got to lay off Putzel. Kill this rumor right here and now."

"You worried about your Fellowship?" I asked, taunting him.

"I'm worried about my A Team. If you keep doing what you're doing, you're not going to make it through. Believe me, I know. I was there."

"Go for the jugular," said Eat My Dust, as if he hadn't heard a word Fats had said, "go for the booby-trapped scope. Kaboom." As he thought it over, Eddie's eyes got big, and he licked his lips, and then he yelled, "KAA-BOOOMM!"

Two nights later, when I was on call again, Berry insisted on coming in. Concerned with what she called my "manic" behavior and my "borderline" descriptions of what the gomers were doing to me and I to them, she thought that seeing for herself might help. She also wanted to meet Fats. Humberto and I took her around Gomer City. She saw them all. At first she tried to talk with the gomers as she would human beings, but recognizing the futility, she soon became silent. After our last stop, the Rose Room, where I insisted she listen through my stethoscope to the asthmatic breathing of a Rose, she looked shell-shocked.

"Hey, a great case, that last Rose, eh?" I said sarcastically.

"It makes me sad," said Berry.

"Well, the ten-o'clock meal will cheer you right up."

At the ten-o'clock meal she watched as we interns played "The Gomer Game," where someone would call out an answer, like "Nineteen hundred and twelve," an answer given by a gomer, and the rest of us would try to come up with questions to the gomer that might have produced that answer, such as, "When was your last bowel movement?" or "How many times have you been admitted here?" or "How old are you?" or "What year is it?" or even "Who are you?" "Who am I?" and "Yippeee?"

"Sick," Berry said afterward in a somber, almost angry tone, "it's sick."

"I told you the gomers were awful."

"Not them, you. They make me sad, but the way you treat them, making fun of them, like they were animals, is sick. You guys are sick."

"Ah, you're just not used to it," I said.

"You think that if I were in your shoes I'd get that way too?"

"Yup."

"Maybe. Well, let's get it over with. Take me to your leader."

We found Fats on Gomer City doing a manual disimpaction of Max the Parkinsonian. Double-gloved and surgically masked to filter out the smell, Teddy and Fats were digging at the endless stream of feces in Max's megacolon, while from Max's huge purple-scarred bald head came an endless stream of FIX THE LUMP FIX THE LUMP FIX THE LUMP. From Teddy's radio poured Brahms. The smell was overpoweringly fresh shit.

"Fats," I said from the doorway, "meet Berry."

"What?" asked Fats, surprised. "Oh, no. Hello, Berry. Basch, you *schlemiel,* you don't want her to see this. Get out of here. I'll be with you in a minute."

"I'm here to see," said Berry, "tell me what you're doing."

She went in. Fats began to tell her what they were doing, but when the waves of smell hit her, Berry covered her mouth and rushed out of the room.

Fats turned on me angrily. "Basch, sometimes you act like a marine at 'brain rest,' a retard. Teddy, finish up. I've got to talk to the poor woman saddled with young numbskull Basch."

When Berry came out of the Ladies', she looked like she'd been crying. Seeing Fats, she said, "How . . . how can you? It's disgusting."

"Yeah," said Fats, "it is. How can I? Well, Berry, when we get old and disgusting, who's gonna doctor us? Who's gonna care? Someone's got to do it. We can't just walk away." Looking sad, he said, "Seeing you react this way brings back just how disgusting it is. It's awful; we're forced to forget. So? So come on," he said, putting his thick arm around her shoulders, "come on into my office. I got a special stash of Dr Pepper. At times like this, a Dr Pepper helps."

They started for the on-call room, and I followed, saying, "Great case, Fats. You know, Berry, most people are like you and me, they hate shit, but Fats loves it. Going into GI work himself."

"Stop it, Roy," Berry snapped.

"When a GI man is looking up the barrel of a sigmoidoscope, you know what you got?"

"STOP IT! Go away. I want to talk with Fats alone."

"Alone? Why?"

"Never mind. Go away."

Angry and jealous, I watched them walk off, and I yelled after them, "You got shit looking at shit, that's what!"

Fats turned and angrily said, "Don't talk like that."

"Hurt your feelings, Fats?"

"No, but it hurts hers. You can't use our inside jokes with the ones outside all this, the ones like her."

"Sure you can," I said, "they need to see—"

"THEY DON'T!" yelled Fats. "They don't need to, and they don't want to. Some things have to be kept private, Basch. You think parents want to hear schoolteachers making fun of their kids? Use your damn head. You got a good woman here, and believe me they're not easy to find and keep, especially if you're a doctor. It makes me angry to see the way you treat her."

265

An hour later they paged me to come in. It felt like a military tribunal. Berry said she and Fats were worried about me, about my bitter sarcasm and rage.

"I thought you told me to express what I feel," I said.

"In words," said Berry, not in acts. Not in taking it out on patients and doctors—Fats told me about your rumor about Dr. Putzel."

"They'll get you, Roy," said Fats, "you'll get it in the neck."

"They can't do anything to me. They can't run the House without interns. I can do whatever I want. I'm indispensable. Invulnerable."

"It's dangerous. Externalization is a brittle defense."

"Here we go again," I said. "What's externalization?"

"Seeing the conflict as outside of you. The problem isn't outside of you, it's inside. When you see that, something's going to snap."

"That's the way it's gotta be, to survive."

"It's not. Look at Fats—he's got a healthy way of dealing with this incredible situation. He uses compassion, humor. He can laugh."

"I can laugh," I said, "I laugh too."

"No you don't. You scream."

"You're the one who used to call him cynical, sick. And he's the one who taught me to call these nice old people 'gomers.'"

"He hasn't killed off the caring part of himself. You have."

"Look," said Fats seriously, "let's stop, eh? We can't tell him what to do. If you can imagine it, last year I was a helluva lot worse than him, and nobody could tell me anything. Even last July I was worse. This year is yours, Roy. I know how it is—it's hell."

"This Putzel thing scares me," said Berry. "Why him?"

"Because every day he stands in front of his mirror, and straightening his bowtie, he says to himself: 'You know, Putzie-poops, you are one great physician. Not a good physician, no. A great physician.' I hate him. You think you're scared? You should see him. Shaking in his shoes! Ready to crack! HA!"

"It's not Putzel, it's you," said Berry. "You hate something inside of you. Get it?"

266

"I don't, and it's not. Fats knows what an asshole Putzel is."

"Don't do it, Roy," said Berry, "you'll only hurt yourself."

"Fats?"

"Putzel's a turkey," said Fats, "a money-grubbing, incompetent piece of *dreck.* True. But he's not the monster you make him out to be. He's a harmless wimp. I feel sorry for him. Lay off. Whatever you're planning, don't do it."

I did it. I'd given the rumor a week to gnaw on Putzel. My time had come. I found Putzel holding a Rose's hand, and I crept up in back of him. I whispered in his ear: "I've had it with you, Putzel. Within the next twenty-four hours, I swear it, I'm going to do you in."

Putzel leaped up off the bed, gave me a panic-stricken look, and ran out of the room. I walked out into the corridor and watched the little emperor of the bowel run, keeping his back to the walls and intermittently ducking into doorways as if he were afraid of a bullet, race off down the hall. I ambled off toward rounds.

I never made it. Two Bouncers from House Security attacked me, twisted my arms behind me, and carried me into the on-call room. They stood me up against the wall and frisked me for a weapon and sat me down facing Lionel, the Fish, Fats, and, quaking in a corner, Putzel. "Hey, what the hell's going on?" I asked. Everyone looked at Putzel until he said, "I heard a rumor about some intern was going to kill me and then . . . and then he whispered in my ear that in the next twenty-four hours he was going to do me in."

I waited until the silence had become unbearable and then in a calm voice I said, "What did you say?"

"You said you were going to . . . to do me in."

"Dr. Putzel," I asked incredulously, "have you gone mad?"

"You said it! I heard you say it! Don't deny it to me!"

I denied it to him, said that anyone who thought that an intern in the House of God would threaten to kill a Private Doctor of the House of God had gone mad and told the Bouncers to let me go.

"No! Don't let him go!" screamed Putzel, hugging the wall like a terrified maniac.

"Look," I said, "I'm just an intern trying to do my job. I can't take responsibility for that nut. See you later, eh?"

"NO! NOOooo!" wailed Putzel, rolling his eyes like a nut.

"What do you think we should do?" the Bouncers asked the Fish.

"I don't know," said the Fish. "Fats?"

"I've never seen anything like this," said Fats. "One thing's for sure: Dr. Putzel is acting mighty strange."

"It's the strangest thing," said the Leggo, as I sat in his office, which was the only place they'd decided it was safe to send me, "yes, the strangest . . ." and he drifted off into that place out his window where the answers to strange things might be found. "I mean, you didn't in fact threaten to kill—no, of course you didn't!" said the Leggo, his consternation turning his horrific birthmark even more purple.

"How could I have, sir?"

"Exactly. It's extraordinary."

"Can I speak in confidence?"

"Fire away," he said, bracing himself for yet another shock.

"To me, this means that Dr. Putzel is a sick man."

"Sick? A House Private sick, Roy?"

"Overworked. Needs a rest. And who doesn't, sir? Who doesn't?"

The Chief paused, as if perplexed, and then brightened and came up with the answer: "Why, no one doesn't. No one doesn't at all. I'll tell Dr. Putzel he needs a rest just like everyone else. Thanks, Roy, and keep right on in there plugging."

"Plugging? For what?"

"For what? Why . . . why, for the Awards. Yes, keep plugging for the Awards."

I felt good. Maybe I even felt grand. My only twinge of regret was that I had stepped out on my own, leaving behind Berry and Fats, the ones who claimed to care, the ones I'd counted on to save me.

17

It was all the rage, that Watergate March, and many Great Americans took the opportunity to explode. Jane Doe, bloated and floated by the infusion of the VA antibiotic, started with a little squeeping fart caught on the Fat Man's alert stopwatch, and then, with the rest of us watching, went on to rage at us with a great cacophony of orchestrated farts and then liquid farts and finally a blasting of her bowels and a continual gushing of what seemed like eternal stool. Richard Nixon, bloated by power and doubt, started with a little bark when named by Judge Sirica as an unindicted co-conspirator of the Watergate Boys, and went on to rage in a farting cornucopia on national TV, convincing almost every Great American by his overreaction and gushing paranoiac railing at other Great Americans that he was as guilty as anyone had imagined. We were all much relieved that no matter what else, we'd all have Nixon to laugh at and kick around for quite a good while longer. In some ways, after Vietnam, it was just what the country needed: a President so lacking in grace.

In Gomer City, we terns exploded as well. First to go was Eat My Dust Eddie. Bent under his own sadomasochism, he broke. He took himself OTC on every gomer until his service was being run by his BMS, and Eddie would talk about gomers only in terms of "How can I hurt this guy today?" or "Some of them want us to kill them and some of them don't, and I wish they'd make up their minds 'cause it gets confusing." The BMS couldn't stand the strain and soon gave in to Eddie's perverted thoughts, and one day when a particularly recalcitrant gomere shrieked PO-LICE! PO-LICE! for several hours, Eddie and his BMS borrowed uniforms and appeared at the bedside and said, "Yes, madam, this is Patrolman Eddie and Officer Katz. What can we do to help?"

"Why are you tormenting them?" Fats would ask.

" 'Cause they're tormenting me," Eddie would say, "they've got me on my knees, do you hear me? ON MY KNEES!"

When his wife started to have labor pains, all hell broke loose. The day his wife delivered, Eddie showed up dressed in his black motorcycle gear: hat and boots and black wraparound reflecting sunglasses and black leather jacket with

***

EAT MY DUST
EDDIE
***

in silver studs on the back, and went around to see his gomers with his flash camera taking portraits "to remember them by." The place came apart. Terrified, the gomers began to shriek. The ward began to sound and smell like a zoo. Every House Hierarchy sent a representative and we found Eddie sitting calmly in the on-call room, boots up on the desk, grinning ear to ear and reading *Rolling Stone*. To any inquiries all he would say was, "They've broken me. I'm OTC." Later, when he asked me if I thought he was being unreasonable, against my better judgment, thinking of what he'd said to me when I was banging on the elevator door, I said, "Unreasonable? Ha! I think you were giving them just what they always deserved."

"He's crazy," I said to Fats.

"Yeah. Delusional. A paranoid psychosis. It's terrible to watch. Ah, well, Basch, they'll have to give him a rest."

"They can't," I said. "There's no one to fill in for him."

"No one doesn't need a rest," said the Leggo to the Fish, as they discussed what to do about Eddie. "No one at all. Why, look at poor Dr. Putzel. I'll tell Eddie he needs a rest just like everyone else."

"And who will fill in for him?" asked the Fish.

270

"Who? Why, the others. My boys will all pitch in and help."

The next day Eddie was not at the cardflip, and when I called him at home he said, "I'm OTC for a while. I'm sorry to do this to you guys, but the Leggo won't let me back into the House. He thinks if I stayed there any longer I might kill one of the gomers and the House would get sued. He might just be right."

"Yeah," I said, "let's face it: you were getting close."

"Wouldn't be a bad idea, though, would it?"

"It's illegal. How's the baby?"

"Oh, you mean the gomere?" Eddie said.

"The gomere?"

"Yeah, the gomere: incontinent of feces and urine, unable to walk or talk, not oriented, and sleeping in restraints at night. The gomere. Room 811. I don't know how she is 'cause they won't let me into the House to see her."

"They won't let you see your own baby?"

"Yeah. I told them I wanted to take some pictures and they took away my camera, so I'm temporarily OTC with my own baby gomere, too."

The Fish told Hooper and me that to pitch in and help take up the slack created by Eddie's snapping, he and the Leggo had decided that we would be on call every other night for our last weeks on Gomer City but that we get special consideration.

"Oh, Christ," I said, "I hope it's not 'the toughies' again."

"Not the toughies," said the Fish. "The 'preferential treatment.' "

Preferential treatment was being skipped in the admission rotation once per day. This sounded good until it turned out that skipping a daytime admission resulted in our being awakened at three A.M. for the gomer beelining it in from the Mt. St. Elsewhere via the Grenade Room to Gomer City, courtesy of Marvin and the Blazers. Every other night, this three-A.M. special was the worst. After a week of the preferential treatment Humberto and Teddy and I were going almost as mad as Eddie. Teddy was first to go. His ulcer had started to act up. Muttering something about "the cramps," or maybe "the camps," he left.

Next to go, for me, was Molly. Strained by Gomer City, my

thing with Molly had been fading for months, and when the preferential treatment had me on call for thirty-six hours and off for twelve, outside the House all I did was sleep. Once in a while I'd see Molly on the upstairs ward, and it was clear that she was losing interest in me. One day I found Howard helping her to make up a bed. I was shocked. Hot oil and myrrh for Howie? I asked Molly what was going on.

"Well, yes, I've been seeing Howard Greenspoon. He's the tern on this ward now. I guess I can't understand you anymore, Roy."

"What do you mean?"

"You've become so cynical. You make fun of these poor patients."

"Everyone makes fun of these poor patients."

"Not Howard Greenspoon. He treats them with respect. I mean, it's like you're making fun of what I do. Remember how you walked out of that arrest on the man dying from multiple myeloma?"

"Yeah, but it was a big mess."

"Maybe, but Howard stayed right until the end."

"Howie? You and me used to make fun of Howie!" I said.

"Maybe so, but people change, you know. Look: I've had to work hard to get where I am. I can't help it if things always came easy to you, and you just coasted into medicine. When you were getting patted on the head, I was getting whacked by the nuns. Do you know how big and scary a nun all in black is to a little girl? Probably not. Well, Howard says he does."

"He does?" I said, thinking maybe Howie wasn't a dumb *shnook* after all.

"He certainly does. He's sincere. No one could call you that."

"So I've got to hand in my gold cleats, eh?"

"Oh, Roy," she said, remembering the loving, snuggling up to me, "I don't know. I still care. I guess it depends on what Howie says."

Jesus! My myrrh depended on Howie! Howie, the tern who felt like a hero every time he put a feeding tube down someone's demented grandmother, who puffed up with pride when he marched into an elevator filled with nondoctors and heard the whispers, "There's one of them, a doctor." Howie, who bought the fantasy that doctors weren't just people, doctors were "better" people. Howie, who would woo Molly and do all those sexual things he'd only imagined doing, with Molly, and think he loved Molly and get back at his parents by marrying Molly the *shiksa* nurse and have three kids and then, and then, fifteen years down the pike when Molly awoke and realized that by marrying Howie she was only getting back at the nuns, and what the hell, why not fuck with the *macho* guy who came to repair her washer-dryer and why not leave Howie, and then, fifteen years down the pike, Howie, awakening to the notion that as a husband-father-lover he'd been screwed by his fanatic dedication to medicine and that even in medicine he couldn't "cure" anyone of anything, he'd check into the motel room alone and for the first time in his life, in shock, have to haggle out his one real decision: whether or not to peg out painlessly with the five grams of phenobarb he'd lifted from the hospital pharmacy when he'd found out that his wife and kids had left. Should I fight? Should I challenge Howie for Molly? Nah, it was too much of an effort now, and she was right: I'd become too cynical, too destructive for her.

Hyper Hooper and I cried differently from Eat My Dust. Although death and Hooper were still going steady and with Eddie on a pitstop at home Hooper was racing even harder for the Black Crow, under the stress of Gomer City Hooper had begun acting like a gomer. He'd gotten thin, almost scrawny, and neglected his personal hygiene. He began to rock, like a schizophrenic or an old Jew at prayer. Having lost his wife, he was now losing his pathologist. On occasion I'd find him sleeping next to Jane Doe in an armchair recliner, mouth in O SIGN, and when the Fish insisted we go on walk rounds, Hooper would slip into a wheelchair and wheel himself around, singing Jane's chromatic scale. If the Fish reprimanded him, he'd turn and say, "Physician, wheel thyself." The real problem arose when Hooper took to sleeping in the electric gomer beds in restraints, and one day when I came in and found him in an ankle cast and asked him what had happened, he said only GOMERS GO TO GROUND. He'd done just that, fracturing a small bone in his ankle, which enabled him to make rounds in his wheelchair every day.

Our final explosion took place at one Sociable C. Rounds.

Rocking, chattering, punning, laughing, Hooper and I managed to blast every House Hierarchy. We fought with Lionel over perverted Sam, the Man Who Ate Everything, who, when we'd found him eating our food stashes day after day, we'd TURFED directly out to the icy street, and refused to readmit. The Blazers had readmitted him to floor eight, trying to convince us to take him back. When Selma, amazed, asked Lionel who was taking care of him, with his diabetes and his sexual perversions, Lionel had said, "We are, the staff of HELP." "You?" asked Selma. "HELP is treating his diabetes? That's illegal." I perked up and said, "From what I know of those petunias in HELP, Selma, they may not know how to treat his diabetes, but they sure as hell will get off on his perversions." Lionel got up to storm out, and lying down on my back in his path, I cried out, "Help, Selma, heelllp! I looked up, and all I saw was Blue Blazers!" We antagonized Salli and Bonni for stopping Eddie's TURF of the Lady of the Lice—he'd neglected to put down on her three-part placement form who would meet her in St. Louis—mentioning in passing the word "cunts," which sent both of them and our female BMS flying out of the room. Finally the meeting turned to mayhem when Hooper and I began rocking in synch and muttering "auto-eroticism, the only way." The Fish, eyes popping like a red snapper's, took charge and organized a STAT field trip to Chinatown for lunch.

How could we have known that during our happy Chinese lunch a rumble had begun in the House of God, and that this rumble had already begun feeding into older, deeper rumbles within the Leggo, our Chief. Each affronted Hierarchy had given the Leggo a buzz, and he was enraged. Returning to the House, fat and happy, imagine our surprise when we saw the Leggo appear at the far end of the corridor, rolling toward us. As he came closer and closer, we could see that he had a smile on his face that no one had ever seen before. Trembling, the Fish turned to Hooper and me and said, "You better watch out, guys, you're really going to get it." Amazed and surprised, Hooper and I stared at each other. In his eyes was reflected my own incomprehension: why would the Leggo get us? What was so bad about what we had done?

The House of God

We braced ourselves for the shock. The stiff legs moved closer, the raging smile spread wider until it looked as if it would split the tight face open and spill whatever hid under that purple birthmark right out onto the floor of Gomer City. When he was so close I could read the brand name on his stethoscope as it ducked down into the jungle of his genitals, in a bizarre fashion that might have been the MSG in the Chinese food, not one but two arms swiveled and two long hands reached out and came to rest on two scapulae, one of the Fat Man and one of the Fish. Staring at them, the Leggo demanded: "Who is responsible? Someone is responsible for these poor interns, for this disaster of a ward. It is my job to find out who. You two, come with me."

"It took all I had," said Fats afterward, "but I did manage to finesse him, at least most of him. Logically, he was trapped. He had two choices: take it out on you terns, or take it out on the ones responsible for you terns. Having already lost Eddie, it was clear that he couldn't take it out on you. He had to take it out on those responsible. While I may be responsible for you, it is also true that the Fish is responsible for me, and guess who's responsible for the Fish?"

"The Chief."

"Exactly. So he was stuck. I managed to finesse that part, the logic, but I couldn't finesse what the Leggo felt. You see, the Leggo didn't mind what you'd done to the Lady of the Lice, or to Sam the hungry pervert, Putzel, the Blazers, the Nurses, the BMSs, to Tina or Harry or Jane or the Roses that Hooper keeps killing. He didn't even mind your setting House records for lowest temperature in a living human being, most organs hit with a single needle shot, or most tests of the bowel run in a single night. In many ways, he thought you'd done a terrific job, especially as regards postmortems. But the thing that he was bullshit about was you guys not liking him. He can't stand your being cool toward him. He suspects you even make fun of him behind his back—imagine that. When you show him you don't like him, you hit a nerve, and when that happens, he goes ape. No one can finesse the ape." Pensively Fats went on, "Of course, for my share of the responsibility, he's delaying

275

writing my Fellowship Letter again. I keep worrying that it'll be Samoa. The last thing he said to me was, 'Whatever you boys do, don't do anything else. Do nothing, understand?' Imagine him saying that to me."

"You told him, of course," I said, "that doing nothing was your greatest invention, the delivery of medical care?"

"Right. Why stop at Samoa. Go for broke and get the Gulag."

Fats fell silent. Hooper left, and I asked Fats what was on his mind. "Well, maybe this is more serious than I think. Maybe this is trouble. All the way from Brooklyn, all those exams and scrabbling, all that effort to land me here in the bigtime, on the verge of the big Hollywood 'Hello Fats!' and I just had the thought that maybe it'll all fall down. I don't like it. This may be good-bye L.A., good-bye dreams. Sometimes it seems like it just doesn't pay, does it, Basch?"

"Does what?"

"To imagine. To dream."

Potts stood before me in the darkness of two A.M. in Gomer City, and mirrored in his gray face was, as always, the Yellow Man.

"What are you doing here at this hour?" I asked, but he didn't reply, he just stood there staring. Again I asked what was going on.

"The Yellow Man just died."

I felt a chill. Potts looked white and chill, and his eyes looked dull and dead, and I said, "I'm sorry. I mean, I'm really sorry."

"Yeah," said Potts, fidgeting as if he wasn't really in the same world with me any longer, "yeah, well, he was going to die, it was just a matter of . . . of time."

"Yeah, he was," I said, and I thought about how much torment Potts had gone through every day that the Yellow Man had been alive. "Are you all right?"

"Who, me? Oh, yeah, I am. It's just a little hard . . . I didn't ask for a post. I didn't want to get one," said Potts, almost pleading with me that it was all right.

"It's OK. I know how you feel. I didn't ask for a post on Dr. Sanders. Sit down and talk about it, eh?"

"No, I think I'll just go upstairs and see him once more and then maybe take a walk."

"Right. I'll be down here if you change your mind."

"Thanks. You know, I should have given him the steroids."

"Stop it. Nothing would have helped."

"Yeah, well, steroids might have helped. Well, anyway, we sure had some fun the other night with Otis, didn't we?"

"Sure did, Wayne. We'll do it again, eh?"

"Yeah. Soon. If I can find the time."

As I watched him slip away down the corridor and disappear into the up elevator, I thought of the fun we'd had. I'd gone over to his house, and although it was depressing with the place a mess and with that loaded revolver by the bed, Potts and I had taken Otis out for a run in the March chill, and we'd talked about the South. Potts had told me about Mrs. Bagley's Dancing Class held at the country club every Friday night. Mrs. Bagley, an immigrant, would come out in a chiffon dress with a cinched waist and pop the needle into the groove and out would come the Charelles. They learned to dance pressing a walnut between their noses, and the big event, year after year, was on the last Friday night when Potts and his less tame but still Old Family buddies would roll B-B pellets onto the polished oak floor during a slam-banging one two three one two three Roll Out the Barrel polka. I'd thought it strange, that day, that Potts hadn't even mentioned his father's recent violent death.

I realized suddenly what was going to happen! Fool! I ran to the elevator and pounded on it, but it wasn't moving, and I raced up the stairs to floor eight, and I kept cursing myself for not realizing it in time and praying that I had or that I was wrong.

I was not wrong. While I'd been cradled in my reminiscences of Mrs. Bagley's, Potts had taken the elevator straight to floor eight, had opened a window, and had thrown himself out to his death. From the window I saw the splattered mess on the parking lot below, and in between my panting for breath and shivering in the chill draft I heard the first siren squeal, and I leaned my forehead on the sill, and I sobbed.

* * *

"Did he leave a note?" asked Berry.

"Yeah. It was pinned to the Yellow Man, and it said, 'Feed the cat.' There was no cat."

"What did it mean?"

"It was meant for Jo. When Potts and Chuck and I were together with Jo upstairs, Jo kept niggling Potts to take better care of his patients, to 'feed the cat.' Jo said that if Potts had been on his toes, the Yellow Man mightn't have died." I found myself thinking of Potts as a tragic figure, a guy who'd been a happy towheaded kid you'd love to take fishing with you, who'd mistakenly invested in academic medicine when he'd have been happy in his family business, and who'd become a splattered mess on the parking lot of a hospital in a city he'd despised. What had been the seductiveness of medicine? Why? "They killed him."

"Who did?" asked Berry.

"Jo, the Fish, the others . . ."

While most of us in the House felt empty and didn't know what to say or do, others had definite ideas. Jo, perhaps thinking of her own pop's leap from a bridge to his death, raised the question of the postmortem exam "to find out if there had been any organic precipitant." The Fish talked to us in a heartfelt way about how "suicide is always an existential alternative." The Leggo seemed upset, puzzled that one of his boys, especially one who he'd thought had loved him more than most, had killed himself. He talked about "the pressures of the internship year" and about "the waste of a great talent." The Leggo reassured us that he wanted to give us some time off to mourn. However, he could not do this. In fact, we'd have to all work a little harder, to fill in: "You'll all have to pitch in and help."

Like many other events in the House of God, this response from our leaders seemed so crass as to be imagined. If imagined, however, it had been imagined by us all. No one mentioned how the House Medical Hierarchy had tormented Potts with the Yellow Man, how it had ignored his pain. We tried hard to forget Potts fast, but for the longest time we could not, for every day when we parked our cars in the parking lot we saw and tried our hardest to avoid the little blotchy discoloration on the asphalt. None of us wanted to run over Potts with our cars, even if he was already dead. At first there was good reason to avoid the blotch, for there was real blood there and bits of hair and bone stuck to the thawing asphalt. As we tried to avoid it, the parking problem increased, and the House sent out some of Housekeeping to scrub it off. Try as they might, although they washed away the hair and bone, they had a lot of trouble washing away the discoloration. Sure it got lighter and lighter, but the hooker was that it also got spread wider and wider over the lot so that it became more and more difficult to avoid it, and we all felt, every day, that we were scrambling to avoid parking on Potts. Everyone tried to park on the perimeter of the lot. Some showed up early so as not to have to park in the middle. All in all it was a worse reminder than before they had spread Potts around. Each of us took the nebulous and faint discoloration and created out of it first an image of bone and blood and bits of hair, and then an image of Potts falling, and then of Potts leaping out, and finally, sadly, of Potts alive, and then, the last, of Potts alive and being crushed by guilt for not having given the Yellow Man the roids. Thinking how they had tormented Potts until he had "bought it," we got mad, for many of us thought that of all of us, Potts, with his compassion and gentleness, might have become a wonderful doc. Of all of us, he was dead. Outrageous.

"What's suicide about?" I asked Berry.

"Here," she said, drawing me to her, "put your head here. Close your eyes. What are you feeling?"

Blank. Then fury: "I'm pissed. I'm so furious I could kill!"

"That's what suicide's about. Under incredible pressure, alone, with no support from your bosses, most of you have found bizarre ways—this role labeling of Hooper with death and the Runt with sex—to project your anger outside yourselves. Potts didn't. He never acted strange, he never got mad. He took his rage and blasted himself. Introjection. The opposite of what you do, Roy."

"What do I do?"

"You rail at everything, you're sarcastic, and even though you're pretty obnoxious, it's the one way you've chosen to survive."

279

Survive? It was not at all certain that I would survive Gomer City. I didn't know much of anything anymore, but I knew that I was in big trouble and acting crazy and that I didn't really care.

Fats and I sat in the on-call room. In the air was death. Fats looked sad, and I asked him what he was thinking.

"Grenade Room Dubler and his HTE Service," he said.

"HTE Service?"

"Yeah. Hold the Elevator Service. When Dubler was here in Gomer City he got so fed up—so the rumor goes—that he knocked off the gomers at a terrific clip. He used intravenous KCL, 'cause it can't be detected at autopsy. Whenever he took the elevator down he'd shout out 'Hold the elevator!' and would wheel in a corpse, and ride down with it to the morgue. They say Dubler seldom made the trip down alone."

"WHAT? He knocked off the gomers?"

"Rumor, Basch, rumor."

We sat there together, my mind on this HTE Service and Saul the tailor and Wayne Potts. I felt numb. After a few minutes I looked up. The Fat Man was crying. Quiet tears filled his eyes, fat wet tears of desperation and loss. They rolled down his cheeks. He sat still, a hero overcome.

"Why are you crying?"

"Roy, I'm crying for Potts. And I'm crying for myself."

From far off I heard a tune in my head: not the bright thunderous Sousa march blared out by the trombones and crunched by the cymbals as the glittering marching band was led down the street by a miracle like Molly, no. No, seeing the Fat Man crying, the tune I heard was the one always played by a lone bugler and wafted out over a grassy knoll littered with alabaster slabs, heard by those weeping as the Kennedy widows and orphans had wept, a tune of an immense numb solitude, taps.

Saul the leukemic tailor was going through hell. Everyone, including the cheery oncologist who'd failed to cure his leukemia, had given up on him and was waiting for him to die. In coma, he was dying slowly, and could last for a long time. The

280

worst part was that he was in terrible pain, his poisoned bone marrow sending shocks and screams straight through his heart and head, and it all came out in moans and tears. Saul didn't shriek. Saul cried. It wasn't a natural, human crying, for several strokes had obliterated his human sleep cycle so that he never slept. The crying was continuous, animal, moans of pain, streaks of tears on cheeks. It was driving everyone mad. I hated it; I hated him.

Without much thought, raging inside, one night I snuck into the medicine cabinet, got the KCL and syringe, and made sure that no one saw me enter Saul's room. He lay there in his own feces, a mass of tubing and tape and bruises and rotted skin and empty bone poking through at the ribs and elbows and knees. I thought of what I was about to do. I stopped. The memory of Dr. Sanders' death rushed through me, and I saw him oozing blood and saying, "God this is awf . . ." and I heard Saul saying to me, "Finish me off, do I have to beg you? Finish me off!" I caught myself thinking of Potts. Saul screamed. Angrily I uncapped the syringe and found the IV outlet and pushed in enough KCL to kill him. I watched him gasp for breath as his heart depolarized, and I watched his breathing become laborious, and his hand give a little twitch, and then a stillness come over him, a peace, but for his agonal breathing, which seemed to last a long time. I put the light out and went to be somewhere by myself. I was paged by the night nurse. Saul was dead.

On St. Patrick's Day I was called down to the E.W. late at night as part of the preferential treatment that the Fish had invented to turn us into lunatics, and I was startled to see a sideshow row of what had to be the worst patients in the world: a dead nun being resuscitated by Chuck; a homosexual murderer TURFED in from prison who thought his tern, the Runt, despite his mustache, was a girl; two roommates who'd overdosed on heroin and were dying; many gomers. I picked up my admissions chart and headed for the Grenade Room. I wondered where Fats was but I didn't really care and I didn't have to wonder long, because I opened the door and saw Fats and Humberto and the two policemen in what looked like green uniforms because it was St. Paddie's Day and a gomere named what else but Rose, and with Fats and Humberto covered in vomit and feces and urine and blood.

"A greatandagrandgood evening tooyooo," said Gilheeny, drunkenly waving a shillelagh, "and itiz true that good officer Quick and I have been while on duty pouring Guinness stout into our bodies and are inebriated."

"For work is the curse of the drinkin' man," said Quick.

"And to cerribrate the Man Who Drove the Snakes from Ireland," said the redhead, "we have foundafittin Rose!"

With the help of the Fat Man and Humberto they hoisted the Rose up to a sitting position and I saw that they had pinned a green sign edged with shamrocks to her nightie, and the sign said:

KISS ME, I'M IRISH

I started to laugh and slipped on a turd and fell down in the doorway. I lay there in the filth, laughing, and the Fat Man came over to me and bent over me and waved a little test tube under my nose and said, "See this? This is all the urine she's made in five days, and half of this is the diuretic I gave her. Her bed has been sold forever. She's had five courses of electroshock therapy for depression, the last in 1947."

A shriek came from the gomere: REEE-REEE-REEEEE . . . and all I did, while they stared at me, was lie on the tile floor and laugh.

"Her neck is so stiff she can lie with her head off the bed and with no pillow, without pain," said Fats. "She is unresponsive to everything we've tried."

REEE-REEE-REEEEE . . .

And I lay on the floor and laughed.

"I stuck a tongue blade in her mouth, and she sucked on it so hard I still haven't been able to pull it out, and neither has anyone else. She has the strongest suck reflex in history, which means, of course, that there is no frontal-lobe function, no frontal-lobe function at all. And do you know why? Because she had a lobotomy in 1948. Ho! Ho! HOO!"

And I lay down and laughed and laughed.

"The ultimate gomere, and you, you ***MVI*** you, she's totally and completely yours! HOOOO!"

REEEE-REEEE-REEEEE . . .

And all I could do then, tears streaming down my cheeks, realizing that these gomers had won, that they had outlasted me and would survive in Gomer City after I'd gone in two weeks and left all of them to try to break my replacement, Howie, and all I could do, then, crying, was lie in the shit on the floor and laugh.

I couldn't laugh when I realized that Potts was gone and Dr. Sanders was still gone and Saul was gone and Molly was going with Howie and Eat My Dust Eddie was gonzo gone and Hyper Hooper was more or less gone and Teddy was gone and half of Teddy's stomach was gone and the Fat Man was soon really going a long way away from me on his Fellowship wherever, and that the only ones who weren't gone were the gomers. I had yet to see a gomer die in the House of God, unless it was with the aid of Hyper Hooper's needle shots or the dummies in dialysis who'd shrunk Fast Tina's brain down to the size of a pea and what the hell mistakes do happen don't they? Almost anyone I cared about was gone, exploded into a billion corpuscular fragments like a Great American Grenade might explode in Vietnam with the shrapnel raining down like confetti except that it wasn't at all like nice soft red white and blue confetti because it brought you to your knees and broke you and hurt you and left wounds that wouldn't heal and watery poisoned blood that wouldn't clot and would never wash out of your whites and images that wouldn't fade like the discoloration on the parking lot that had once been Wayne Potts. We were mostly gone, caught in a net of silence and pain where it might just be that the dead did lie, restless, and even in death fearing worse death or something worse.

I lay on top of my bed. Berry came in. I was silent. Berry sat on the edge of my bed and talked to me, but I was silent. I was not tired or sad or mad. She cradled my head in her lap and looked into my eyes and started to cry. She tried to leave. She came back a couple of times between the doorway and the bed and finally, hesitating at the door a final time like a mourner might hesitate before allowing the casket to be closed, she left. Her sad footsteps echoed down the stairs and died, and I did not feel sad. I was not tired or mad. I lay on top of my bed and did not sleep. I imagined I felt what the gomers felt: an absence of feeling. I had no idea how bad I might be, but I knew that I could not do what Dr. Sanders had told me to do, to "be with" others. I could not "be with" others, for I was somewhere else, in some cold place, insomniac in the midst of dreamers, farfar from the land of love.

III. THE WING OF ZOCK

*But how is the poor wretch to acquire the ideal
qualifications that he needs in his profession?*

—Sigmund Freud, *Analysis Terminable and Interminable*

18

I was ready to be taken over by machines. On the morning of April Fool's Day, I found myself just outside the hermetically sealed double doors of the MICU, the Medical Intensive Care Unit, what the Fat Man had called "that mausoleum down the hall." Like a suburbanite in a fugue state who starts out heading for Wall Street and turns up three days later, blank, in Detroit, I had no past or future, I was merely there. I felt scared. For the next month I would have to take responsibility for the intensive care of those perched precariously on the edge of that slick bobsled ride down to death. I would be on call every other night, alternating with the resident. A bronze wall plaque caught my eye: THROUGH THE MUNIFICENCE OF MR. AND MRS. G. L. ZOCK, 1957. Zock, of the Wing of Zock? When would I meet a real Zock? With the technocratic dispassion of an astronaut, I pushed through the double doors, sealing myself hermetically in.

The inside was ultraquiet, ultraclean, ultraunbusy. MUZAK shirred the crisp atmosphere as gently as a French chef might shir a sleepy egg for an early-rising guest. I wandered through the deserted eight-bed unit, searching for intensive care. The patients were in their beds, quiet, at peace, at home with all they touched in this calm sea, happy fishes floating, floating. I found myself happily humming along with the MUZAK: "Some enchanted eeee-veniiiinng . . ." and stopped in front of a computer console, which filled me with a mixture of awed childhood memories of Cape Canaveral and adolescent fears stirred up by *2001*. I watched the bright lights blink, the oscilloscope flicker with what looked like something like rows of heartbeats. As I watched, there was an unpleasant buzz from the console, lights flashed, one of the rows of beats froze in space and time, and like ticker tape, out spewed the pink blue-gridded tongue of an EKG strip. At that, from a nearby room, out spewed a nurse. She looked at the EKG, looked at the oscilloscope screen, did not look at the patient, and with a mixture of pique and cajolery said to the console, "Shit, Ollie, wake up and get it together, will you, for Chrissakes?" As if for punishment, she poked a few keys *fortissimo*, which sent the thing humming along again, almost in syncopation with the fresh aria from MUZAK, a samba: "When they begin, the bee-geeene . . ."

Relieved to see a warm-blooded being in this freaky reptilian lab, I turned to her and said, "Hi I'm Roy Basch."

"The new tern?" she asked suspiciously.

"Right. What's this thing?"

"Thing? Not hardly. He's Ollie, the Computer. Ollie, say hi to Roy Basch, the new tern here," and with a few prompting punches in the vital parts, Ollie spewed out a pink blue-gridded tongue of an EKG strip, on which was printed: HI, ROY, AND WELCOME, I'M OLLIE. I asked the nurse where I could put my things, and she said to follow her. She was dressed in a green cotton operating-room wraparound, open in the back from neck nape to lumbar-4, that region of the back where the spine begins to make a delicious *contrappunto* curve into what used to be a tail, and what now begins the beegeeene of the fullness of the upper insertion of the *gluteus maximus*, the ass. As she walked, her spine traced imaginary curves in the MICU space. How fitting, I thought, that these firm young muscles, bathed in MUZAK, should dance together so perfectly in neurophysiological synch.

> . . . There's nothing more magnificent than the human body and by now you are an expert in dealing with it . . .

The small staff room was filled with nurses, doughnuts, and

gossip. My arrival punctured the bubble of chat, and out leaked silence. Then Angel, the Angel of the Runt, stood up, came over to me, gave me a hug, and said, "I want to"—gesture toward me—"introduce Roy Basch, the medical intern. I told"—gesture toward nurses—"them about"—gesture toward me—"you. We're"—gesture toward heaven—"glad you're"—gesture toward earth—"here. Wanna"—gesture toward doughnuts—"doughnut?"

I chose cream-filled. Forgetting work, I eased into this friendly group, relieved that things were so relaxed. I flipped my mind-flop to OFF.

The gossip was about the resident in charge of the Unit, Jo. In the weeks she'd been there, Jo had amazed, frightened, and ultimately antagonized the nurses, in that archaic pattern still so familiar when women doctors worked with women nurses. Although Jo usually started her own pre-rounds rounds before usual, on this particular day she was nowhere to be seen.

"She spent all last night—her night off—here," said a nurse. "She sat up with Mrs. Pedley, wondering why Pedley was still alive. And the only thing wrong with Pedley, really, is Jo's treatment of her. She must have overslept. Will she be mad!"

Jo came in sizzling. She looked at me suspiciously, remembering our debacle when Chuck and the Runt and I had tormented her on the upstairs ward, but she stuck out her jaw and stuck out her hand and said, "Hi, Roy. Welcome aboard. Never mind what happened upstairs, you'll like it here. It's high-powered medicine. Tight ship, the tightest ship in the whole House. Fresh start. No gripes, no hard feelings, eh?"

"No hard feelings, Jo," I said.

"Good. Cardiology's my specialty, I'm going on my Fellowship to the NIH in Bethesda in July, so stick with me and you'll learn an incredible amount. In the Unit, we've got total control of all cardiac parameters. It's high-pressure, but if we work hard, we save lives, and we have good fun. Let's go."

Just as Jo, the head nurse, and I were wheeling the chart rack to the first room, in skipped Pinkus, the Consultant to the Unit, ready to start his teaching rounds. Pinkus was a tall, emaciated-looking Staff cardiologist, heading toward forty. A TURF from the U. of Arizona to the BMS and the House of

God, Pinkus was a legend, fanatic in his personal and professional life. Pinkus, it was said, rarely left the House. I myself had seen him, night after night, prowling the corridors, in the guise of following up consults on cardiac patients. Whatever the hour, I had found him patient, helpful, courteous, ready to produce an article, ready to put in a pacemaker, ready to chat. Such was his dedication to being in the House that an apocrypha had arisen about his home life: married, with three daughters, it was rumored that the only way that his wife or daughters knew he'd been home was to notice the toilet seat flipped to the UP mode.

The other part of Pinkus' fanaticism was his obsession with cardiac-risk factors. Smoking, coffee, obesity, high blood pressure, saturated fats, cholesterol, and lack of exercise were like death to him. Rumored at one time to have been sedentary, anxious, overweight, stuffing doughnuts and slurping coffee, Pinkus now through much effort, was on the verge of emaciation, was phobic to cholesterol, and had run himself into incredible shape, for the past two years finishing close to the time of three hours in the April Marathon. Somehow Pinkus had managed to reduce the final risk-factor variable, personality type. In a total turnabout, he'd gone from Type A (anxious) to Type B (calm).

Pinkus and Jo, in a short excoriation of the fuck-up of rounds times, had reached the decision that on this day all rounds would be one rounds, beginning at once. Despite more pressing problems, both Pinkus and Jo were interested in the woman Jo had spent the night with, Pedley. A pleasant seventy-five, Pedley had been TURFED into the House by Putzel, for the usual, the bowel run, for complaints of burping and farting after Chinese food. The bowel run had been negative. Unfortunately, some red-hot noticed on the screening EKG that Pedley was walking around in V Tach, according to the textbooks, a "lethal arrythmia." Whisked by a nervous tern in the MICU, Pedley had fallen prey to Jo, who'd taken one look at the EKG, decided Pedley was dying, and had hooked up the electrodes of the cardioverter, and without anesthetic had burned the skin off Pedley's chest. Pedley's heart, affronted at having been jolted into normal sinus rhythm, stayed there for only a few minutes and reverted to the beat of its own drummer, V Tach. Frantic, Jo scorched Pedley's chest four more times before Pinkus arrived and stopped the barbecue. For the past week Pedley had remained in V Tach. Except for the festering burns on her chest, she was fine, a LOL in NAD. Pinkus and Jo, sniffing a publishable article, had employed Pinkus' fund of expertise: cardio-pharmaco-therapeutics. Pedley had been put on every cardiac drug, to no avail, and by the time I arrived Pinkus was into drugs only he would dare use, ranging from remedies for such noncardiac diseases as systemic lupus erythrematosis (an autoimmune disorder) to *tinea pedis* (athlete's foot). Pedley, held prisoner and suffering the side effects of these meds, wanted out. Daily, Pinkus and Jo would coerce Pedley into a trial of something new. That day it was "Norplace," a derivative of the grease used to stick Ollie's EKG monitor leads to a patient's thorax.

"Hello, dearie, how's the gal today?" asked Pinkus.

"I want to go home. I feel fine, young man. Let me go."

"Do you have a hobby, dear?" asked Pinkus.

"You ask me that every day," said Pedley, "and every day I tell you: my hobby is my life outside of here. If I had known that Chinese food would lead to this, I'd never have called Putzel. Wait'll I get my hands on him—he won't visit me, you know. He's scared of me."

"My hobbies are running and fishing," said Pinkus. "Running for fitness and fishing for calm. I heard you had Jo worried last night."

"She's worried, I'm not. Let me go."

"There's a new medicine I wish you'd try today, dear," said Pinkus.

"No more medicines! That last one had me thinking I was a fourteen-year-old girl again in Billings, Montana. I came in here in good faith, and you're giving me trips to Montana! No more meds for Pedley!"

"This one will work."

"There's nothing wrong with me for it to work on!"

"Please, Mrs. Pedley, try it for us," pleaded Jo sincerely.

"Only if you get me some fish chowder for lunch."

"Done," said Jo, and we left.

291

In the hallway, Pinkus turned to me and said, "It's important to have a hobby, what's yours, Roy?"

Before I had a chance to answer, Jo whipped our caravan forward again. Of the other five patients, none could speak. Each suffered in the throes of some horrible, incurable, lingering disease that would almost certainly kill, usually involving major organs like heart, lung, liver, kidney, brain. The most pathetic was a man who'd started with a pimple on his knee. Without culturing it, his House Private, Duck's Ass Donowitz, had given him the wrong antibiotic, which had eradicated the bacteria that were containing the spread of the resistant *staph* in the pimple, allowing the *staph* to spread, producing total body sepsis, and turning a happy forty-five-year-old successful broker into an epileptic, mute, debilitated skeleton who could not speak because of the hole that had rotted through the cartilage of his trachea from his months on a respirator. In our rounds, he looked at me, dumbfounded and terrified, pleading to be saved. His only hope now would be the hope of a dream, his only solace, dreamsolace, a time when his dream of his voice, of his full life, would comfort him until the daily awakening to the nightmare of his crushed life. It was obvious malpractice by Donowitz. No one had told the man who'd started with the pimple on his knee that he could sue for millions. At his doorway, I heard his story from Jo in clipped dispassionate argot like Ollie's. I saw his eyes fasten on me, a newcomer, someone who might bring a miracle, asking me to give him back his voice, his Saturday-afternoon game of squash, his piggyback rides under his kids. I was overwhelmed. As if by fate, with a little help from an incompetent and lazy doc, a man's life had taken a sharp permanent turn down. I turned my head away. I never wanted to look into those mute eyes again.

He was not alone. Four more times I was shaken by the horror of ruined life. One after the other, totally immobilized, lungs run by respirators, hearts run by pacemakers, kidneys run by machines, brains run barely, if at all. It was terrible. The smell was that of lingering death: sickly-sour, feverish, sliding away far off on a horizon I could barely see. I didn't want any part of it. I would not touch these putrid ones, no. It was all too sad for me.

Not for Jo. At each room she riffled her three-by-five cards and rattled off numbers, and then had the nurse hoist the body up to sitting, so she could listen to the chest. Pinkus looked distractedly out the window, unable to ask or tell about hobbies, and I felt dead inside. Jo asked me didn't I want to listen to their chests, and reflexively, I did. The last was a second-year BMS student who, while on a pediatrics rotation, had caught a cold from a kid, which turned into a cough, then a flu, then a something beyond the realm of the known or the treatable that had hit his lungs, heart, liver, and kidneys and left him driven by respirator, pacemaker, and kidney machine. Despite this, despite the MICU's "4-plussing" him—going all-out—he was dying. The stubble on his cheeks was blond. Jo had the nurse hoist him up, put her stethoscope on him, and motioned for me to join in. I said I'd pass.

"What?" asked Jo, surprised. "Why?"

"I'm afraid of catching what he caught," I said, leaving.

"What? You're a physician, you've got to. Come back here."

"Jo, get off my back, huh?"

Later, Pinkus and I went down to lunch, leaving Jo to tend to the Unit. Pinkus always "brown-bagged" it—brought his own—so he could regulate his diet while in the House. As he picked gently at his cottage cheese, alfalfa, and fresh fruit, he inquired first about my hobbies, telling me his were running for fitness and fishing for calm, and second about my attitude toward the cardiac-risk factors. In one lunchtime I learned more about how I was destroying my life, narrowing my coronary arteries, falling prey to the endemic atherosclerosis sweeping America, than I'd learned in four years at the BMS. Pinkus suggested that, given my clear family history, I had an obligation to exert as much control as possible over my cardiac destiny, by refraining from eating what I liked (doughnuts, ice cream, coffee), smoking what I liked (cigarettes, cigars), doing what I liked (lazing around), and feeling what I felt (anxious).

"Even coffee?" I asked, not aware of this risk factor.

"Cardiac irritant. Latest *Green Journal*. Work done right here at the BMS by intern Howard Greenspoon."

Finally, after a lengthy discussion of running, informing me that he was up to sixty miles a week at present in preparation for the Marathon in three weeks, Pinkus invited me to his office to feel his legs. We adjourned there, where he directed my examination. From the waist up, he was toothpickoid; from the waist down, Mr. Olympia. His *quadriceps*, hamstrings, and calves were sleek and rippling, fastened to tendons of steel.

Returning to the MICU, repulsed by the disease and boggled by the machines, I had an urge to escape. Jo cornered me, insisting that I learn how to pop a big needle into the radial artery of the wrist, a brutal, dangerous, and more or less unnecessary procedure. After that, I escaped as far as the staff room, saying I had to read up on the patients. I picked up the chart of the BMS with the total body wipe-out of unknown etiology, and started to read. He'd started with a sore throat, a cough, a cold, a slight fever. I had a sore throat, a cough, a cold, a slight fever. My red throat was a plowed field, getting a viral seeding from the BMS. I would catch what he had. I would die. I looked around me and realized it was the nursing change of shift. The nurses came in in their street clothes and used an alcove off the staff room, where there were lockers, to change. Since there was a mad crush at about three, when everyone rushed in, there were too many nurses for the alcove, and with a nonchalance, a few spilled out into the room, slipping out of their blouses and skirts or jeans, radiating the light of their bras and panties and other undies into the staff room, and then wrapping around the green cotton MICU uniform. Even the braless ones would spill out and change in my sight, smiling at my gawking, and I was thrilled with that ease of body I'd grown to know so well, that was somehow connected with doctors and nurses who dealt, day after day, with the decay of other human flesh.

I left. As I drove through the chill April rain, my mind stuck on the Unit. What about it had been so different?

Quintessence. That was it. The Unit was the quintessence. There, after all the sorting had been done, lay the closest rep-

294

resentation, in living terms, of death. That was to have been expected. That was the bronze Zock plaque on the wall. And there, also, lay the closest representation, in living terms, of sex. I could not fail to notice. I did not pretend to understand. Amidst the dying, these nurses were flaunting life.

Berry asked me how it had been, and I told her that it had been different, high-powered, kind of like being part of the manned space program, but that it was also like being in a vegetable garden, only the vegetables were human. I was down about it because of course they were young and would die, but that didn't matter because I too was going to die from whatever tropical virus had attacked the little BMS. Berry suggested that my fear of dying was yet another "medical-student disease" and that she was more worried about my heart. Thinking of Pinkus, I said, "Oh, yeah, how'd you know I was going to key more on controlling my cardiac-risk factors?"

"No, I don't mean the mechanics, I mean the feelings. It's been weeks since Potts's suicide, and you haven't said anything about it. It's as if it didn't happen."

"It happened. So?"

"So he was a damn good friend of yours and now he's dead."

"I can't think about it. I got a new job to do, in the Unit."

"Amazing. In spite of everything that happens, there's no past."

"What's that supposed to mean?"

"You and the other interns obliterate each day, in order to start the next one. Forget today today. Total denial. Instant repression."

"Big deal. So what about it?"

"So nothing ever changes. Personal history and experience mean nothing. There's no growth. Unbelievable: all across the country, interns are going through this, and going on each day as if nothing had happened the day before. 'Forget it; all is forgiven; come home; love, the Medical Hierarchy.' It rolls on, greater than anyone's suicide. That's what makes a doctor. Terrific."

"I don't see what's so wrong with that."

"I know you don't. That's what's so wrong. It isn't the medical skills you learn, it's the ability to wake up the next day as if nothing had happened the day before, even if what happened is a friend killing himself."

"There's a helluva lot new to learn in the Unit. I can't afford to think about Potts."

"Stop it, Roy—you're not some dumb clod, you're a person."

"Look, I'm not your red-hot intellectual anymore. I'm just a guy out to learn a trade and make a buck, OK?"

"Wonderful. All the shadows have been taken from your sun."

"How can you ask me to think when tomorrow I'm gonna die?"

19

I awoke the next morning with my throat more sore. I drove to the House coughing, oblivious to all but the tightness in the center of my back. I was about to follow the BMS into a premorbid coma. Jo had just completed examining the night's excretia, but before we started on work rounds, I insisted she listen to my chest. She said it was clear. Despite this, I was so worried I couldn't concentrate, and TURFED myself to X Ray for films. I went over them with the radiologist, who said they were normal. I got beeped to the unit for a cardiac arrest, and ran on up.

It was the BMS. Fifteen people had crowded into his room: a Messarabian breathing him; a nurse perched on her knees on top of the bed pumping his chest, every systolic compression lifting her skirt to her waist; the Surgical Chief Resident with wiry black chest hairs curling up over the V-necked green scrubsuit; barely in the room, Pinkus and Jo. Pinkus had been paged from his morning trot, and was in track shoes and gym shorts, looking distractedly out the window. Jo was all icewater, eyes riveted to the EKG machine, choosing medications, barking orders to the nurses. In the midst of all this, the BMS was meat.

Despite all efforts, the BMS continued to die. As usual at arrests, as if at a dud party, after about half an hour people got bored and wanted to stop and call it a day and let the patient really die, the heart following after the dead brain like a car motor stopping a few internal combustions after the ignition had been turned off. Jo, angered at the idea of failure, shouted out: "With this kid we're four-plussing it, all the way!" and wouldn't stop. When the heart finally did stop, Jo ordered the broiling of the chest, and when four shots of that didn't work, she paused, at the end of her medical bag of tricks. This was where the surgeons began, and the Chief Resident, sensing the chance to turn carnage into drama, got hot and said, "Hey, want me to open the chest? Manual cardiac massage?" Jo paused, and then, in the hush, said, "You bet. This kid walked in here. We're going all out. Four-plus!" The surgeon ripped the chest from armpit to armpit and spread the ribs. He grabbed the heart and began to pump it with his hand. Pinkus left the room. I stood, frozen. It was clear that the BMS was dead. What they were doing was being done for them. The surgeon, hand tired, asked me if I'd like to take over. Foggy, I did. I got my hand around the back of the young lifeless heart and squeezed. Tough, slippery, the sinewy muscle was a leather bag, filled with blood, rolling in the steamy chest cavity, tied to the tubes of the major vessels. Why was I doing this? My hand hurt. I gave up. The heart lay like a grayish-blue fruit on a tree of bones. Sickening. The face of the BMS was blue, turning white. The gash in his chest was bright red, turning to a clotted black. We'd ruined his body, even as he'd died. As I left the room, I heard Jo yell out with crisp authority: "Any BMS students here? This is a chance you don't often get in your training, to learn to massage the heart. Great teaching case. Come on." Sick, I retreated to the staff room, where the nurses were chattering, eating doughnuts, as if nothing had happened outside.

"Glad to see you're not wrecking your coronaries with doughnuts, Roy," said Pinkus. "I've tried to tell the girls, but they won't listen. They're lucky, of course, in that the estrogens lower their incidence."

"I'm not hungry," I said. "I think I've caught what the BMS had. I'm gonna die. I just timed my respirations: thirty-two a minute."

"Die?" asked Pinkus. "Hmm. Say, did that BMS have a hobby?"

The head nurse picked up the chart, turned to the special section created by Pinkus, called "Hobbies," and said, "Nope. No hobby."

"There," said Pinkus. "See? No hobby. He didn't have a hobby, do you understand? Do you have a hobby, Roy?"

With some alarm I realized that I did not, and said so.

"You should have at least one. See, my hobbies are directed to the care of my coronary arteries: fishing, for calm, and running, for fitness. Roy, in my nine years on this Unit, I've never seen a Marathon runner die. Not of an MI, not of a virus, not of anything. No deaths, period."

"Really?"

"Yes. Look: if you're not fit, your heart beats like this," and Pinkus made a motion with his fist, slowly moving his fingers toward his palm as if he were in slow motion waving someone good-bye. "But if you run, your cardiac output goes up dramatically, and you really pump and I mean PUMP! Like this!" Pinkus clasped and unclasped his fist so hard that his knuckles turned white and his forearm musculature bulged. It was dramatic. I would be converted. I grasped his hand and asked, "What do I have to do to start?" Pinkus was pleased, and went right to shoe size. Instead of viruses and atherosclerosis, my mind filled with New Balance 320s, anaerobic glycolytic muscle metabolism, and a subscription to *Runner's World*. We planned out a schedule with which to begin, which would get me to Marathon distance within a year. Pinkus was one great American.

Except for frolicking in the occasional erotic fondle, I spent the rest of the day avoiding Jo and running scared. Jo wanted to teach me everything about everything so that when she left that night, my first night alone, I would be able to handle things. Apprehensive about turning her Unit over to me, she loitered around, and telling me "I never turn off my beeper," she finally left. As usual in my medical training, knowing little, I was put in charge of all. I needed someone who knew the nuts and bolts of the Unit. I ran to the night nurse, and made it clear that I was her pawn. Pleased, she used me, and began teaching me things never mentioned in my four rarefied BMS years filled with enzyme kinetics and zebraic diseases. I became a technician, getting off on how to set a respirator's dials.

Just before the ten-o'clock meal, I was called to the E.W. for my first admission, a forty-two-year-old man named Bloom, with his first MI. He was coming to the Unit because of his age. If he had been sixty-two, he would have been fending for himself on the wards, his chances of immediate survival halved. Bloom was lying on his stretcher in the E.W., white as a sheet, puffing with anxiety and cardiac pain. His eyes showed the terrified longing of a dying man wishing he'd spent his last days differently. He and his wife turned to me, their hope. Uncomfortable, I was surprised to find myself thinking of Pinkus, and asking Bloom if he had a hobby.

"No," he gasped, "I don't have a hobby."

"Well, after this you might think of developing one. I'm taking up running, for fitness. And there's always fishing for calm."

The risk factors were weighted against Bloom. He'd suffered a serious MI, and for a period of four days he'd camp on death's door, courtesy of the Unit. I wheeled him into the MICU, where the nurses swarmed over him, wiring him for sound, light, and whatever else they could grab onto. Ollie's face lit up with Bloom's ratty EKG. What was I doing for poor Bloom's heart? Not much. Watching for when Bloom stopped.

The Runt and Chuck, knowing what a strain my first night on call in the Unit would be, stopped by to talk. Even though it had gotten increasingly hard to make contact with each other, what had happened to Eddie and Potts had made us try to be with each other more. I said to the Runt, "I always meant to ask you, Runt, what's the matter with Angel's language centers. I mean, she starts to talk, fades out, and waves her hands around. What's it all about?"

"I never noticed," said the Runt. "She seems to talk fine, to me."

"You mean you still haven't talked about anything?"

Thinking it over, the Runt paused, and then broke out in a wide grin, walloped his knee, and said, "Nope! Never! HA!"

"Damn," said Chuck, "you sure come a long way from that poet."

"I think I do love Angie, but I don't think I'll marry her. See, she hates Jews and she hates doctors and she says I whistle too loud and that I follow her around too much when we're not in bed. I think I might . . . Oh, hi, Angie-Wangie, I was just tell—"

"Runt," said Angie, "you know what"—gesture toward self—"I think?" Gesture toward Runt. "You talk too"—gesture toward cosmos—"Goddamn much. Roy, Mr. Bloom wants to"—gesture toward mouth—"talk to you. We need"—gesture toward heaven—"help."

Chuck and the Runt left, and left me to the shocks and thrills of my first solo night in space. Walking a tightrope with Bloom and the other patients, balancing over their catastrophies, I passed the evening. At eleven came the striptease, the nursing change of shift: smooth leading thighs, a black lace panty rolling down as the tight dungarees came off, flashing pubic hair, the side slope of a jiggly breast, the full frontal of two firm ones, errant nipples, the works. Testosterone storm. Who had each been abed with, how had each been abed with, before coming to work, to me? When I'd calmed down, I went to bed. A nurse awoke me at four A.M.: new admission, age eighty-nine; small MI; no complications.

"We don't take them that old," I said, "she goes to the ward."

"Not if her name's Zock. Not if it's Old Lady Zock."

Old Lady Zock turned out to be a typical gomere except for her money, which was three bags full. I was impressed. I would be nice to this Zock, she would give me a bag of money, I would leave medicine and marry the Thunderous Thigh and promise not to whistle, ever, or follow her around. I wheeled Old Lady Zock—whose shriek was MOO-ELL MOO-ELL—up to the Unit. If Bloom and Zock were to have clamored over the last intensive-care bed, who would have gotten it? No contest.

When a Zock gets admitted to the House of God, the whole ice-cream cone of Slurpers shakes and shimmers like a belly dancer in a hall of mirrors. The Leggo gets a call, and he calls on down the cone to the lower Slurpers, and as the nurses were settling Old Lady Zock into her bed, in trotted Pinkus. I looked at him and said, "Great case, eh?"

"Does she have a hobby?"

301

"Sure does. Moo-elling."

"Never heard of that one," said Pinkus, "what is it?"

"Ask her."

"Hello, dearie. What's your hobby?"

"MOO-ELL MOO-ELL!"

"What a funny joke, Roy," said Pinkus. "Say, look at this." Pinkus unbuttoned his shirt, revealing a running shirt on which was a giant-sized full-color healthy heart. He took off his trousers, revealing pink shorts on which, in blood red, was the slogan YOU GOTTA HAVE HEART. PINKUS. HOUSE OF GOD. "Here," he said, motioning the nurses' and my attention to his calves, "just feel these."

We fondled the steel cords that were his *gastrocs* and *soleus*. Pinkus reached into his tote bag and produced a pair of running shoes and said, "Roy, these are for you, a pair of my shoes that I don't use anymore. Already broken in, so you can start right away. Here, I'll teach you the stretching exercises. I'm on my way out for my A.M. six miles."

Pinkus and I performed the ritualized stretching of the muscles from the pelvis to the toes. Warmed up, he began to walk out of the Unit as dawn was beginning to break. He passed the room with the lights on, Bloom's, and asked, "Who's that?"

"New admission. Name's Bloom. No hobbies. None at all."

"Figures. So long."

The next day I was surprised that I was not tired. I felt excited. I'd been in control of the sickest, deadest patients alive. By watching the numbers and occasionally giving a med or turning a dial, I'd averted disaster all night long. Bloom had made it through the night. My biggest thrill that morning was Pinkus turning to me at the end of rounds and saying, much to Jo's chagrin: "Roy, good job on your first night on call. And not just good job, no, I mean darn good job, Roy. Darn good job indeed."

For the rest of the day I rode the backs of the rolling waves of intoxication at my competence. Before I left, I went to "M and M Rounds," which stood for "Morbidity and Mortality." At this conference, mistakes were aired, with the idea of not repeating them. In practice, it was a chance for the higher-ups to shit on the lower-downs. Given the propensity for mistakes on the part of some of the terns, the same terns would appear over and over again. That day, again it was Howie, being shat on for mismanaging someone with disease in his future specialty, renal medicine. Unfortunately, Howie had missed the diagnosis, and had treated the man for arthritis until he died from renal failure. I entered at Howie pronouncing the death.

"Did you get the post?" asked the Leggo.

"Of course," said Howie, "but I'd made a mistake—the patient was not dead after all."

Covering his eyes with his hand, the Leggo said, "Oh. Well, what happened next?"

"I called the resident," said Howie, as the audience laughed.

"Yes?" asked the Chief.

"Then the patient really died and we got the post. The dying words were something like 'the nurse is incompetent' or 'the nurse is incontinent.'"

"What difference does that make?" asked the Leggo harshly.

"Why, I don't know," said Howie.

And Molly loves that asshole? I dozed off, and awakened to the Leggo discussing the case, saying, "Most people who have glomerulonephritis and spit blood have glomerulonephritis and spit blood." I thought I'd been dreaming until, awakening again, I heard the Leggo's next pearl: "There is a tendency for healing in this fatal disease." How pedestrian. Poodling around with kidney disease, and I was doing high-powered medicine with exact regulation of every known body parameter, in the Unit. I left M and Ms, signed out, drove home. I was surprised to find myself whistling, happy, thinking of the musculature of the leg. I would become like Pinkus. The deadness I'd felt in Gomer City was being replaced by the excitement of the Unit. Like the E.W., it was not a place where the gomers could come to linger and outlast me, no. From the Unit, unless they were rich or young, they would be TURFED elsewhere. The thrill of handling the complexity of disease, of running the show well and with power, on top of the pile, the elite of the profession. I was king. Hotcha.

I couldn't wait to slip into my shorts and Pinkus' old shoes. Well-worn, they cradled my feet. Tired as I was, I put myself through the Pinkus stretching maneuvers, and trotted out to the street, and with the sun lowering in front of my eyes, with the soothing PLONKA PLONKA of the wide cushioned soles against the asphalt, I was carried a few miles farther toward the land of dilated coronary arteries, patent to rich red well-oxygenated blood. I was a child, free after supper, floating on Icarus wings in the first warm evening breeze of Daylight Saving Time, of spring.

I came back with chest pain, worried that I had *angina pectoris* and that I had started exercising too late in life. I would die from an MI while running. Pinkus would view my corpse and say wistfully, "Too bad. Too late."

Berry was waiting for me at home, and given my usual sedentary life, she couldn't believe her eyes.

Taking her hands, I put them on my *gastrocnemius* and said, "Here, feel that."

"Yeah?"

"That's BEFORE. I want you to form a clear mental image of that, for when you get to feel AFTER."

20

By the end of the first two weeks I was doing four miles a day. To my relief, what I'd feared was anginal pain was, according to Pinkus, pain referred from the stretching of the intercostal ligaments as the rib cage expanded, common to beginning runners. I began to run the four miles to work, floating along the cycle path—named in honor of a famous marathoning cardiologist who'd died of old age—next to the river, the dawn breaking over the awakening city, my PLONKA PLONKA a soothing affirmation of my lifebeat.

But all was not Pinkus yet. Unlike him, I had yet to come to terms with the Unit. One side of me was filled with the horror of human misery and helplessness; the other was exhilarated, king in an erotic diseased kingdom, competent to run machines. Being on call every other night meant that there was never time to think about the world outside the House, and the conflicts of the Unit became the main conflicts of life. The nurses? Like the background in Vermeer's *Lady with a Guitar,* the empty black highlighting the glow of candle on lithe fingers, the disease highlighted the sex.

Often I'd find myself entwined in variants on the same erotic theme: late at night, the eerie artificial Unit light punctured only by the green-flashing BLEEP BLEEP of the cardiac monitors. The nurse calls me from my bed to see a comatose patient whose body is being run by machine, one parameter of which had gone awry. Following her to the bedside, I notice her bralessness, that she wears no pantyhose. I put a stethoscope on the body. I need to listen to the chest, and ask the nurse to help me. She bends over, the two of us hoist the body to sitting, tubes dangling down. I listen to the clogged lungs, inflated by respirator, my fingers on the waxy skin, fighting the stench of chronic disease. I smell her perfume—coconut. Our heads are close together. I drop my stethoscope, put my free hand around her neck, kiss her. Her tongue and my tongue slither together. I lean my shoulder against the patient's body, freeing the other hand. The kiss prolonged, I fondle her breast through her cotton dress, feeling the coarse fabric scratching against the skin, pulling the nipple erect. We part, the body falls back—THUMP—on the bed. Later, on her break, she comes to the on-call bunk bed, hoisting up her green surgical skirt because there isn't time to undress. We two begin to take out our hatred, our loneliness, our horror with human suffering and our despair at human endings in the most tender of human acts, making love. Knowing that she hates me for being a doctor, for forgetting her name three times that shift, for being a Jew who views her eunuch Pope's pronouncements on "Human Life" as comical at best, for running her Unit, for her being trammeled on by men like me, for my always being the smarter one in the class, for all those hates and for the arousal bred by hates, we bash away at each other savagely, skin on skin, cock in cunt, with the desperation of two space travelers on a journey of light-years, with death at the far end and no way back, imprisoned in a spacecraft of chrome and lights and computers and MUZAK. She will not talk to me about her hatred, she will not even gesture to me about her hatred, she will only fuck me for her hatred, and let it go at that. Groaning, we rattle the springs of the bunk bed, secured by the vigilance of two machines: her IUD; and each of our abilities, the next morning, to forget. California, here I come! We finish. Blushing from the clitoris and not from the heart, she goes back to work.

In tune with this spring theme of sex and death, like eight vultures, the days of Passover swooped down upon the House of God. Despite the false hope offered by Good Friday and Easter Sunday, with the coming of Passover there was no question of God's intent: death. Despite the technocratic thrust toward life, God flexed his *biceps* and *triceps* and, for all we knew, *infini-omniceps*, and began to mock us, with death. During Passover, patients began to drop like flies.

It was eerie. We'd work like hell on someone, who'd appear to have made it, and then—BLEEP—a cardiac arrest and death. I'd pick up a patient in the E.W., and as I put my stethoscope on him, he'd clutch his chest, turn blue, and die. I'd be sleeping peacefully, and—BUZZ—the arrest button would sound and I would run, blinking and trying to hide my sleep erection, into the bright neon and MUZAK searching out the room with the panic, and sure enough God had made his move and another had cooled on us. Afterward, looking back over the recordings stored up by Ollie, we'd find that despite our preparations, an aberrant beat would have landed at the vulnerable period and—BLEEP—ranting, arrogant, in strutted death.

All of us were shocked. The families of the dead, set up with hope and then smashed with despair, suffered beyond words. Blitzed, their own hearts cut from their moorings and rolling and floating in their chests like balls of wool in empty bags, they washed us with their tears. Jo, the perfectionist, was hard hit. By Day Four of Passover, she was frantic. Fighting the specter of what she took as a personal failure to keep her patients alive, Jo adopted a sort of phlogiston theory, deciding that there was something contaminated somewhere in the Unit. When Pinkus arrived, she assaulted him with this idea and insisted that the Unit be torn apart, top to bottom, to find the noxious agent that was killing her patients. Pinkus, phlegmatic, told her she could do as she wished, although he didn't think that was it. He asked me to feel his legs, and I did, and said, "Amazing."

"The Marathon's only six days away. Carbohydrate loading starts today."

"Pinkus," said Jo with great intensity, the circles under her eyes even blacker, "I want to make one thing perfectly clear: we are going to win this war against death."

The penultimate setback for Jo was at four o'clock in the middle of the Fifth Night. Jo usually stayed up most of the night, but the stress of being the first woman resident to wrestle directly with the Angel of Death had worn her out, and with things seemingly under control, she'd gone to bed for an hour. Shortly thereafter, all hell broke loose, with a man named Gogarty, a spanking-fresh virgin MI, having a cardiac arrest. Jo was called, and with a fanaticism hardly ever seen in the Unit, spent an hour 4-plussing the victim back toward life. Unfortunately, Gogarty turned out to be a smokescreen, for as Jo and the nurses left his room what sight should greet their eyes but Old Lady Zock spread-eagled nose-down on the tiled Unit floor, stone dead. It turned out that, having heard the commotion in Gogarty's room, Old Lady Zock, in a final philanthropic gesture, had wished to pitch in at the arrest, and following the most heart-rending of House LAWS: GOMERS GO TO GROUND, had done so, in the process dislodging the cardiac pacemaker which was prodding her generous heart, and had died. The final irony, of course—the story of Jo's life—was that Jo's insisting all nurses tend to Gogarty had caused the neglect of Zock. When a Zock gets neglected, it shakes God's House.

The next morning, there was much commotion. It was Zocks versus Medicine. Recrimination City. Although in the confrontation the Leggo restrained himself from asking for a postmortem, Jo did not, and things got sticky. The Leggo told Jo to "get the hell back inside," and we watched as the caravan led the flock of Zocks away to one of the green plush "function rooms" donated by the Zocks and used only for the stroking of philanthropists of the House of God.

Fed up with Jo's "contamination" theory, I announced that I was going another route. Jo asked what it was, and I said, "Fight fire with fire." I picked up the phone and told the operator to page the Rabbi on call, STAT. Alarmed that his beeper had gone off, and STAT at that, huffing and puffing, young Rabbi Fuchs arrived. I told him about the Reign of Death, and about my conviction that this was, in some way, a Visitation of the Lord God, over Passover, mistaking us for Egyptians.

"I don't understand," said Rabbi Fuchs.

"Isn't it just possible that God is punishing us with these deaths, and that we should do everything within our power to follow his Passover Laws? Like paint the doorposts of the

Unit, use special Passover dishes, leave a cup of wine for Elijah the Prophet, and so on?"

The black-bearded intellectual Fuchs looked puzzled, peered through his granny glasses at Ollie's sempiternal flickering console, and said, "The Haggadah, the Passover Story to which you refer, is not literal, it's homiletic. Yes, that's it: the exigesis of the Haggadah, since the eleventh century, has produced commentaries that are mostly homiletic, although sometimes mystical, in character."

"Did you understand that, Pinkus?" I asked.

"Nope."

"Me neither. What do you mean, Rabbi?"

"Don't take it literally. It is myth. God doesn't work that way anymore. These deaths have to do with physiological fact, not with the whims of Deity. Body, not soul, is what's dying here."

Leave it to the House of God to produce some red-hot Theology student as its Rabbi. I turned to him and asked, "What denomination are you anyway, Rabbi Fuchs?"

"Me? Why, Reform."

"Figures," I said, picking up the phone. "Thank you very much. I'm calling the Orthodox boys, the Hassidim."

The Orthodox Rabbi was an aged, white-bearded patriarch from a half-abandoned synagogue in the black ghetto. Excited by my idea, he quoted cabalistic writings about "the homes of the sick during the Exodus," telling me about the timeliness of the Passover teachings, as in the Mishnah: "In every generation let each man look on himself as if he came forth out of Egypt." Unfortunately, this Rabbi suffered from congestive heart failure, and before we could get on with the chanting and painting, he wanted some *gratis* medical advice. This took us up to lunchtime, and the Rabbi said he must stop and eat. He produced a small screwtop jar, sat down with the nurses and me, and as he opened it, I knew what it was.

"Herring," he said to the nurses, "piece herring."

"I thought you were low salt?" I asked.

"Yeh, I em. Would you believe: the whole low salt for one day is in this tiny piece herring?"

Finally, Maintenance delivered the can of bloodred paint,

and with the Rabbi belching herring, beginning to pray, chanting and *dovening* back and forth, I slapped the red paint around. I wished the Rabbi well, made a small donation to his *shul*, and reentered the space lab. That evening, as I listened to the Runt blather on about his ecumenical fornications with Angel, befittingly menstrual during Easter and Passover both, I listened also for the wingbeats of the Angel of Death passing over my Unit.

For a night it worked. The main threat that night was Dr. Binsky, a middle-aged Private, who'd suffered a serious MI. I knew that he knew he might die, and despite the pull of being colleagues, my fear of getting involved pulled me away from him. During the night Dr. Binsky served up most of the cardiac arrythmias known to man. Luckily, miraculously, each responded to my efforts, and dawn saw Binsky, and vice versa. The Orthodox boys had come through.

The next morning, the Seventh Day, Jo was ecstatic. Seeing none dead, she beamed from ear to ear, clasped my hand, and affirmed that, "by God, we're going to win, and if it takes painting the doorposts, why of course we'll paint the doorposts, in the interest of patient care." We went to see Dr. Binsky, and Pinkus, his old friend, said, "Hi, Morris. How's Morris today?"

"I feel OK, Pinkus. What's it been now, forty hours?"

"Just about."

"How's my rhythm strip today?" asked Morris.

"Dr. Binsky," said Jo, putting her hand in an older-brother fashion on his shoulder, and with a crinkle in her voice, "it's normal sinus rhythm again. NSR, at last."

"What a relief," said Dr. Binsky, "what a gigantic relief."

Ten seconds later he had a cardiac arrest and despite our efforts, within the half-hour he was dead.

Jo broke. She sat in the staff room with Pinkus and me, crying, repeating over and over, "He couldn't have died, he was in normal sinus. Normal sinus rhythm and now he's dead? It doesn't make any sense, statistically. I can't take this absurdity anymore."

"People do die in NSF," said Pinkus calmly. "It shows that we did all we could, right, Roy?"

I nodded my agreement. Of course Pinkus was right.

"Look, Jo," said Pinkus, "he went out in perfect, normal sinus rhythm. With class. Yes, he went out the House of God way."

I thought of a House LAW: THE PATIENT IS THE ONE WITH THE DISEASE. It was his heart, not mine. I was immune from responsibility or concern. My world was for running, eating right, and staying calm. I left Jo to puzzle it out, and tended to the others of the Unit. Later that afternoon I said goodbye, wished Jo good luck, and on the four-mile run home filled my mind with Pinkus and God. I had done all I could, and Dr. Binsky had died. To get anxious about it, to eat away at myself, would only increase my stress, and boy did I know about the risk factor, stress. Personality Type A, the cardiac grenade. No thanks.

After dinner that night, Berry and I were walking home. She was surprised at my energy, given the fact that I'd been averaging only three hours' sleep a night since I'd begun in the Unit.

"Pinkus says that within limits, fatigue is mental, not physiological. Every other night is not bad. I kind of like it."

"Like it? I thought you hated being in the House at night."

"Outside the Unit, I did. Inside the Unit, I like it. In fact, I almost could say I love it. Like the surgeons say: 'The only drawback to being on call every other night is that you only get to admit half the patients.' That's how I feel too. I might become a cardiologist."

Berry stopped, grabbed me by the shoulders, and forced me to look at her. She seemed far away as she said, "Roy, what's the matter with you? For nine months you've been telling me how the internship is wrecking your life—your creativity, your humanness, your passion. What the hell is going on with this Unit, anyway?"

"Don't know. Lotta deaths. Jo cracked. Cried. High anxiety level. Type A. Even with estrogens, bad news for her."

"Jo cracked? And what about the effect of these deaths on you?"

"These deaths? So what?"

"So what?" asked Berry, in a tone that came from the bottom

of a well, far off, ringing of dismay and regret, "I'll tell you what—the more deaths, the less human you become."

"You shouldn't worry. Like Pinkus says, 'anxiety's a killer.'"

That night in bed, as I turned to her and touched her shoulder, I could feel her tension. She stopped me and said, "Roy, I'm worried. I could understand your shutting yourself off from grieving Potts's death, but this is too much. You're isolated. You never see your friends, you never even mention Fats or Chuck or the policemen anymore."

"Yeah. I think I've left them all behind."

"Listen to me: you don't love the Unit, it's a defense. You don't love Pinkus, it's a defense. You're hypomanic, identifying with the aggressor, idolizing Pinkus to save yourself from falling apart. It may work in the House, but it won't work with me. For me, tonight, you're a dead man. There's no spark of life."

"Gee, I dunno, Berry. I feel healthy and alive." Thinking of Hal, the computer in *2001*, I said, "Things are going extremely well."

"How much longer does this MICU rotation last?"

"Ten days," I said, and caressed her hair, thinking calmly of our supreme primeval exercise, sex. She pulled away, and I asked why.

"I can't make love to you if there's this distance between us."

"You mean you can't stand the thought of another woman? Because that's all ov—"

"NO! I can't stand you! I've just about had it with trying to get through to you. I've got to start thinking of myself. I'll give you the benefit of time, let you finish the Unit, to see if you can snap out of this. Otherwise, it's all over. After all this time, we're through. In your terms, it's ROR, Roy, ROR."

As if from far off, I heard myself saying, "Better ROR than anxiety, Berry. Better that than Type A."

"Goddamn you, Roy!" she screamed, in tears. "You are a jerk! Don't you realize what's happening to you? Answer me!"

"At this point in time," I said, trying to remain calm in the

312

face of all this turmoil of emotion and stress, "that's all I have to say."

Berry let out a hissing sound, like a train makes braking into a station, and she said, "You're not a jerk, Roy. You're a machine."

"A machine?"

"A machine."

"So what?"

21

She was wrong. I was not a machine. I was not dead. I was alive. I was doing extremely well. My life was full. The PLON-KA PLONKA of my feet on the bicycle path beside the river basin helped to beat out an affirmation of these reassuring thoughts. My head felt clear, like a sleek coronary artery lumen, a sleek woman in a maillot bathing suit, wet from a tropical sea.

That night was my masterpiece. A nurse and I had been told to do a marvelously difficult and intricate medical procedure. A young mother of two had been lingering toward death for months. Now, with end-stage liver disease, she was finally about to die of massive infection and failure of her heart, liver, kidney, brain, and lung. She had been sent to the Unit, and we had been told to drain the infected fluid out of her belly and replace fluid in her circulation. Since the fluid that we put back into her circulation would, because of the low serum protein, soon migrate back into her belly, this procedure, if successful, would do no good. So what? Long ago I'd given up the idea that what I did to these bodies had any relevance to whether it did any good. I would do it well. Why should I mind being the final expiation for the failure of House medical care?

I put in big lines everywhere, monitored everything, and the nurse and I got ourselves rigged up, ready to launch. This would be my moon landing, my techno-Lisa, my grenade.

Over the orange belly of the young mother of two we slaved away in erotico-synch, taking fluid out, putting fluid back, watching numbers, setting dials, bathed in the eerie space light of the Unit, humming the melodies dished up by MU-ZAK. Hushed admiring others, doctors and nurses, dropped in to observe. Time turned timeless. The husband, having suffered the treatment and having lived with the death that the House red-hots had been denying his wife, informed us that he wanted us to stop, to do no more. Knowing that this last prolongation of life was worthless, done out of collective impotence and guilt, I convinced the husband to let us continue, assuring him—falsely?—that her suffering would not be prolonged. Too enraged to cry, he left. I watched him go, hugging his little boy and little girl. They had quizzical looks in their eyes.

At about midnight the arrest alarm sounded in room 5, where a pithed-frog woman died. In confirmation, Ollie spewed forth a flat-line EKG. I walked into her room. Her husband sat there, content with the illusion of life provided by the respirator inflating and deflating the corpse that had been his wife. I asked him to let me see her. He looked at me and began to weep. I helped him up and led him out to a cup of coffee. A nurse asked me what to do. Heading back into the young mother's room, I told the nurse to turn off the pithed woman's respirator.

"I don't turn off respirators," said the nurse.

I was puzzled. Why not? She's dead. I looked at the nurse in silence, trying to understand. I went into the room with the body. I looked at it, a female, now turned a waxy death-white, without heartbeat or blood flow, dead-brained with a skull filled with clotted blood, the lungs rippled by machine. I searched through the wired undergrowth in back of the bed for the respirator plug. I paused. *Bona fide* dead. Saul the tailor flashed through. It was easy enough. I did it. Time turned timeless again.

The pleasing symmetry of the shape of that night continued through the next day, the day of the Marathon. I was doing extremely well. I felt extremely good for Pinkus, and planned to get off work early to watch him run up the worst hill, the Humbler. On rounds that morning, things went as smoothly as the MUZAK. A single incident, with the hepatitis woman, made it hard for me to do extremely well for a minute or two. Having spent much of the night completing the tricky hyro-digito-technics of the Unit's equivalent of the moon walk, at about noon the nurse and I—she working a double shift out of compassion for this poor "salvageable" woman—were accosted by the husband, who got real red in the face and said, "I think you're both incredibly callous for keeping my poor wife alive!" The nurse burst into tears. I, in agreement with the husband, fell silent. The nurse and I stood there with the dying woman who stank of disinfectant and infection and bilirubin and ammonia, until the husband had done his punch-drunk catharting and left. For a few minutes I felt as if I were on the edge of some disaster, some abyss that seemed familiar from a nightmare. Then it passed, and again I felt calm.

From noon until I left, I was to work in my Outpatient Clinic downstairs. With some apprehension I left my Unit and entered the hopelessly inefficient world of the rest of the House of God. As I was going into my office, I ran into Chuck going into his. He looked even worse than usual.

"Well, man," he said, "bad news. I been found out."

"Found out? Found out what?"

"Well, you know how I always had the amazin' luck that the old ladies would never seem to show up at my Clinic, no matter what appointments they made?"

"Yeah, it was amazing," I said.

"Well, the reason they never showed up was that they was daid."

"Dead?"

"Un-hun, daid. See, I used to go over to the record room and pull charts, use daid names for appointments. Hardly any of 'em showed."

My own Clinic was ridiculous. I employed a useful anatomical concept for Clinic medicine, called Scruffy's Rhomboid Space, which was formed by unbuttoning the fourth button down on the shirt or blouse, forming a diamond-shaped opening for my stethoscope. With clever wrist action, the stethoscope could be rotated and pushed in such a way that all majcr organs could be examined without having the patient undress. Using this technique, I waded through my familiar patients with their trivial complaints, my mind filled with the precision and elegance of the techniques of the Unit, like popping a steel needle into a virginal radial artery. My outpatients seemed wary of me, and many of them kept asking me if I was sure I felt all right. I told them I was feeling extremely well. One in particular, my basketballing Jehovah's Witness, was insistent: "Why, Dr. Basch, you nevah for months used that stethelscope on me. We allas used to jes' talk. I knows in mah heart that there's sumpin' gone wrong. What is it?" I told her there was nothing wrong, and finished examining her. Shaking her head, she left.

I muttered to myself as I walked through the fresh April afternoon toward the Humbler, all this education just to write prescriptions for padded bras with pockets? What the hell was I in, anyway, ladies' lingerie?

The gaily colored marathoners began to pass. The first, the leaders, looked fit and eager even after these twenty miles, even facing the terror of the Humbler. The build of the leaders was like that of Pinkus: thin to the waist, solid below. They ran through waves of applause. How jealous I was! The blur of color went on and on and after about five hundred had gone by, there came Pinkus, in a determined sure style that might well bring him in under three hours. I shouted, "Go get 'em, Pinkus!" and he looked up, without waving or smiling, and trudged on up the Humbler, with calm, deliberate strides. He looked good. He was doing extremely well, and I watched him go wistfully, the GOTTA HAVE HEART on his rear end disappearing over the crest. My man Pinkus hadn't even broken stride. The Humbler? Ha!

Later that evening, at the high-school gym after playing some hoop, I ran into a Unit nurse, whose name I'd always forgotten and couldn't recall then. Wearing a tight black Danskin, she was working out with weights. I was surprised and delighted with her body and with her interest in her body. Dripping sweat, we chatted. I asked her out for a drink. In the bar, we watched Nixon, who, even though Haig thought that Nixon "didn't sell on TV anymore," had gone ahead with a prime-time TV address from the Oval Office, something about "edited transcripts" of the tapes. The packaging was terrific! On a side table to which the camera intermittently panned were shiny black vinyl binders, each embossed with a gold presidential seal. "I am placing my trust in the basic fairness of the American people."

Nuzzling the nurse's sweaty neck, I said, "Damn good idea. It's about time. Get the goddamn thing straightened out, once and for all." To me, the locker-room aroma of this tough nurse was more enticing than perfume. I loved it.

After the drink, before the bedding, she went with me to an all-night sporting-goods store, where I bought myself my first ever fishing rod and reel.

22

Having done extremely well in the Unit, it was difficult for me to say good-bye. I felt sad. I wanted to stay on. How do astronauts say good-bye? As befit a pro, my good-byes were unemotional. Neal Armstrong saying good-bye to Frank Borman. John Ehrlichman saying good-bye to Robert "Bob" Haldeman. Good-bye to Pinkus, my hero, who had run two hours fifty-seven minutes thirty-four seconds and who said, "Cardiology can be very rewarding in financial and personal terms, and with the implementation of hobbies, a very healthful life. Think about it, Roy, you're a young man with a bright future."

I left.

Later that afternoon, Berry and I, ROR, were driving out into the countryside to relax. I was reading a letter from my father.

> . . . Your experience undoubtedly is stimulating and I am sure that you are totally absorbed. Soon it will be over and you will have to decide about your future life . . .

"You know," I said to Berry, "after all these years of disagreement with him, I finally think he's right."

We sat on the edge of a park, the spring blushing chaotically all around us. The swath of green, lush with a fresh rain, swept across in front of us, from the pond reflecting the mansion on the left, past the hundred-year-old oak under which the WASPs held their weddings, to the old stone wall and in back of it, the symmetric and rooted old houses. A dog came up to play, dropping a twig closer and closer until I threw it and he chased it. After a while I got tired, and he sensed it, and left. My mind, like a missile, kept homing to the Unit.

On the drive back, I felt restless, and Berry noticed and asked, "What's the matter, Roy? You're done with the hardest part of the year."

"I know. I miss it. It's hard to relax. Even fishing would be easier than this. Did I tell you I bought a rod and reel? You know, I need your help. With your psychological expertise, maybe you could tell me how I can change."

"Change what?"

"My personality. I want to go from Type A to Type B."

Berry didn't comment. We separated, planning to meet again that night. We had tickets to see Marcel Marceau.

I was restless. I missed something. I was not doing well. I didn't want Marcel Marceau, I wanted the Unit. It would be strange if I went back there tonight, my first night off. After I had finished. But wait: Jo had done it. My first day there, she'd spent the night with Mrs. Pedley. I would do it too. Under the guise of concern for the old lady in V Tach, I would go and spend the night on the Unit. It wasn't until the hermetic doors slushed shut behind me, and I heard the ethereal "A-round the wurrld in aay-tee dayzz . . ." and I had settled into a chair in Pedley's room, that I felt calm again.

This calm was not to last. Berry appeared, dressed to kill, and said, "Roy, what the hell are you doing here? We're supposed to see Marcel Marceau. You bought the tickets, remember?"

"Here, feel this," I said, indicating my *gastrocs.*

"What about Marcel Marceau?"

"Inoperative."

"All right, Roy, it's either this or me: take your pick."

I heard myself say, "It's this."

"That's what I thought you'd say," said Berry, "and I don't buy it, 'cause you're sick!" She made a motion out into the hallway, and in walked the two policemen, Gilheeny and Quick. Following them were Chuck and the Runt.

"A good evening to you from the depths of my nervous

stomach," said the redhead, limping in. "We have not seen
you since you became a red-hot intern in this weird Unit."

"We have missed you," said Quick. "Finton here, with his
bolloxed leg, cannot pursue your company as once he could."

"What the hell are you doing here?" I asked suspiciously.

"Your girlfriend said that you have been crazy and were refusing to leave this Unit and go to the show with her," said
Gilheeny.

"I'm not going," I said. "It's ROR with her and me. Face it.
We're through."

"Hey, man," said Chuck, "you don't want to stay here with
these pitiful patients. You're done with this Unit shit, get out,
get on down."

"They're not pitiful. They're salvageable."

"Roy," said the Runt, "you're acting like a donkey."

"Thanks a lot, my fairweather friends. I'm staying here.
None of you can understand me anymore. Please leave me
alone."

"Trespassing is an offense," said Gilheeny, "and so we shall
remove you. Boys, let's begin."

With a good deal of furious struggling and cursing on my
part, under Gilheeny's direction Quick, Chuck, the Runt, and
Berry hoisted me up and carried me out, ushered me down the
stairs, and helped me into the police car, which, sirens blaring, raced through the downtown traffic and delivered Berry
and me to the theater door. I sat there, bullshit. While I
thought I'd escape when left alone with Berry, once again I
had underestimated these policemen.

"You're coming in with us?" I asked, amazed.

"We are admirers of true genius," said Gilheeny, "and true
is the genius of M. Marceau, a Jew of the French Catholic denomination, combining the better attributes of both."

"How the hell did you get tickets on such short notice?"

"Graft," said Quick simply.

With Berry and me sandwiched tightly between the bulky
Gilheeny and the sinewy Quick, I realized I was trapped, and I
resigned myself to sitting there until intermission. I watched
as the lights dimmed and the mime began. At first I was indif-
ferent, my mind on the Unit, and yet, as Marceau went on,

with Berry pressing my hand and the policemen reacting with all the spontaneity of kids, I couldn't help getting interested. The first mime was the Balloon Seller, giving a free balloon to a child, who, clutching it in his hand, is floated up and up out of sight. Everyone around me laughed. On my left I heard a chortle, erupting into a roar, and I realized from the smell of fat and sweat from a uniform that it came from Gilheeny. A hefty elbow slammed into my ribs, and the redhead turned to me, flashed his huge hippo smile, and screamed, flooding me with onions and hash. I laughed. Next, a mime I'd seen Marceau do in England: in thirty seconds he walked through the successive stages of youth, maturity, old age, death. I sat, hushed, with the others, touched, enthralled, as we recognized our lives ebbing past us in a matter of seconds. Blasts of applause crackled through the theater. I looked at Quick. Tears were in his eyes.

All of a sudden I felt as if a hearing aid for all my senses had been turned on. I was flooded with feeling. I roared. And along with this burst of feeling came a plunging, a desperate clawing plunge down an acrid chasm toward despair. What the hell had happened to me? Something in me had died. Sadness welled up in my gut and burned out through the slits of my eyes. A handkerchief was placed in my hand. I blew my nose. I felt a hug.

The last mime skewered me: The Maskmaker switched back and forth a smiling mask, a crying mask, faster and faster, until finally the smiling mask got stuck on his face and he couldn't remove it. The human struggle, the frantic effort to be rid of a suffocating mask; trapped, writhing, wearing a smile.

The theater erupted. Ten encores, twelve. BRAVO! BRAVO! we screamed, and flowed out with the rejuvenated crowd. I blinked, confused. Inside me, all was chaos. My calm had been the calm of death. More than anything, I wanted to jackboot Pinkus in his plump pink *soleus*. Thank God for Berry, for my orthodox samaritans, my policemen. As we parted from them, Gilheeny, touched, said, "Good night, friend Roy. We'd been worried that we'd lost you."

"We've seen it happen before to interns," said Quick, "and

if it had happened to you, it would have been a singular loss. God bless."

Later, Berry welcomed me back to her, and I felt her caring arms around me as if for the first time. Awakening, I began to thaw. I began to feel a trickle, then a rush of feeling that was scary and overwhelming. Choked up, I began to talk. On and on into the night I talked about the things I'd blotted out. The theme, over and over, coating my bedroom walls with a grayish-white mottled skin, was death. I talked about the horror of the dying, and the horror of the dead. Guiltily I told her about injecting the KCL into Saul. She couldn't hide her shock. How could I have done that? Even if my head told me, Yes, it had been for the best, my heart cried out, No! I hadn't done it for him, for the humanity of it, no. Angrily, to shut him up and to get back at them, I'd done it for me. I'd killed a human being! How that phrase would haunt me, tail me like an Israeli agent a Nazi, search me out when I was least suspecting, clamor after me in sleepy tropical courtyards of my new life where I'd thought that I'd found peace. Finding me, it would accuse me, and I would say: "I must have been out of control, crazy." Coldly, rightly, it would say: "That can be no excuse."

I talked on, about the families of the patients in the Unit, coming in, searching my eyes for hope. What had I done? I'd done everything I could to avoid them. I had been as far from the world of humans as I could get. Disgusted, I talked about how, in the face of suffering, I'd been professionally nonchalant. Where compassion had been needed more desperately than any medicine, I had been sarcastic. I'd avoided feeling everything, as if feelings were little grenades blasting off a fingernail, a toe, a fragment of a heart. Tears in my eyes, I asked Berry, "Where have I been?"

"Regressed. I thought I'd lost you for good."

"Why? Why did I get like that?"

"The more the hurt, the more the fantasied need for defenses. Potts's death rocked you. You imagined yourself to be so fragile, you wouldn't let yourself grieve. Like a two-year-old scared of the dark, you locked onto rituals—your machines, your crazy idolization of Pinkus—to protect you."

323

She was right. Since Potts's suicide, all of us had gone around like zombies, stunned, numb, too scared to cry. Each of us had been strung out trying to save ourselves, fighting against going really psychotic like Eddie or really killing ourselves by leaping from real buildings and splattering on a real parking lot eight stories below. We knew that it could have been any of us. Lethal, this becoming and being a doctor! Denying hope and fear, ritualized defenses pulled up around ears like turtlenecks, these doctors, to survive, had become machines, sealed off from humans—from wives, kids, parents—from the warmth of compassion and the thrill of love. I realized that it wasn't just that they'd kept on riding Potts about the Yellow Man, no. They'd ignored his suffering, his months of fatal depression. And because I felt helpless and didn't know what to do, I'd ignored it too.

"This internship—this whole training—it destroys people."

"Yes. It's a disease. The kind of stress you're under, unless you can find some safety, some caring, you've got only a few choices: kill yourself, go crazy, kill someone else. Potts had no one, no way to survive." Berry paused, took my head in her hands, and more seriously than I'd ever seen her, said, "Roy, you're a survivor. You'll make it now, to bear witness, to record the ones who didn't survive."

All across the country, interns were killing or going crazy, trying to survive. The medical hierarchy would continue. The new residents would say to the new interns: "We did it, now you do it." It was the scaly underside of the American Medical Dream. It was Nixon, in these "edited transcripts" shocking Americans with "I don't give a shit what happens, I want you to stonewall it . . ." And it was my own arrogance in the face of the most feeling human events: a loved one's sickness, a loved one's suffering, a loved one's death. No more. I would not pay the price. Having felt the first tantalizing suckings of this leech, this doctor's disease, I'd burn the fucker off. How?

"I'm here, Roy," said Berry. "Don't shut me out. I care, and your friends care too. Sharing the experience is what will get all the rest of you through."

"Fats!" I cried out. Apprehensive, worried that by fighting with him in Gomer City and by avoiding him while in the Unit

324

I'd wrecked something with him, I got up. I had to see him right away and tell him. "Gotta see the Fat Man," I said, heading for the door. "Gotta tell him before it's too late!"

"It's three A.M., Roy. What do you want to tell him?"

"That I'm sorry . . . And that I like him . . . And thanks."

"He won't like it if you wake him in the middle of the night."

"Yeah. Damn," I said, sitting back down, "I hope that there's still time."

"There will be. There always is, with people like him."

That was a beginning. To repair, to re-create the human took some time. And it wasn't for many months—no, years—that I was free from a recurrent nightmare: strapped down upon an icy metal slab, writhing back and forth to break free, running and running and running away, in a marathon race, from death. As I began to repair, I asked myself what had been missing. From another time, another, almost tropical country plagued by civil war, like a man with his chest thrown out proudly toward a firing squad who thinks back to a clear young summer and a gilded beribboned love letter ringed with doves, I realized that what had been missing was all that I loved. I would be transformed. I'd not leave that country of love again.

23

"What are you going to do on July the first?" I asked Chuck.

"Who knows, man, who knows? All I know is I don't want to do no more of this."

It was May Day. I was in the on-call room of my final ward rotation, 4-South. I was lying in the top bunk. This was unusual. The tern always used the bottom bunk so that he wasn't at risk of GOING TO GROUND from the Orthopedic Height and breaking his hip. For some reason I'd had the urge to lie in the top bunk, up under the ceiling, far back from the leading edge. I'd gathered pillows, climbed the ladder, and settled into a peaceful horizontality, snuggled up against the back wall, staring at the pea-green, sea-green ceiling. Very nice. I wished that the top bunk had side rails, like a gomer bed or crib. I wished food, a breast, a nipple, why not?

There I was to stay. Others would try to move me, and at times, others would succeed, but I had work to do. Having recognized the doctor's disease, I wasn't sure that I could escape. Oh, yes, I had work to do, on compassion, on love. Like a park attendant with a steel-tipped stick, I had to patrol the darkening seaside summer park, browsing around the bandstand in the wake of the wedding, stabbing, stabbing, collecting the shredded scraps of self scattered among the rainbow of confetti, ruffled in the breezes from the bay. From my top bunk I could see in through the windows of the fleshed-out Wing of Zock. With the spring, the workers seemed renewed, and in the plush GI radiology suite across from me, imitation gold toilet fixtures lay scattered on the thick green carpet like mushrooms. This pristine Wing of Zock offered hope, for the House of God, for the People. My hope was to finish the year in one piece.

On July the first, the medical profession acknowledged its only game, musical jobs. You had to play this game in advance. All of us terns in the House of God had tacitly agreed not only to the one-year ternship, but to the second year as residents. For some of us, like Howie, this was terrific, two years of being "a real doc" being twice as good as one. Smiling, puffing, Howie seemed to love the ternship. Cautious, indecisive, Howie was acknowledged to be the worst tern. Terrified of harming patients or of taking risks, he practiced a homeopathic, almost phantom medicine.

"You know," I said to Chuck, "that dose of antibiotic Howie was giving that woman downstairs is like giving a millionth of an aspirin."

"It's like pissin' in the wind, man, is what it is. It's amazin,' though, he's still happy in Gomer City."

"Impossible."

"No it ain't. I came in this mornin' and Howie was whistlin.' He went there a month ago, whistlin,' and he's still whistlin,' Puffin' that pipe and whistlin.' They won't break that dude, no way. He loves it."

Others of us felt differently. Hooper, Eddie, the Runt, Chuck, and I clung together in our disillusionment. Having agreed to do another year come July the first, we were sure of one thing: we did not want to do another year in the House of God. None of us knew what to do. What would we say to Leggo when he called us in to ask us—thinking he already knew the answer— what were our plans for July the first?

The two months to decide were to be spent on ward 4-South with Chuck and the resident, a shade named Leon. Leon, finishing two years in the House, had perfected the technique of the LP—Low Profile. Leon's profile was so low that no one saw him, ever. Having watched people screw up their life plans at the House by being visible, Leon had perfected invisibility. Slim, common-featured, commonly and neatly dressed,

Leon reckoned on only two more months of LP-ing it until musical jobs and the ultimate city, Phoenix, the ultimate Fellowship, Dermatology. On 4-South, outside myself, only the most extraordinary could hold my interest. The extraordinary took shape in 789 and Olive O.

789 was my new BMS. A mathematician who'd gone to Princeton, and who'd done his senior honors thesis on the numeral 789, he'd been nicknamed by Chuck and me "789" or, for short, "Sev." A bepimpled intellectual prodigy with few social skills—just the kind of draft pick the BMS adored—789 always had a scared-rabbit look in his eyes. A rare genius for numbers, he was a dullard in common sense. His body coordination was beneath contempt, and all but the most loxed-out gomers soon banished him from doing any procedure upon their bodies.

Olive O. was just as rare. Olive O. was a gomere extraordinaire, who'd been TURFED to the House in some secrecy by her family. Told by flunky Marvin in Admitting that there was a TURF from Orthopedics, I'd sent Sev to investigate. Sev had looked through Olive's chart, had talked to the surgical resident, and had found out that for some godforsaken reason the surgeons, overcome with an early-summer rutting zeal, had made Olive the proud recipient of a hemipelvectomy—they had ripped off half her pelvis—which had left her with only one leg. They had used the orthodox TURF-tool from surgery—replacing too little blood—which had made Olive the proud recipient of an MI, and in need of medical care. Proudly showing me a series of EKG traces, Sev explained to me, with vector diagrams and with herds of those imaginary numbers that had outgrazed my IQ in grade eleven, how he had succeeded in obtaining an electrophysiologically sound EKG using three of Olive's extremities, the fourth being in a can in the morgue. How could I fail to have been impressed? Sev and I, proud son, proud father, went on down to Ortho.

Tied down in her personal Ortho jungle gym of rods, poles, bells, and chains lay our Olive. A nest of white hair cradled her balding head. Eyes shut, breathing calmly, whitely, she was reveling in her penultimate stillness. From the top of her head to the tip of her ten toes, she was at peace. Ten toes? I un-

328

covered her feet further and counted toes. Ten. I counted feet. Two. Legs? Two. I brought Sev to the bedside, and together the little polymath and I counted: "All right, now we count legs: one—"

"I don't think that's funny," said Sev. "I know how to count."

"Well, then, what happened?"

"I got the wrong chart."

"You didn't look at this patient?"

"Yes, I did," said Sev. "I looked, I just didn't see the other leg, that's all. My cognitive set was for one leg, not for two."

"Terrific," I said. "Reminds me of a very famous House LAW: SHOW ME A BMS WHO ONLY TRIPLES MY WORK, AND I WILL KISS HIS FEET."

The rareness of Olive was her humps. As I did my brief incursion into the realm of her body, I noticed, under the bedsheets, two protrusions from the vicinity of her chest-belly. Curious, I fantasized about what they might be. Breasts? Hardly. Supranumerary growths? No. I rolled down the sheet and rolled up her nightie, and there they were. Sprouting from her abdomen, below her low-slung flat breasts, were two humps.

Sev, at the foot of the bed, enjoying the luxury of putting EKG leads on both legs, glanced up, and his eyes lit up with horror, and he blurted out, "Ugh! What are those . . . those things?"

"What do they look like?"

"Humps."

"Good, Sev, good. That's what they are."

"I've never heard of humps in humans. What's in 'em?"

"Don't know," I said, seeing my own disgust mirrored in 789's eyes, "but by God we're gonna find out," and I began to examine them.

"UGGGHhhh!" said Sev. "Excuse me, but I feel . . . I fee—ecch—"

I watched him rush out of the room. I too felt repulsed, vomitoid. And that, Basch, is what you've learned this year in the House of God: when you feel like vomiting, you don't.

Later, in the on-call room, Sev had come up to me and apologized for getting sick, and I told him it was understandable and that he never had to confront the humps again. I was surprised to hear him say, "Yes, but I'd like to work them up."

"The humps? I thought they made you sick?"

"They did, but I'll take an antiemetic if I have to. Doggone it, Dr. Basch, I'm going to work up those humps, you just wait and see."

"Suit yourself," I said. "In spite of the fact that you couldn't tell how many legs or toes she had, Sev, from this day on she's all yours."

"I don't know how to say this, Dr. Basch, but, well, thanks, thanks a lot. I'll need a prescription for Compazine."

And who were we, anyway, to imagine we knew what these gomers felt, to be so hot on saving them? Wasn't it ridiculous for us to imagine that they felt as we did? As ridiculous as it would be for us to try to imagine what a child felt? We were putting into these gomers our fear of death, but who knew if they feared death? Perhaps they welcomed death like a dear long-lost cousin, grown old but still known, coming to visit, relieving the loneliness, the failing of the senses, the fury of the half-blind looking into the mirror and not recognizing who is looking back, a dear friend, a dear reliever, a healer who would be with them for an eternity, the same eternity as the one long ago, before birth. Wouldn't that be death, for them?

"You know, Roy, I wanna be so rich!" said Chuck. "That's it! Maybe in July I'll start one of them equal-opportunity foundations to find out why we're such good guys and nobody else is, huh?"

"Do you really hate medicine?" I asked.

"Well, man, put it this way: I know I hated this."

A sloth from Transportation poked his nose in, delivering the mail. I picked up a throwaway journal called *Doctor's Wife*, addressed to "Mrs. Roy G. Basch." Chuck looked at his mail, his eyes lit up, and he said, "Damn! It just happened again!"

"What did?"

"The postcards. Here, look," he said, and handed me a postcard: WANT TO HAVE A LUCRATIVE PRACTICE ON NOB

HILL, SAN FRANCISCO? IF SO, FILL OUT AND RETURN
THIS CARD.

I left the House of God and drove to the suburbs. I stopped in
front of a large turreted Victorian house, opened the door, and
suddenly realized why the Fat Man had never let me see his
house before: I was in a crowded waiting room; the first floor
was his office; the Fat Man had a booming private practice in
general medicine! The receptionist greeted me, said that Fats
was a little behind schedule, and led me past a lab and an examining room to what seemed to be a workshop. There I sat,
waiting. I couldn't help noticing the signs of many abandoned
projects, and in one corner was a pile of lenses and stainless-
steel tubing, and hand-lettered slogans: OWN YOUR OWN
ASSHOLE; GAY ASSHOLES, GRAY ASSHOLES, ASSHOLES
OF FOREIGN WARS; and finally, the conundrumical: SOME
OF MY BEST FRIENDS ARE ASSHOLES.
    "How goes the Anal Mirror?" I asked as he came in.
    "Ah, yes," said Fats dreamily, "Dr. Jung's. An idea whose
time might just have come, eh, Basch? If only I had the time."
    "What's keeping you so busy?"
    "Diarrhea."
    "I'm sorry to hear that."
    "Not mine, the Vets'." Haven't you heard?"
    "No," I said, thinking this would be a way to introduce what
I'd planned to say. "No, we've been out of touch. That's why I
insisted on—"
    "Yeah, over a month. So much has happened! Back then, I
was on the ropes, not knowing if I'd get my Fellowship Letter
from the Leggo."
    "Yeah," I said, trying to stick with my feelings, "I want to
tell—"
    "Wait'll you hear what's been going on, Basch. Oh, Christ,
wait'll you hear about this!" Settling in, he began telling me
how—like one of those weighted clowns that you punch down
and watch bob back up—he'd rebounded with a smile, but
then he noticed the anxious look on my face and stopped.
"You've come to say you're sorry? Is that it?"

How had he known? Looking into those familiar dark eyes, I felt choked up. Ashamed, I blushed. My face twisted toward sadness.

"I know, I know," said Fats quietly. "There'll be time to talk about it. But hey—a guy like me can't wait on telling an old-friend–new-protégé about the latest fortoona, can he? Basch, stop sniveling and tune in to this: right now, at this very moment, that diarrhea I inadvertently unleashed is going through God only knows how many hundreds of thousands of U.S. Vets' colons, ripping off the mucosal linings, and sluicing the *villae* out through the anus. The worst! Remember that Colonel who cornered you in the Unit, snooping around about me?"

"Yeah," I said, hearing again the Colonel asking me all kinds of questions about Fats and Jane Doe's diarrhea, and whether the Fat Man's extract had cured it. In the midst of our conversation the Colonel had gotten a painful look in his eyes and asked for the Men's Room. "Yeah, I remember the Colonel—the one with diarrhea himself?"

"Exactly. It's all over: NATO, SEATO, they say even Tito's caught the goddamn stuff. See, it's a virus. To date, there's only one cure. And the one inventor of the one cure is Fats."

"You invented a cure?"

"I invented the disease, so I had to: the extract. A cure not only for the diarrhea but also for the Fat Man's GI career." Musing, he picked up a lens and, toying with it, asked playfully, "Will I, like Lincoln, be the one to bind up our nation's bowels? I ask you, Basch, as a citizen, is it not time to put this Watergate of diarrhea behind us and go on with the great task of world peace?"

"How is it a cure for your career?"

"Oh. Well, the Leggo is a military man, right? And what military man wouldn't jump when a higher-up military man says 'Jump'? Why no one, Basch, no one wouldn't jump at all. You should have seen it! Beautiful! Last week, the Leggo and I walk down the corridor together, and there's an arm around my shoulder. There's also an arm around his shoulder, Basch, because in between us is a six-foot-three two-sixty-pound gorilla of a Four Star General of the U.S. Army. Made me feel like

I'm in a parade in a Banana Republic: the Colonels had won."

"And so he wrote you a good Fellowship Letter after all?"

"Not exactly. Delighted as he was by the promise to the House of a big GI Research grant, the Leggo has some pride. He told me to write my own letter. He signed it. My Fellowship is assured."

"Not Hollywood?"

"Yes, Hollywood. The bowel run of the stars!"

I was overwhelmed. Never before had I encountered such sustained application of genius. I felt small. "Fats, it's mindboggling. And you've had this private practice going all year?"

"Sure. Ever since I got my license last July. What's the sense of being a licensed doc if you don't use it 'to relieve pain and suffering'? This GP work is terrific—these are my neighbors, my people. JFK said it: 'Ask not what your country can do for you, ask what you can do for your country's bowels.'"

"So it all worked out just as you planned?"

"My life story, Basch: everything always works out."

"Fats, you might think it's stupid, but I did come here to say I'm sorry for fighting with you. And . . . and to say thanks."

"It's OK, Basch, you don't have to say—"

"Shut up, you fatso, and listen!" I said, smiling, watching him curl down into his roly-polyness and smile sheepishly. "You got me through it—"

"Berry got you through it. Marvelous woman. I wish I had—"

"SHUT UP, FATS!" I shouted, hurling a piece of an Anal Mirror at him. "Gradually, over the year, I threw away all the others, until you were the only one left. When I threw you away last month, things just fell apart."

"No, Roy," said Fats seriously, "things fell apart when Eddie cracked and Potts jumped. None of us stayed on our feet after that."

"True. But you showed me that a guy can stay in medicine and still be himself, that besides the Leggo and Putzel, there's another way." I paused, gathered myself up, and said, "Fats, you're fantastic. Thanks. Thanks for everything." I fell silent

333

and watched the steady eyes show their happiness. We sat together for a while in silence. Then I sighed and said, "The only problem is that your way is not for me. I can't do GI medicine. I doubt if I can stay in medicine at all. It's not for me."

"You mean you can't think of an organ you can see yourself dealing with every day for the rest of your life?" Fats asked sarcastically. "Kidney? Spleen? Rectum? Tooth?"

My father the dentist. Unimaginable. Even my grandfather, an immigrant, hadn't stuck himself into anything particular. I remembered my mother telling me about the time her mother took her and my aunt Lil to watch him, their father, at work: like a bee in a golden metal honeycomb high up in the sky, they saw him etch the sparkling arcs and curved sunbursts on the spire of the Chrysler Building, at the time the tallest in the City, maybe the world. And now, after all these years, I should choose a tooth?

Feeling hopeless, I said, "I can't see it."

"I know. It's clear that it's not for you."

"Well, then, what is?"

"You think I know? Big deal. Fly high. Have a blast, Basch. Great minds—like ours—can't be just one thing."

"Yeah, but I've got to decide soon," I said, feeling lost, cast out alone after so many programmed years. "I don't know what to do."

"Do? Well, in Brooklyn we always did this," said Fats, and reached out and hooked my pinkie in his. "Linking pinkies."

"Linking pinkies?"

"Sure. That's what we did in Brooklyn whenever we didn't know what to do."

A joke? No, his face was serious, sincere. I felt his fat pinkie hugging mine. Suddenly I knew what he meant. It was perfect, a magical moment. A tingling current of feeling zinged through me. He'd sensed my emptiness, and he'd responded. His touch meant I wasn't alone. He and I were connected. I squeezed back. It was love. No matter what, Fats and I would be friends.

Laughing, I said, "You know, for a fat kid, you don't sweat much."

"Right. Life's tough, but even a fat kid can fast on Yom Kippur."

Berry and I were laughing over the lead article in *Doctor's Wife,* a tribute to a terrific doctor's wife who, "becoming aware of the depth charges in a doctor's dinner" such as her terrific doctor hubby getting called out on an emergency case that might keep him away until his food gets cold, had learned "a foolproof operation to keep roast beef deliciously rare for hours," namely, wrapping it in Aluminum foil and warming it on a hot plate. I told Berry about my top-bunk posture and asked if she thought it was another regression.

"No, I think it's integration, working out what to do with yourself. Now that you know you can be a doctor, you've got the option of discarding medicine and moving on. What are you thinking of doing?"

"Going on vacation to France with you. Maybe taking a year off."

"But what are you going to tell the Leggo about July?"

"I don't know. I hated this. The whole year sucked."

"Not true. Fats, the policemen, your buddies—you liked them. And you liked listening to your patients in the Clinic, right?"

"As long as I didn't have to do anything medical, it was fun."

"In the E.W., you were fascinated by the psych resident, Cohen." Tantalizingly she asked, "Why not become a psychiatrist?"

"Me?" I said, surprised. "A shrink?"

"You." Looking me squarely in the eyes, she said, "Being with people was all that kept you going this year, Roy. And 'being with' is the essence of psychiatry."

CLICK. In my head, CLICK. I asked her to repeat what she'd said.

"'Being with' is the essence of psychiatry. You've always perched yourself at a slight angle to the universe. Psychiatry might be perfect for you."

Being with. CLICK. Dr. Sanders, dying, telling me that what

335

doctors did was to "be with" patients. "You mean 'being with' patients?"

"I mean being with," she said. "Even being with your family."

Family? My grandfather, TURFED to rot in a home, never again to be with anyone: my father?

. . . There is nothing more comforting during illness than a loved one to be with you and a good physician can serve that role . . .

"You're saying that psychiatry really offers something to patients? That it's different from medicine in that you can cure?"

"Sometimes. If you catch a life early, yes."

"So the big thing is that you can offer something to patients?"

"No. You can offer something to yourself."

Stunned, I asked her: "What can you offer to yourself?"

"Growth. Instead of forgetting, you'd try to remember. Instead of defensive, obsessive superficiality, you'd try to become open, looser, deep. You'd create. Your only tool as a therapist is who you are and who you might become."

It was hard for me to think. Somehow, in the chaos, something was clearing. I might become someone I might not despise? Escape being strapped into the rocker of past, culling my memories for trinkets? Be rid of my avoiding, my exploding, my contempt? Trembling, I asked her if there was anything I could start to read.

"Freud. Start with *Mourning and Melancholia.* In it Freud says, 'The shadow of the lost object falls across the ego.' You've been under that shadow for a solid year."

"What shadow?"

"You. The shadow of yourself."

My lacuna of humanity, my Berry. How I'd grown to love her, my accepting, caring, clear-sighted soft one, during this abrasive year.

"I love you," I said. "I lived through this nightmare because you were with me."

"Yes, partly. And you're right: this internship has been like

336

the stuff of dreams, like the overpowering nightmares of childhood: aggression, fear of retaliation, and then the resolution,
where you don't win, you live. It's the straight Oedipal theme:
mother, father, child."

. . . Hope you are finishing up well and glad to be finished
with your experience. Could not understand your premise that
now you can handle all medical problems and there is so much
to know. I am very worried over the worldwide economic situation meaning the inability of the brains of the world to solve
inflation and the monetary crisis and it is not even worth having money in the bank. I don't know what mother told you but I
know it was basic and true. I know you care for us as a son and
that will never change. Distance and circumstance have inter-
fered with our keeping close, and that is inevitable in this day
and age. Would love to play golf with my son number one again
and that is just a hope. Mom really has such a short controlled
swing and it is a picture. My passion for the game is unlimited
and I do enjoy it . . .

24

Disillusioned, not wanting to go on as House residents but not knowing what to do, we needed help. We turned to Fats. At the ten-o'clock meal, we asked him what we should do.

"About what?"

"About what specialty to go into on July the first."

"Do what's always done nowadays," said Fats, "do a colloquium. Never fails."

"What on?" asked Eddie, his eyes a bit dull, tranquilized.

"On 'How to Choose a Specialty,' what else?"

"Who the hell's gonna run it?" asked the Runt.

"Who?" asked Fats, smiling. "Me. The star of the bowel run of the stars."

Word spread rapidly. On the day, from all over the House of God, terns and BMSs appeared. Even Gilheeny and Quick were there. The crowded room hushed, and the Fat Man began: "The whole pattern of medical education is backwards: by the time we realize we're not going to be TV docs undressing ripe-titted beauties, but rather House docs disimpacting gomers, we've invested too much to quit, and we wind up like you poor slobs: stuck. The sequence of training should be reversed: on day one, bring the puking BMSs right into the House of God and rub their noses in Olive O.: turn off potential surgeons with her humps, potential internal-medicine red-

338

hots with her numbers incompatible with life and her inability to be cured or dead; even potential gynecologists will take one look at the terrain of their future speciality and transfer into dentistry. And then—and only then—let the ones who still have the stomach for it start on the preclinical years."

It was brilliant, as expected. But how did it help us now?

"But that doesn't help you now, 'cause now you've invested, and now you're trapped. So? So there are many different specialties you could choose. Most of them involve the same close contact you've had with patients all this year—touching, being tortured, killing yourself with night call. These are the 'PC—Patient Care' specialties. PC specialties will not be considered here. The masochists may leave."

No one left.

"I myself am going into a PC specialty, Gastroenterology. I have my reasons. I am a very special case. Where I'm headed, GI is what's best for me. A rare gift, eh? Right. But the NPC—No Patient Care—specialties number six and only six: Rays, Gas, Path, Derm, Ophthalmology, and Psychiatry."

The Fat Man listed these six on the blackboard and told us he would list, with our suggestions, the advantages and disadvantages of each. "Game theory," he called it. This chart would "optimize" our specialty choice.

"First," said Fats, "is Rays. Advantages of Radiology?"

"Money," said Chuck. "Big money."

"Exactly," said Fats, "a veritable fortoona. Other advantages?"

Aside from the assumed "No Patient Care," no one could think of any other advantages, and Fats asked for disadvantages.

"Gomers," I said, "you do bowel runs on gomers."

"Narcolepsy," said Hooper, "you're always in the dark."

"Gonads," said the Runt. "X rays can fry your sperm. Your first kid comes out with one eye, two teeth, and eight fingers to a hand."

"Terrific!" said Fats, writing them down. "Men, we're on our way!"

We proceeded to construct a table of the NPC Specialties:

SPECIALTY	ADVANTAGES*	DISADVANTAGES
RAYS	Money (100K/annum)	Gomers. Dark offices, narcolepsy. Damaged gonads; 8-fingered progeny. Barium enemas and bowel runs.
GAS	Money (100K/annum)	Gomers. Boredom punctured by panic. Astronomical malpractice premiums. Noxious gases, producing bizarre personalities. Contempt, daily, of surgeons.
PATH	No live bodies. Low malpractice premiums	Gomers (rare). Dead bodies. Smell of dead bodies and formalin-type picklers. Basement office. Contempt, daily, of all but other pathologists. Depression.
DERM	Money (100K/annum) Travel to sunny conventions. Naked skin—attraction.	Gomers. Contagion. Naked skin—repulsion.
OPHTHAL-MOLOGY	Astronomical money (millions/annum) Opportunity, daily, to torment GAS.	Gomers. Astronomical malpractice premiums Surgical internship required. Occasional patient care.
PSYCHI-ATRY	NO GOMERS! Never touch bodies except in sex-surrogate therapies.	Hourly wage. Hard on lumbar spine. Multiple accusations from right-wingers, cf.

SPECIALTY ADVANTAGES*	DISADVANTAGES
Voyeurism, perversion, eroticism, autoeroticism, polyeroticism. Easy on feet. Long lunch hours. Cure—alleged** (many others . . .)	'communist,' 'queer,' 'pervert.' Contempt, daily of other doctors except when they are in therapy.

*Each specialty has advantage of NPC: No Patient Care, in the Fat Man's sense of the term.

**Berry, Clinical Psychologist and Psychotherapist.

By the end of the Fat Man's colloquium, the remarkable had happened: on paper, Psychiatry was the clear winner.

On the canoe trip, Psychiatry loomed even larger. Chuck had organized this final intern outing, and one bright, sweet-breezed summer day we signed out to the House residents, loaded the beer, and headed for the shore, into the foothills of the marshland to the tidal river, winding through the grasses to the sea. As we paddled lazily downriver, Berry and I found ourselves in a race with the two policemen for last. Gilheeny, a great red-feathered mallard in the bow, continued to curse his rudderman, Quick, as their listing canoe smacked first one bank and then the other. And yet what could have been better than drifting along, drinking cool beer, listening behind us for the deep carmine baritone of the redhead and the insistent tenor of his mate crooning "a lament from the Emerald Isle"?

We stopped on an island for a picnic. In a pine grove dappled with shadow, we found ourselves drawn to Berry. She listened to our discontent; she agreed that the year had been a horror:

"It's been inhuman," she said. "No wonder doctors are so distant in the face of the most poignant human dramas. The tragedy isn't the crassness, but the lack of depth. Most people have some human reaction to their daily work, but doctors don't. It's an incredible paradox that being a doctor is so degrading and yet is so valued by society. In any community, the most respected group are doctors."

"You mean the whole thing's a deception?" asked the Runt.

"An unconscious one, a terrific repression that makes doctors really believe that they are omnipotent healers. If you hear yourselves saying, 'Well, this year wasn't really that bad,' you're repressing, to put the next group through it."

"Well, then, my clever woman," said Gilheeny, "why is it that these fine young men do this at all?"

"Because it's so hard to say no. If you're programmed from age six to be a doctor, invest years in it, develop your repressive skills so that you can't even recall how miserable you were during internship, you can't stop. Can a star take himself out of a ballgame? No way."

She was right. What could we say? We sat, still, absorbed, hushed, as the afternoon shadows inched on. Berry answered some questions about psychiatry, and as we awoke to what she was saying, she turned our picnic into a sort of group session. The theme was loss.

"What all loss do you mean?" asked Chuck.

"What each of you has lost this year. I know it firsthand only from Roy, but I've heard about the MORs and RORs and . . . and Eddie's break and . . . " She paused, and then, her voice trembling, said, "And Potts. You lost Potts. If you felt that loss, you'd still be crying. You're crippled by your guilt, the guilt of killing off the cherished parts of yourselves."

In the darkening grove, silence hung somber as a shroud. I felt choked up. What had I killed off? Days like this one, my creativity, my ability to love. Gloom. Stasis. Doom. Finally, with the sun curdling down into the reddening hills, Gilheeny asked softly, "These men are wounded. Can anything still be done?"

"Guilt's a hot potato—whoever holds onto it gets burned. You're all doing a slow burn. Give it up. Get mad. Give it back to the ones who infantalized you. Is there a House shrink to talk to?"

There was: Dr. Frank, the psychiatrist at the B-M Deli lunch on our first day in the House. He'd mentioned suicide, and the Fish had canned him. He'd stayed canned the whole year. Why? Returning to the canoes, we floated toward the sounds of oceans, each wondering what had been lost, how this Dr.

Frank might help find it, and finally, as the lightning bugs began their dance, wondering how to take this rage and stick it to the ones who'd ripped off parts of each of us, these House Robber Barons, the House Bosses of Loss.

I was on call that night, and arrived from the canoe trip with blistered hands, my drunkenness beginning to hang, preoccupied with what Berry had said, and mad about being back inside the House. It was hot and humid, and my sweatiness brought back memories of the terrifying summer I'd spent as a new tern a year before. Everything had happened. An admission was awaiting me in the E.W. It was to turn out to be extraordinary in that it was to be redeeming. I was greeted in the E.W. by the Pearl, who wanted to warn me about this particular patient, but I wasn't in the mood and I picked up the clipboard and read: "Nathan Zock, 63; bloody diarrhea;? benign polyp." No wonder the Pearl had wanted a word with me. Zock, of the MICU Zocks and of the Wing of Zock, which had shut out summer from my on-call room.

Irritated, I entered the room, the Pearl rolling in at my heels. I had never seen so much flesh. Six bovine Zocks, overinflated flesh balloons, hovered around the stretcher, chomping, sucking, nibbling, snacking, smacking in a tribute to Freud's oral stage of development. Gems glittering, the Pearl introduced me to Nate Zock's fat kids, in an effort to herd them away from the stretcher on which Nate Zock allegedly lay. As they edged back, they dislodged a nasty-eyed chalk-voiced macaw of a woman with artificially black hair, who, hearing my name, said, "Well, young Dr. Kildare, it's about time—"

"Trixie," came an authoritative voice from the stretcher, "shut up!"

She did. There lay Nate, a rubbery-faced sixty, a bit booze-riddled, but with wealth in his manner and decisiveness in his mien. Even hassled by the herd, he was calm. The Pearl introduced me and left. Immediately I was besieged by the non-Nate Zocks. Everyone wanted feeding, about the diagnosis, prognosis, and the portending emergency: that Nate might not procure the best room in the House. To work on the latter problem, Trixie kept hinting in my ear the name Zock and "do you know who Nate is, have you heard of the Wing of Zock, eh?" After being sucked on for about three minutes, I'd had it and said loudly, "OK, everyone but Nate, get out of this room now!" Shock. No one moved. To talk like that to Zocks?

"You wait a minute, young Dr. Kil—"

"Trixie, shut up and get out!" said Nate, and when Nate Zock talked, even other Zocks listened. The room cleared fast. As I began my exam, Nate went on: "They're too fat. We tried, but nothing worked. You know, Dr. Pearlstein told me about you, Basch, he warned me, he said you're a tough guy, that I shouldn't try to cross you. Said you're very good, but straightforward. I like that. Docs should be tough. When you're rich as I am, people don't treat you tough enough."

I nodded, and continuing my exam, asked what his business was.

"Nuts and bolts. Started with five hundred bucks in the depression, and now . . . millions. Nuts and bolts: not the best, but the most."

I told Nate that as long as we didn't do anything much to his bleeding gut, it would probably heal. As I finished, Trixie poked her head in, upset, saying that Nate would get only the second-best room in the House. Nate told her to scram, and said, "So what? I always get the best room; nobody visits you in the best room. So I'll rough it for a night, so what? That's what happened to those kids: all the time the best, and what happens? Fat. Too goddamn fat."

789 had had a rough day. Caught in a maze of tests ordered by Olive. O.'s Private, Little Otto, whose name still—still!—rang no bell in Stockholm, Sev was discouraged about making any headway with the humps. His first admission of the day had seen Sev and the radiology resident decide that the patient had a lesion on chest X ray, and when he presented the case to me, I dismayed him by quoting a House LAW: IF THE RADIOLOGY RESIDENT AND THE BMS BOTH SEE A LESION ON THE CHEST X RAY, THERE CAN BE NO LESION THERE. Despite Sev's insistence, the lesion turned out to be the technician's bracelet, and Sev was crushed. I tried to cheer him, but he'd have none of it, so I gave up. I'd try no more for anyone that night. "Sev," I said, hoisting myself down from the top bunk to the bottom, "I'm going to sleep. I want you to

get your scrub suit and change into it now, so that you won't come barging in here later, turn on the light, and wake me up." Through half-open eyes I saw the short bearded scholar strip down, bare his pimply and already flabby body to the neon, quickly and scurrilously slip on his morgue-gray scrub suit, and then pause. I asked what was the matter. After the thoughtful pause so characteristic of him, he said, "Dr. Basch, I've got several hours' more work to do tonight, and you don't. How come you're always going to sleep, and I'm always staying awake?"

"Simple. You're a mathematician, right? Now, I get paid a fixed salary by the BMS, no matter how many hours I'm awake. You pay a fixed tuition to the BMS, no matter how many hours you're awake. Therefore, the more I sleep, the more I earn per waking hour, and the more you stay awake, the less you pay per waking hour. Got it?"

There was a pause, and then Sev's QED: "So you get paid for sleeping, and I pay to stay awake."

"You got it. Hit the light on the way out, eh, good buddy? Oh, and remember: Nate Zock is not a BMS case. If you talk to him—even say 'Hi, Nate' or 'Hi, Mr. Zock' to him—you die. Nighty-night."

I heard the ataxic shuffle of the little polymath, I felt the puzzled look back at me, and then the lights went out, and I slept.

By the next morning, something had changed. A small epidemic had begun. Never in the House of God had there been anything like it. Starting as a murmur, a trickle, a loss seen full-face on a dusk-dappled island, the epidemic spread, and was soon many rivulets streaming around many islands, sounding louder and louder, an ululation of a river against a sea. Suddenly, urgently, five of us terns in the House had become infected with psychoanalytic thought. We had begun to BUFF ourselves for the possibility of TURFING ourselves into a residency in psychiatry on July the first.

Together we five began to study *Mourning and Melancholia*. We sought out Dr. Frank, who at first was delighted with Eddie's interest in a psych residency at the House, but who, when four more of us followed suit, ran to the Leggo with the news. We ordered psych consults on our patients, and we attended psych rounds, our dirty whites conspicuous amidst the psychiatric fashion show, our rudimentary questions on anger, loss, and guilt demonstrating our ignorance. At a case conference on an obscure autoimmune disease, Hooper startled us by letting fly a psychoanalytic interpretation based on Freud's "Death Wish." Eddie, still racing Hooper down the stretch for the alleged Black Crow, was delighted to find Freud so tight into anal sadism, and developed a facial tic. Chuck grooved on the passive-aggressive personality, and discovering his pathological closeness to his momma while his poppa was reading cowboy novels at work, came out with, "Man, it's amazin' I ain't queer, 'cause everythin' in my upbringin' points right to me bein' a fag." The Runt, of course, plunged deepest into the one whom Fats had tagged "that red-hot from Vienna": obsessing about what the hell he'd been letting Angel do to his face, he'd look dazed and say, "Holy cow, is there ever something wrong with me!" I kept on self-analyzing in my top bunk, finding and stashing these pieces of myself.

The day came for our "future-plan-Leggo-chats." The Leggo had heard of the epidemic and had discounted it. He harbored no doubts about our future plans: the House residency year. With July less than a month away and a year full of residency on-call night slots to fill, the Leggo was a little surprised to hear the Runt, Hooper, and Eddie, one after the other, say: "Well, sir, I'm thinking of starting my residency in psychiatry."

"Psychiatry?"

"Yes, sir, on July the first."

"But you can't. You've agreed to stay in medicine for your residency year. I'm counting on you, on all of you boys, to stay."

"Yeah, but you see, I feel kind of urgent about this. Lotta things to work through, and some things, sir, well, they just can't wait."

"But your contract says—"

"There is no contract, remember?"

The Leggo didn't remember that the House had refused to

write us a contract—the only way it could legally treat us like shit—and he said, "There isn't?"

"No. You said we didn't need one."

"I said that? Hmmm . . . " said the Leggo, drifting out the ·window. "Why, no, one doesn't need a contract. No, one doesn't, at all."

When Chuck mentioned psych, the Leggo burst out with "WHAT!? YOU TOO?"

"No foolin', Chief. What this country needs is a high-class black shrink, right?"

"Yes, but . . . but you've done so well so far in medicine. Up from the poverty of the rural South, your father a janitor, to Ober—"

"Ezactly, man, ezactly. And get this: today I was in my Clinic, and this chick got mad at me and threw this textbook across the table and hit me in the ear, and instead of smackin' her up side of her haid, I go: 'Hmmm, gurl, you mus' be angry, huh?' So right then I knew I was gonna think about shrinkin'. I'm talkin' to Dr. Frank again tomorra about goin' under analysis myseff."

"But you can't start this July, I need boys like you."

" 'Boys'? Did you say 'boy'?"

"Well I . . . What I meant was—"

"Want me to send in Roy now?"

"Basch? Hmmm. You wouldn't know his future plans, would you?"

"Yup."

"Psychiatry?"

"Really."

"Yes, well, no, you don't have to bother to send Roy in."

And so he didn't call me then. Despite Berry's formulation that the Leggo couldn't help it, that he too had been damaged by the system, I was too angry not to see him as Nixonesque, getting squeezed by us as Nixon was getting squeezed by Sirica and the Supreme Court for the tapes. Couldn't it have been the Leggo himself, standing with St. Clair on the bow of the yacht *Sequoia* at Mount Vernon, listening to the ceremony of ship's bells and the National Anthem, who, when it was over,

347

drunkenly spilled out: "They pay you nickels and dimes, but this is what makes it worth it"? Berry was right—it was pathetic. But these pathetic men were powerful men, and soon the Leggo began to pressure us to stay. Through the Fish, at first by insinuation and then by clear threat, the Leggo made it known that to leave in July "would seriously—very seriously—jeopardize one's future plans and career." We didn't budge. The Leggo got more vicious. Vulnerable and powerless, we got madder. As July came closer, all his retaliations having failed, the Leggo began to panic.

None of us knew what he would do.

25

Why, he would call an emergency B-M Deli lunch.

On the morning of the emergency lunch, I walked into the House to find Howie, calm "Social Medicine" Howie, the last tern to have gone to Gomer City, standing in front of the elevator door, IBM cards scattered at his feet, hair disheveled, biting on his pipe stem and kicking and pounding on the closed steel door, screaming, "GODDAMNIT, COME DOWN, COME DOWN!" So, I thought, the last happy tern has been broken.

The only patients I went to see were Nate Zock and Olive O. My relationship with Nate had rocketed along on a remarkable trajectory. All the Zocks—Nate, Trixie, the kids—suffered under the illusion that my "taking charge" in the E.W. by kicking them all out of the room was what had saved Nate's life. I did not relieve them of their suffering under this. For the first few days Trixie, thinking that Nate was at death's door and that I had the key, had shadowed me all over the House. I'd shaken her only by mentioning that in fact Nate still did not have the best room in the House. Trixie had gone one-on-one with the daughter of the rich gomere who did have the best room and was never to give it up. Trixie had done a thumbnail calculation and ascertained that this gomere was not in the League of Zock, especially while the interior of the Wing of Zock was not quite finished. The major medical complication in Nate's case had been how to implement what Nate needed, the Fat Mannish LAW: DO NOTHING. I'd encountered much resistance, and had had to use all my hard-earned House skills—lying, false-BUFFING the chart, keeping the Low Profile—to be sure of doing nothing on this important personage. I liked Nate, which made my holding on to doing nothing a little easier. And so the potentially lethal bleeding polyp of Zock had healed over, and he got better. That day, he was to go home, and wanted to talk to me.

"You're a good guy," Nate said. "I'm a real judge of talent. I look at a guy and I know if he's got it or not. Know what I mean?"

"Sure," I said.

"You got it. The Pearl warned me about you. The way you kicked my wife out of that room I'll never forget. You and me are similar: started with nothing, and now . . ." And Nate made a wavy motion with his hands, as if playing a huge accordian stuffed with money, expanding to fill the world. "Now, listen: I like you, Basch, and the people I like, I reward. I know you don't make shit for money here, but now, with your internship almost over, you can start in private practice. I can help. You know the Pearl? With that ritzy office and the Muzak playing *Fiddler*? You know how he got started? My old man. So listen: your sneakers tell me you play tennis. Come to the house, play on my court, use my pool. Here's the card: NATE ZOCK: NOT THE BEST BUT THE MOST. You call this weekend, OK?"

I thanked him and started to leave.

"Oh, and one more thing: I'm writing a letter to the Chief of Medicine, Dr. Leggo, with copies to the Chief Resident and the BMS and House Board of Trustees. I been a patient here eight times and I never been treated so good. Usually my intern is some whiny kid from the Bronx who's so scared of a Zock pegging out that he's in the room every ten minutes doing tests, taking blood, and I get worse before I get better. By the time I'm out of here I'm so exhausted I've got to fly straight to the condo in Palm Springs for a rest. Bad for business. But you—you had enough savvy to let me heal. And I knew you were there in case anything went wrong. Basch, you were with me man to man. You handled my wife, my fat kids, and you handled me. So I'm going to tell your bosses, eh? Give a call Saturday. I'll send my man around."

A letter to the Leggo? Fight power with power! Not even the Leggo would be dumb enough to stand up to Zock, a family dealing in monstrous steel beams and knockwurst-sized nuts and bagel-sized bolts holding together the brand-new Wing of the House of God. Excited, I checked out humpy Olive O. She seemed to be doing just great.

Yet LP Leon still refused to let me present the humps to the Leggo, and so I climbed into the top bunk, pried open my can of Freud, and soon found yet another Viennese bombshell recalling leaping into the sack with her pop. Chuck came in, took his bottle out of his bag, and began to sing. Hooper wandered in and opened a book called *How to Pierce an Ear,* which turned out to be not another quest for a post, but a requirement for a moonlighting job in a department store downtown. Eddie stopped by and started reading out loud from my old "internship novel" *How I Saved the World,* but after a few passages that had us laughing at the idealized deception, the book sailed into the trashcan for good. The Runt ambled in and greeted 789 cheerfully: "749, how are you? Did you ever find out what was in those humps?"

"Excuse me, but you misspelled my middle name," said Sev. "No, I have not yet found what is in 'those humps.'"

"Man, maybe they're breasts," said Chuck. "Extra breasts."

"Doesn't help," said 789, "no one knows what's in breasts either."

"They're spiritual humps," I said, "filled with the milk of human kindness."

"The leading theory," said Sev, "is that they're filled with oxygen. It's said that the oxygen in her humps is what's keeping her alive."

"That's it," I said, "she's not human, she's a plant. Her humps are cotyledons. In her altruism, she makes oxygen for us all."

"Nah, you're all wrong," said the Runt, "I know what's in the humps, and it's not altruism or oxygen either."

"Well, man, what's in 'em?"

351

"Pimento. Olive's humps are big pimentoes."

After the laughter had died down, Chuck drifted into a song by Mississippi John Hurt:

When my earthly trials are over, cast my body down in the sea;
Save all the undertaker's bills, let the mermaids flirt with me.

Each of us had heard another tern sing that song. The other tern had been Wayne Potts. We were ready. It was time for the B-M Deli lunch.

Gilheeny and Quick stood by the door. As we entered, they sent back two winks: one fat, red, and bushy; the other thin, wiry, and black. Little did the Leggo realize whom he'd chosen to protect him. We dug into our B-M Deli sandwiches. The Leggo ate standing, in front. Sensing the tension in the room, and with only two weeks to go until his Chief Residency year was successfully completed and he would be assured a spot on the House Slurper staff, the Fish was determined to avoid an explosion. Standing before us, he began to announce the event that Hyper Hooper and Eat My Dust Eddie had been awaiting, the presentation of the Black Crow Award.

"You mean the thing really exists?" I asked Chuck.

"If'n it don't, it sure did fool the Leggo and the Fish."

". . . and so, since there has already been one award this year, the ***MVI*** won by Dr. Roy G. Basch and symbolized by his silver tiepin, we've decided to have a tiepin for the Black Crow." The Fish held up a silver tiepin with a black crow perched on it, and said, "I know there's been fierce competition, and right up until last night the contest was a dead heat between Hooper and Eddie for the most posts. In fact, it wasn't until the early hours of the morning, with the death of Rose—"

"KATZ! ROSE KATZ!" screamed Hooper, leaping up. "YAYYY! I KNEW IT! ROSE KATZ PUT ME OVER THE TOP! I WON IT AT THE POST!"

"Yes," said the Fish, "it was Mrs. Rose Katz, the postmortem was done this morning, and it gives me great pleasure to announce that the first annual House of God Black Crow Award goes to Dr. Hooper."

"YEE-AYY!" said Hooper, running up to the front of the room to accept his tiepin and his free trip for two to Atlantic City. He did a little victory dance and burst out with "Underr the boo-arrd-walk, down by the seee-eeeeee—"

"Wait just a second," said the Runt angrily. "Rose Katz was my LOL in NAD. I claim credit for the death and for the post. I worked hard for that death, and Hooper robbed me of it. He came in last night when he wasn't even on call and I was home asleep. Eddie was on call, and since Rose died when Eddie was in charge, I know she'd want him to get credit for her post. Eddie's the winner, not Hooper."

"HEY HEY HEY!" cried Eddie, standing, running up to the front. "HEY, GUYS, IT'S EDDIE! HOOPER, YOU CAN EAT MY DUST! I'M THE BLACK CROW, FAIR AND SQUARE! LET'S HEAR IT FOR EDDIE, EH? HEY HEY HEY!"

Well, at that, all hell broke loose. Eddie and Hooper started arguing and then were pushing and shoving and then really started in swinging at each other, and with all of us screaming like at a prizefight, finally the policemen broke it up. The Leggo marched center-ring and said that unfortunately the decision of the judges was final and Hooper was the first House Black Crow. Hooper, relieved, shook hands with Eddie, and then, turning to the rest of us, with moisture in his eyes, said, "You know, guys, I just can't believe it. This is like a dream come true. I want you to know I couldn't have done it without your help, each and every one of you. You put me where I am today, and I'll never forget it. From my heart, guys, thanks. YAY! Under the boo—"

The Leggo and the Fish canned the second verse of Hooper's song, and we settled down to the serious business of the day: "All of you, when you came here almost a year ago," said the Leggo, "agreed to do two years, and yet some of you are thinking of not going on in medicine. Boys, I'll be frank: I'm banking on your being here with me for the rewarding House residency year. One year isn't enough. One year is nothing, almost a waste. It's the second year, built on the foundation of the first, that makes it all worthwhile." He paused. Angry silence filled the room. A waste? "Now, how many of you are considering psychiatry? Raise your hands."

Silently, five hands went up: the Runt, Chuck, Eddie, the Crow, the ***MVI***. And then the Leggo's eyes and the Fish's eyes bugged out, staring at the back of the room. We turned. Both Gilheeny and Quick had raised their hands.

"What?" asked the Leggo. "You too? You're policemen, not physicians. You can't become psychiatrists on July the first."

"Policemen we are," said Gilheeny, "and strictly speaking, psychiatrists we cannot become. At first this seemed a singular limitation for us, so taken as we are with the warped and criminally perverted—"

"Get on with it, man. What's the point?"

"The point is that we shall become lay analysts."

"Lay analysts? You cops are thinking of becoming lay analysts?"

There was a pause, and then, out of it rolled a familiar question: "Would we be policemen if we were not?"

"Yes," said Quick, "for lay analysis was introduced to our minds by our old friend Grenade Room Dubler. Dr. Jeffrey Cohen also—"

"WHAT?!" yelled the Leggo. "DUBLER A PSYCHIATRIST?"

"Not just a psychiatrist, no," said Gilheeny, "a Freudian analyst."

"THAT MADMAN? A FREUDIAN PSYCHOANALYST?"

"And not just a psychoanalyst," said Quick, "but the bearded President of the Psychoanalytic Institute, a preeminent humanist and scholar."

"Yes," said Gilheeny, "having left the House of God directly after his internship year, Dubler never looked back, and has risen to the very top. At this moment, he is pulling strings for us, giving us 'a leg up.'"

"And with Finton's banjaxed leg anyway," said Quick, "it is time for us to change careers to a less ambulatory one. Lay analysis is perfect."

"For did not the great Sigmund Freud in 1912 conclude a symposium on masturbation with the statement: 'the subject of onanism is inexhaustible'?"

"And will it not take time to work out our Church dogma that masturbation will render the Catholic lad blind, hairy-

palmed, insane, doomed, and with the leg bones bent like an
orphan with the rickets?"

"And so excuse us, Chief," said Gilheeny, folding his big
arms across his chest and leaning back against the door, "we
will now resume the free associations," and he closed his eyes
and lapsed into silence again.

The Leggo was shaken. Turning back to us, anxiously tugging the stethoscope deep-sixed in his trousers, he asked,
"Psychiatry? All of you five? I don't understand. Hooper?"

"Well," said Hooper sheepishly, "I got to admit I was thinking Path most of the year, but for some reason, right now
Psych seems a better deal. Lot to work through, Chief—the divorce, splitting up the furniture, saying good-bye to the wife's
old man, the works—anyway, the fiancée's a pathologist,
she'll keep me up on the stiffs."

"Chuck? Even you?" asked the Leggo.

"You know how it is, man. I mean, just look at me. When I
firs' came here, I looked great, didn't I, guys? I was thin, ath-a-
letic, dressed like a Bluenote, remember? Now I'm fat, and I'm
dressin' like a janitor, a damn bum. Why? You dudes and
them gomers, that's why. And mostly you—you made me
what I am today. Thanks, man, thanks a lot. I be good god-
damned if I stay here for round two."

We were startled by Chuck's outburst. The Leggo looked
hurt and puzzled. He began to question Eddie, but the Runt,
more and more angry, exploded: "Damnit, Leggo, you don't
realize what we've been going through this year. You don't
have a clue!"

There was an ominous hush. The Runt, wild-eyed, looked
like he was about to strangle the Leggo, and the Fish shielded
his Chief with his body and gestured toward the policemen.
Snarling, the Runt continued: "There's some good news,
there's some bad news: the bad news is there's shit around
here; the good news is that there's plenty of it. You've broken
us this year, with your pious version of medical care. We hate
this. We want out."

"What?" asked the Leggo incredulously, "you mean you
don't enjoy doing medicine here at the House of God?"

"Get it through your fucking skull!" shouted the Runt at the

Leggo, and, according to Freud, at his mom and pop in the Leggo, and sat down.

"It's just a small radical nucleus."

"Nope," I said in a somber tone. "It's all of us. This morning I saw Howard Greenspoon bashing and screaming at the elevator door like a maniac."

"Howard? No!" said the Leggo. "My Howie?"

The attention turned to his Howie. Silence. The tension billowed out. Howie squirmed. The tension hung, taut. Howie cracked: "Y-y-yes, Chief, sir, I'm sorry, but it's true. It was the gomers: one named Harry and a flatulent woman named Jane. See, it's my admitting days that kill me. Each admitting day— knowing that the total age of my admissions will be in the four hundreds—I get depressed and I want to kill myself. The tension had been incredible: those M and M Conferences where I get roasted every two weeks for my mistakes—I can't help making mistakes, can I, Chief?—and then Potts splattering and his mess being spread around so we had to park right on him, and all these gomers. And then the young patients dying no matter what we do. The truth is, Chief, well . . . well, since September I've been on antidepressants, Elavil. And I'm staying on here; imagine how the other guys feel. Like the Runt: he used to be a fun guy, and now . . . why, just look at him."

We all looked at him. The Runt was staring at the Leggo with a gaze as ferocious as Crazy Abe's. The Runt looked extraordinarily mean.

The Leggo, shocked, asked, "You mean you don't look forward to your admitting days?"

"Look forward?" said Howie. "Chief, two days before my admitting day—just after my last admitting day—I'm nervous, and I up my dose of Elavil twenty-five milligrams. One day before my admitting day, I add fifty of Thorazine. On my admitting day, as I start to see the gomers, I start to shake, and . . ." Shaking, Howie took out a silver pillbox faced with mother-of-pearl and popped a Valium into his mouth. ". . . and it's Valium all the way. On real bad days . . . well, it's hits of Dex."

So that was Howie's smile: the guy was a walking pharmacopoeia.

The Leggo had gotten stuck on something Howie had said,

and asked the Fish: "Did they say they don't enjoy their admitting days?"

"Yes, sir," said the Fish, "I do believe they said that, sir."

"Strange. Boys, when I was an intern, I loved my admitting days. All of us did. We looked forward to them, we fought for those 'toughies' so we could show our Chief what we could do. And we did damn well. What's happened? What's going on?"

"Gomers," said Howie, "gomers are what's going on."

"You mean old people? We took care of old people too."

"Gomers are different," said Eddie. They didn't exist when you were a tern, 'cause then they used to die. Now they don't."

"Ridiculous," said the Leggo emphatically.

"It is," I said, "and it's true. How many guys have seen a gomer die under his own steam this year, without medical interference? Raise your hands."

No hands went up.

"But surely we help them. Why, we even cure."

"Most of us wouldn't know a cure if we found one in a Cracker Jack Box," said Eddie. "I haven't cured anybody yet and I don't know an intern who has. We're all still waiting for number one."

"Oh, come, now. Surely. What about the young?"

"They're the ones who die," said the Crow. "Most of my posts were on guys my age. It was no picnic, Chief, winning your Award."

"Yes, well, you are all my boys," said the Leggo, as if he had forgotten to turn on his hearing aid that day, "and before I close this meeting I'd like to say a few words about the year. First, thanks for the terrific job. In many ways it's been a great year, one of the best. You'll never forget it. I'm proud of each and every one of you, and before I end, I'd just like to say a few words about one of you who isn't here today, a physician with a tremendous potential, Dr. Wayne Potts."

We stiffened. Leggo was asking for trouble if he messed with Potts.

"Yes, I'm proud of Potts. Except for some defect that led to his . . . accident, he was a fine young physician. Let me tell you about him. . . ."

I tuned out. Instead of anger, I felt sorry for the Leggo, so stiff and so clumsy, so out of touch with the human, with us, his boys. He was another generation, that of our fathers, who in restaurants before paying, added up the arithmetic of the check.

". . . maybe this year has been a little difficult, but all in all it was a pretty typical year, and we lost one in the middle, but sometimes that happens, and the rest of us will never forget him. Yet we can't let our dedication to medicine suffer because . . . "

The Leggo was right: it had been your standard internship year. All across the country, at emergency lunches, terns were being allowed to be angry, to accuse and cathart and have no effect at all. Year after year, *in eternam:* cathart, then take your choice: withdraw into cynicism and find another specialty or profession; or keep on in internal medicine, becoming a Jo, then a Fish, then a Pinkus, then a Putzel, then a Leggo, each more repressed, shallow, and sadistic than the one below. Berry was wrong: repression wasn't evil, it was terrific. To stay in internal medicine, it was a lifesaver. Could any of us have endured the year in the House of God and somehow, intact, have become that rarity: a human-being doctor? Potts? Fats had done it, yes. Potts?

". . . and so let's have a moment of silence for Dr. Wayne Potts."

After about twenty seconds the Runt blasted off again, shouting, "DAMNNIT, YOU KILLED HIM!"

"What?"

"YOU KILLED POTTS! You drove him nuts about the Yellow Man, and you didn't help him when he was crying for help. If an intern sees a shrink, you stigmatize him, you think he's nuts. Potts was scared that if he saw Dr. Frank it would damage his career. You bastards, you eat up good guys like Potts who happen to be too gentle to 'tough it out.' It makes me want to puke! PUKE!"

"You can't say that about me," said the Leggo sincerely, looking crushed. "I would have done anything to save Potts, to save my boy."

"You can't save us," I said, "you can't stop the process. That's why we're going into psychiatry: we're trying to save ourselves."

"From what?"

"FROM BEING JERKS WHO'D LOOK UP TO SOMEONE LIKE YOU!" screamed the Runt.

"What?" asked the Leggo shakily, "what are you saying?"

I felt that he was trying to understand, and I knew he couldn't but that he was crying inside because we'd pushed the button that had him hearing the tapes of all his failings, as father and son, and I said as kindly as possible, "What we're saying is that the real problem this year hasn't been the gomers, it's been that we didn't have anyone to look up to."

"No one? No one in the whole House of God?"

"For me," I said, "only the Fat Man."

"Him? He's as kooky as Dubler! You can't mean that, no."

"What we mean, man," said Chuck forcefully, "is this: how can we care for patients if'n nobody cares for us?"

At that, for the first time, the Leggo seemed to hear. He stopped, still. He scratched his head. He made a gesture with his hands, as if to say something, but nothing came out. He bent at the knee, and sat down. He looked hurt, a kid about to cry, and as we watched, his nose twitched and he dug into his baggy trousers for his handkerchief. Saddened, sobered, yet still mad, we filed out. We'd played for keeps. The door closed behind the last of us, leaving our Chief alone. Boozy, babbling, Nixon was coming apart in public places. People were filing out. What he was feeling, no one wanted to know.

Berry, Chuck and I were at the mansion of Nate Zock. We sat in the fake Elizabethan garden basking in the late-afternoon summer sun, looking back up toward the multimillion-dollar palace, a mixture of millennia of architectural vogue. Nate finished retelling the "Basch's a tough guy, don't cross him" story. Berry and I excused ourselves to play tennis, leaving Chuck to booze it up with Nate and Trixie and the overweight bovines grazing on the hors d'oeuvres and low-calorie celery tonic. The tennis court was wind-sheltered by beech and poplar, and roses coated the fence enclosing it. The splash of color and waves of scent made it like playing tennis inside a rose. We sweated. We stopped, and Nate urged us to cool off in the indoor pool. We hadn't brought swimsuits.

"That's OK," said Nate, "no one's going to watch."

"And no one's keeping track of the time," said Trixie, "we know all about the sex lives of our young Dr. Kildares."

We wandered up the lawn to the house, and I realized that unlike the rich, I was unused to privacy, to being unwatched, to things—pools and tennis courts—coming in ones. We passed the garage, where the butler was waxing Berry's Volvo, trying to match the shine on Nate's white El Dorado. In the indoor pool, tile-echoing, secluded, we stripped, embraced, dived down into the perfectly right water. We played. Delight delight. Splash splash not the best splash splash but the most splash splash not the splash best but the splash fuckin' most.

At dusk, after dinner, continuing with drinks, we chatted about the Letter of Zock. Nate had sent his letter about me to the Leggo, and had gotten a cordial reply. Not one to be satisfied with anything short of "the most," Nate had called up the Leggo and the Fish "to find out why those guys didn't think you—both of you—were as great as I thought you were, 'cause I'm a helluva judge of talent or I wouldn't be where I am today." After some discussion with the Leggo and the Fish and a few other Slurpers, Nate had cleared it right up. Not only that, but to make sure that this clear area would remain clear, Nate had decided on something more permanent: there would be named, in my honor, in the Wing of Zock, a Room of Basch. Not only that, but in addition to the ***MVI*** and the Crow, there would be, annually, the Basch Award, a free trip for two to Palm Springs for the tern "who best exemplified the qualities of Roy G. Basch, M.D.," the principal one being "how to leave the patient alone." On hearing of the Room of Basch and the Basch Award, both the Leggo and the Fish had been filled with emotion, too choked up to speak. My Redeemer, Zock, liveth. My name would live on in the House of God.

Cigars were lit. The night was so still, the match flames stood upright. Chuck and Nate related their life stories. Chuck told the story of the postcards, the latest: WANT TO BE AN OFFICER IN THE NATIONAL INSTITUTE OF HEALTH? IF SO, FILL OUT AND RETURN THIS CARD. Nate loved it. Nate told the story of "out of the valley of the Depression rode the five hundred bucks to manufacture not the best but the most nuts and bolts," and ended with tears in his eyes. Chuck loved

360

it. The long June evening ushered in a serenade of crickets, and the dusk lingered in the air like a dozing kitten's purr. Berry leaned her head on my shoulder. Nate and Trixie loved her. They suggested she be a weight-control therapist for their fatties. Nate suggested, about me and Berry, that, as he'd been told by Trixie's father years ago: "If you milk the cow, you gotta buy it," that we should get married. Chuck chimed in, warning me, "Like they say back home, man, if'n you plant it, you gotta watch it grow." Arm around me and Berry and Chuck, Nate kissed us good night, tears in his eyes, wishing we would accept his offer to start us in a private practice. At peace, at the level of love, I watched the silver liquid moonlight flow over the orange stucco roof of the House of Zock, reminding me of the stuccoed farmhouses of France.

26

In the House of God, whosoever had sighted the humps had been repulsed. These pneumatic, stupendous, astounding humps had stirred up even more speculation than a Zock. Given her rate of respiration—six breaths per minute—the oxygen theory was much favored, and many thought that the slightly green gomere had turned into a plant. And so, the last week of the ternship, LP Leon, his Fellowship secure, relented, and I lay on the top bunk going over her chart, the full story of Olive O., formulating how best to spring them on our Chief. I wanted to see if he'd show any human emotion upon sighting the horrible humps.

After the eye-opening lunch, the Leggo had in fact made some concessions and it looked like all but two or three terns would stay. The Runt and I were definitely leaving; Chuck hadn't yet said. The others were staying. In years to come they would spread out across America into academic centers and Fellowships, real red-hots in internal medicine, for they had been trained at the Best Medical School's best House, the House of God. Although a few might kill themselves or get addicted or go crazy, by and large they'd repress and conform and perpetuate the Leggo and the House and all the best medical stuff. Eat My Dust had been promised by the Leggo that he could start off the second year as ward resident, with "a free rein" on his new terns. And so, saying already that the tern-

362

ship had been "not so bad," Eddie was preparing to indoctri-
nate his new charges: "I want them on their knees from day
one." A year later it would be back to California for his Fellowship in Oncology. Hyper Hooper was staying as well. He'd
sent us a postcard from Atlantic City, signed with a picture of
a black crow. Upon returning to the House, he'd shown he
hadn't lost his touch: walking into a room containing a LOL in
NAD who'd been getting better, Hooper had said, "Hi, dearie,"
she'd gasped, clutched her chest, and five minutes later was
dead. The post showed a massive pulmonary embolus. Hooper
had been promised by the Leggo that he could start off the second year in a Path elective, doing his own personal autopsies
on his own personal patients. And so, saying that the ternship
had been "not so bad," Hooper was also dreaming California
Fellowship, in "Thanatology." The Runt was going west for a
"classic Eastern" psychiatric training program on the "mountain campus" of the U. of Wyoming, run by a guru named
Grogyam with a Ph.D. from the U. of Kansas. The Runt was so
emphatic about his entry into psych being diametrically op-
posed to the psychoanalytic viewpoint of his parents'—"classic Western"—that it seemed pretty clear that this "Eastern"
jag was a penultimate step that the Runt had to take in order to
rebel against it and come on back to mom and pop and Freud
to roost. Thunder Thighs had told the Runt that she would not
miss him. The Runt imagined this was OK with him. Little did
he know how lonely Wyoming could be.

My Clinic patients had been sad to hear I was leaving.
They'd brought presents, brought family members, wished me
good luck. One, who I'd recently told had incurable cancer
and who continued to deny that it exists, had asked me,
"Where will you hang up your shingle?" When I'd told her I'd
be taking a year off, she'd said, "That's OK, I'll be your patient
when you get back." No. She'd be dead. It was hard, too hard. I
went through my last Clinic taking deep breaths to keep back
the tears. Mae, my black Witness, concerned about my puffing,
asked, "Oh Doctuh Bass, you ain't done caught my asthma
from me, has you?" When I'd told people I was thinking of going into psychiatry, many were surprised.

. . . NOT GOING ON IN YOUR MEDICAL RESIDENCY?!
YOU PROMISED THEM! HOW WILL IT LOOK ON YOUR REC-
ORD? RECONSIDER! I AM AMAZED! . . .

My father. For the first time, he'd been nudged out of his
conjunctions. But then, calming himself again, he embraced
his grammar, he embraced his son, and went on:

> . . . I can't understand your taking a year off and it is a waste
> of a potential year's income. I'm amazed at your going into psy-
> chiatry and it seems a waste of your talent. I hope I am explain-
> ing the point well and probably not. I know that you will al-
> ways give yourself over to your new field of medicine and I am
> sure you have all the attributes to make an outstanding practi-
> tioner of psychiatry. Your deep interest in people and what
> makes them tick will be a great basis for your work and I do
> hope you will be able to make a living at it. The new philoso-
> phy for people of all ages is to enjoy each day and do what you
> plan on doing within the limits of responsibility, work, and
> commitment, and mom and I will try to do this as we have al-
> ways tried to, only more so now.
> The weather has been wet, and remember, dear son number
> one: IT NEVER RAINS ON A GOLF COURSE . . .

I finally realized what all these conjunctions meant: hope.
What was my hope now? To take a year off, to risk, grow, be
with others, even to be with parents who'd loved me despite
my shabby treatment of them, through so many arrogant years.
Was the Fat Man my hope any longer? In what he'd taught me,
yes, in showing me the one truly great American Medical Invention: the creation of a foolproof system that took sincere
energetic guys and with little effort turned them into dull,
grandiose docs who could live with the horror of disease and
the deceit of "cure," who could "go with" the public's fantasy
of the right to perfect health devoid of even the deterioration
of age, a whole nation of Hyper Hoopers and other Californians who expected the day to be sunny, the body young, to be
surfing along always on the waves of vitality, and who, when
the clouds come, the marriage fails, the erection wilts, the
brown blotches of age break out like geriatric acne on the
backs of the hands, in terror, wipe out.

364

And so I'd succeeded in keeping Olive O. from being killed by the Privates and Slurpers and BMSs and Blazers and even Housekeepers of the House. In a few days a dew-fresh tern would get the gomere. We had survived. The Leggo arrived for rounds. As I began to present the case to him, I realized that ever since the emergency lunch he'd been out of sight, withdrawn, secretoid. In his rare appearances, he'd seemed down, sad yet bitter, vulnerable and suspicious. For some reason, it troubled me. And yet Olive, a real "fascinoma," seemed to perk him up. I made no mention of the humps, and the Chief's questions were mainly to 789 about Olive's diabetes. Why, the Leggo wanted to know, with Olive's blood sugar three times normal on admission, had Sev infused more sugar, raising the level to nine times normal, a new House record? Sev gave a brilliant mathematical exigesis, drawing vector diagrams of enzyme action, which left us confused and subdued. In a rare burst of excitement the Chief said, "Great case! Come on, boys, let's go see her!"

We fairly ran to the bedside. Chuck and I positioned ourselves at the head of the bed. Getting no oral response from Olive, the Leggo proceeded to physical exam. In hushed expectation we watched him gently peel back the bedsheet and then pause. It was not clear if he'd caught sight of the humps. As if communing with the dead, he rolled up the nightie, and there, suddenly, were the two homungus, smooth, fluctulant, translucent, greeny-veined, and mysterious, almost cabalistic humps. Did the Leggo so much as bat an eyelash, no. Many eyes focused on him, and none could detect any reaction at all. Even well-prepared strong-gutted terns had felt the queasy slosh of nausea on first sighting the humps, but our Chief never turned a follicle. And then what did he do? Silently, as cautiously as a cat around food, didn't he take his right hand and put it on her right hump and then take his left hand and put it on her left hump, and it was all we could do to keep from screaming DON'T DO THAT! in amazement, revulsion, and disdain. And what did our Chief say was in them? Well, he didn't say. He just stood there straight-legged palming her humps for two minutes or more, and no one could figure out what for, but the only things we'd ever seen him go after like that were Moe the Toe's toe and God-given things filled with piss.

And then it was the last day. Relieved, happy, we bopped around the House saying good-bye, doing loopy nutty things, a carnival of interns. I searched out the Fat Man, and found him in an on-call room standing at a blackboard in front of three new terns, talking into the telephone:

"Hi, Murray, what's new? Hey, great! What? A name? Sure, yeah, no problem, hang on." Turning to the terns, Fats saw me, winked, and then asked, "OK, you turkeys, what's a catchy doctor's name for an invention? I'll be with you in a minute, Dr. Basch."

So that was it: the reality of his inventions was only that they involved us with him, showing us that someone could stand outside the drudgery of the Hierarchies and create. He'd given us his inventions as a way of helping us through. How I would miss him! More than anyone else, he knew how to be with patients, how to be with us. Finally I understood why he stayed in medicine: only medicine could take him. Burdened by his precocity, all his life Fats had hurt people by being too much. From his puzzled parents through his grade-school teachers and chums to his college and med-school classmates who'd gather at dinner, where he'd scribble notes and equations with such prodigal brilliance that as he rose to leave there'd be a mad dash for the napkins, the Fat Man had found himself separated from others by his power and his genius. All his life, he'd had to hold himself back. Finally, after two years of testing it at the House, he knew that here at last was something even he couldn't dent, that would not, in awe, in jealous anger, reject him and play with somebody else. He could dish out anything and not hurt anyone. He was safe. He would flourish. He would bloom.

Fats finished, escaped from the throng wanting to say good-bye to him, grabbed me and rushed me into the Men's Room, locking the door. He was beaming: "Isn't this great! I love it! It's like being at Coney Island on the Fourth! And tomorrow, Basch, it's the STARS!"

"Fats, I figured out why you stay in medicine."

"Terrific!" he said. "Hit me while I'm hot!"

"It's the only profession that's big enough for you."

"Yeah, and you know what the damn thing is, Basch?"

"What?"

"It might not be, after all."

We were interrupted by a banging on the door and the cries of the Fat Man fan club, and feeling rushed, I asked, "Really?"

"Sure. But that's the game, isn't it?"

"What is?" I asked, feeling that this wily fatso had foxed me again.

"To find out. To see if it matches our dreams."

The noise at the door grew louder, more insistent, and, panicky, I felt in my gut that this—right now!—was our good-bye.

"This is it," said Fats, "for now."

"Fats, thanks. I'll never forget—"

Big fat arms hugged me, and the smiling fat face said, "Basch, come to L.A. Be 'beautiful' like all the rest of us Californians. Even car crashes and rectums are 'beautiful' out there. So? So listen, Roy Gee Basch, Emm Dee: do good, support your AMA, and once in a while, to remember where you come from, put money in the *pishke* to plant a tree in Yisro-el."

He unlocked the door, was embraced by his crowd, and was gone.

I went to the Telephone and Beeper Operators and handed in my beeper. Walking down the long fourth-floor corridor, I passed Jane Doe and ignored Harry the Horse's HEY DOC WAIT. I found Chuck doing an invasive procedure on a go-mere. He was wearing a bright orange shirt and a green tie with a heart of gold in the middle of which was the word LOVE. I asked how he felt and he said, "Man, it's been pitiful, but like this tie says, I loved it. C'mon, Roy, there's somethin' I want to show you." We went into the on-call room, sat, and poured ourselves shots from the bottle in his bag.

"You know, man, I been thinkin' about what to do next year."

"You mean tomorrow?"

"Right. I keep gettin' these postcards, see," he said, showing me the pile he'd collected, "and I been puzzlin' out what to do. I come a long way from Memphis. I could keep right on goin', startin' tomorrow, again. But look where it got me, huh? You know what, Roy?"

"What?"

"I figure I gone about as white as I can go. Watch this." He took the postcards and one by one ripped them to shreds. He finished and looked at me. For once his eyes weren't that fake dull soft, no. They were sharp. They were proud.

"Good for you, baby," I said, full of pride, "good for you."

"An' look at this," he said, handing me a piece of paper.

"A bus ticket?"

"No foolin', man. Tomorrow mornin'. Back to Memphis. Back home."

"Great!" I said, grabbing him. "Great!"

"Yup. It ain't gonna be easy, it's a whole differn' worl down there, and I been away since that bus ride to Oberlin, lemmee see, yeah, nine years ago. Folks are differn' there, and, well, man, the only cotton I ever picked was out of a aspirin bottle. But I'm gonna try. I'm gonna get back in shape, find a black woman, be a regular old black doc with a lotta money and a big bad lim-O-zeene. And that'll jes' about do it for old me."

"Can I come visit you?"

"I be theah, darlin'. Don't you fret none, 'cause I be theah."

Getting up to go, feeling sad and happy both at once, I asked him: "Hey, ace intern, notice anything different about me?"

He looked me up and down and then said, "Damn, Basch! NO BEEPER!"

"They can't hurt me now."

"There it is, man."

"There it is."

I walked out of the on-call room, down the corridor, down the stairs. I stopped, feeling uneasy. Something had been left undone. The Leggo. He had never called me in. For reasons I didn't understand, I had to see him before I left. I went to his office. Through the open door I saw him staring out his window. Separated from the happy bustle in the rest of his House, he looked lonesome, a kid not invited to play. Surprised to see me, he nodded hello.

"I just thought I'd say good-bye," I said.

"Yes, good. You're starting psychiatry?" he asked nervously.

"After I take a year off, yes."

"So I heard. Three of you leaving this year, yes."

"Five if you count the policemen."

"Of course. You know, you may find this hard to believe, but I had the same thought once, to take a year off. Even to try psychiatry."

"Really?" I said, surprised. "What happened?"

"Don't know. I'd invested too much by then, and . . . and I guess it seemed like a risk," he said in an almost quavering voice.

"A risk?"

"Yes. Now I almost admire the ones who do it, take that risk. It's so strange: at my previous hospital, my boys had great affection for me, but here, this year . . ." And he trailed off, searching the sky in quiet amazement, like a man watching his wife run over his dog. Turning back abruptly, he said, "Look, Roy, I'm upset. Things are out of order: three of you leaving, what you all said about House medicine at the luncheon, Potts killing himself like that. This has never happened to me before—never!—where my boys didn't love me, and I don't know what the hell's going on!" He paused and asked, "Do you? Why me?"

Suddenly I realized how much he was hurting, how vulnerable, at that instant, he was. Did I know why him? Yes. It was my knowing that was setting me free. Should I tell him? No. Too cruel. What would Berry do? She'd not tell, she'd ask. I'd ask him, give him a way to talk about it, a way out of the judgment he was begging from me.

"Never before?" I asked. "Not even in your family?"

"My what? My family?" he said, startled. He fell silent. His face showed concern. Perhaps he was thinking of his own son. I hoped that he would find a way to talk about it. As I watched, his face got sad. I began to hope that he wouldn't say anything, scared that if he opened up, he'd dissolve. The Chief in tears? That would be too much for me. I waited, my anxiety rising. Time seemed to have died.

369

"No," he said finally, looking away, "nothing like that. Things are fine at home. Besides, in many ways my family is here in the House."

I felt relieved. Somehow he'd pulled things back up around him, and could go on, impenetrable, cold, the tough little *pisher* he'd always been before. I felt sorry for him: I was going free; he was in a cage. As had happened so often before in my life, the tiger had turned out to be a paper tiger, a dream tiger: worn, bored, timid, envious, sad.

He held out his hand in good-bye and said, "In spite of everything, Roy, it's, well, it's not been all that bad having you here this year."

"It's been difficult for me, sir. There were times when I did things that just about drove you ape, and I'm sorry for that."

"Nothing to be sorry about. I know. I went through it too, by God. But you know something, Roy, I'll tell you from my experience: you wait and see, you'll look back on this year as the best year of your life."

I didn't know what to say. I shook his hand and left.

Finally free, and more free for having glimpsed the fear and jealousy of those trapped inside, I left the House of God for the last time. These men were so vulnerable. Poor Nixon, with a severe phlebitis that might kill him, and probably would if he had Hooper for his doctor, floundering so bad. I found myself standing on the microfilm of human tissue coating the parking lot that I still regarded as Potts. Feeling the warm sun on my face, I felt a weight in my hand: my black bag. I didn't want it or need it anymore. What should I do with it? Give it to the nearest six-year-old kid and start him on his way to the top? Give it to an underprivileged? No. I knew what to do. Like a discus, round and round and round it went, gathering momentum, until with a scream of bitterness and joy I launched it up and up into the hot fresh summer breeze and watched the glittering chrome instruments fall out in a rainbow and smash on the pavement below.

Later that evening, the policemen picked up Berry and me and loaded our luggage into the squad car and with sirens blaring and lights ablaze rushed us to the airport.

"You're really becoming lay analysts?" asked Berry.

370

"The couch awaits the excretia of our unconscious processes," said Gilheeny.

"And like other rare Catholic candidates—the latest being a horny nun," said Quick, "we are celebrities. Our brains are being picked neatly for our reactions to so many years on the beat."

We arrived at the airport, and Gilheeny said, "Brevity is not my forte, and yet I shall try to be brief." Rambling on, the flashing red light of the squad car highlighting his bushy features, he finally concluded: "And so as Quick and I place this final bookend on our shelf of time at the House of God, the three we will always cherish are Dubler, the Fat Man, and Roy G. Basch."

"Your like will not be seen again," said Quick.

"From the libidinal heart, the oracle of the ventricle, we wish you both good-bye, Shalom, and"—he was interrupted by a gush of plump tears streaming down his cheeks—"and God bless."

"And God bless," echoed Quick.

My first thought when I saw the bulging face of the jumbo jet was that it looked like an obese or edematous gomer. Sinking into the seat for the short night flight to Paris, Berry at my side, thinking of the train ride that would take us to the south of France the next day, I told Berry what the Leggo had said to me, about the year being "the best year of your life." After a moment's thought she settled into the snug of my neck, yawned, and said, "You told him, of course, that there have been twenty-nine others that have beaten it so far."

Damn, now why couldn't I have thought of that? I yawned and closed my eyes and slipped down into the dark.

I am a blind cave fish, thrown into a river of light. My senses are readjusting. As I learn to live in this strange full spectrum, day after dazzling day, at the same time I am drawn back to the horrific dark. I am split, filleted by the knife glare of the French summer sun. Berry and I will be dining in a garden under a trellis of woven branches, our table dressed with heavy silver and starched white linen and monogrammed crystal, the perfection completed by a red rose in a silver vase, and my eye will catch the aged waiter, standing, napkin over his tremoring arm, and I will think back to a gomer with a senile tremor in the House of God. We will be sitting on a bench in the village square, in silence but for the Clack! Clack! of the *boules*, bathed in the scents of orange, garlic, river musk, and walnut, and I will focus on an old man heaving *boules* from his wheelchair, and I will think back to Humberto, my Mexican-American BMS wheeling Rose Nizinsky to X Ray the night we set the House speed record for the bowel run. On market day I will see two black-clad LOLS in NAD carrying a pole to which are tied, by the feet, three squawking geese; behind them, dawdling home, fingers looped through the green ribbon loops tied round the boxes of *patisserie*, two white-clad little girls. There is no escape. Even the bikini-clad luscious bodies at our river are not safe. I dissect them into tendon, muscle, and bone. At least, I think to myself, I have yet to see the incapacitation, the complete horizontality of posture that goes with being a true gomer, here in the south of France.

And yet I know it is only a matter of time. One lazy and succulent day, I am sitting by myself in the graveyard at the top of the village. A little girl's grave is inscribed "*Priez pour elle*"; upon the stone vault lies a supine Crucifixion, the arched breast of Christ so lifelike in glazed, flesh-toned ceramic. As I leave, "*Priez pour elle, Priez pour elle*," rings on and on in my ears. I am walking down the catnapping winding road overlooking the château, the church, the prehistoric caves, the square, and far below, the river valley, the child's-toy poplars and Roman bridge indicating the road, and the creator of all this, the spawn of the glacier, our river. I have never taken this path before. I am beginning to relax, to know what I knew before: the peace, the rainbow of perfection of doing nothing. The days are beginning to feel smooth, warm, pebbled with the nostalgia of a sigh. The country is so lush that the birds can't eat all the ripe blackberries. I stop and pick some. Juicy grit in my mouth. My sandals slap the asphalt. I watch the flowers compete in color and shape, enticing the rape by the bees. For the first time in more than a year, I am at peace.

I turn a corner and see a large building, like an asylum or a hospital, with the word "Hospice" over the door. My skin prickles, the little hairs on the back of my neck rise, my teeth set on edge. And there, sure enough, I see them. They have been set out in the sun, in a little orchard. The white of their hair, scattered among the green of the orchard, makes them look like dandelions in a field, gossamers awaiting their final breeze. Gomers. I stare at them. I recognize the signs. I make diagnoses. As I walk past them, their eyes seem to follow me, as if somewhere in their dementia they are trying to wave, or say *bonjour*, or show some other vestige of humanness. But they neither wave, nor say *bonjour*, nor show any other vestige. Healthy, tan, sweaty, drunk, full of blackberries, laughing inside and fearing the cruelty of that laughter, I feel grand. I always feel grand when I see a gomer. I love these gomers now.

That night is the worst. I awaken, bolt upright, at attention, drenched in sweat, screaming, as the church bell tolls three. My mind is filled with horrific images of the year in the House of God. My screams awaken Berry, and I say, "I finally saw where they keep them."

"Keep who?" she asks, half-asleep.

"The gomers. They call it a 'Hospice.'"

"Calm down, love. It's over."

"It's not. I can't get them out of my mind. Everything reminds me of the year in the House. I don't know how to forget. It's wrecking my whole life. I never realized it would be so bad."

"Don't try to forget, love. Try to work it through."

"I thought I had."

"No, it takes time. Here," she said, holding me, "talk to me, tell me where it hurts."

I tell her. Again I tell her about Dr. Sanders bleeding out in my lap, about the look in Potts's eyes that night before he jumped, about my pushing the KCL into poor Saul. I tell her how ashamed I am for turning into a sarcastic bastard who calls the old ones gomers, how, during the ternship, I'd ridiculed them for their weaknesses, for throwing up their suffering in my face, for scaring me, for forcing me to do disgusting things to take care of them. I tell her how I want to live, compassionately, with the idea of death clearly in sight, and how I doubt I can do that, ever again. As I think back to what I'd gone through and what I'd become, sadness wells up and mixes with contempt. I put my head into Berry's folds and weep, and curse, and shout, and weep.

". . . and in your own way, you did. Someone had to care for the gomers, and this year, in your own way, you did."

"The worst thing is this bitterness. I used to be different, gentle, even generous, didn't I? I wasn't always like this, was I?"

"I love who you are. To me, underneath it all, you're still there." She paused, and then, eyes sparkling, said, "And you might even be better."

"What? What do you mean?"

"This might have been the only thing that could have awakened you. Your whole life has been a growing from the outside, mastering the challenges that others have set for you. Now, finally, you might just be growing from inside yourself. It can be a whole new world, Roy, I know it. A whole new life." Eyes wet with tears, she said, "I'm going to love you even more, Roy, because I've been waiting a long time for you to begin."

Overwhelmed. Speechless. Excited, even happy. Yet it seemed too easy. "I want to believe you, but it all seems so painful. The whole year seems like a nightmare now."

"Not all of it. There was pleasure in it, too: the pleasure of the mastery of medicine, the pleasure of your group of guys, of latency."

"Latency? What's latency?"

"Latency is the lull before adolescence. Latency is the time of clubs, groups, teams, when baseball is the most important thing in your life and the days are too short for all that you want to do. Latency is caring. This year's been a latency trip: during your internship, with all of you scared and brutalized, the caring in your bunch of guys sustained you."

Cradled in her arms, I think back to then, to the tree house in the overgrown shallow ravine, to the early-summer nights running out of the house leaping up and up in the warm dusk, to the baseball games when the pepperpot shortstop pegged a two-hop bouncer over to first base to just nip the runner in time, and as I begin to curl down into the river must of sleep, like a song hummed by a tyrant and picked up by the birds and spread all along and away, a blanket of soothing ideas spreads itself over me, and I think of days so still that a match flame won't bend and I think of blind fish in the black world of a mammoth-painted cave who somehow, even in their icy smooth-walled limestone pool know about the flat hot slabs of summer slapped against the mime-white walls to warm a dozing cat in the middle of a street of a French hillvillage overlooking a rivervalley laced with châteaux of the real sort and of the mirrored marbled butchershop sort caressing chilled meat laced with ribbons of lard and a box of *patisserie* tied with a green ribbon with a loop looped for a child's finger and a market ebbing quiet as the words flow louder from the mouths of the cafés where men caricaturing French peasants sit with their cigarettes stuck to their lips and a cemetery which chimes *"Priez pour elle, Priez pour elle"* in deathly silence and then I think that outside the House of God even in a cemetary there is no result just process and that here at last, with my love holding me, each day might be filled with all things and all colors and the eternal repetition of all colorful things renewed, and I feel that it just might be that in the flow of time the layers of bitterness might begin to peel away, until bitterness itself had become but a faint etching on a glass wall, layers of etched glass walls leading down a life toward a latency, a summergame, a summer of fun, and as I struggle to rest the layers of bitterness are beginning to peel off, are peeling off, leaving me homing upriver toward innocence and nakedness and rest, as in the time before the House of God with Berry thank God for Berry and except for Berry where would I be for without her I could never learn to love as once I did love and will love and love.

Humbly, I ask her to marry me.

LAWS OF THE HOUSE OF GOD

I. GOMERS DON'T DIE.

II. GOMERS GO TO GROUND.

III. AT A CARDIAC ARREST, THE FIRST PROCEDURE IS TO TAKE YOUR OWN PULSE.

IV. THE PATIENT IS THE ONE WITH THE DISEASE.

V. PLACEMENT COMES FIRST.

VI. THERE IS NO BODY CAVITY THAT CANNOT BE REACHED WITH A #14 NEEDLE AND A GOOD STRONG ARM.

VII. AGE + BUN = LASIX DOSE.

VIII. THEY CAN ALWAYS HURT YOU MORE.

IX. THE ONLY GOOD ADMISSION IS A DEAD ADMISSION.

X. IF YOU DON'T TAKE A TEMPERATURE, YOU CAN'T FIND A FEVER.

XI. SHOW ME A BMS WHO ONLY TRIPLES MY WORK AND I WILL KISS HIS FEET.

XII. IF THE RADIOLOGY RESIDENT AND THE BMS BOTH SEE A LESION ON THE CHEST X-RAY, THERE CAN BE NO LESION THERE.

XIII. THE DELIVERY OF MEDICAL CARE IS TO DO AS MUCH NOTHING AS POSSIBLE.

Glossary

Admission: a patient entering the House of God; two types: emergency, through the emergency room; elective, scheduled.

Agonal: just before death, as in "agonal" respirations.

Amyloidosis: chronic degenerative disease with increasing deposits of a starchy substance, amyloid, in many organs; rare; incurable.

Anal: pertaining to the anus, as in fissure (tear), sadism (a Freudian concept whereby a sadistic urge is related to early anal activity), and Mirror (cf. Dr. Jung's).

Aneurysm: a ballooning out of a vessel, especially an artery, before it bursts.

Angina pectoris: a pattern of cardiac pain, often felt in the chest, signaling severe disease of the coronary arteries, often a prelude to a heart attack.

Ascites: fluid in the abdominal cavity, always abnormal, often associated with liver disease or infection, resulting in distended belly.

Attendings: private doctors affiliated with the House of God.

A-V node: Atrio-Ventricular node, a collection of pacemaking cells in the heart, between the atria and ventricles, which can, if the normal sinus node fails, take over the initiation of the heartbeat.

Black Crow: the House Award given to the intern who collects the most postmortem permissions in the course of the year; prize is a tiepin and a free trip for two to Atlantic City, for AMA meetings.

Blue Blazers: House Administration; often tanned, blond, gold-buttoned; comprising the staff of HELP; origin and function unknown.

BMS: Best Medical School (in the world).

BMS: a BMS student

BUFF: polish to make look good, as BUFF a car, BUFF a chart, BUFF a gomer; part of BUFF and TURF.

BUN: Blood Urea Nitrogen; indirect measure of heart failure.

BOUNCE: to return to: "I BUFFED her and then TURFED her to Urology, but she BOUNCED back to me."

Bowel Run: part of the Gastrointestinal Workup, a series of tests, including upper GI series with small bowel follow-through, barium enema, sigmoidoscopy, liver scan, gallbladder series etc.; a specialty of the House; prior to the bowel run the "cleanout" is necessary, a series of enemas and cathartics to render the bowel, in the words of a surgeon, "so clean I can drink the stuff coming out"; The Emperor of the Bowel Run: Dr. Putzel; The Bowel Run of the Stars: the Fat Man's dream.

Cardiac catheterization: threading catheters through veins and arteries into the heart so that radioopaque dye can be injected and the structure of the vessels and the chambers can be seen.

CHF: congestive heart failure, progressive incurable decay of the heart, in which it can't pump blood efficiently; leads to renal failure, pulmonary edema, stasis ulcers, death.

Cirrhosis: chronic degeneration of the liver; usually fatal.

Clavicular: of the clavicle, bone at the top of the chest running between the shoulders.

CVP: central venous pressure, the pressure in the vein feeding directly into the heart; CVP line, a catheter placed in that vein to measure pressure.

Cytology: study of cells, especially cells suspected of being malignant.

Defibrillator: machine used to attempt to shock the heart back into normal rhythm or to start it again after it stops; electrodes are placed on chest wall; also called cardioverter.

DERM: Dermatology, the study of skin; an NPC Specialty.

Disimpaction: using a finger to dig impacted feces out of the rectum.

Dr. Jung's Anal Mirror: allegedly the Fat Man's Great American Medical Invention, allowing the user to view his or her own anus "in the comfort and privacy of the home."

Dyspareunia: pain during intercourse; especially in the female.

Ectopic nodal pacemaker: abnormal initiation of the heartbeat from the A-V node instead of from the sinus node.

Ectopic pregnancy: abnormal location of the fertilized ovum, often in the fallopian tubes; upon rupture, often fatal.

Egodystonic: a thought, feeling, or action which causes discomfort to oneself; opposite of egosyntonic.

Episiotomy: incision in vagina during labor and delivery to allow baby to be born without damaging the mother unnecessarily.

Feeding tube: polyethylene tube put into stomach through nostril, through which pureed food is injected.

Flatulence: farting.

Foley catheter: tube put into bladder through urethra to assure flow of urine.

France: a country.

Fulminant necrotic hepatitis: inflammation of the liver, acute; various causes; virtually always fatal.

GAS: Anaesthesiology; an NPC Specialty.

Gastrocnemius: muscle of the calf; soleus is another calf muscle.

GI: Gastro-Intestinal, pertaining to the gut.

Glomerulonephritis: inflammation of part of the kidney; often fatal.

GOMER: Get Out of My Emergency

Room; "a human being who has lost—often through age—what goes into being a human being"— (the Fat Man).

Gluteal: muscle forming the ass.

GOMERE: feminine of GOMER.

HELP: organization in the House of God, comprised of Blue Blazers, summoned by dialing H-E-L-P; origin and function unknown.

Hospice: French word; home, asylum, poorhouse.

Hotel-Dieu: French word; literally "House of God;" hospital.

House of God: hospital affiliated with the BMS; founded in 1913 by the American People of Israel when their medically qualified Sons and Daughters could not get good internships because of discrimination; competitor of MBH (See MBH).

House Staff: interns and residents of the House of God.

HTE Service: Hold The Elevator Service; allegedly promulgated by Grenade Room Dubler as an intern, to transport the allegedly murdered gomers down to the morgue.

Intercostal: between the ribs.

Intertrochanteric: between the protrusions of bone at the head of the upper legbone, the femur; often synonymous with fracture of the hip.

Intubated: with a rubber tube inserted through the mouth down into the trachea, by which to artificially respirate a patient.

IV: intravenous, inside a vein.

Lasix: a drug; diuretic often used to treat congestive heart failure.

LAWS OF THE HOUSE OF GOD: a series of rules, almost commandments, many formulated by the Fat Man.

Lay analyst: a psychoanalyst who is not an M.D.

Limbic: primitive part of the brain, thought to be a center of aggressive and sexual impulses; allegedly linked to cortex.

LOL in NAD: Little Old Lady in No Apparent Distress; not a GOMERE.

LP: Lumbar Puncture, the introduction of a needle into the spinal column to procure a sample of spinal fluid; also Low Profile, the intern technique of not being seen.

M and M: Morbidity and Mortality; a regularly scheduled conference of the medical hierarchy at which mistakes are aired; an opportunity for the higher-up Slurpers (See SLURPERS) to roast the lower-down.

MBH: Man's Best Hospital; a BMS-affiliated hospital founded by WASPs; competitor of the House of God.

MI: Myocardial infarction, heart attack.

MICU: Medical Intensive Care Unit.

Monilia: a species of yeast, causing infection, often with swelling of lymph nodes; common cause of vagitch.

MOR: Marriage On Rocks; frequent event during internship; cf. ROR.

Mt. St. E.: Mount Saint Elsewhere, generic term for any hospital not affiliated with the BMS; often used to denote small community hospital.

Multiple myeloma: one type of bone cancer; fatal.

MVI: Most Valuable Intern; allegedly the House Award given to the intern who is most valuable; alleged prize is a tiepin and a free trip for two to Atlantic City.

Narcolepsy: disease in which the main symptom is sleepiness; endemic to radiologists.

NIH: National Institute of Health; a step up the Slurper cone.

Nitro: nitroglycerin, tablet placed under the tongue to relieve the pain of angina pectoris.

NPC Specialty: No Patient Care Specialty in medicine, numbering, according to the Fat Man, six: RAYS, GAS, PATH, DERM, OPHTHALMOLOGY, PSYCHIATRY.

NSR: Normal sinus rhythm, the normal working of the heart, in which the heartbeat is initiated in the pacemaking cells in the sinus node.

Onanism: masturbation.

OPHTHALMOLOGY: surgical specialty dealing with eye; an NPC specialty.

ORTHO: Orthopedics, the surgical specialty dealing with bone.

Parotid: gland in jaw that produces saliva.

PATH: Pathology, an NPC Specialty.

Perineum: Genital region, especially that between the anus and scrotum or vulva.

Pishke: Yiddish word; tin box into which to place coins for charity.

Placement: process of finding a home for a gomer or gomere, especially, finding a nursing home; a possible TURF.

Primum non nocere: first of all, do no harm.

PRIVATES: Private doctors of the House of God; "Double O" Private is one "licensed to kill."

Psoriatic: pertaining to psoriasis, a disease producing scaly skin.

PSYCHIATRY: an NPC specialty.

Psychoanalysis: the Freudian technique of psychotherapy.

Pulmonary edema: flooding of the lungs with fluid, often from a backed-up flow of blood during congestive heart failure; along with the bowel run, a specialty of the House.

Pulmonary embolus: a bloodclot lodging in the lung; often a sudden event in bedridden patients which produces death.

Putzeled: to be treated as Dr. Putzel, House Double O Private, would treat; colloq.: "screwed."

Q.E.D.: Quod Erat Demonstrandum, "which was to be demonstrated," "thus."

Quadriceps: four large muscles of the thigh.

RAYS: Radiology, an NPC Specialty.

Redhot: hotshot, whizkid, ace, young mensch, "my man."

Renology: medical specialty dealing with kidney and urine.

Respiratory tech: respiratory technician, in charge of machines to aid respiration of patients.

ROR: Relationship On Rocks; frequent event during internship; cf. MOR.

Rounds: meetings to discuss patients.

Scapula: shoulderblade.

Septicemia: infection of the blood, leading to infection of major organs, and to septic shock, in which the blood pressure falls.

SICU: Surgical Intensive Care Unit.

SIEVE: an intern in the Emergency Room who admits too many patients, who does not BUFF and TURF patients out to the street (the process known as MEET 'EM AND STREET 'EM); opposite of WALL.

Sigmoidoscopy: process of introducing a long, lighted, straight tube, the sigmoidoscope, through the anus into the dark, twisted lower bowel to look at the feces and the pathology; a specialty of the House.

SLURPERS: House Academics, striving to lick their way up the academic medical cone toward the one position at the top—the Chief.

Stasis ulcers: erosion of the skin caused by pressure, often from lying in one position for too long; seen in debilitated patients who are unable to move themselves.

STAT: at once, immediately.

Steatorrhea: foul-smelling and oily diarrhea.

Straight bendover: nursing maneuver in which, legs held straight, nurse bends over bed, flashing ass.

Subarachnoid space: layer of spinal cord where cerebrospinal fluid circulates; aimed at in lumbar puncture.

Superior mesenteric insufficiency: syndrome in which an artery of the gut, the superior mesenteric artery, becomes blocked, resulting in loss of blood supply to bowel, necrosis, and foul-smelling infected stool.

Systolic: contraction of the heart; opposite of relaxation or diastolic; systolic murmur is one which appears during contraction.

TBC: Total Bowel Control, a concept of the Fat Man's, implying complete regulation of all bowel function.

Tern: Intern, the first of a series of House Staff members, including Resident, Junior Assistant Resident, Senior Resident, Chief Resident, Fellow, Junior Fellow, Senior Fellow.

Thorazine: A drug used to decrease anxiety, especially the severe anxiety related to psychosis; one of a number of mind-bending drugs used by the House Staff, others being Stelazine, Valium, alcohol, Elavil, Dexedrine, etc.

Triage: to sort according to severity of injury, so that the more severe are attended to first.

TURF: get rid of, as TURF a gomer to Urology; often preceded by a BUFF, as in BUFF and TURF; occasionally followed by a BOUNCE, as "I TURFED my gomere to Urology, but she BOUNCED back to me"; to BUFF and TURF, according to the Fat Man, is the essence of the delivery of medical care, the concept of the "revolving door."

Uremic: a stage of renal failure in which waste products flood the blood.

UROLOGY: surgical specialty dealing with the urinary tree; "plumbing."

Vagitch: itch in the vaginal region; nonspecific; common.

V.D.: Venereal disease.

Villae: Fingerlike projections of gastrointestinal mucosae lining the gut, main function being absorption of nutriments.

Visit: a medical teacher assigned to a team of interns and residents on a ward of the House of God; selected from the pool of Privates, Slurpers, and Fellows.

VTach: Ventricular tachycardia, rapid heartbeat in which the pacemaker is in the ventricle, is chaotic, and which often signifies impending death.

WALL: an intern in the Emergency

Room who keeps patients from being admitted to the House of God, mainly by using the TURF known as MEET 'EM AND STREET 'EM; opposite of SIEVE.

Wing of Zock: addition to the House of God, financed by the astronomically wealthy philanthropoid Family of Zock, expressly dedicated to the bowel run of the rich, to contain the Room of Basch, and, ultimately, signifying hope.

Zebra: an obscure diagnosis.

Zock: hope.